THE LOVE GENES

Claudia J. Severin

THE LOVE GENES

Copyright © July 2023

Claudia J. Severin

Published by Pella Road Publishing

Lincoln, Nebraska

ISBN: 979-8-9873408-2-0

All rights reserved. No part of this publication may be reproduced, distributed, or transmitted in any form or by any means, including photocopying, recording, or other electronic or mechanical methods without prior written permission.

The Love Genes is a work of fiction. Any references to historical events, real people, or real locales are used fictitiously. Other names, characters, places, and incidents are the product of the author's imagination, and any resemblance to actual events, locales, or persons, living or dead, is entirely coincidental.

Claudia J. Severin

https://claudiaseverin.net

DEDICATION

For Wilhelmina, Dietrich, and Elizabeth
Their untold secrets inspired me

Contents

PROLOGUE: DARCY 1
CHAPTER ONE: ADELAIDE 5
CHAPTER TWO: ANSELM 9
CHAPTER THREE: ADELAIDE 12
CHAPTER FOUR: ADELAIDE..15
CHAPTER FIVE: ADELAIDE 18
CHAPTER SIX: ANSELM..26
CHAPTER SEVEN: ADELAIDE 31
CHAPTER EIGHT: ANSELM 38
CHAPTER NINE: ADELAIDE 45
CHAPTER TEN: ANSELM 48
CHAPTER ELEVEN: ADELAIDE 53
CHAPTER TWELVE: ADELAIDE 66
CHAPTER THIRTEEN: ANSELM..75
CHAPTER FOURTEEN: ADELAIDE 80
CHAPTER FIFTEEN: ANSELM 85
CHAPTER SIXTEEN: ADELAIDE...89
CHAPTER SEVENTEEN: ANSELM 92
CHAPTER EIGHTEEN: ADELAIDE..99
CHAPTER NINETEEN: ANSELM 104
CHAPTER TWENTY: ADELAIDE 110
CHAPTER TWENTY-ONE: ANSELM...................................113
CHAPTER TWENTY-TWO: ADELAIDE 126
CHAPTER TWENTY-THREE: DARCY 131
CHAPTER TWENTY-FOUR: DARCY 139
CHAPTER TWENTY-FIVE: DARCY 151

CHAPTER TWENTY-SIX: DUSTIN	154
CHAPTER TWENTY-SEVEN: DARCY	158
CHAPTER TWENTY-EIGHT: DUSTIN	162
CHAPTER TWENTY-NINE: DARCY	168
CHAPTER THIRTY: DUSTIN	172
CHAPTER THIRTY-ONE: DARCY	183
CHAPTER THIRTY-TWO: DUSTIN	185
CHAPTER THIRTY-THREE: DARCY	192
CHAPTER THIRTY-FOUR: DARCY	197
CHAPTER THIRTY-FIVE: DUSTIN	206
CHAPTER THIRTY-SIX: DUSTIN	211
CHAPTER THIRTY-SEVEN: DARCY	216
CHAPTER THIRTY-EIGHT: DARCY	221
CHAPTER THIRTY-NINE: DUSTIN	229
CHAPTER FORTY: DARCY	234
CHAPTER FORTY-ONE: DUSTIN	255
CHAPTER FORTY-TWO: DARCY	262
CHAPTER FORTY-THREE: DARCY	272
CHAPTER FORTY-FOUR: DUSTIN	276
CHAPTER FORTY-FIVE: DUSTIN	283
CHAPTER FORTY-SIX: DARCY	297
EPILOGUE: DARCY	302
AUTHOR'S NOTES	304
ABOUT THE AUTHOR	305
WHAT'S NEXT?	306
Also by Claudia J. Severin	307

THE LOVE GENES

PROLOGUE: DARCY

Lancaster County, Buda Township, Nebraska
April 2022

At times, I thought I was living someone else's life—my mother's life perhaps. The life she discarded when she left her husband and two children. At my age, if I were eating dinner with a man, he should be a sexy playmate who might whisk me off to the bedroom before dessert. *Guess I'll keep that fantasy to myself.*

"Your meatloaf is delicious, Darcy girl," my father told me. "As usual."

The grizzly man seated at the kitchen table was a responsible, hard-working farmer, who still lived in the house his great-grandparents built a century ago. He loved me enough to let me return to the nest after my last romance detonated.

"I'm happy you like it. It's the old family recipe." I slipped off the sweater I'd worn over my shirt to work that day. I liked working as a supervisor at an insurance company call center, but they kept the temperature a little cool for me.

"How were the crazies today?"

I laughed. "The crazy customers or the crazy employees? Both were calmer than usual." I took a bite of a roll and waited until my mouth was clear to continue. "I did get a strange email and it involves you."

"Me? I have nothing to do with your job," Dad retorted.

"No, this was a message from a woman who saw our family tree on Ancestry.com. You can contact someone if you want info about an ancestor in their tree. I have most of the Schulz line entered as far back as when the homesteaders emigrated from Germany."

"You're using the information I had written up from when I went to Salt Lake City years ago?"

"Yes, but now you can verify a lot of material with things other people have found. Anyway, this woman wrote to me, Tasha somebody. Wait, it's on my phone." I pulled my iPhone from the back pocket of my jeans and read the message aloud.

> "I was excited to find your family tree including Samuel and Helene Schulz who lived in Lancaster County, Nebraska, in the early 1900s. I believe they are my great-grandparents. I have had trouble tracing back to this generation because my grandfather and his twin brother were adopted and were given different surnames. My mother was able to get their birth certificates with the biological parents' names and they match people in your tree. These twins were born in 1926 in Sacramento, California. Do you have any information about this? Tasha Edmonds."

My dad dropped his fork on the table. "That can't be right! What does she think, that my grandparents decided they had too many kids and went all the way to California to give some away? That's ludicrous. They probably never set foot outside of Nebraska once they settled here. Write back and tell her she's as crazy as your customers! Makes no sense at all."

I hadn't considered that. He had a point. I'd hoped we had some long-lost cousins somewhere. "Okay, my response will be more polite than that, but she must have the wrong family."

I wrote a quick note back to Tasha and forgot about the whole thing until three days later when I received another email. This one was from a man. I read it to my father that evening.

"Dear Darcy,

I know this seems like it is out of the blue, and we don't mean to shock your father or any of the Schulzes. Tasha is my second cousin, but we grew up together and attended the same schools, so I think of her more as a first cousin or sister. Her mother has the birth certificates for these twins, but we have more reasons to believe in our connection. I work at Family Tree DNA in Houston. Since I receive a discount on DNA tests, I have had all living relations of Tasha's and mine tested. We uploaded the raw data to Ancestry's site and it came back with a familial match for Donald Schulz. It looks like your father, your brother, Archer, and you tested through Ancestry's DNA program. If you are not familiar with the potential of these tests, this may not mean much to you, but based on the autosomal results alone, we are related.

"Since I am in the business of DNA analysis for ancestral research, I would like to offer all three of you some additional testing at no charge. I would be happy to visit you in Nebraska and administer the tests myself. Some of these are more precise than the ones you took. They are all done using saliva and are no more invasive than those you took previously.

"Please don't hesitate to call me or email me with questions. Trevor Wood."

"I don't understand what these people are getting at," Dad said.

"I think they are trying to figure out if they're really related to the Schulz family. They are going to a lot of trouble. Trevor says your DNA matches somehow. He didn't mention my DNA or Archer's matching, just yours. I don't know what to make of that. Should I tell him we'll do the testing?"

"Don't answer yet. I'd rather do a little research of our own." Dad blew his nose into a bandana handkerchief. "And let's talk to Archer about it. I'll go through my old box of ancestral records this weekend. Maybe something will stand out that we didn't see before."

THE ANCESTORS

CHAPTER ONE: ADELAIDE

Lancaster County, Buda Township, Nebraska
July 1925

I raced Emil Hoffmann across the newly plowed wheat field to the blackberry brambles. I used to be able to beat him handily when we were children, but now that he had sprung up like a corn stalk, his long legs easily pushed him ahead.

It was hardly a competition when my skirts got in my way. I hiked them up as much as I could, but then I lost the power of using my arms to help propel myself forward.

I could see him stop and turn around when he reached the brambles. Emil had gotten so cocky and confident the past few years. I barely recognized the flaxen-haired boy I'd taught to sing hymns and do multiplication. He was not only tall and lean, but his shoulders had also become broad, and his beard and hair had darkened. Soon, he and his brother, Henry, would be looking for their own farms and women to start families with.

I couldn't see the point in running once he'd won the race, so I slowed to a brisk walk. By the time I reached Emil, he had slipped off his suspenders, unbuttoned the top two buttons of his muslin shirt, and pulled the shirt hem out of his pants, billowing the shirt to create airflow in the sun-fueled heat. His wet light-brown hair clung to his forehead.

"Where you been, Addie?" he drawled, biting on a piece of straw left by the harvest. "I'd about given up on you."

"You try running in a long skirt and petticoat. It not only hampers your movement; it is very hot. Some days I would prefer to wear trousers, but Mama would turn over in her grave."

"How many petticoats you got on under that skirt?" Emil walked around me as though trying to guess.

"Emil! That is no question to ask a lady. If you're going to be courting a girl soon, you need to know what is proper conversation."

He shrugged. "All right. Don't tell me. Show me. Lift your skirt."

Sometimes boys were so crude. But I wasn't about to let him see me riled. "Not on your life. Now we'd better be getting on with the blackberry picking."

He moved toward me and pushed a strand of my hair behind my ear which had come loose from my braid. For a moment, it felt oddly intimate, looking up at him at close range, both of us breathing deeply from the exertion. Why should that bother me? Emil was only twenty years old, five years younger than me. He wouldn't know how to flirt. And even if he did, he was like family. My older brother, Samuel, had married Emil's mother, Helene, a widow lady. Sam and Helene now had more children: my niece and nephew. Emil seemed like the same sort of relation.

But he wasn't looking at me as his favorite aunt. He meant to…I took a big step backward and picked up my pail for the blackberries.

"Addie, Addie, what's wrong? I'm sorry, I teased you about the petticoats. But here we are a long way from the farm. No one can see us. Don't you fancy me?"

"Fancy you?" My jaw dropped. The heat blossoming on my cheeks had nothing to do with the soaring July humidity. "I couldn't fancy you if I wanted to. We're family."

Emil shook his head. "We're not blood kin. I ain't your brother's son. I'm his stepson and I was half-grown when he married my mother. I've always thought you were pretty as a daffodil, Addie Mae. Even when you were just a girl."

"Emil, you shouldn't speak this way. It's wrong. You'll be looking for a girl to court in a year or two. Save your sweet talk for her." I wiped the perspiration running into my eyes with my sleeve.

"I have plenty of sweet words to go around. I think of you when I lie in bed at night, Addie. I dream of how you used to sing to me. Your voice is like a nightingale's, gliding on angel wings through the springtime dusk. Your golden hair makes the wheat fields bow with envy. Your blue eyes sparkle like the dew in the new morn, a thousand stars wouldn't shine so bright. Your lips are—"

"Stop! Emil, stop saying those things." I plastered my palms over my ears. "You can't mean them! Your mother would be horrified to hear you speak to me thus."

"I am a man, Addie. I don't give a hoot about what horrifies my mother. I'm sure the list is very long." Emil pulled his suspenders back onto his shoulders and stood up taller. "I know what I feel for you, what you do to me whenever I gaze upon you."

"I'm asking you to stop. Or I shall leave, and you will be picking all the blackberries yourself. And we need a lot of them to make jam."

"As you wish. I won't tell you what's in my thoughts today. But soon, Addie. Soon, you will understand that we are meant to be more to each other than you expected."

I marched over to the nearest bramble and set to work furiously collecting berries. *What's wrong with him? Are young men always confused by their yearnings? Doesn't our self-control set us apart from the lesser beasts?*

"Ow!" I didn't mean to cry out, but a thorny branch pierced my thumb. Without thinking, I stuck my thumb into my mouth.

And he appeared before me in a flash, examining my injured thumb, then kissing it tenderly. For a brief moment, I forgot to admonish him. His comfort was innocent, and my heart welcomed his intentions. Yet my pulse quickened when he held my hand. Why did he affect me the same way he'd been describing?

"Taste." He picked up one blackberry and put it in my mouth. I closed my eyes and parted my lips, rolling the juicy berry on my tongue. Sweet. Tart. It tasted like July and all the forbidden flavors she evokes.

"Delicious," I admitted.

Emil grinned and ambled twenty feet away to pick blackberries with renewed concentration.

CHAPTER TWO: ANSELM

My brother, Anton, and his wife, Mary Elizabeth, were celebrating their twenty-fifth anniversary. The whole extended family attended, including the Schulz clan. My wife, Matilde, was Mary's much older sister. That's right; my brother married my wife's sister. Not an unusual thing when so many families homesteaded nearby.

Of course, I wanted to salute my only brother and his lovely wife, but I had another mission today. I needed to find a new caretaker for Matilde. A neighbor, Mrs. Hintz, had been coming over to help every morning until after the noon meal. Now they were moving to be near family in Omaha, so I was losing my helper.

I couldn't afford to be home with Matilde all the time. Her deteriorating condition required nursing care. A family member assisting her with personal hygiene matters would make her more comfortable if only someone would agree. I knew I had to figure this out. Matilde had done a lot for me as a young man finding my way in the world. I owed her. Ours had never been a love match, but we had meant a lot to each other and I wasn't about to let her down.

I walked around the various gatherings. Some folks were at long wooden tables, others stood in clusters, and some sat on blankets under the Osage orange trees eating sandwiches and drinking tea or lemonade. The younger children ran in the yard chasing chickens and dogs.

Finally, I spotted her—little Adelaide Schulz. She wasn't so little anymore; she must be in her mid-twenties. Addie was the youngest child of Herman and Lillian Schulz. Herman had been my wife's brother, making Addie Matilde's niece. She'd been over to our house with her older brothers many times when they were growing up. Matilde favored Addie since we had no children of our own.

Addie had some experience with nursing relatives. Her mother died when Addie turned twelve, and when her father took ill, she became his nursemaid for the last three years of his life. I suppose that must have ruined her chances of finding her own husband. She helped her dad at a time when most women her age would be marrying or perhaps going to college to get a teaching certificate.

I was in luck. Addie sat alone under a tree; a worn book open in her lap. She leaned her head back on the tree trunk as though she was napping, her eyelids closed.

"Good afternoon, Addie." I squatted down next to her, not sure if I was interrupting her solitude. "I have something to discuss with you if you have a few moments to spare."

She opened her eyes and shielded them from the sun. I moved deliberately in between so the glare didn't blind her. "Uncle Anselm. Nice to see you. I hope Matilde's better. Is she with you?"

"No. Matilde's not well, Addie. That's what I want to talk about."

"With me? I'm afraid I'm not a doctor or a nurse."

"Oh, no. She's seen a lot of those. Ever since she fell off that horse years ago, she's had rheumatoid arthritis. It's getting more painful for her to even get out of bed. I hate to see her like this, but there isn't much I can do. Except find someone to come in to help her. Mrs. Hintz was a godsend, but she is moving next month. I wanted to persuade you to come to take care of Matilde. I think we need someone who is a live-in helper now. I would pay you, of course, and it would include room and board, and any expenses you might have."

Addie's eyes widened. "You want to hire me to care for my aunt?"

"You did it for your pa. And you didn't get paid for that until the estate was settled. I know because when I bought the Schulz homestead, you were paid with funds from the land sale. I'm offering to pay you monthly at the going rate as a live-in nurse and housekeeper. You could save that and you might have enough to buy a house in town or go to school if you wanted. Of course, I don't know how much longer Matilde has. She's seventy-six and not in good health."

"I'd live with you and Matilde then?"

"That's the idea. It's a very big house, with five bedrooms. You'd have private quarters." I studied her face. She'd never dreamed of living in a house so grand. I dropped to kneel facing her, so we were eye-to-eye.

"So, what do you think about my offer? I'll be honest. I'm kind of desperate. If I must stay home with her, I can't do my work. I travel quite often. I have a ranch out west that I go check on about once every two months. And I attend auctions and land sales in the surrounding townships all the time. That's what the real estate business is about."

"Is that what you call what you do? Real estate?"

"Yes. Sometimes I buy and sell land or farms with my own money, but mostly I buy and sell for clients. I got the land out west for a very good price, but if I don't check on the cattle operation frequently, they might take advantage of my trusting nature. Unfortunately, I'd have to sell that at a loss if I have no one to care for Matilde."

Addie patted my arm. "I hate to see you do that. Let me think about this some. I need to talk to Samuel and Helene. I help them a lot with their children and some of the farm work. If I take your job, I wouldn't be any use to them."

"You take a few days to think about it. If there is anything else you need to sweeten the deal, just let me know. Maybe you'll need a car to drive, or a puppy to keep watch. I'll wait to hear from you."

CHAPTER THREE: ADELAIDE

"You can't be honestly considering moving in with Aunt Matilde and that man, Addie! Tell her, Samuel. Tell her what kind of reputation Anselm Roth has!" Helene Schulz fisted her hands on her hips, standing in her sparse kitchen.

"Now, Helene. Most of what I've heard is idle gossip from years ago. I don't put much stock in it. Folks have been jealous of Anselm because he's worked hard and made good money. If he wants to spend it on nice clothes and a fancy car, why should anyone else care?"

"I suppose you don't care how he made that fortune either! Swindling poor farmers who depend on their land. He claims to get them top dollar but we all know whose dollar he's talking about. What about the way he took your land away, Samuel? The Schulz family homestead. He owns the land we live on." Helene was on a roll. I had learned to take my cue from Sam to stay out of her way until she blew it all out.

"Anselm hardly stole the homestead," my brother answered. "You know as well as I do, he had the funds to buy the 160 acres when Pa died. Twenty-four thousand dollars was a lot in 1920. It's a lot five years later. I reckon he had some bank give him credit because he owned so much property." Samuel lit his corn cob pipe and sat back in his cane-backed chair.

"Addie, Darlin,'" Helene took me by the shoulders and looked me square in the eye. "There are things in life that a woman knows. You're old enough to be able to sense things yourself. I know you haven't been around many men who aren't in our family, but some of them cannot be trusted. Anselm was just your age when he married your Aunt Matilde after her first husband died. Ask yourself, what kind of twenty-five-year-old man marries a woman twice his age? I was just a girl then, but I remember a lot of talk about it. He was the hired hand on their farm."

"Well…" I stammered. "Matilde must have liked him. I remember as a little girl I always thought they made such an elegant couple when they would come over in their horse-drawn surrey. I guess I knew he was younger than she was, but I didn't think it was that much of a difference. You said yourself he has money. He's going to pay me to serve as a nursemaid for her. I should do it for free as my Christian duty to care for the sick, but he's willing to pay me every month."

"Hmmph!" Helene wrinkled her nose. "Where do you think he got that money? It started with Matilde's land that her husband homesteaded and purchased from the railroad. She owned 320 acres. Once Anselm had his hands on that, he used it as collateral to buy more land. I heard he got a lot of it cheaply by charming trusting widow ladies who wanted to move off their farms. Now they say he owns more than one thousand acres just in this county. And another two thousand acres of ranch land in western Nebraska. He got that on the cheap too, once the farmers who got free land under the Kincaid Act realized it was no good for dryland farming."

"I thought you liked Uncle Anselm. Maybe he's just a good businessman." I spoke softly, wringing my hands behind my back.

"That's exactly right, Addie. People gossip about him because they are jealous." Sam nodded. "Matilde saw his potential, and she was right."

"Aren't you even worried about your innocent sister, Samuel? Anselm is a handsome man even at fifty. He might turn that charm on her one day if she is living under his roof. Don't you remember that business about the missing woman, Sam? That must have been twenty years ago. The sheriff questioned Anslem about it."

"Yeah, they questioned him. He was talking to her on the street in Hallam. I think he might have given her some cash to escape her crazy husband. They charged the husband with her murder a year later, as I recall," Samuel said.

Helene sniffed. "They say Anselm has a woman in every town in Lancaster and Gage counties. And who knows what kind of mischief he gets into when he stays in hotels on his travels to his ranch."

I'm sure my eyes got bigger. I had no idea what went on in hotels. Did women go there to entertain male travelers? Anselm didn't seem like the rogue she was describing. He was taller than average and had the strong build of a younger man. With his dark hair and neatly trimmed beard, I suppose he could be mistaken for a dandy. I'd seen him dressed in expensive clothing, and driving extravagant cars.

Samuel came over to me and put a reassuring hand on my shoulder. "Don't be putting nasty ideas in her head, Helene, just because he used to flirt with your older sister. He married Matilde, and she was a fine-looking woman in her day. She's had a comfortable life in that big house. I don't think their relationship is anyone else's business."

Helene picked up the broom and began to sweep the floor furiously.

I smoothed my hands over my apron. "My concern is entirely different. If I was living across the section with them, I wouldn't be able to help you with little Nelle, and Josef. I might not be able to do canning or collect the eggs for you, or help plant the garden. I know I don't do as much work as the two of you do, but I don't wish to increase your burden…"

Sam said, "Adelaide, we knew you would be leaving to go find your own life. We thought it would be with a husband, but there is no shame in taking employment. At least this way you'd be close by, so we can keep an eye out for you, and you might be able to put away some cash for a rainy day. Who knows, it might only be for a year or so. Don't worry about our family. We've got two strong young men to help us, Henry and Emil. If you want to take this job, don't let us stand in your way."

Helene went outside to shake out the broom without another word. Samuel winked and tried to hide a smile.

CHAPTER FOUR: ADELAIDE

I was still making up my mind about the job offer the next evening when I was taking my dry clothes off the clothesline. When Pa got sick, Samuel and my other brother, Christian, built a second house next to the big house that my parents built in 1900, about the time I was born. The new house had only two bedrooms and a small kitchen. Christian lived there until Pa died, then he moved to Oklahoma when he received his inheritance. He and his wife farm there.

Samuel and Helene needed the big house for their growing family. When Christian moved away, I moved into the cottage. It was cozy, private, and suited me for the past five years. If I left this place, someone else in the family would take it over. Maybe Henry, as the oldest, or perhaps Emil. It bothered me to think of leaving the first home I could call my own.

As I walked back into my house, Henry stood in the doorway. Not as tall and lean as his brother, Emil, Henry was stocky with dark curls clustering around his ears and clean-shaven face. And strong as an ox. Whenever heavy lifting was needed for farm work, they summoned Henry to assist. An unfamiliar intensity glowed in his dark eyes.

"Oh, hello, Henry. You startled me."

"Don't move, Addie. The light is shining on your hair just right, you look like you're aglow."

I laughed. "I'd better get inside then; I don't want to catch on fire." I brushed past him to lay the wicker basket on my table.

Henry reached for my arm. "I think I might be the one burning up."

I whirled to face him. "Are you feverish? What's—"

His mouth pressed tightly against mine. I had no idea why he decided to kiss me. He held my upper arms fast, and it was a few moments before I could think clearly.

"Henry! What was that for?" I stumbled back when he released me.

"I had to do it, Addie. Don't you see? I couldn't listen to my stupid brother go on and on about the poetry he was writing for you. Some nonsense about how your smile lights the sun. You are the sun, the moon, everything. You can't be distracted by silly Emil. You belong to me."

"I belong to you? Why would you think that?"

"Don't you remember, Addie? You said you wanted to marry me when I was eight years old. I said you had to wait for me to grow up and you promised you would. I'm twenty-one now, we can make some plans together."

I started to laugh. I couldn't help it. When he winced and glanced toward the door, I saw he was serious. "Oh, Henry! I assumed you were teasing me. Just back up here. You thought we were supposed to be married for real?"

"You don't want a husband who writes silly love notes, do you? I'm more the kind of man who believes in action, not words. The kind who can give you many, many sons and daughters." Henry fisted his hand in my long hair and pulled my face to his. His grip was powerful but his lips brushed mine gently this time, kissing me long enough to steal my breath.

I pushed back on his solid chest, and he let me retreat. "I don't think you're ready for this, Henry. I think you're feeling something all right, but you need to consider your options more carefully. No one should rush into marriage, it's too important."

Henry wiped his mouth on the back of his hand. "I have no intention of rushing. I just didn't want your head turned by my impulsive little brother." He jammed his thumbs around his suspenders. "I don't know if you heard, but our neighbors, Gustav Hintz and his wife are moving to Omaha. Gustav asked me if I wanted to go along. His nephew works in the stockyards and he said they want men who can handle livestock. He said it was a good job and paid well. I haven't told my Ma and Samuel yet, but

I'm going. I figured I could save for a place of my own and send for you."

I blinked. Twice. I knew better than to laugh this time. His hands shook when he took one of mine. "I don't know what to say, Henry."

"You don't have to say anything now. I'll write you a letter every so often so you'll know how things are going. I should be back to visit the rest of the family in the fall if I get time off. I'm just telling you; this is my plan. My plan includes you."

He walked off and left me standing there with my mouth open. *What am I supposed to do now?*

CHAPTER FIVE: ADELAIDE

I needed to talk to Matilde. After all, if I accepted Anselm's job offer, she would be principally involved. Maybe she didn't want anyone else living with them.

It was only three-quarters of a mile up the road to the big house, an easy walk. I brought some of the blackberry jam I had canned with Helene. Mrs. Hintz greeted me at the door.

"Why, Addie, how are you doing on this beautiful morning? Is Mrs. Roth expecting you? She didn't mention it."

"No, ma'am. I brought her some fresh blackberry jam. I was hoping I might visit with her." I was admitted to the cool foyer. A stained-glass window cast shades of blue and green from above.

"Just let me go check with her. She was feeling rather poorly earlier, but sometimes the pain is better after she's been up and moving a little." Mrs. Hintz went into one of the large rooms in the rear of the house. I had heard they had fashioned a bedroom on the first floor for better accessibility.

After a few minutes, I was ushered into Matilde's room and sat in a horsehair-stuffed chair by her bedside. She was propped up in bed wearing a shawl over her nightgown and a smile.

"Adelaide, my dear. How long has it been since I've seen your sweet face? At least a year. Tell me everything that is going on with your kin."

I took her hand. Aunt Matilde always made me feel special, as though I was the sunshine of her world. She must have had the same effect on Anselm. No wonder he cared for her so much. "Let's see. I'm sure you've heard about most of the comings and goings. We got a letter from Christian and Grace last week. They are raising pigs. A twister nearly destroyed their pig pen though, and the pigs got out. Um, Henry told his mother and Samuel last night that he intends to move to Omaha when the Hintzes go next week. Helene had a few choice words to say about that."

Matilde laughed. "I'm sure she did. If it wasn't Helene's idea, it wasn't a good idea. What does Henry aspire to do in Omaha?"

"He said he wants to work in the stockyards. I hope he likes it."

"That's a booming business, at least that's what Anselm's heard. It will be a good way for Henry to settle down."

I glanced around the room, avoiding her eyes. I was immediately drawn to a large oil portrait of a woman with a mass of dark curls circled by a dozen big loops of golden ribbon. Her dress was trimmed with ecru lace and slid off her shoulders. The billowing sleeves were translucent, covering shorter sleeves. Beneath her coy smile flowed a long neck and radiant ivory skin, and it was shocking how exposed she looked, as the painting must have been quite old. But the most striking thing about the portrait was her captivating eyes, a midnight blue that penetrated the years and sought the truth in your soul.

"Who is the woman in that painting? I think I remember seeing it before," I asked.

Matilde smiled. "She's lovely, isn't she? It's my mother, Carolina Kraus Schulz when she was about sixteen. My sister, Mary, resembled her when she was that age. I've always loved that portrait. It was done by a well-known apprentice of Joseph Karl Stieler, who did commissions for the royal court."

I turned my attention away from the painting to the rest of the room. It must have previously been a parlor, adorned with pale lavender-flowered wallpaper and fancy crown molding below the vaulted ceiling. The chairs and a small davenport were covered with rich lavender silks and burgundy velvet. I imagined it was like living inside the queen's crown. All it lacked was some sparkling gemstones. Very lush compared to my meager wooden furniture.

"This room is beautiful. Did you pick out everything yourself?"

"Oh, Honey. You've seen most of it before. You children used to play in here. Of course, that was before I was stuck in this bed most of the time." She shifted the quilt covering her legs. "You know, my first husband, Roderick Meier built this house. He was an expert carpenter and built fifty or sixty houses in different states. Most of that was before he married me. At our wedding, he was already thirty-two. I was a girl of eighteen. He helped other homesteaders build their homes and barns. But he promised he'd build me the finest house he'd ever built, and he did. I was only sorry I couldn't fill it with children."

"Didn't you have a child?" I wondered if this question was impertinent.

"Oh yes, I was with child several times, and when I was about your age, I gave birth to a darling angel, Bernadette. She was a golden-haired beauty, just like you were, and so strong-willed. She loved to run outside and ride on the wagons."

"If it is not too hard, tell me what happened to her." I leaned closer to hear her frail voice.

"She was riding with her father sitting on the box of the wagon behind the horse team. Something went wrong with the harness and Roderick had to get down and adjust it. He told her to sit very still. Then the horse started, and she jumped up and screamed, he said. The team started to run, knocking Roderick down. Bernadette fell off the wagon and struck her head. He rushed home with her in his arms but it was too late. We were heartbroken, as you can imagine. She was almost four."

"I'm so sorry. You and Anselm didn't have any children?"

"Oh no. I was fifty when I married him. He could have had children if he'd married a younger woman. When Roderick died, I was so crushed. Anselm was here every day taking care of the farm. We had some animals then, milk cows, chickens, goats, and horses. I think I would have shriveled up and died myself if it hadn't been for Anselm. He encouraged me to do more every day, to learn how to do some of the outdoor work. He reminded me that my Roderick was looking down from heaven watching me, wanting me to be strong. And after a while, I did start to want to live again. I sold some of the livestock, we bought more land, and figured out a way for me to have some financial security in my later years."

I smiled. Matilde's face brightened when she spoke of Anselm. "And how long was it before you remarried?"

"It was only a little more than a year. I decided to grab what happiness I could before it was too late. You realize at some point that life is too short and precious. It was a good choice for me. I'm still not sure it made any sense for Anselm."

I patted her hand. "He loves you. I can see that by how he tries to handle your needs now."

"He feels obligated. Of course, he cares about me. He told me he asked you to come to live here and help us out." Matilde gave me a steady stare.

"Oh." I looked away. "I'm glad he asked you. What do you think about it?"

"I think it is more important what you think. I need a nursemaid; I can't deny it. I need help getting to the privy, especially in the morning. They call it rheumatoid arthritis. I was thrown from a horse seventeen years ago. She was a beautiful animal; Anselm was so proud he was able to find her for me. But one day she threw me off. My whole body hurt awhile, but I got better. Then a year or so later, arthritis set in and the doctors said it was because of my fall. Anselm blamed himself and sold that horse the first chance he got."

For a moment, we were both quiet. Matilde stared down at her misshapen fingers. When her eyes rose to meet mine, she forced a smile.

"There is no one I would rather have in the house than you, Addie, but what will this do to your outlook? I already told you I probably ruined Anselm's chance at having a family. I don't want to rob someone else of that possibility."

"I don't think you will, Aunt Matilde. Can I tell you a secret?"

"Of course, my darling." Matilde leaned closer.

"Henry told me he would like to send for me once he has money saved up after he starts his job in Omaha. It will be a year or more before he has that kind of savings. I need to think about whether I want to marry Henry. I aim to find a life for myself and not be beholden to my brother and his wife, but Henry feels more like a brother than a suitor. And then there is Emil. He claims he's sweet on me too. That could lead to big trouble between those boys and I don't want to be caught in the middle. So, I figured I should just take my time, and make them take their time. In the meantime, it might be smarter if I was not living over there. Less awkward. It would give Henry and me a chance to write letters and see if it is a good idea to be married."

"Nothing like a little competition to bring out the best in a man, I always say. Does that mean you will accept Anselm's offer?"

"I'm inclined to if you agree. I need to speak to him again. Are you sure it won't bother you to have a younger woman around your husband?"

"You've heard the gossip then!" Matilde scoffed. "I suppose it was inevitable that people would think Anselm was chasing other women, younger women. In the early days of our marriage, I knew I could trust him. He traveled a lot, but he always came back to my bed. Once I started getting feebler, I told him he shouldn't worry about the gossip. Some crows just like to hear themselves caw. If he wanted to spend evenings in the company of a young woman, he had my permission. He has made me happy in the second portion of my life, I have no complaints about him. He ought to enjoy some comforts with other women. He's been discreet, I think, and has never discussed any details with me, nor have I made any accusations."

My hand flew to my mouth. "I wouldn't dream of being involved like—"

"Oh, I know. I didn't mean to imply that. What I'm saying is that he can handle himself with young women. I don't think it will be a problem. You referred to him as your uncle. He's gone quite often, and it appears this arrangement may only be temporary for you. Just promise me that you won't sacrifice your future happiness to wait on an old lady like me."

I had to give her a hug. Most women would not be so understanding. I looked forward to many long talks with Matilde.

It was three days before Anselm returned from a trip. He found me in my little cottage reading the Bible in the waning light. Two candles lit the corners of the room.

"Good evening, Addie. Forgive me for disturbing you. Matilde said you wanted to talk to me about the live-in helper position." Anselm removed his cap and took a seat in the chair facing me.

"Yes, I do. I'm earnestly considering it. You should know that it might be temporary. I may be moving away at some point. I haven't made that decision yet."

Anselm shrugged. "The job is temporary too. I hope Matilde will live a long time, but not if she's in pain. No one should live in pain forever." He put his forearms on his thighs and looked at the floor. "Was there anything else you needed to consider? I mentioned an automobile or a dog. Maybe you'd rather have a horse or carriage available?"

"Anselm, what do you value?"

His head snapped up. "What do I value? Gee, I don't think anyone ever asked me that. I guess life, love, good health, family…honesty, loyalty, faith…"

"No, I mean, what if you were doing a business deal with another man and you had the advantage? You had something he wanted at any price. What would you ask for? What would be valuable to you?"

He blinked. "Oh. That's different: land. I always believed land was the finest commodity. It always increases in price eventually, and there's a limited supply."

I nodded. "Land. Right. That's what I need to make the deal."

His brows knit together, giving him deep wrinkles in the shadowed room. "I don't understand. What land?"

"The Schulz homestead land. My parents homesteaded this quarter-section right where we are sitting more than forty years ago. I want it back for my children and my nieces and nephews."

"You expect me to give you 160 acres of land? I bought that as a favor for my wife, her brother's legacy. It's worth close to $27,000 by now. You could never make that much as a live-in helper."

"I still want the wages you offered. This is in addition to that. I don't expect it right away. Maybe a few acres every year, or put it in your will. It's your land but it used to be our land. I want to be able to leave it to the descendants of Herman and Lillian Schulz who risked everything to move here and carve out a life for our family."

"Oh, you want me to include that in my will? That might be feasible."

"You're a clever businessman, or so I am told. Talk to a lawyer, if necessary, or the banker you're such close friends with. Make me an offer you can live with that includes returning that land to me."

Anselm shook his head. Then he laughed. "And Matilde was afraid I was taking advantage of a poor innocent youngster. You drive a hard bargain, my dear."

I pursed my lips. "If I agree to this, I will be going against the advice of my sister-in-law. She thinks you might corrupt me. I haven't even consulted my fiancé. He likely won't approve either."

Anselm's brows lifted. "You have a fiancé? You hadn't mentioned him."

"Well, nothing is settled. It's possible. I don't want to go into details until it's certain. The point is, that this venture involves some risk and discomfort for me. I want to be sure it is worth it down the line. I mean the point is to help my aunt, I know, and I'm willing to do it. I also need to think about my interests. She told me that herself."

"All right. Let me work on this and I will present you with some options, Miss Schulz. I think I'm going to take Matilde on the train to Hot Springs, South Dakota, at the end of the week. We were hoping you could start when we return. Or if you would like, you can go along and enjoy the springs yourself. They are quite soothing, even for someone without arthritic pain. You can let me know next time we talk."

Anselm stood up and put his hat back on. Then he bowed politely as though we had been dancing. *Maybe that's what he thinks we were doing. A negotiation is similar to a dance with its ebb and flow.*

I blew out my breath and got ready for bed. I couldn't believe I'd had so much nerve. I asked for exactly what I wanted. It appeared he took me seriously. Well, we'll see what he comes back with.

CHAPTER SIX: ANSELM

What is wrong with me? I am losing my touch!

No one would believe I would consider giving up land I came by fair and square. I stood on those icy courthouse steps and outbid everyone else five years ago. I bought it for my wife because it was her family's land. Now this audacious girl thinks I'm not good enough to own her parents' homestead. Well, she's liable to get some real-world comeuppance.

Except, damn it. That took some nerve. She tricked me into revealing my own Achille's heel. I've never met a girl so shrewd. You wouldn't know to look at her. She looks like she could use her feminine charms to dazzle a man. She's a feast for the eyes, but she hasn't tried to use her beauty at all. She tried to outsmart me, outmaneuver me. Nobody gets away with that—Nobody except maybe Matilde. Years ago, Matilde could do that to me. She could wrap me around her little finger and I wouldn't know what hit me until it was too late.

But I've had lots of experience with women since then. Women always want something, usually money. Sometimes just affection, someone to keep them warm for the night. Someone to pour them a drink and keep alive their fantasy of love until the morning light.

I'm too tired. I can't let this girl get into my head. Tomorrow I'll determine what needs to be done to secure her cooperation. I've done dozens of deals with stubborn old men, sometimes with shotguns at their side. I've done deals with unfortunate widows who needed time, conversation, and sympathy before they could sign papers. But never have I been bested by a mere girl. A girl who claims to have a fiancé. Maybe. She didn't even want to involve him in this business arrangement. She wanted to handle it herself. And why? For her future children, nieces, and nephews. Doesn't she know that's a man's job?

Doesn't she realize she's a simple wisp of a girl? She should be thinking about combing out that lovely blonde hair of hers. I can imagine her small graceful fingers gripping her silver hairbrush as she sings softly. She should be pouting those full pink lips and batting her extremely long eyelashes at someone. Her fiancé, I suppose. She should—*what is wrong with me?*

I had my wits about me three days later when I returned to meet with Miss Schulz. It was better to think of her more formally, as we were conducting a business arrangement. I found her weeding the garden in a patch between her house and that of Samuel Schulz. She was so intent on her vigorous hoeing that she didn't appear to be aware of my approach. I had driven up in my Dodge Roadster, hens squawking and scattering before me.

"Miss Schulz?" It was hot standing there in the August sun in my three-piece suit and straw boater. Perhaps she intended to make me wait.

She lifted her head, perspiration running down her cheeks and forehead, giving her a radiant sheen in the glistening sunlight. She ran one dirty hand across her brow, leaving a streak of dirt framing one eye. "Mr. Roth? Have you made progress?"

"Yes, I believe so. It looks like you've been hard at work as well." I surveyed the plot she'd been toiling over, with clumps of dirt turned up in a twenty-foot radius. I adjusted my hat, but it provided little shade. "I have just met with my attorney, Clark Jeary. Perhaps we might adjourn to your cottage to look at the papers he drew up for us."

She nodded and headed toward the cottage with me on her heels. As living quarters go, her place was humble. It looked to me as if her brothers had cobbled together some leftover lumber from building a barn or other projects. The roof was a little off-kilter and her porch was rotting. A fresh coat of paint would have improved the facade.

As soon as she entered the kitchen, she pumped water at the sink and drank heartily from a tin cup, dribbling liquid down her cotton blouse.

"I'd offer you a drink but I'm afraid I only have one cup."

I nodded and smiled. I took the cup from her hand and pumped more cool water, sipping it leisurely and leaning on the cabinet housing the sink.

"As I said, I had my attorney revise my will so that—"

"You should know I changed my mind."

"You did? Oh, well that's a relief. Because Mr. Jeary suggested that leaving the land to a woman made little sense—"

"I don't want you to put the land in your will. I want you to put it in Aunt Matilde's will."

"In Matilde's will? She doesn't have a will. Everything she owns is jointly owned by me. If we were to die at the same time, say a fire or something, my last will names certain heirs. As of this morning, you were added to my list of heirs."

"No, that won't work. I've been thinking about it. You will likely live another ten or twenty years. I don't know where I'll be then. I need to have this taken care of sooner."

I wrinkled my brow. "The problem with your notion is that Matilde doesn't own that particular piece of property outright. It's in my name. She owns the acres we live on, she inherited that from her first husband. I'm not giving that up, the house is too valuable."

"Nor am I asking for that. Just transfer the title to Matilde for the 160 acres that comprised the Schulz homestead. You said you bought it because of your wife. She should have the deed. When that is done, you can have a will drawn up for her estate that leaves that parcel to me. Certainly, anything else in her name is yours. If you agree to those terms, we have a deal."

I unfolded the papers I held in my hands. "But my attorney has just made the previous revisions this morning."

"I'm sure he will be happy to prepare the other papers. Isn't that what you pay him for?"

I sighed. "You don't understand. What you're suggesting will take time. Weeks, maybe a month to transfer the deed. It must go through the offices in Lincoln. Then another week or two to create a will for Matilde. I need your assistance with her much sooner than that."

Addie plopped down on her wooden chair. "Then you should make haste. Don't stand around jawing with me. I'll bet you could have the lawyer work on the will while waiting for the deeds to be finished. I am willing to trust you to get it all done. If you still want me to, I would like to travel with you to Hot Springs. I've never been there. I really haven't traveled at all."

As I rocked back on my heels, some of the tension I'd held all morning began to ease. "You're taking the job then?"

Adelaide rose and stood in front of me. "Yes, Mr. Roth, as long as you provide me with room and board in your home for as long as my aunt needs my care and the monthly wages you mentioned. And you will start the process to transfer the title of the Schulz homestead quarter to Matilde and prepare a will for her that leaves that land to me alone. Upon her death, our contract will be terminated, as we will have both fulfilled the provisions."

"Are you sure it doesn't make more sense to put the land in your brother Samuel's name? He is farming it, after all."

"He is leasing the land from you. He can continue to lease it from me as long as that is practical. What I do with the land won't be your concern. Have we agreed on terms?"

Her steely gaze was one I'd rarely seen from the most astute adversary.

"I believe we have a deal, Miss Schulz." I gave her the once over just to gain some psychological advantage. Then I stuck out my hand. I was betting she wouldn't shake it.

But she shoved her right hand into mine and gripped it firmly. She looked me solidly in the eyes. Those big blue eyes were confident, almost out of place on a face so gentle. Eyes a man could wade in for hours. Perhaps in time, I could spend evenings lost in those eyes, pushing those errant blonde strands away from her delicate face. I wondered how she would look blushing in the candlelight over the evening meal.

I held onto her hand a moment longer than necessary. Did I imagine it, or had we both shortened the gap between us?

"I have work to do. I believe you do as well." Addie took a step back and moved toward the doorway.

"Yes, you have made more work for me. I expect not for the last time. I will pick you up early Friday morning to catch the train for the trip to South Dakota."

She nodded and turned to leave. I looked at my palm and found it caked with sweat and more than a little soil.

CHAPTER SEVEN: ADELAIDE

"What do you mean, you didn't bring a bathing suit? What did you plan to wear in the sulfur springs?" Anselm studied me, hands on hips.

We gathered in the hotel room I was sharing with Aunt Matilde, my small bag piled on the bed. "I don't own a bathing suit. I've only been swimming in the pond, and haven't even done that for a few years. I suppose I wore my knickers."

Anselm's pinched lips and upward glance appeared to be his default expression, as though there was no end to the things a simple farm girl did not know. Yet here stood the same young man who had gotten his start at Matilde's farm all those years ago. He flaunted his acquired sophistication like a fine pocket watch.

He turned his attention to his wife. "I'm sorry, my dear. You can rest while Addie and I go to the bath shop and purchase a swimsuit and cap for her. We shall return in plenty of time to enjoy the springs today." He helped her settle on her bed, covering her with a blanket.

I could not have imagined what awaited me in the bathing shop. All sorts of wildly bright and printed fabrics adorned most of the ladies' swimwear. Some looked like dresses with pantaloons; others were more like underthings, jumpers, or wool knit bloomers with sleeveless tops attached. Anselm stood at a rack looking at men's swimming wear, primarily all-in-one sleeveless knit shirts and short pants.

"Pick out whatever you like," he muttered.

"I don't know. There are different sizes. How would I know which size to pick?"

He frowned. The condescending scowl was practically stuck on his face. "Excuse me, Miss!" He'd addressed a saleswoman nearby. "My girl doesn't know what size to choose. She looks about the same as you. Can you give her some guidance?"

"Your daughter, then?" the clerk smiled sweetly at Anselm. "Let's try the medium. If it is too small, we'll go up. If it's too big, we'll go down." She pulled a few garments from the rack and herded me into a dressing room. "Just call out if you need any help."

It was enough of a chore just to remove my long skirt, petticoat, and blouse. Was I supposed to wear my underthings with the bathing suit? I didn't want to get them wet; how could I wear them afterward? I had seen some of the more modern fashions, even right here in this hotel. Women were abandoning corsets and long column dresses skimmed over their waists. These swimsuits looked like that too: tight, straight, and shapeless.

I tried on a wool knit contraption first. It was a conservative dark shade but looked much like the styles shown for men, with a hint of gold decorating the arm holes and a sash around the waist. Although it fit, without the added cinch of my corset, I appeared bottle-shaped from my shoulders to my knees.

The salesgirl wandered back and opened the dressing room door. "Very stylish. You have the perfect shape for that style. Do you want to show your father?"

"My uncle, not father," I said, "And no, I do not need to show him." I closed the door to sample the next option.

"Your uncle! Ha. I have heard that one before, Dearie. Pretty young ladies often have older uncles shopping with them."

My face reddened at her implication. No matter. We would be on our way as soon as I found something I could live with. The next suit the clerk had chosen was green satin with blue trim. It was a little fuller with a flared skirt. The knee-length pantaloons that went underneath were ruffled blue and green. I supposed this was better.

"Miss? I have a question." The salesgirl appeared at my door again.

I pulled the loose scoop-necked bodice away from my chest. "What do you wear underneath this suit?"

She smiled. "You should be naked under a swimming suit. However, I see your concern. You're afraid too much will show under your arms. Let's try the size smaller. It might fit better there."

The smaller size was tighter, but it still allowed some movement. I settled on that one. Then I had to go through the whole rigmarole of putting my regular clothes back on, just to reverse the process again in the bathhouse.

I forgot my awkwardness with my apparel when I was helping Matilde navigate from the bathhouse to the spa pool. Anselm had to meet us at the pool. He came forward immediately when he saw us emerge, and together we lowered Matilde down the wide steps into the springs. Ledges were spaced where one could sit submerged to the shoulders in the warm water. It was truly pleasant until I noticed my suit billowing upward like a bubble.

"You like the warm water, Addie?" Matilde asked, leaning back to relax. She moved her arms in a figure-eight motion which helped her balance on the ledge.

"It feels wonderful," I said. "It's like you're weightless. I could sit here for an hour."

"Do you like Addie's suit, Matilde?" Anselm asked. He finally seemed to be enjoying himself. His black wool swim jumper showed off tan arms. For someone who didn't do much physical labor, he had broad shoulders and a trim waist.

"Let me see your suit, Honey," Matilde said.

I stood and realized what didn't show in the store dressing room. The wet satin fabric clung to my bosom in a way that defied modesty. I refused to glance at Anselm but felt the heat of his stare as I sank back into the water.

Matilde must have sensed my embarrassment, but she tried to make light of it. "You look very modern, Addie. Like a fashionable 1920s girl. Maybe we can do some more shopping while we're here. You could use a party dress."

"I don't know. It's a nice idea, but I have clothes I can work in."

"We may invite some of the neighbor women to tea when we get home. Wouldn't you like to have a modern style to wear for an occasion like that?"

I didn't think you were up to entertaining. I know I can't afford a new dress. Anselm already paid for the swimming suit; I can't expect him to buy anything else.

"Let's just see how you do with the spa treatments, Aunt Matilde."

After a big hotel breakfast, Anselm and I took Matilde to a special treatment area. The attendant put her in a Turkish towel robe and they lowered her into a big vat with swirling water. The murky water had a strange odor from some type of salt additive. I stayed to watch but this pool was intended for just one patient.

"I have some meetings this morning, Adelaide. You stay with Matilde. If she is finished, and you think you can get her back to the room yourself, go ahead. Sometimes an attendant is available for that purpose. Otherwise, stay in the waiting area until my return."

I was worried we might wait for him for hours, but as it turned out, Matilde did so well with the treatments that we got back to the hotel room on our own.

Matilde lay down on her bed. "I feel so much better after that. The therapists help me move my joints around under the water. It always wears me out though. I'm going to take a nap, but you should feel free to explore the hotel or the grounds. There are lovely walking paths through the gardens."

The gardens were in full bloom, and I soon found a comfortable bench where I could read the book I had brought along. Although late August meant blistering hot temperatures in southern Nebraska, the weather in Hot Springs was much milder, partly due to its higher elevation. I found myself caught up in the story until I felt the wooden slat bench bend with a newcomer's weight. I looked up into Anselm's face.

"I guessed I might find you out here. It's a beautiful day," he said.

"You finished your meetings?

"Yes. I was exploring for part of the time. I'm learning more about the real estate market here in Hot Springs. The town is growing."

I put my book down. "Are you thinking of buying property here?"

He shrugged one shoulder, stretched out his legs, and leaned back onto the bench. "I'm considering options. I might want to sell some of my lands in the country and buy property in a city. Maybe Hot Springs, maybe Lincoln, or Kansas City. Unlike you, I don't have a sentimental attachment to any piece of land."

"Your parents didn't homestead then? I don't know where you came from."

"I came over to this country when I was eighteen. Worked on the ship to earn my passage. I didn't even speak English very well. My parents stayed back in Prussia. Two years later, they sent Anton over here. We were both lucky enough to find families who would hire us to help with the farming. Roderick Meier took me under his wing. He was a tough one, much stricter than my father back in the old country." Anselm laughed. "Of course, I suppose I was an uppity boy who thought he knew everything. I did have a good education, but I knew nothing about the prairie, the crops here, raising animals, or carpentry. He taught me a lot."

"Your parents didn't come over to America?"

Anselm shook his head. "I think they tried to make it once or twice. They wrote and said they were coming, but my mother got sick before they got on a boat. They died in Germany. I never saw them again after I left."

It made more sense now. Matilde and Roderick were his substitute family.

"I suppose I got comfortable with Roderick and Matilde. He was quite a bit older than she was." Anselm's face tightened and he looked out at the horizon. "I saw how they struggled to have children. Then when little Bernadette died, I don't know who took it harder. Rod blamed himself, of course, for the accident. He was never the same afterward, but he wouldn't speak of it. Not even to his wife. I guess that's when I started to get closer to Matilde. Not in a romantic way, more like a brother might. She would talk to me about her pain, losing her child, and her husband pulling away. I tried to make him see what he was doing but then he turned on me. We got into a terrible fight. I can still see how angry…well, it was the pain talking. I feared he meant to fire me…"

I can't believe he's telling me this. Here's a different side of Anselm I haven't seen before. How hard this must have been for all of them.

He looked back at me and huffed out his breath. "Lord knows what brought that on. I meant to say they sort of pulled me into their family. I tried to help Matilde heal after Roderick died. It was platonic at first, but after about six months or so, I guess we both recognized we were lonely, and things changed."

"It's been good for you, then? Your marriage?" I knew I had no right to ask such a personal question, but I wanted to know.

"Yes, it has. Does that surprise you?"

"Not anymore. Not after what I have heard in the past few weeks."

He slid forward on the bench resting his arms on his legs and looked down. "This next part is going to be tough. I guess that's one reason I am making some plans for later. She won't want to leave that house she loves. After she's gone, I don't think I will want to live there. Too many memories. Ghosts maybe." He swiped his cheek and chuckled. "I remember after I married

Matilde, I was afraid Roderick would come back and haunt our bedchamber."

I laughed aloud, then covered my mouth. "Oh my! He didn't!"

"No," Anselm smiled. "Are you hungry? Should we go find some lunch? We can check on Matilde first."

CHAPTER EIGHT: ANSELM

Addie and I bundled Matilde warmly for the train trip back home, per the spa staff's instructions. We had brought extra shawls and blankets for the ride. The cool outside night air contrasted with the stuffy train car, and I found myself overheated in my usual clothing without any of the extra layers my wife wore. I saw beads of perspiration trickle down her face when the lamplight flashed through the windows.

Would this be like the last time we went to the springs? When we visited six months ago, she felt better while we were there but by the time the train ride ended, she was right back where she started. Did I waste our time and money again? Did these futile attempts exasperate the defeat we both felt?

I tried to sleep in the seat across from Matilde, but I couldn't relax. The catfish dinner I'd eaten earlier churned with the clattering of the train wheels over the track. I couldn't shake the feeling Matilde's prognosis was only going to get worse.

I watched Adelaide out of the corner of my eye. She had curled up on one of the seats across the aisle with a shawl wrapped over her shoeless feet. We were fortunate that the car was almost empty so we had room to stretch out. I wondered if I'd done her a great disservice bringing her in on this. She was so young and caring and had already had to watch one ailing parent descend to the grave.

After an hour, I gave up trying to sleep. Not wanting to disturb the others, I went to the smoking car behind us. I lit one cigarette after another, staring into the black void outside the open window.

Matilde didn't fare well on the car ride home and stayed in bed for most of the next two days, rarely even eating or drinking. The evening after we returned, Gustav and Zelda Hintz came to say goodbye. They were leaving for Omaha the next morning. I was surprised to see they brought Helene Schulz's son, Henry Hoffmann.

"Is Matilde up for visitors today?" Mrs. Hintz asked.

"For anyone else, I'd say no. Considering you are leaving tomorrow, I think she would like you to look in on her, Zelda. Why don't you go on back?"

I took the two men out back. Adelaide had been in with Matilde but came outside when Zelda went in.

"Oh, Henry. I didn't know you were here," Addie said to him. She didn't even look at Gustav or me.

He took her hand and guided her to the barnyard, out of earshot.

That puzzled me. Addie had mentioned a suitor, a possible fiancé. Surely, she didn't mean Henry! He was practically a schoolboy.

"We've got everything packed up to start tomorrow…brother is coming to feed the cattle…be back in three weeks for the sale…Omaha has lots of opportunities…" Gustav was prattling on about God knows what. I think I'd heard him tell the same story twice before.

I cocked my head when Addie and Henry moved into the shadows near the barn's entrance. He put his hand on her face. Was he kissing her? Did she need help to ward him off?

"Anselm, what's wrong?" Gustav said.

"Huh?" I turned to face him now. His back was to the barn.

"You looked alarmed." Gustav turned around. "Oh, Henry wanted to say goodbye to Adelaide. He wanted to take her with him, but they should wait."

"Wait?" My mouth went suddenly dry. I stepped a few feet to the side to try to see if Addie was all right. "Wait for what?"

"To be married. He can get established—"

"Married? He can't be thinking about marriage yet!" I let out a sound like a strangled chortle. "You mean to Adelaide? That's ridiculous. She's…she's much too…I don't see how. I don't see them as ever being married."

Gustav grinned. "Ah well, young love. You can never tell how it will work out. I still have chores to do to wrap things up. We'd best be going. I'll go fetch Zelda and give Henry a few more minutes to…" Gustav just raised his unruly brows.

As soon as Gustav went around to the front of the house, I headed for the barn door. I caught sight of Henry holding a folded paper out to Addie. She smiled sweetly. At least she appeared to be safe.

They both looked up at me expectantly when I drew near.

"I needed to get…something. Something from the barn." That didn't make much sense. I had no choice but to enter the barn and cast around for something worth fetching. A horseshoe. I spotted a horseshoe hanging over one of the pens. I grabbed that.

I started whistling as I neared the barn door again. It appeared they might have been in an embrace. Henry was moving away from Addie and his hand trailed from her waist across her backside.

"Gustav is ready to leave, Henry," I grumbled. "You don't want to make him wait."

Henry tipped his hat as he walked toward the house. I stopped to search Addie's face as a frown spread across it.

"Are you good?" I asked.

"I'm fine. Henry just wanted to say goodbye before he moves to Omaha. What was so important in the barn?"

I held up the horseshoe. "Something Matilde wanted in her room. Good luck I reckon." I whistled on my way back to the house.

My work kept me busy the next few days, and I spent two nights in Lincoln, meeting with investors in one of my projects. When I returned late in the day, Addie and Matilde both toiled in the yard. I found Matilde sitting in a wicker chair with a large flower urn between her knees. Despite the clumsiness of her misshapen fingers, she was digging with a hand trowel. Excess dirt was spilling onto her white apron. Addie stood by watching.

They both turned smiles on me.

"What's going on?" I asked, surveying the mess Matilde had made of her clothing.

"We're gardening!" Matilde declared. "I told Addie that I missed working in my garden, and she found these big pots behind the barn. I guess we haven't used them for years. Emil came over and helped her get them closer to the house. Then we mixed in some chicken manure and dug up the old foliage. We should have these ready for flowers in the spring."

"You're digging in the dirt and chicken manure! Tilde! Addie can do that for you, or I can tomorrow."

"I know that, but I want to do it. It feels good to do something useful again even if I make a mess."

"When I left, you'd been in bed for days. You started feeling better?"

Addie put her hand on Matilde's shoulder. "We tried some new things. Stone therapy, more movement, dandelion tea. We've gotten her walking around the outside of the house ten times today."

She could have punched me in the gut. The sickening blow radiated up to my chest. "You made her walk around the house ten times? Do you have any idea how painful that must have been for her? Have you ever looked at her feet?"

Adelaide's face lost its color. "Her feet? What's wrong with her feet?" She grabbed onto her braid and looked from my face to Matilde's.

I snarled at her ignorance. I yanked the wicker chair away from the urn and rotated it around to face me. Putting Matilde's dirty right boot on the leg of my clean trousers, I untied the laces and pulled off her boot and stocking. Matilde's soiled toes were red and blisters were forming. Her big toe had long ago taken a detour pointing toward the midline of her foot. Her third toe curled atop the second, and there were pronounced nodules on all three of the first toes. I picked up her foot by the heel.

"This! This is what she is walking on! How do you imagine that feels, Adelaide?"

Addie stared at Matilde's foot, then her frightened gaze moved to Matilde's face. She backed up quickly, then turned to run to the barn.

"Wait! Addie." Matilde called after her. "It's not as bad as it looks. Most of my foot is numb!"

"I'm so sorry, Tilde." I began to gently put her stocking and shoe back on. "This was a mistake. I should have never left you in the care of someone so inexperienced—"

"No! It's not a mistake. It was hard at first." With her shoe tied, she rose, holding onto both my hands. "Addie made me do more than I knew I could, but don't you see what's happened? I can do more. I want to do more. When I push through the stiffness, I feel better. I can move more than I thought possible. No, I can't stand up as long as I used to, but I can walk farther every day. My feet might hurt but my back and knees feel stronger. And her stone therapy is a wonderful idea. I can get up in the morning without pain."

I helped her take a tentative step, then she took my arm and walked gingerly without using her cane.

"What is stone therapy?" I asked.

"I think she might have invented it. She had been heating big pots of water on the stove for my bath. The next day, she put little rocks in a frying pan and heated them instead. The rocks went into two pillow cases and she put them on my hips in bed with me. I put my aching hands on the bundle of rocks. In no time, my hips and hands both felt better. We talked about using kidney beans but she was afraid they'd split open. Very resourceful, that niece of mine. I think she's the one you should apologize to, Anselm."

I scowled. I'd scowled a lot more lately. We entered the house and I helped her sit on a chair at the dining table. "Did Addie prepare dinner?" I asked.

"No, we were working in the garden. She said she'd make a late supper when I was ready. I need to wash my hands. To my astonishment, Matilde pushed herself out of the chair and walked carefully to the kitchen pump. Before our trip to the springs, she'd needed at least her cane to traverse the room. "You do seem better. I suppose I will have to go find Adelaide."

Matilde called after me as I went out the door. "Apologize, Anselm!" she called. I winced.

Addie wasn't in the barn. I wondered if she might be hiding up in the hayloft like a child, but I didn't find her there either. I whistled loudly as if calling a dog, but it brought no response. *Where in tarnation had she run off to? Why must women resort to such hysteria?*

Then it struck me. Would she return to her brother's farm? It was within walking distance. Heaving a sigh, I got back into my roadster. I spotted her about half a mile away.

I tooted the horn to make sure she knew I was behind her. "Addie, get in the car. I shouldn't have yelled at you. I'm sorry. Matilde explained what you were doing. Stop walking. Addie, stop!" She didn't stop though, and I felt my temper flaring up like a firestorm again.

I stopped the car in the middle of the road. Then I jumped out and spun her around to face me. "Get in the car."

"I won't!" Her eyes had darkened to match the enveloping dusk.

I'd had enough of this errant behavior. I bent quickly and hoisted her over my shoulder. She squawked like a prickly hen. I dumped her onto the passenger seat, then climbed over her and the gearshift to get to the driver's position, keeping one hand on her arm until we were back in motion.

"Let me go! You can't force me to go back with you!" she cried, trying to wrench her arm free.

"I can and I will. You've been bought and paid for."

She turned her fury on me. "You have not yet paid me a cent, I'll remind you!"

"My Lord, Woman! Do you expect me to pay for your services in advance now? Has anyone ever offered you a deal such as that? You'll be paid when the month is out." I released her arm, hoping she wouldn't jump from a moving car. "In the meantime, my wife and I need our supper."

Addie stuck her nose in the air. "You implied I tried to injure her."

"I was mistaken. I apologized. Get over it." I hoped my stern tone would end any future discussion.

She crossed her arms and glared at me out of the corner of her eye, but said nothing.

Supper that evening involved a lot of heavy pans banging loudly behind my back as I waited at the kitchen table. I supposed I should be pleased none of them whacked me across the skull. In time, a plate of fried eggs and potatoes appeared in front of me. I chose to be appreciative and silent. Arguing only makes me hungry.

CHAPTER NINE: ADELAIDE

It was harvest time. Anselm stopped wearing his business clothes, as I thought of them: his suit jackets and silk vests with starched white-collar shirts and stiff trousers. Instead, he left soon after dawn wearing the kind of clothing my brother Samuel favored: overalls or work pants over a union suit with overshoes on his feet and a brimmed hat shading his face.

"Is Anselm actually going to do some farm labor?" I asked Matilde the first morning when I brought the warm stone packets into her bed for her hips. I had perfected the process somewhat, after having sewn smaller pockets to hold the stones, held tight with a drawstring. I had even ventured down to a nearby pond to retrieve smoother stones that would be less likely to tear the fabric or poke Matilde's skin.

"Don't tell anyone, but I think he looks forward to doing this every season. He gets a chance to talk to all his neighbors and see the fruits of their labor. He takes a share of the profit on the farms he owns, so his labor helps reduce the expense. They should be picking corn today, and he hopes to bring in a corn sheller machine in a few weeks once the corn has dried in the cribs."

"I don't think I know what that means, a corn sheller. Don't they shell the corn by hand?"

"You'll have to ask him. It's new, that's all I know."

Matilde and I kept working on improving her mobility. While we were at the sulfur springs, I picked up a few pamphlets at their library on ways to reduce inflammation. I heard the doctors talking about how rheumatoid arthritis causes one's body to attack itself. I could see evidence of that in Matilde's deformed feet and hands. If you looked closely, you found some twisting in her knees and hips. No wonder she was in pain.

As she was able to sit or stand for longer periods, we did some baking and canning to prepare for the winter months.

"I must confess, Addie. It is such a joy to have you here. Anselm is gone so often during the day, especially this time of year. I appreciated Zelda Hintz, but she preferred to have me sleep so she could clean the house and prepare food. She prepared meals for her family's household here, sometimes. I didn't mind; she worked hard. I only had her company for an hour or so every day. I didn't realize it, but I was sad."

"I'm enjoying being here with you too, Aunt Matilde. It reminds me of when I used to visit as a child. After my mother died, it was not the same living with Helene. She means well, and she has done a great job with her own children but…"

"Say no more, my dear. I have fond memories of Lillian. You remind me of her. She shone like a star."

Anselm returned home at about dusk. I heard his car when he drove in and saw him do an unexpected ritual in the backyard near the barn. He filled a large black caldron from the pump, then hoisted it to some sort of metal stand. Directly below that sat an iron barrel. It must have been filled with something flammable, as he lit the contents of the barrel.

He came in and ate supper without mentioning the fire he had burning outdoors. Neither Matilde nor I commented on the fact that his clothing and face were covered with dirt and remnants of the cornfield. Up to this point, he'd been so fastidious, that I was amazed he ate supper wearing dirty clothes.

I got Matilde put to bed after supper as usual, then returned to tidy up the dishes and kitchen area. I spotted Anselm through the window. He was returning to that burning barrel and carrying a blanket and gloves. As I watched, he stripped off all his clothing except for the gloves and picked up the caldron, and dumped the water over his head. I gasped in surprise at his wet naked form shining in the moonlight. The heat rushed to my face as I spun away from the window.

I scurried to the sitting room and lit a lamp so I could read my book. He came in shortly, wrapped in the blanket. I didn't want to look up, didn't want him to know I'd witnessed anything, but I couldn't help it.

When our eyes met, I saw the recognition. He knew what I'd seen. He nodded and slipped his shoes off. He must have left his dirty clothes on the porch. He went up the stairs to his room and I heard a faint chuckle.

CHAPTER TEN: ANSELM

Before we had all the corn picked, it started raining. We could have worked in the rain except for the lightning. I took advantage of the free day to head to the nearby town of Hallam, where my attorney and banker were. I was glad I'd stored my car in the barn overnight, but I had to put the side curtains on due to the dampness.

In mid-afternoon, I returned home and found Matilde and Addie in the drawing room, the largest room on the main floor where the player piano was located. Strains of a polka filled the air before I'd even closed the front door. Matilde sat on the piano bench pumping the pedals with her stocking feet. Adelaide jumped around the floor barefoot doing what I would describe as a jig. They were both laughing.

"What have we here?" I bellowed, to be heard above the noise.

"Oh, Anselm!" Matilde said. "You're just in time. Show Addie how we used to polka to this!"

"All right, Tilde. But rest a moment. I have a gift for you."

Matilde beamed. "What are you hiding?"

I realized how long it had been since I had brought her any kind of trinket. I once did that when I traveled, but the house became cluttered and I stopped buying her things on impulse.

I opened an envelope in my hand and thrust the papers in front of Matilde.

She looked up at me. "What is this?"

I took a deep breath, giving Addie a sideways glance. She was pacing the floor catching her breath. "I transferred some property into your name. The land across the road that Samuel Schulz is farming now."

"You mean the land that used to belong to my brother, Herman? The 160 acres that Herman and Lillian homesteaded?"

"Yes, that's right." I waited for her to understand.

"Why, thank you, Anselm. It's a sweet gesture, but isn't it kind of pointless? It will go back to you sooner or later." Tears rimmed her eyes behind her spectacles. She pushed to her feet, clutched my arms, and kissed me on the cheek.

"Well, actually no." Apparently, Adelaide had chosen not to discuss this maneuver of hers with her aunt. "This other set of papers…" I laid the envelopes on the piano and pulled out the new will. "This is your last will and testament. Since you have property in your name alone, you need a will. It bequeaths that property to one Adelaide Schulz."

Matilde held onto my arms for balance but peered around me to look at Addie. Addie had the good grace to look uncomfortable. She studied the view out the front window.

"Adelaide? Were you aware of this?" Matilde asked. "You don't appear surprised."

"Hmm? Oh, yes. Anselm and I discussed it. I hoped to keep the property in the Schulz family."

Matilde narrowed her eyes, looking from Addie back to me. "Why didn't you just give it to her, if that's what she wanted?"

I hadn't expected that. "Um, this is more…appropriate. I mean you were born a Schulz and um…I think it will be more palatable for her brothers, Samuel and Christian, if we do it this way."

"But Samuel and Christian both have wives and children. Addie does not." Matilde turned her gaze back to Adelaide. "How would you pass the property along to the next generation?"

Addie walked up to Matilde and put her hand on her arm. "I'm sorry we have sprung this on you. I just wanted to have some control over what happens with the property. If you are opposed to this, we can just tear up these papers right now." Addie reached for the will.

I pulled it away. "No. I paid to have this done. If you don't like it, I'll have to have the deed transfer rescinded."

"I don't want you to do that, Anselm," Matilde said. "Do I have to sign something?"

"We will go to Clark's office tomorrow and sign the papers in front of a notary. I wanted you to have time to examine them first."

"As you wish. Now, it's time to dance." Matilde sat back down at the piano and began pumping the mechanism with the foot pedals to build up pressure. In a moment, the lively polka began playing again.

Addie spoke loudly to be heard over the music. "We found this was good for her knees, pumping the pedals. She said the two of you used to—"

When I placed one hand on her waist and took the other, her feet began flying as quickly as mine did. We spun around the room at a lively pace while Matilde powered the piano. We bumped into a few chairs, and I stopped to scoot the furniture all against the walls. When the music stopped, we were both winded.

"You two should dance," Addie insisted. "I'll bet you did this in the old days."

Matilde smiled. "We once danced every night, but I can't polka like that anymore. I'll change the music." She pulled out a different piano roll from the cabinet and loaded it. "All you have to do is pump your feet up and down, Addie."

Addie took over at the piano and a slow waltz began playing. I took Matilde's right hand in my left hand and placed my right hand on her shoulder blade. She may have been somewhat frail, but she was still lightweight and I could hold her up to a certain extent, keeping pressure off her swollen joints. Matilde smiled coyly. It had been a long time since we held each other in such an intimate manner.

"Look at me, Tilde," I said.

She met my eyes and I saw the passion that had faded over time. The robust woman who had once blossomed in my arms now was disintegrating before me. When I pressed my lips together, they tasted bittersweet.

"I think I need to sit down," Matilde said when the song ended. I helped her into one of the chairs now lining the perimeter.

I went back to the piano and folded the papers, returning them to the envelopes.

Matilde got up again and shooed Addie away from the piano bench, taking her seat. "I want you to show Addie how to waltz. A young girl should be able to dance more than one way." Matilde rolled the paper on the piano and started the song again.

I showed Adelaide the basic steps, and we practiced just a bit. Then we were gliding around the floor with Matilde clapping at our progress. Dancing with an energetic girl took me back twenty years at least. It had been so long since I'd held someone who could flit like a swallow, soaring effortlessly across the floor. It was like trying to contain a hummingbird.

When I looked into Adelaide's glowing eyes, she took my breath away. Was it more than her youthful exuberance that made my heart race? Those blue eyes always fascinated me. I pulled her closer so we could move as one. I could feel her pulse beating against my chest. I stroked my fingers across her back. Her smile faded and her lips parted as if the dance itself had become a seduction. I wasn't ready for it to end.

When the music stopped, we stood frozen for a second. She leaned her body away but I didn't release her immediately. I shook my head to clear the trance and dropped my hands.

"Thank you for the dance, Miss Schulz," I said, bowing slightly to break eye contact. When I looked back up, Addie was walking to the kitchen.

"You looked marvelous together, Anselm. You're a good teacher," Matilde said. I didn't miss the way she scrutinized me, as though nothing escaped her notice. I walked over to take my wife's hand to help her up. "Don't worry about Addie. She'll come around." Matilde glanced toward the kitchen at the sounds of Addie making tea.

"How are you feeling, My Dear? That was strenuous. Do you need a nap?" I asked.

"Yes, would you take me back to my room?"

I settled her down on her bed and covered her with a quilt. When I turned around, I glanced up at the portrait of Matilde's mother, Carolina. It struck me then that she was also Addie's grandmother. I'd swear her faint smile had turned to contempt.

CHAPTER ELEVEN: ADELAIDE

It had taken me a few days to feel comfortable around Anselm after that waltz. While dancing, I detected a subtle change in the way he held me and the way he looked at me with longing. Afterward, he appeared to have gotten over it. Thank goodness the wintery weather made it too cold for him to shower outside in view of the kitchen window.

Before I knew it, Thanksgiving had arrived. Now I had a new problem: the brothers. Henry had written that he expected to be home for Thanksgiving dinner. He'd been writing about once a week, and began signing his letters "with love, Henry." I enjoyed hearing about his work and travels. Henry and I became closer than before, but I couldn't say I felt attracted to him. Was I wrong to want that before marriage?

Helene had invited Matilde, Anselm, and me to her home for the Thanksgiving meal. I arrived carrying two pies and a loaf of bread in one of Matilde's ribbon-festooned baskets while Anselm helped Matilde from the car to the house. I had barely set down the basket when Henry was upon me, pulling me out the back door. I wore my hair loose for the festive occasion, and he cupped the back of my head with his hand and kissed me as though we were long-parted lovers. I was going to have to rethink our attraction. He might have stored up enough for both of us.

"Did you miss me, Addie?" he whispered, leaning his forehead on mine.

Before I could answer, the door opened and six-year-old Nelle emerged. "Did you see the kitty come out here?" she asked.

I hustled her back indoors and Henry followed. When we gathered around the table, I found myself with Henry on my left and Emil on my right. Anselm was seated directly across from me, next to Matilde. We placed our hands in our laps while Samuel gave the blessing, and right afterward, Henry grabbed my hand beneath the tablecloth. When I looked at him, he smiled innocently and pretended to be listening to the table conversation.

The food was passed, forcing him to release my hand. When we began eating, Emil leaned over to whisper in my ear. "You look lovely today, Addie. I wish to share the new poem I wrote for you. I'll show you later." Emil wasn't very subtle.

I took a deep breath as he moved back. When I glanced at Henry out of the corner of my eye, I caught him glaring at his brother. I assumed it would be safer to look across the table, but both Anselm and Samuel were scrutinizing our exchange too. *Oh boy.*

If Henry and I did marry, it would change my place in this family. I would not remain sidelined as my brother's spinster sister. I'd become the matriarch of the next generation of Hoffmanns. Helene would be my mother-in-law. More importantly, we would live in Omaha: a city with countless opportunities to make our own choices and grab more from life.

The conversation turned to other topics such as the harvest and how Henry's work was going. Henry liked living in a boarding house in Omaha. I rose when it was time to clear the dishes for dessert.

"I have an announcement to make," Henry said in a confident voice.

What now? I hope this is not involving us, not the right time or—

"Addie and I have been writing to each other," Henry said. "I guess you'd say we are courting. I mean to spend time with her tomorrow since I must be back at work the next day. I just thought the family should be aware."

I released my breath. At least he said nothing about marriage. I forced a small smile and couldn't look at Emil. My feet felt stuck to the floor next to the sink.

But Emil was not to be ignored. He bolted to his feet, throwing his napkin down on the table. He scowled at Henry and gave me a traitorous glare before hastening out the back door.

"Henry," Helene began with a tremble in her voice. "We should discuss this later."

"There's nothing you can't say in front of everyone, Mother. We're all family here." Henry sat up straighter in his chair.

"Yes, I hoped to remind you of that. We're family." Her pointed look at me was understood by everyone.

Samuel said, "Henry, don't you remember when Addie used to read to you? Taught you arithmetic too, as I recall, when you were in school together."

"Look, you don't need to approve. I know I'm younger than Addie. But look at Uncle Anselm and Aunt Matilde. He was a lot younger 'n her and they've been married—"

"Married?" Helene's head recoiled; eyes wide.

Several people began talking at once. My head started swimming from the commotion.

"I don't think Tilde and I have anything to do with—" Anselm began.

"You need to hear your mother out, young man," Samuel said.

"Are we having pie?" Nelle asked.

Henry stammered, "This is only up to Adelaide and —"

Three-year-old Josef began pulling on his father's sleeve, "I need to go—"

Matilde gasped and choked, but no one heard her above the din. Her face went ghastly white. I rushed to her side as she slumped unconscious toward Anselm. Her head thunked the table before I had my hands on her shoulders. Anselm knocked over her teacup when he wrapped his hands around her head, propping her back up.

Between Anselm, Samuel, and Henry, they picked up Matilde and laid her on Samuel and Helene's bed. I got a cold compress and laid it on her forehead. By that time, she'd opened her eyes and appeared lucid.

"How do you feel, Tilde?" Anselm clutched her hand. "You gave us all a scare."

"I think I'm all right. I couldn't catch my breath. Then everything went black."

"Should we take you to the hospital?" Samuel asked.

"No, no. I'm better now. Just let me rest a moment." Helene and I propped up pillows so that Matilde was half-sitting.

"I'll stay with her if the rest of you want to go eat dessert," I offered. "Then we'd better take her home."

Anselm studied Matilde's pale face, then shifted his gaze to me. He nodded, and a glimmer of a smile played on his lips. He patted her hand.

The rest of the group went back to the table. I sat on the edge of the bed stroking Matilde's forehead. "Does your head hurt? It looked like you whacked it went you fainted."

"It hurts a little bit. The cold cloth helps."

In about thirty minutes, we bundled her up and drove back to the Roth's farm.

Once we were inside, Anselm said, "I'm calling the doctor in Wilber. Samuel said it is probably your heart. He said Herman had chest pains."

Matilde peeled off her fur stole. "Don't call anyone tonight. Let the doctor enjoy his Thanksgiving. If I'm not right as rain tomorrow, you can call. And Herman only had angina right before he died. I suppose everyone's heart fails them when they die."

I was alone in the Roth's house when Henry knocked the next afternoon. I hesitated to let him in.

"What's the matter, Addie? You look like you've been crying. Is it Matilde?"

I leaned on the door. "I'm worried about her. The doctor came this morning, and he insisted they take her to the hospital in Beatrice to do some tests. They've been gone for a couple of hours. I assumed I'd have much more time with her."

"Do you think she's dying?" Henry pushed the door open wider and engulfed me in his arms. "She's a tough old bird; she'll pull through."

I leaned my cheek on his shoulder and inhaled the smell of burned wood. His arms felt strong holding me. It was nice to have someone to share this burden. He closed the door behind him, with the cold November wind forecasting the approach of winter.

"I have a pot of soup on the stove. Do you want soup and biscuits?" I moved back from him to lead him to the kitchen, but he wasn't about to break our touch entirely. He reached for my hand.

"Have you learned to cook then? That's a nice switch!" Henry smiled as he took a seat at the table.

"You didn't think I could cook anything?" I asked, ladling him out a bowl of steaming potatoes, barley, and beef.

"I remember a time you tried to cook soap." Henry grabbed a couple of biscuits from a plate on the table.

"I was only a teenager. And I didn't know Helene had used the pot on the stove to make soap so I cooked porridge in it."

"Porridge with bubbles. It was hard to get the taste out of my mouth." He spooned soup into his mouth. "This is rather good. Which is a relief if you're going to be my chief cook."

I took a seat across from him. "About that…"

"Oh, we had quite the family discussion about our impending marriage last night after you left. My mother and brother were up in arms. I hoped Emil had gotten over his crush on you, but I guess not. My mother wants us to wait a few years. She thinks I'll find another girl in Omaha. Samuel tried to be neutral but he didn't like me upsetting Mother. I told them all it was not up to them. If we want to wed, we will. Unless you're content to wait two or three years, we may have to marry without inviting them."

"Oh." I pondered this a moment. *This may work in my favor.* "I don't think it makes sense to rush. I don't know what's happening with Matilde. I was expecting this job to go on for a year or more. I'm content to leave things as they are for now."

Should I mention the land that I might be inheriting soon? No, that's ill-advised with Matilde's health so precarious. I don't want that to influence Henry.

Henry reached for my hand on the table. "You're one in a million, Angel Face. Not every girl would postpone marriage to nurse an elderly relative. But the more I can save up, the better off we will be when our wedding day comes. And you're getting paid something too. It will all come in handy. Although," he said softly, letting his gaze trail from my head to my blouse, "you may want to invest a little of your earnings in a new dress. You should see the short frocks women wear in Omaha. Maybe you can take the train to visit me and show off your legs."

"You expect me to wear a dress that shows my legs? I've never done that, Henry. And I don't think I could come to see you without a chaperone."

He shrugged. "Maybe old man Roth will bring you. We can talk about it later. How long do you reckon we have until someone returns home?"

"I don't know. I'm happy you came by, Henry, but I think it wise if you leave soon. I don't want to upset your family more."

"Why don't I fetch some extra wood for your fire in the parlor? Do you need more upstairs? It is likely to be cold and sleeting tonight. I wish you'd let me stay. I can sleep on the sofa or the floor in front of the fireplace."

If only I knew what was happening at the hospital. I don't want Anselm and Matilde to return and find Henry here. How would that look?

Henry went out back to the woodpile and brought in more logs for the parlor hearth, supplied the kitchen, and carried more up to my room on the second floor. I appreciated that he wanted to take care of me. When he was done, he moved the davenport so it was facing the blazing fire. He sat on it and pulled me next to him.

"I need you to warm up my face." Henry pulled my mouth to his. I braced my hands on his shoulders. The sound of the front door opening tore us apart.

"Addie!" Anselm called. "Are you keeping warm in here? It's gotten worse outside."

Henry rose before Anselm made it to the parlor. Anselm clenched his teeth and his eyes swept the room. He strode over to the fireplace and stoked the logs with the poker. He didn't return the poker to the stand right away.

"I just brought in more logs from outside. I put some in here and in the kitchen. Upstairs in Addie's room. Should I go get more?" Henry looked down and put his hands behind him.

Anselm stretched to his full height. He was taller than most men, taller than Henry by about three inches. "It's fine. If we need more, I can get it." He glanced at me. "You should get home, Henry, before the weather gets even worse. Do you need a ride?"

"No, I brought one of Samuel's horses. It's in the barn."

"Very well." Anselm stomped off to the kitchen. It sounded like he was helping himself to the soup.

Henry took my hand again and pulled me to the foyer with him. He put his hands on either side of my face and kissed me softly. "When will I see you again?" he asked.

"Christmas?" I stepped back to look at him. "Are you coming home for Christmas?"

He smiled. "If my mother hasn't disowned me by then." Henry backed up and went outdoors. I turned around and Anselm was standing two feet in front of me.

He scowled. "Do you love Henry?"

My brows arched. "Love him? I don't know."

"You let him kiss you. You let him spin fairy tales about marrying you. Is he the one you want to spend your life with?"

"I think that's what we're figuring out. Were you spying on us?"

"Spying? Of course not. I ought to know what's going on under my roof. You two were here alone. Did he try to compromise you?"

"No! Henry is too much of a gentleman."

"Henry is still a boy. And you should be grateful for that today."

I stepped closer to Anselm. "Grateful. What do you mean by that?"

His eyes grew dark. "Most men who found themselves alone in a house with a beautiful woman would—" He closed his eyes and took a deep breath. "You need to be careful. What would you have done if he'd tried to…force himself on you?"

My eyes must have been as big as saucers. "Henry? He wouldn't. No, he wants to marry me, he wouldn't do something so untoward." When I felt my cheeks get hot, I escaped back into the parlor.

Anselm followed me. "Adelaide, do you want to marry Henry?"

"Why do you keep asking me that? I don't know! You should not concern yourself with my affairs."

"Your affairs affect me too. I need to know if you can fulfill your duties." He swallowed hard.

"Matilde! She's not with you. What happened at the hospital?"

"They still think her heart is involved. They think that's why she passed out. She'll have more tests tomorrow. I'll go back in the morning."

I sank onto the sofa, trying to understand. "But she'll come home again, right?"

Anselm sighed. "I think so. Time will tell. Your soup is delicious. I'll go finish my bowl."

I had trouble drifting off that night. I found it odd sleeping in that house with only Anselm there and not Matilde. If it was not proper for me to entertain Henry in a house by ourselves, why was it okay to sleep in the same house with only Anselm? Sometimes these rules of society made no sense at all. Anselm used the largest bedroom on the second floor, the one he had shared with Matilde until she had trouble with the stairs. I had a smaller room next to his. Sometimes I could hear him snore or snort in his sleep.

Could it be legitimate because he was so much older than me? Did everyone look at him as a father figure? I suppose I looked at him that way until I started working here. Now that I'd gotten to know him better, he was more like an elder brother, like Samuel or Christian. Sometimes, it felt like something else, like the day we danced. When he'd taken me in his arms, it felt natural.

Around Henry, I felt flustered and clumsy. I didn't know if I should rebuff his advances or acquiesce. Surely it was a man's place to initiate romantic overtures, but how could Henry even know what to do? Had someone taken him in hand and shown him the appropriate way to kiss or hold a woman tightly? Is this something I should guide him through as I did when he was learning to sound out his words as a child? Of course, it's not like anyone had given me any training. True, I had been kissed a couple of times in the schoolyard by young men who were soon forgotten. But never like Henry, never someone who meant to claim me for his own.

My relationship with Henry was already causing strife. His mother clearly opposed our match. I'd tried to get along with Helene, but it was always forced. She'd moved into my parents' house when she married Samuel. My mother had been gone for five years by then and my father was failing. Helene had swept in like a summer windstorm and we all had to adapt to her housekeeping, cooking, and rules. She didn't need to tell me that she thought I wasn't good enough for her oldest son.

And Anselm didn't approve of the courtship either. He looked at me oddly when he questioned my feelings for Henry, as though he had anything to say about it. It was almost as if he were jealous. Of course, that was ludicrous. Anselm, as a long-married man had no interest in me that way.

Anselm undoubtedly knew something about romance. Helene said he had a reputation as a lady's man. Even Matilde implied she ignored whatever liaisons he chose to pursue. How tempting would that be for a man in his prime, to have both a loving marriage and the freedom to enjoy relationships with other ladies? Helene had been right about one thing. He knew how to be charming. I'd seen it with Matilde. And on occasion, briefly, he'd directed his charm on me. Disarming was a better word—like a sneak attack. When we were dancing, I'd let my guard down concentrating on my feet, and suddenly I became aware of how he was touching me giving me highly inappropriate feelings.

I threw aside my blanket and quilt. How was it so warm in here suddenly when the wind howled outside?

In the morning, I heard Anslem go outdoors early. I had breakfast started before he came inside.

"I'm getting ready to go to Beatrice. With any luck, I can bring Matilde home today." He stood near the table blowing across his cup of coffee.

"I'd like to go along. I'll feel better knowing she is being cared for. A hospital room can be a daunting place."

"I guess that will work. We just need to make sure there are plenty of blankets in the car so all three of us can be kept warm if she comes home."

He brought the car around to the front of the house, explaining that it needed to run for a few minutes before our departure. I'd ridden in his car before, but never as far as Beatrice, twenty-four miles.

There had been some snow and sleet the night before, leaving the roads bumpy and ice-packed. A couple of times we fish-tailed across the road.

"Are you sure this is safe?" I asked Anselm. It was cold enough that I was wrapped in a blanket covering my skirt and a heavy shawl over my woolen coat. I wore a sturdy felt hat and a muffler circled my neck.

He had an iron grip on the steering wheel and didn't take his eyes off the road. "If I'd known it was this treacherous, I would have left you home. I'm going to have to slow down."

Just then, we hit something in the road. I couldn't tell if it was a branch that blew off a tree or something else covered in snow. All I know for sure is that we went airborne for a moment. It seemed like a long moment. When we hit the ground again, I bounced forward, crashing onto the dashboard and then the floor.

Anselm's forward motion was halted rudely by the large wooden steering wheel. He grunted in pain. He hit the brakes and let out the clutch. The car stalled.

"Addie! My God, Addie! Are you okay?" He jumped out of the driver's side, ran around to open the other door, and carefully lifted me back into the seat. He put one knee on the floor of the car, and the other foot on the outside floorboard. His bare hands were on my chin and jaw.

I didn't want to cry like a child who'd fallen, but I knew I was trembling; I couldn't stop. My nose was running and I tasted something metallic. Was I bleeding? My pulse was pounding in my temples, my breaths came hard and fast. I closed my eyes and had visions of the car rolling over me.

"Look at me, Adelaide." When I opened my eyes, his face was right in front of mine, searching my eyes for injury and pain. I didn't expect his fear, concern, and guilt perhaps. And yearning. That couldn't have been true; I must have looked like a mess. He brushed away tears from my cheeks that I didn't know had fallen. Then his thumb moved to my bottom lip. When he withdrew it, I saw blood. He pulled a white handkerchief from an inside pocket and pressed it to my wound.

"Your lip is bleeding. Where does it hurt?"

I shook my head. I felt hot tears fill my eyes this time. He pulled me to his shoulder and I tried to assess the damage myself. My knees hurt; they must have taken the impact. One hand and the other forearm must have landed on the dashboard. I suppose I bit my lip on impact. I don't know why I wrapped my arms around his neck. Fear still gripped me. It's a natural reaction when someone embraces you to pull them close. I didn't think; I reacted.

"If something happened to you, I'd never forgive myself," he whispered.

I leaned back into the seat. "I don't think it's anything serious. Just a few bumps and bruises." I took the handkerchief from him and wiped my nose and face.

Concern still wrinkled his forehead. He took one of my arms in his and ran his fingers under my woolen coat from my hand to elbow. "Nothing feels broken?" He repeated this with my other arm with the question lighting his eyes. Then he moved the blanket aside and lifted my skirt to examine my knees. He put his hand around one knee, rubbing my patella with his thumb. "Do your knees hurt?"

I took a big breath. "They're sore, I hit both knees. Just the kind of pain you'd expect. I think we can get going again."

He continued his probing, running his hands down both my legs to the top of my boots. I shivered when I realized I had goosebumps. His touch felt comforting. And strangely exciting. My gaze flitted out the door behind him.

He pulled my skirt back down and wrapped the blanket over my lap and legs again. Then he climbed into the driver's seat. "I don't know whether to take you back home now or if it makes more sense to continue to the hospital. I think we are more than halfway there, and they can check you out."

"You don't need to take me home. You didn't get hurt at all?"

"Oh, my ribs hurt where I fell into the wheel. It'll be okay. If it gets worse, I can have a doctor check me too."

CHAPTER TWELVE: ADELAIDE

It was three days before Matilde was released from the hospital. The day after she returned home, she told Anselm she wanted to speak with both of us. She was able to get out of bed by then, and we all sat at the kitchen table.

"I considered talking to you individually but I don't want any misunderstandings." Matilde began, as she stretched her hands across the table to each of us.

I took her hand, and Anselm did likewise.

"Now take each other's hand," Matilde said.

"Are we making a prayer circle?" I asked.

"Well, yes. That's a good idea. Let's pray. Dear Lord, please help these two younger people, whom I love dearly, understand my words. Open their hearts to all that you have in store for their future happiness. Amen."

Anselm dropped my hand when she finished. He snorted and studied Matilde's face. "What's this about?"

She tightened her grip on my hand and pulled the hands she clasped closer together. "I want to talk about what is going to happen one of these days. The doctor cleared me to come home but he said my heart muscle will continue to grow weaker. It's not something that can be cured."

Anselm shifted in his seat and looked at their clasped hands. "I don't want to talk about—"

"No. You need to let me have my say. Just wait until I'm done. Please."

He sighed, in the way of husbands everywhere.

"One of these days, I will be gone. Dying is part of life, it's not so scary once you approach a certain age. Anselm, I have told you before that I want you to remarry."

He rolled his eyes and opened his mouth, but closed it again.

"You married a woman who was experienced in the ways of marriage but was limited in other ways. You should have a chance to be with someone young, just as I did. A young woman can give you children and can bring energy and joy into your life in a way you don't expect. I remember what that was like. It felt forbidden, but thrilling just the same. You must take this chance while you can, or you are destined to waste away as a lonely old man with only his riches to warm his nights."

I watched Anselm's brow furrow more deeply with every word she spoke. I had to suppress a laugh. She had a good point. Surely, he could see that.

"And you, Adelaide. What are you going to do after I leave? Are you already engaged to young Henry?"

My cheeks reddened. "Engaged? No. I mean it's not like he asked me to marry him. He said he had a plan and the plan included me."

"What about your plan, Addie? Do you intend to marry Henry?" Matilde pulled on my hand again and pulled Anslem's hand closer toward mine.

Anselm raised one brow waiting for my response.

"Um, I don't know yet. I don't feel like I have thought about him like that long enough. I can't quite imagine Henry as a husband. I need more time. He's willing to give me time."

"Do you think of Henry every hour?" Matilde squinted at me. "When he is close by, do you want to be in his arms? Are you dreaming of a future with him, in his bed, having his children, moving into his home?"

I scoffed. "Nooo." I wrinkled my nose.

"You're not in love with Henry Hoffmann," Matilde stated.

"I might learn to love him. People don't get struck by Cupid's arrow. It happens gradually sometimes. He might be in love with me. I think he's at least attracted to me."

Anselm pursed his lips. "Well, he's a healthy young man. How could he not be?"

I ran my free hand along the length of my braid and studied the loose end.

"You should marry Anselm," Matilde said, brushing the backs of our hands together.

"What?" I know my mouth dropped open, then I felt paralyzed. *What was she talking about?*

Anselm broke her grasp, scraped his chair back, and stood, turning away from us. He huffed out air from the back of his throat in a half-growl. He clutched the side of the sink and looked out the window.

"Anselm, come back…" Matilde began.

He whirled around to face us. "You're not my damn matchmaker, Tilde. You can't tell either one of us what to do with the rest of our lives!"

Matilde squeezed my hand, then released it. "I'm not telling you what to do. I'm telling you what I would like you to do. Because sooner or later, you're going to realize that you have feelings for each other. Don't think I can't see that myself. You're not that subtle! But then you are liable to feel misdirected guilt regarding me. Like being together would betray my memory. Hogwash! I love you both and I want you to be happy. Addie can give you things I never could, Anselm. And Anselm can give you a better life than Henry could, Addie. Both of you need to take the blinders off."

"Tilde, it is not right to speak of such things," Anselm said, putting a hand on her shoulder.

"No. What is not right is that people are afraid to speak of such things. You'll see, Husband. After you have looked death in the eye, you see some things more plainly. You must speak your mind, even to those who won't want to hear you."

I wanted to curl up into a ball and hide. I propped my elbows on the table and covered my face with my hands.

Matilde pushed herself to her feet. "That's all I'll say on the subject. Addie, would you help me back to my bed? I'm feeling weary now."

I leveled a glance at Anselm, got up, and took her back to bed. She didn't say anything else and acted as though nothing unusual had happened.

When I returned to the kitchen, Anselm had gone outside. I saw him leaving in the car a few minutes later.

Anselm didn't return by supper time. Matilde and I were having chicken stew and bread.

"Do you know where Anselm went, Matilde? Is it a good idea to leave the stew on the stove for him?"

She smiled. "I think he's having a snit. I'll bet he went to Hallam. He doesn't like to be told what to do. And he doesn't like it when I talk about my death. He's not angry with you; it's me. I'm not surprised. Men are pig-headed. You'll learn that soon enough."

"I don't think Anselm and I are going to be married." I looked her directly in the eyes.

"I don't see why not. Don't you think he's still handsome?"

"Well...I suppose he is handsome, but he is old enough to be my father."

"Your father was forty years older than you are. Anselm's not so old that he can't give you babies if that's what you're thinking. He is well off. He wasn't when I married him. You're lucky you missed young Anselm when he was cocky one minute and investing in some risky scheme the next. If I recall, you asked him for the Schulz homestead quarter-section. This is a chance for you to inherit a great deal of land."

I gasped. "I would never marry a man for his wealth. Or land, or anything besides love."

"Love doesn't mean you can't have wealth too. I was a catch when he married me. And we found a way to make each other's lives better." She pushed her plate away. "I know neither of you wanted me to be so frank. The main thing I wanted to say is that I am not opposed to the two of you getting together. It makes sense to me. Whatever happens, happens. Just be honest with each other about your feelings."

It must have been past midnight when I heard the door bang. I crept out of my room fearing a break-in. I hadn't locked the door as I wasn't sure if Anselm had taken a key. I felt better when I heard his voice, although he was laughing and it sounded like he was bumping into things. I wrapped my cloak around my nightclothes and ventured downstairs in my stocking feet.

Anselm was in the parlor with a younger man. His guest had a red beard and messy red hair sticking out of his knit hat. They were having trouble removing their coats. The red-haired man took hold of Anselm's sleeves and pulled his coat off, stumbling onto the floor in the process. Anselm fell onto the davenport in a fit of hilarity. I didn't think I'd ever heard him laugh so.

"Is everything all right?" I asked. Both men stopped laughing and stood up with a marked degree of effort.

"Oh, A-del-laide" Anselm said. "Are you still awake?"

"The noise woke me." I glanced from one man to the other.

"Noise? Did you hear a noise, Patrick? I didn't hear a noise. This is Pat Patrick. I found him in Hallam."

"I thought you said your wife was older." Patrick squinted.

"My wife is older. No, this is wife number two, right, Ah-del-laide?" Anselm laughed at his own joke. "You know what, Patrick? How old are you? You could marry Adelaide."

"I'm thirty, Mr. Roth. I've been married for four years already. We live down near Dewitt."

"Oooh. Sorry, Maddy Addy. Are you maddy? You look mad." Anselm gave me an odd crooked smile.

"I'm fine. I don't understand what Mr. Pat Patrick is doing here in the middle of the night."

"We're sorry to disturb you, Miss. My name is just Patrick. Patrick Tucker. Mr. Roth here asked me to drive his car home for him. He said I could stay the night. I can sleep here in front of the fire."

I shrugged. "It's his house. Just try to keep the noise down. I don't want Matilde to wake up."

I started back up the stairs.

"Who's Matilde?" Patrick asked Anselm.

"She's my first wife. She sleeps like the dead." That struck him as funny and he started laughing again.

When I got to my room, I locked the door. I hadn't seen many drunks in my time. Samuel and Helene were opposed to consuming alcohol. I'd seen my brother, Christian, drink too much once, the day before his wedding. That was before Prohibition. As far as I knew, neither Henry nor Emil ever drank moonshine. I had heard about a backroom in Hallam that some of the farmers frequented.

For the second time, a noise awakened me. Dawn was painting its first faint strokes across the window pane, but my room was nearly dark. I lit the candle by my bed and slipped into the hallway. The door to Anselm's room was open. He must have made it up the stairs finally. But some instinct made me walk a few more steps.

A candle flickered on Matilde's elaborate Queen Anne dressing table. Near the brass candle holder sat a large silver jewelry box. The lid was open, and someone was removing items and putting them into his pocket. He turned slightly, and I saw the red beard. It wasn't Anselm at all. Then I noticed that drawers had been left open and contents scattered.

My breath caught in my throat. I dashed to the stairs.

"Anselm! Come up here!" I cried.

Later I would wonder what would have happened if he hadn't heard my scream. What if Anselm were dead to the world or literally dead?

But Anselm bounded up the stairs with his shirt askew and his suspenders trailing from his pants. I motioned toward the room he'd once shared with Matilde. Patrick was prying open the window.

"I saw him take something from Matilde's box and put it in his pocket," I said.

"Empty your pockets, Mr. Tucker!" Anselm demanded. Patrick turned hesitantly but didn't comply. Anselm snatched open the closet door, pulled out a pistol, and aimed it at Patrick's chest.

"Let me see the insides of your pockets, or I'll plug you full of holes. Your choice."

Is this the same man who was stumbling around like a fool last night? His hand was steady as an anvil.

Patrick grumbled something under his breath, then turned his coat pockets inside out. The jewelry clattered onto the wood floor.

"All of your pockets. Let's see those pants."

Patrick pulled his trouser pockets out and set a couple of rings on the dressing table.

"You might still be hiding something. Here, Addie, you hold the gun on him." Anselm thrust the revolver into my hand and positioned it so it faced Patrick. "If he tries anything, shoot."

I had never even touched a gun before. If I had to pull the trigger, I might hit the wrong man. I took a steadying breath and narrowed my eyes.

Anselm grabbed Patrick's coat roughly and stuck his hand in Patrick's pants pockets. Finding nothing more, he shoved Patrick toward the bedroom door. "I ain't taking you back to town after this. You can walk. I don't care how cold it is. Just get out."

Patrick descended the stairs. I handed the gun back to Anselm and knelt to pick up Matilde's jewelry. I carefully returned the pieces to the spots where she'd kept them. When Anselm's roadster started, we exchanged looks. Anselm raced to the steps. By the time we made it to the front porch, Patrick Tucker was driving onto the road.

Anselm's thunderous stream of curses finally woke Matilde.

"Addie, what's going on?" Matilde yawned.

Anselm gave me a side-eye warning. He marched into Matilde's bedroom. "Addie is going to have to drive the wagon into Hallam with me, so I can pick up my car. Can you wait a little bit to have your breakfast? We can all eat together when we get back."

"And why is your car in Hallam?" Matilde asked.

"Uh, somebody else gave me a ride home last night." Anselm pulled on his boots.

"Hmmm. That's odd. You didn't wind up the night at that moonshine place, did you?" Matilde's puckered lips twitched from side to side.

"I might have," Anselm dropped his chin. "You see the thing about getting drunk is you don't remember all the bad decisions you made."

I went back upstairs to get dressed to drive the horse-drawn wagon. By the time I had helped Matilde get her day started, Anselm had the horses and wagon ready.

He helped me up and let me take the reins. I let the horses trot a little faster than necessary. It wasn't long before he began choking.

"Stop the wagon!" He gripped the handle on the wagon seat.

I smiled to myself. "Whoa!" The horses got the message when I tugged on the reins.

Anselm jumped off the wagon and bent over on the side of the road. Listening to someone retching was not my favorite way to start my day, especially outdoors in December.

When we arrived in Hallam, Anselm's car had been abandoned smack in the middle of Main Street. He jumped off the wagon and got into the car. It appeared the keys were left in the ignition. Before I could figure out how to turn two horses and a wagon around, he was already heading back the way we came.

I need to learn how to drive that darn car. Next time, I won't be the one riding out in the frigid wind. Right now, Anselm Roth is the last man I'd want to marry.

CHAPTER THIRTEEN: ANSELM

I couldn't bring myself to broach the subject that Matilde had raised with Addie and me. I'd expected to talk to Addie about it, but then that whole foolish night with Patrick Tucker came about, and I was too embarrassed after that. Two days later, I made a trip to my cattle ranch in western Nebraska and stayed there for two weeks. I hoped Addie and Matilde would have forgotten all that nonsense.

Then it was Christmas. Adelaide spent some time over at the Schulz's place when Henry was home. It looked like she was making plans and I expected to hear that they had set a wedding date for the summer. When he returned to Omaha, I noticed a letter from him appeared in our mailbox at least four times a week. Henry was certainly thinking about Addie. *It looked like Matilde got this one wrong.*

Addie planned to take the train to Omaha to visit Henry in March, but when Matilde took a turn for the worse, she canceled. Matilde was hospitalized for a week, and she was weaker when she returned.

One evening, when it was unseasonably balmy, I found Addie sitting out on the stone bench reading a letter from Henry. I took the seat beside her.

"What are you drinking?" she asked when she saw my glass of lemonade. I also had a bottle of vodka stuck in my pocket.

"Just some of your delicious lemonade," I said. "Of course, I'm making it a bit more delicious by adding some zing to it." I set the glass on the bench, then added a finger of vodka.

"Where did you get that?" She sniffed the open bottle, making a face.

"From the doctor. Since you can't buy liquor otherwise, a doctor will prescribe it. I just had to tell him I was feeling low."

She tilted her head and leaned closer. "Have you been feeling low?"

"How else should I feel? My wife is slowly dying. Nothing I can do to stop it." I took a big sip. "I guess I have been feeling a little lonely."

She smiled. "I find that hard to believe. From what I have heard, you have plenty of girlfriends hidden away. Is that all just gossip?"

"I've had a few women, but not until Matilde suggested it. A long time ago, before we married, I had some girlfriends. My first assignation was a few months before I got on the boat for America. Heidi, her name was. We both had a few beers and got carried away. Anyone can drink beer in Germany. Even children."

"But no romance lately? Not even when you've been traveling?"

I shook my head. "Maybe I'm waiting for something that's never going to happen." I pressed my lips together. "But you and Henry. That's going well, yes? I see you're getting lots of mail." I'd tried to stop thinking of Adelaide as the beautiful young maiden whose presence in my home had been the only glimmer of joy. The homey scents of her cooking were eclipsed by the fresh smell of her skin and hair when caring for my wife put us in close contact.

"He writes me almost daily. He wanted me to come and stay in a hotel in downtown Omaha for two nights. What do you think he had in mind?"

I clicked my tongue. "I know what I would be intending if I were asking a woman to spend two nights in a hotel. If you aren't sure, you should ask him."

"Well, he says something about it in this letter." She skimmed through the two-page letter in her hand. "He writes, 'I want to start kissing you at the nape of your neck and work my way down to cover every little bone in your back. Wear a blouse that unbuttons all the way.' You don't think he means to kiss my bare skin, do you?"

I shifted on my seat just imagining her exposed back. It had been too long since I'd done anything remotely like what he described. "Yes, he means to get you naked."

Her eyes popped. "But we're not even married yet! We can't…that is he can't…I don't even think I want to do that."

I chuckled. "You might like it. I guess he wants to take your relationship a bit further."

Addie shuddered and picked up my glass of lemonade, taking a big gulp. "Ooowee. That's strong."

"You don't need to be afraid, Adelaide. Just tell him to take things gradually."

She folded the letter back into the envelope and tucked it into her waistband. Then she pulled the ribbon off her braid and began untangling it, letting her long blonde hair flutter free in waves. She ran her fingers through it and it was all I could do not to touch it myself.

"Your hair," I tried to catch my breath. "looks like ripples in a stream where the water tumbles over the rocks."

She turned to me with an innocent smile. "Your hair is getting long. Should I cut it for you?"

My brows arched. "Would you? I haven't had a haircut for months." I stood. "I'll go take a bath and find the scissors and comb. Meet me upstairs in about twenty minutes."

I took a hasty bath, not even letting the water on the stove in the bathroom heat sufficiently. I shaved my face and neck and put on my muslin nightshirt, which hit me mid-calf. The bathroom was still a bit warm and steamy when Addie came up to find me.

I sat on a wooden stool facing a long mirror. She ran her fingers across my scalp through my wet hair, which was halfway to my shoulders. I tried not to moan, but it came out more like a growl.

"Are you all right?" Addie asked, switching to using the comb.

"Fine." I picked up one of the Turkish towels I had used and placed it on my lap.

"How much do you want me to cut?"

"Whatever you think looks good. You have done this before, haven't you? Or will I end up looking like a clown?"

"Oh, turning you into a clown might be fun." Addie giggled. "I used to cut Samuel's and Christian's hair before they were married. And then Henry's and Emil's hair when they were boys."

She set to work on the haircut. I watched her progress in the mirror. She was comparing the length from one section to another. It wasn't like what I was used to at the barber shop. The best thing about watching her work was that she often brushed her bosom against the sides of my head without even noticing. I might start drooling. From now on, only women should cut my hair. With any luck, only this one.

When she was done, she mussed my hair up to loosen the cut ends, then combed it carefully. "What do you think? Is it short enough to suit you?"

I inspected it in the mirror, leaning forward and turning my head back and forth. She'd trimmed a good two inches off. "It's good. You did a nice job, thank you. I suppose I'll have to increase your stipend." I looked back at Addie. "Oh, come here. There's some hair stuck to your face."

She leaned over me and closed her eyes. With the towel, I brushed stray hairs off her cheeks, chin, and nose. Then I ran my thumb over her bottom lip, that full rosebud that had been haunting me for so many months. She opened her eyes in time to watch me kiss those lips. My hand slid around to the back of her head and pulled her tighter to me. Her loose hair curtained over my arms as I pulled her into my lap.

This was a risk. If she'd rebuffed my advances, it would make our living arrangement awkward. I hadn't even thought about what might happen if she didn't. *But I was thinking about it now.* I covered that sweet mouth of hers with kisses over and over. She wrapped her arms around my neck and ran her fingers through my hair.

I picked her up and carried her to my bedroom. I set her on the bed and lit two candles then climbed onto the bed behind her. Adelaide wore a gingham apron over her standard "wash dress." I untied the apron and unbuttoned the back of her dress. She wore a camisole and a shorter corset than was currently popular. The corsets I'd seen advertised in 1926 flattened a woman's shape to fit into the slim tunics that were gaining popularity. I was pleased to see that Addie was still wearing the kind of underclothes that emphasized a womanly shape; cinched somewhat at the waist and allowing the figure above and below the corset to expand freely.

I was no stranger to corset-lacing or unlacing. I'd learned it from helping Matilde, and I could keep a steady hand. When Addie's corset was removed, I turned her back to me. She still wore a camisole, petticoat, and stockings.

I put my hands on either side of her face. "Is this what you want? If we do this, it means you're not going to marry Henry."

She kissed me. "Who's Henry?"

CHAPTER FOURTEEN: ADELAIDE

Sometimes life makes no sense. Just an hour earlier, I was squeamish at the very idea of Henry touching and kissing me the way Anselm was doing now. So why did I welcome it so unabashedly?

It was obvious. I'd come to care about Anselm. It may have happened over time, over stolen glances in the candlelight, casual touches here and there. I learned I could depend on him, admire him, work alongside him, and ease his sorrow if necessary. I was ready to surrender everything to him, at least for this one magical night.

He untied my petticoat and slipped his hands beneath it onto my hips. I thought my heart might beat out of my chest. His kisses were intoxicating and unending. Then he gently laid me on the bed on my stomach and pulled my camisole over my head. He chuckled as he pushed my hair to one side and kissed me on the bottom of my neck and gradually moved down, pressing his mouth over every vertebra with skillful attention.

I didn't recognize the sound I made, sort of a high-pitched whimper. I expected him to stop at my waist, but no. The petticoat inched down gently as he went, his fingers moved from gliding across my ribcage to embracing my hipbones. Everywhere he touched me, my skin felt ignited. Finally, when I didn't think I could stand much more of this, I rolled over to a sitting position, pulling forward my long hair to cover my breasts.

Anselm just laughed and shook his head. He pulled his twisted nightshirt over his head and tossed it aside. In one fluid motion, he pushed my hair back over my shoulders and cupped the back of my head with both hands. We were kissing again as he pulled me to my knees. Everything about him felt hard and hot. His shoulders and back tensed rock solid under my hands. I watched the muscles and tendons flex in his neck as he bent over to caress my shoulders.

It struck me that this was what life itself was about. The rugged maleness of him over the tender softness of me. The dark and light, the rain and the sun, the joy and the sorrow. All contrasts blended in harmony with nature. It was unimaginable now that I considered saving this moment for young Henry. I knew my future lay in the dark mystery of Anselm Roth alone.

I awoke at dawn with Anselm's hand spread across my stomach. We were warm in his bed layered with quilts and blankets. I didn't think I'd ever slept without my nightgown before; it felt unusually liberating. When I started to sit up, he stirred.

"Where are you going?" He rubbed the sleep from his eyes.

"I should go check on Matilde. I hope we didn't disturb her last night."

"She's a sound sleeper, but she wakes up early sometimes."

"We can't tell her anything about this." I waggled my finger to indicate the bed.

He sat up. "She knows."

"What?" I pulled my hair forward again to cover myself when the covers fell to my lap.

"Well, she may not know yet, but as soon as she sees either one of us, she'll know." He pushed my hair over one shoulder and ran the back of his index finger down the middle of my chest.

"How would she if we don't tell her?"

Anselm shrugged. "She has uncanny perception. I've never gotten a thing past her."

I felt a shiver ascend my back as I picked up my clothing and headed to my room. *Was he right? Would she see it on my face somehow like I had a scarlet letter on my dress?*

I had breakfast started before Matilde began calling me. She was feeling well enough to come to the table to eat. Anselm appeared in the kitchen a few minutes later.

"I have to go to Lincoln today," he announced. "There's an auction I want to attend."

"Are you buying more property, Dear?" Matilde gave him a tight smile.

"Only if the price suits me," he answered. He didn't look prosperous; he had on ragged overalls and an old shirt, as though trying to appear unfortunate. After we ate, he stooped and kissed Matilde on the lips. I jumped up and turned toward the sink so she wouldn't notice my shocked expression.

I tried to busy myself with the dishes as Anselm left. He searched around for his keys and boots, and then before he went out, he started singing to himself. That whirled me around. I'd never heard him sing.

"Anselm is acting peculiar this morning, ain't he?" Matilde said.

"I don't know what you mean." I picked up the plates from the table to wash.

"He kissed me. He hasn't kissed me in four years. Did Anselm go out last night?"

Why did he have to do something to arouse suspicion? "I couldn't tell you. I was tired and went to bed early."

"And what was that song he was singing? I don't think I recognize it." Matilde drummed her fingers on the table.

"I think it was 'It Had to Be You.' Helene plays that on her gramophone. I've seen Samuel and Helene dance to it." I sang the first few bars for her.

"Funny, you know it too."

"It's a very popular song, I think. Sweet. Romantic."

Matilde just stared at me. I saw what Anselm meant. I broke eye contact and continued to clean the kitchen.

My nerves were on edge the rest of the day. When I picked up the mail from the box, there were two letters from Henry. One of them must have been delayed. I felt like a stone had formed in my stomach. I put all the mail on the hall table and didn't open his letters.

By the time Anselm returned, Matilde was already down for the night, and I had taken a bath and put on my nightgown. I was combing my wet hair sitting on my bed.

He lit the gas lamp on my dresser. He stood smiling at me in the lamplight. "Are you going to sleep in my bed again tonight?"

I rolled my eyes. "I don't think that's wise. Matilde commented that you were acting very curiously this morning."

He pointed at me and snickered. "Didn't I tell you? She's got it figured out already."

"Aunt Matilde said you hadn't kissed her in four years. That was sad to hear, but that also made her think you were guilty of something."

He just winged his brows.

"Then you had to start singing!"

"What's wrong with singing? I like that song." He started singing it again and took my hands to pull me to my feet. "Dance with me." He switched to humming. He might not have known all the words.

I didn't want to dance with him wearing only my nightgown. I felt too exposed and it reminded me of the night before. When he laid his hand on my back, I remembered how he put those hands all over me, how he'd kissed my back, my shoulders, my mouth—"

"Anselm, I'm going to bed now." I pulled my hands away from his.

"Okay." Then he rolled me down onto the bed with him. The bedsprings creaked.

"Quiet!" I whispered forcefully.

He laid on his back and stretched his arms out. "This bed is terrible. It doesn't have enough stuffing. We'd better go back to my room."

"No! It's fine. I'm sleeping here alone. You need to leave."

He got off the bed and started for the bedroom door. I scooted my way up to the head of the iron-framed bed and got under the blankets. Then he smirked and leaned over me and kissed me. Not just once. He braced his hands on the bed on either side of my shoulders and kissed me repeatedly. The euphoric yearnings of the night before were pounding my senses demanding to be freed. I put my fingers on his lips to push him back.

"You'll miss me." He smoothed down his shirt as he stood up. "I don't think I'll even tell you what I bought you today." A smile teased the corners of his mouth.

I sighed, running my palm over my forehead. "What did you buy me?"

He shrugged and turned off the lamp. "A house." Then he walked back to his room.

I had a hard time getting to sleep.

CHAPTER FIFTEEN: ANSELM

The house I bought was a good investment—my first real foray into the real estate market in a city. I didn't want to live in it right away, but I could see how it might be a nice family home. In the meantime, I needed to get it ready to be rented to renters.

I could see that Addie was a little uncomfortable with our relationship. I mean, it was kind of strange, living with a husband and wife and sleeping with the husband. Then she had that whole presumed engagement with Henry to divest herself of. I was determined not to pressure her. She'd come back to my bed when she was ready. The wait, however, was interminable.

It's not as though I had meant to seduce Adelaide. I'd been charting out my next steps after Matilde left me. Focusing on the future was the only way to cope with the heartache I was anticipating. But Matilde herself had shoved Addie in my path, and after my initial resistance, I had to admit my attraction. I feared I may have eliminated Addie's other options. In time, I could help her find other employment if she no longer wanted me.

I spent many days and nights in Lincoln in a hotel, getting the paperwork handled for the house sale and lining up workmen to do some updates. I got a good price on the house because it needed repairs, and this way, I could decide on the specifics. Turning one of the small bedrooms into a nice bathroom was the major reconstruction, and I had to find just the right crew who knew how to add modern plumbing without destroying the integrity of the structure. Once the proper drainage was connected to the city sewer system, the kitchen plumbing needed a major overhaul. This was just the kind of work that would take my mind off things at home.

Two weeks later, I returned to find Matilde and Addie gardening again. This time, Matilde was sitting in a chair and digging with a short-handled shovel, dropping seeds into the ground, and using her feet to push the soil back over the seeds.

Addie was letting Matilde do most of the work. She just helped her move the chair along to the next plot.

When they declined my help, I went into the house to get something to drink. I checked my mail, which had been piled on the hall table. My letters were the usual assortment of updates from my tenants, invoices, and documents to sign. I couldn't help but notice about a dozen letters addressed to Adelaide from Henry Hoffmann. She hadn't opened any of them.

Later that evening, I put on my nightshirt after bathing and saw Addie in the backyard in the moonlight. She was kneeling in the dirt.

I went downstairs and slipped on my boots and went out to find out what she was doing.

"Everything okay out here?" I asked.

Addie jumped up, startled. "Oh, I was just fixing a few of the plants Matilde worked on today. She said she couldn't see well enough to tell if they were all straight. They weren't. It will be hard to keep the rabbits and deer away from the carrots and spinach."

"Addie, come sit with me. We need to talk."

She wiped her dirty hands on her apron, and we both sat on the stone bench. "We talked at dinner, didn't we?"

"Yes, we talked about the farm, the house in Lincoln. Why haven't you opened all those letters from Henry?"

"Oh, you saw those." She rubbed the dirt off her fingers. "Matilde asked me the same thing. I have no way to clarify this for Henry. Those letters will be full of plans he wants to make or he'll be asking me to visit him. I just don't want to know. Matilde says I must write to him to break it off, but what can I tell him?"

"Maybe he wrote to say he's met another girl."

"That would be ideal, but if he'd done that, I think he would have stopped writing by now."

"It's cruel to let him deal with uncertainty."

"I know! I know, but what am I going to say to him? I changed my mind? I don't think I ever loved you? There's someone else?"

I brushed the back of my fingers across her cheek. "Is there someone else?"

She looked up quickly. "Anselm? Maybe I'm not sure about you either. Were you just looking for a quick fix to your loneliness?"

I exhaled. "That's harsh. No, of course not. You and me…I mean somewhere down the road, after…I think we'll be together."

She looked at the full moon. "Somewhere down the road. Someday. That's not what a woman can count on."

I frowned. "Well right now, things are a little complicated. You see that as well as I do. Tilde acted more like herself today. More energy, less pain."

"Yes, today was a good day. She seems improved. Tomorrow she'll lose ground again. She'll stay in bed, she'll be a little confused, or she'll say it hurts her. This pattern has been repeating itself. I'm not sure she's aware of it."

"Has she been to the doctor recently?"

Addie shook her head. "She doesn't want to go. I think we should make the most of the good days."

"Yes, we should all make the most of our good days." Our eyes met and I leaned over to kiss her.

She stood up. "I need to take a bath; my hands are dirty."

"Go on then. Come to my room afterward."

After that night, Addie slept in my bed regularly. We both made that choice.

The Saturday evening before Easter, Addie was helping Matilde in the bath, and I was standing by, ready to lift her out of the tub. We all heard loud knocking on the front door.

I flung open the door to find Henry standing on the porch. Fury was stamped all over his face. *Oh boy. Guess she put off writing back to him.*

Henry merely nodded to me before pushing inside. "She here?" He walked to the middle of the house near the stairway and hollered, "Adelaide Schulz, where are you?"

"I'm upstairs. I'm busy right now," Addie called back.

Henry started up the stairs.

"No, Henry, come back. She's helping my wife with her bath. Let me go up and help Matilde and I'll send Addie down."

Henry turned and came down the five stairs he'd climbed. His attention was fixated on the hall table. I waited as he walked over and recognized all those unopened letters.

"Has someone been keeping my letters from her?" The pain in the glare he shot me was intense.

"No." I looked at the letters and then back to Henry. "She's just been…you'll need to ask her."

CHAPTER SIXTEEN: ADELAIDE

Henry was pacing at the base of the staircase as though he meant to intercept me if I tried to escape to another room. He had his letters in one hand, his other balled into a fist. He didn't look at me until I was in front of him. The ice in his eyes sent a chill up my spine. Or perhaps I was just cooling off from leaving the humid bathroom.

"Adelaide." Henry shook the wad of letters at me. "You owe me an explanation."

I nodded. "Yes, of course." I tried to brush past him to get to the kitchen but he body-blocked me. "Let's go into the kitchen. It will be more private."

The muscles in his jaw tightened. He let out a forceful breath and let me lead him to the back of the house.

"Why have you not even opened my letters? The first one was postmarked more than three weeks ago."

"I don't know."

"Whaddaya mean, you don't know? Something must have happened around that time."

Something like Anselm kissing me? Spending that first night in Anselm's bed? "I don't think it was anything specific. I just realized that we were never going to be together. I didn't want to read your letters because they'd be full of dreams and sweetness and…things you would wish you'd never said to me."

His lips twitched and curled into a sneer. "You're right about that. I did write some tender words that should not have been so wasted. Told you things I've never told anyone else. I believed you were as enamored with me as I was with you, but it looks like my mother was right."

"Helene? What does she have to do with this?"

"I heard her that night telling you not to take this job. She warned you about what might happen." His eyes rose accusingly toward the ceiling.

"No, Henry, this is just about the two of us. I don't think we want the same things. At any rate, I am not interested in moving to Omaha and being your wife. Isn't that what you wanted?"

Henry glanced at the big stove for the first time. The fire was still crackling from when I'd made supper an hour earlier. He stared at the letters in his hand.

"I did want that," he said, "and I assumed you were just getting cold feet. Now I see that you were never enthused about me from the start, you were just stringing me along."

"No, I never intended to. I hoped we'd learn to love each other over time."

He held up the letters. "That's why we were writing, Addie! To learn more about each other, our daily routines, our deepest thoughts, hopes, and fears. But you stopped wanting to understand…anything about me." He stepped to the stove, opened the door, and threw the letters onto the burning embers. The edges of the envelopes curled into gold ribbons.

Henry sighed. "It's ironic. Emil finally was happy for us. He told me when I got home. And my mother and your brother," Henry smirked, "announced they're having another baby."

"They are?"

"It feels odd to think my mother is still bearing children when I expected to marry and have offspring of my own." Henry's mouth grew pinched and his tone was hard. "But maybe I was rushing it, depending on a girl like you. Maybe I've never really known my step-auntie at all."

"Henry—"

He moved toward the door. "I don't think you'll be welcome at the Schulz and Hoffmann gatherings, at least not for a while. Give Emil a wide berth. I don't want my brother's heart broken too. As for little Nelle and Josef, someday they might remember they had an Aunt Adelaide."

A single tear rolled down my cheek before I could stop it. Anger at his mocking tone began to replace the guilt. He can't ban me from my own brother's family. I will give them some space for now.

I stood frozen in the kitchen next to the stove, warming my chilled bones. Henry slammed the front door and was gone.

A few minutes later, Anslem brought Matilde down and put her to bed. I went in to help. When I sat next to Matilde's bed, she took my hand.

"You told him, didn't you, that you didn't want him?" Her voice cracked with concern.

I nodded, tears heating behind my eyes. "I told him."

Matilde squeezed my hand. "He'll find another love. He's young and bold. He'll be good as new in time."

I sighed and just sat with her, holding her hand until she fell asleep.

CHAPTER SEVENTEEN: ANSELM

It was frustrating how Matilde wasn't heeding the medical advice. Although, how could I blame her? She didn't have a lot of time left and she wanted to choose how to spend it. Sometimes it put me at odds with Adelaide, who was doing as well as she could following Matilde's lead.

We'd made a shopping trip to Lincoln to buy Adelaide some new clothes. Matilde had enjoyed seeing the latest fashions, but for three days afterward, she barely left her bed. Dr. Carson had suggested we take her to the hospital in Lincoln, but she refused to go. I was forced to accept that her time was approaching quickly now.

Addie made a big breakfast to celebrate Matilde's return to the kitchen table. She served bacon, eggs, fried potatoes, and cinnamon bread. The kitchen was filled with an aromatic cloud of spices, coffee, and fried food.

"This is wonderful, Adelaide. Better breakfast than I've had at restaurants." I took a big bite of the eggs.

Matilde nodded her agreement. Addie set her fork on her plate.

"You're not hungry this morning?" I buttered my piece of hot bread.

Adelaide jumped out of her chair, spun around, and vomited into the sink. Then she pumped water to wash her face and rinse the sink.

"I'm so sorry! I don't mean to ruin your breakfast." She rushed out to the front porch and sat on the steps.

Matilde raised her brows and hurled a pointed look at me. I rose and went to check on Addie, abandoning my delicious food.

"Are you all right? Are you coming down with something?" I stuck my hands in my pockets and surveyed her holding her head.

She shook her head. "For some reason, I keep getting sick to my stomach. I've been throwing up almost every morning. The car ride back from town made me nauseated. I may have to go to the doctor if it doesn't stop."

I was headed to Hell in a handbasket. I saw my luck running out as though my blood was seeping from my veins onto the porch and out onto the grass. My breakfast was forgotten. She may have been the one with the upset stomach, but my gut was scolding me loud and clear.

I dropped to a squat next to her. "You're pregnant."

Her head jerked around; eyes wild. "That can't be true. I'm not even married."

I scoffed. "That isn't a prerequisite."

Adelaide glanced back at the door as though Matilde had suddenly gotten the energy to come up behind us and eavesdrop. She lowered her voice. "Before you can have a baby, you have to perform something called the marital act. I remember the minister talking about this when my brother was married. I think it's like a sacrament in the church, like communion or baptism."

I put my feet down on the step and sat next to her, struggling to contain my incredulity. I looked away and shook my head. I covered my mouth to disguise my smirk. A guffaw slipped out before I could gain control. "You can't be serious."

Her stern look told me otherwise.

"Oh boy." I took a deep breath and cleared my throat. *Was she in denial about this or had she not understood what had happened between us?* "What you referred to as the marital act is the same as a couple…engaging in certain intimacies." I nodded pointedly hoping she would comprehend the rest.

"Intimacies?"

"Yes. Which you and I have done frequently. Upstairs in my bed." I kept nodding like a hen pecking the ground.

Her mouth fell open and her eyes jumped up and down, back and forth, as though searching for meaning. "You mean when we—when you…" She looked out toward the road as her brow crumpled. "You knew this might happen!"

Pain seared the back of my throat. Her naïveté no longer was amusing. "Well, I suppose I knew it might. However, I shared a bed with Matilde for years, and there have been at least five other ladies I have associated with, and this has never happened to me before."

"Then maybe it's a false alarm. Maybe it is something else that will go away on its own."

I took her hand. "We could wait a few days, a week or so even, but you should see a physician."

I stewed in the doctor's waiting room. There were only three chairs, and a woman came in pushing a wailing baby in a carriage and pulling a little boy by the hand. The poor lad's nose ran like a waterfall, and the mother was in the throes of a serious head cold too. I wanted to give them plenty of space, so I moved to the opposite wall and tried not to breathe in any germs. Addie had been back in the examining room for twenty minutes or more. She didn't want me to go in with her.

When the woman began sneezing, I went outside. It was a beautiful spring day, and the temperature was climbing. I tried to shake the image of the pathetic children in the waiting room. Was this what it was like to live with offspring? I stood near the window so Addie could spot me when she emerged.

Her face was grim when she joined me outside. I helped her into the car.

"You were right. The doctor said I was expecting. I asked him what people do to avoid this condition. He said he'd heard about something that men used when we were at war overseas. But there is also a law here in the United States that prevents him from sharing any information about contraception. That the correct course of action to prevent pregnancy was enforced by morality. Of course, within a marriage, procreation was the expected objective."

I scratched my head. "So, what did he say about you? When are you having a baby?"

She sighed. "He couldn't be specific, sometime in November or December."

"That gives us a little time."

"Time for what?"

"It's obvious, isn't it? My wife is not long for this world, but she might live for months yet. We could be married if she was gone, but certainly not before then."

Addie narrowed her eyes at me. "Take me home."

She didn't speak to me after that. When I stopped the car, Addie went directly to her room and closed the door.

I checked on Matilde, who was in bed but not asleep.

"Did the doctor give Adelaide some medication?" Matilde asked.

"She didn't mention that," I said. How was I supposed to explain this to Matilde? "I think Addie isn't feeling well. She went to lie down."

I ascended the stairs quietly, not knowing whether Addie was sleeping. I heard her weeping through the closed door.

I couldn't help her. I hadn't had much guidance from my father on how to deal with women. Roderick Meier was more of a mentor, but he rarely offered advice on the fairer sex. I did recall one time he told me that if a woman starts to cry, it's prudent to leave her alone until she's finished. It was like a rainstorm, sometimes with lots of thunder and lightning. You're better off waiting until the calm has returned and then you can deal with the problem rationally.

That's what I did. I left the women alone and went outdoors to the wood pile. Only hefting my ax to splinter a section of cedar tree eased my remorse.

I spent the next five days and nights in Lincoln working on the house I'd purchased. When I got home in the late afternoon, I found Matilde in bed. Addie had just changed the bedsheets and was settling her in.

"I'm glad you're home, Anselm. I want to tell you both something." Matilde reached for my hand. I rolled my eyes remembering the last conversation that started like this.

"What is it, Matilde?" Addie said, sitting on the bed next to her.

"I'm bound to get worse. No matter what happens, don't call the doctor. I don't want to go to a hospital. I propose to die at home."

I studied my shoes. The lump in my throat tried to choke off my words. "What if you're in pain? We don't want you to suffer."

"Ask the doctor to prescribe something for pain, just in case. If he refuses, I still don't want to leave my house. Tell me you understand what I'm asking."

I nodded. "I understand. I'd feel the same way. How are you feeling today?"

Matilde gave a half-shrug.

"She's been weaker since you left. I've only gotten her out of the room once."

Matilde closed her eyes. "You two go have some dinner. I'm just fine right here."

I went back out to my car to fetch my things. Then I went into the kitchen where Addie was frying chicken.

"How have you been feeling, Addie?"

"Well, the nausea is better. If I eat a piece of bread in the morning, that helps. At first, I thought I should be careful and not do anything too strenuous. Women sometimes lose their babies if they fall or lift something heavy. For any reason, really. The pregnancy doesn't always last. Then I realized that might be a good thing in this case." Her voice caught in her throat. "Because I don't know how this is all going to work out and…"

I wrapped her tightly in my arms and let her tears fall on my shoulder. "We have to wait and see now."

"Wait." She pulled back and looked at me with red eyes. "We should have waited before."

I shook my head, then nodded. "Oh, I bought you something." I strode back into the foyer and hefted a large box wrapped in brown paper and twine.

Her face brightened and she swept the tears from her cheeks. She put the box on the table and cut the string with a knife. When she saw the fur coat, her jaw dropped.

"Anselm! What did you do?"

I helped her pull the coat from the box and slid the sleeves over her arms. "It's imported from Paris. Dark muskrat with a fox collar and cuffs. Silk lined."

Addie giggled. I hadn't even seen her smile for weeks. She wrapped the luxurious ankle-length coat around her and spun in a circle. The red fur collar kissed the nape of her blonde hair, which was drawn into a bun. The coat was a little loose on her, but it was better than too small.

"You like it?" Obviously, she did, but I needed to hear the words.

"Do I like it? It's the most fabulous thing I've ever seen! Or felt. Feel how soft it is!" She held her arms out, inviting me to touch the sleeves.

I ran my hand across her forearm, then through the collar. I'd sampled different furs at the store, so I already knew I liked this one best. "It's very soft. Like petting an animal. A muskrat, I guess."

Then a cloud passed over her eyes. "This is too fancy for me. When would I ever—"

My hand slid up to cradle her jaw. "How do you think women become fancy? When they wear extravagant furs. You'll get there." She let me pull her into a kiss then, and she wrapped that soft muskrat around my neck.

Afterward, she stepped back and let the coat slide off her shoulders. I helped her fold it to set it in the box.

"You bought this because you felt guilty." Her lips formed a tight line.

"I bought you this because I care about you. And I put you in an untenable situation. That was selfish of me."

She picked up the fork and rotated the chicken in the skillet. "Why is it so hard for men to simply utter an apology?"

I walked up behind her as she stood at the stove and slipped my hands around her waist. It still looked as slim as the first time I'd touched her. I pressed my mouth behind her ear. "I'm sorry."

She smiled. We stood like that for a long time.

CHAPTER EIGHTEEN: ADELAIDE

It was hard to know what to wish for. I suppose life is like that sometimes, full of contradictions: hopes mingled with regrets. My relationship with Anselm had gotten much better in recent weeks. I had returned to his bed and it appeared that we had a future together. The downside was that for us to share our lives, his wonderful wife had to claim her reward in heaven.

I tried to forget all of that on this Saturday night in July. Anselm had brought me to a lavish affair that marked the opening of the new Cornhusker Hotel. A month ago, when Matilde was feeling up to it, the two of them had taken me shopping in Lincoln to purchase new clothes. Tonight, I wore one of the new outfits, a pretty peach voile frock with the deep V exposing my back, a matching cloche hat, and black patent-leather shoes. I felt like a genuine flapper. I might even have a chance to learn the Charleston.

We were whirling around the dance floor after a marvelous dinner in one of the ballrooms. Thankfully, my persistent nausea was gone by the end of May. Even my frequent exhaustion had abated. Tonight, I felt more awake and light-headed than I had in months. Anselm had even engaged his sister-in-law, my aunt, Mary Roth, to stay with Matilde while we were gone so that we could be the first couple to spend the night in one of the hotel rooms.

"I'm so glad Matilde is having a good week," I said brightly. "If she was doing poorly, I don't think either of us would have wanted to leave her in someone else's care."

Anselm looked over my shoulder. "It is remarkable to me how she keeps rallying. Just when I get used to the idea that she is at death's door, she improves for a week or so."

"I'm thankful for—" It was hard to have a conversation with Clive Davis and his Hotel Cornhusker Orchestra playing so loudly. *Live music, dancing, and beautiful couples everywhere you looked.*

Brand new hotel, romance in the air. I don't think I have ever had such a magical evening.

Anselm took my gloved hand and steered me toward one of the lovely terraces with curated flower pots and plantings.

"Are you having fun tonight, Addie?" he asked.

I grinned. "I'm not sure I've ever had so much fun. Thank you for bringing me."

He put my hand to his lips. "I hope you'll remember tonight for a long time. It will be a long time before we can do this again."

I beamed at him. "I will remember this, but I don't expect—"

"We won't even be seeing each other for a long time."

I jerked my head back, "What?"

He bit his lip. "There's no good solution to our problem. I delayed as long as I could. Tomorrow morning you're catching a train to California."

Had I heard him correctly? He said I'm taking a train, not we're taking a train.

"I realize this is unexpected but I have it all arranged. You don't have to worry about a thing. I found a place where you can go. No one will know you there. You can have the baby and they will handle the adoption. I've already paid for your room and board. After you've had a chance to recover, I'll send you a train ticket to come back. Surely by then, Matilde will have…" he swallowed hard.

No, he couldn't mean this. He might as well have told me he was sending me to Antarctica.

I must have gone deaf because I couldn't hear the music or the conversations around me anymore. I needed to flee, but my muscles froze. I backed up a few steps staring at Anselm. My sweetheart, my protector—my banisher. My breathing was getting ragged.

He doesn't want me at all. He wants to protect his reputation. I've become a disgrace.

The adrenaline hit me like lightning, propelling my limbs into action. I remembered how I raced Emil in the wheat field just a year ago. Now I was running as fast as my stylish Cuban-heeled shoes would carry me, thankful for the shorter skirt. I raced out of the courtyard, into the hallway, and out the nearest exit. When I reached Thirteenth Street, I pivoted, not sure where I was. I almost plowed into a white-haired man wearing a tuxedo.

The gentleman grabbed my arms to steady me. "Stop, Miss. What's wrong?"

I opened my mouth but no words came out. I needed to catch my breath. I shut my eyes and stood there panting. Before I could say anything, Anselm had his hands on me.

"Thank you, Sir. I've got her now. Sit down a minute, Addie." He steered me to a bench in front of the hotel. My hat had gone askew so I removed it and smoothed my hair. I had no intention of meeting Anselm's eyes. He held onto my wrist to prevent further escape on my part.

Now I'm sitting out here in plain sight of this crowd of important people. Not people I know, of course, but Anselm probably knows some of them. They saw me running like an unruly child, with him trying to corral me. I hope he's embarrassed. I'm beyond caring.

"Adelaide…" he began. I felt his gaze on me but I kept looking down the street.

I pressed my lips together so they wouldn't tremble. I would not give him the satisfaction of seeing me cry. I had to think. Just because he made plans didn't mean I had to follow them.

"Maybe we should go up to our room where we can have some privacy." Anselm stood up. He released my wrist and took my hand. I kept my eyes diverted.

This beautiful setting suddenly felt unfriendly and portentous. As we wound our way to the elevators, I surveyed the Georgian architecture of the ten-story building. Ivory-colored pillars in the lobby were topped with what looked like thistles and sheaves of wheat. I heard one of the tour guides say that the marble and travertine floors were imported from Italy. My gaze was drawn to the centerpiece of the lobby, a crystal and silver fountain that featured water sprayed from the mouths of frogs around the fountain rim. The huge chandelier played colored light over the cascading water. An hour before, this had felt magical. But like Cinderella, my fairy tale was ending abruptly.

When we got to our room, I sat on the ornate bedspread. "How long have you been planning this?" My mouth tasted sour; our marvelous dinner was a distant memory.

"Planning what? This stay at the new hotel? I heard about it in April."

"How long have you been planning to send me away?"

He shoved his hands in his trouser pockets. "I hoped to avoid it. Then last week I talked to my banker and my attorney. They helped me locate a broker in Sacramento that they've used before. Their guy knew a guy. This place is supposed to be very well-run. They will take good care of you."

"I don't have my clothes. This dress is not a good one to travel in, it's too thin."

"I agree. I packed most of your regular clothes in a trunk of Matilde's. It's not like she'll need it. The trunk is in the car, ready to load on the train."

"Why didn't you talk to me about this ahead of time? Maybe I don't want to go to California. Maybe I don't want to put my baby up for adoption."

"What choice do we have? You can have other babies. You could go somewhere closer, but there's no chance of running into anyone you know in Sacramento. If you went to Kansas City or Denver—well, it seemed riskier."

"What about Matilde? Who will help her if I'm gone?"

"I don't know. I'll try to hire another girl. I might not be able to find one."

That snapped me out of my mental fatigue. "Another girl? You're going to start this whole thing up with some other girl? Introduce Matilde to a new person when she's only got a short time left? Are you meaning to entice another girl into your bed?"

"Now wait just a minute! I didn't expect any of that to happen. I didn't expect to fall for you at all. I would not make that kind of mistake again."

I stood up to meet his eyes and fisted my hands on my hips. "A mistake. Is that what this was? I was a mistake? Or is it the baby that was a mistake?"

Anselm held up his index finger. "Do not put words in my mouth." He paced across the floor. "I think if you realized how much effort and expense went into arranging this trip, you'd be a little more appreciative."

"You want me to be appreciative like I was when you bought me a fur coat? You're just trying to convince me to cooperate. Which is what you've done from the start."

"Oh, I left the fur at the house. I was afraid it might get stolen. I packed your wool cloak. It's warmer in California they say." He put his hands on my shoulders. "I understand that you don't want to go. I don't want you to go either, but it is the best solution for everyone."

I shrugged off his hands and went into the state-of-the-art bathroom with electric lighting and hot and cold running water. I ran water into the built-in tub, which the hotel boasted could be filled in two minutes. I had to prepare for a long and uncomfortable journey.

CHAPTER NINETEEN: ANSELM

En route to Sacramento, California
Late November 1926

I looked out the window at impressive mesas in western Colorado. The mountains had mostly given way to smaller outcrops, and the threat of snow covering the tracks this time of year was dismissed from my mind, if only briefly. I wish I knew what I'd find when I reached Sacramento.

Matilde had finally succumbed to her heart condition brought on by rheumatoid arthritis in early October, in the middle of the corn harvest. We held the funeral early in the morning while the dew was still coating the fields. Dear, thoughtful Matilde would not have wanted to inconvenience anyone. It was the first time I'd ever started drinking before noon. It would have been more bearable if Adelaide had been by my side.

I had sorely miscalculated the effect of her departure. I missed her more than I supposed I could miss anyone. I knew I had gotten used to her, but after I sent her away, it was as though the sun never shone again. Every time I smelled pie, Addie's hard-working hands came into view. When a gentle breeze blew the sinking sun from the amber sky, I saw her tresses waving at me. When the cool night air stole the warmth from my toes, I wished with all my soul that she was snuggled in my bed.

As Matilde's illness began to overtake her, she became unrecognizable. Her mind had discarded the recognition of who I was or what went on around her. I was sorely tempted to turn her over to the hospital staff, but I knew how she felt about that, and I didn't want them to prolong her suffering. I cared for her myself as well as I could.

What I didn't anticipate was that Adelaide's absence would become a mystery. I had given her the name of Albert Fischer, the broker I had spoken with on the phone. He promised to meet her train and escort her to the Claremont House, an upscale facility that provided temporary lodging to pregnant women and arranged adoptions with prosperous couples. Three weeks after Adelaide left, I received a letter from her saying she had gotten settled, and they were treating her well.

I was certain I had done the right thing for her. Then a few weeks later, my letters to her came back unopened. Someone at Claremont House had written on the envelopes, "return to sender, addressee unknown." I contacted Mr. Fischer by telephone, and he assured me that he had taken her there per my request. But every letter I sent came back to me the same way. The next time I called Mr. Fischer, his telephone number had been disconnected.

Panic set in, but I couldn't do much to alleviate my concern. I was obliged to stay at home and care for Matilde. I finally obtained a telephone number for the Claremont House and made a person-to-person call to the director of the facility, Mrs. Bodine.

"I'm sorry, Mr. Roth. We do not have anyone in Claremont House by the name of Adelaide Schulz. Could your party be using another name?"

"Maybe Adelaide Roth or Addie Schultz. Is there anyone there named Adelaide at all?"

"I'm sorry, no. We have over forty girls here right now, but no one using the name Addie or Adelaide."

"But she was there in July? Do you know where she might have gone?"

"We have no record of anyone with that name ever registering here. Could it be a different home for women? There are others across town."

I had no luck when I took down the names of two other facilities. Addie's first letter stated she was at Claremont House and had their return address. She hadn't put her name on the outside of the envelope. I assumed she didn't want our local postmaster to report her whereabouts.

It just about drove me crazy not knowing whether she was safely in the care of the Claremont House, especially in her condition. About every two weeks, I received a letter from her. She began to complain that I had not written back to her.

If that wasn't bad enough, her disappearance began arousing suspicion from her family. She had not written to any of them. The first time I went over to Samuel Schulz's farmstead was in August.

"I haven't seen Addie out in the yard of late when we go to Hallam," Helene said, offering me a cup of coffee. "Is she getting on all right with Matilde?"

"Adelaide is out of town," I muttered. I should have prepared a story in advance.

Samuel scoffed. "Out of town? Where would Addie go? Isn't she a nursemaid to your wife?"

"Well, something came up and I needed her to handle it for me. She went out to my ranch in Lincoln County."

Samuel and Helene exchanged looks. They weren't buying this for a moment.

Samuel frowned. "You got a telephone at that ranch out there?"

I could feel the sweat forming on my forehead, but mopping it seemed like a bad idea. "Yes, the house has a telephone. Addie has been writing letters though. She said she's doing well."

"What is she doing there? Ain't that kinda isolated? I'd suppose there'd be nothin' but a bunch of cowhands living on a cattle ranch."

I scratched my nose. "Yeah, it's about a baby. One of the cowhands had a wife and she got sick. They had a baby and needed someone to help until the woman recovered."

"Ain't that funny." Samuel crossed his arms. "Addie didn't tell us she was going anywhere. Haven't gotten a letter neither. Why don't you just tell her to write us a note when she has a chance. When is she coming back?"

I stood up. I was running out of tall tales. "Not sure. When the wife is better, I guess. I'd better go look at that field."

"Mighty peculiar when she had a sick woman right here that you hired her to care for," Helene said, taking my cup from my hand as I made a hasty retreat.

Of course, I couldn't ask Addie to write to her brother when my letters weren't getting through. Sheriff Thompson spotted me on the street in Hallam a few weeks later and asked me to stop by his office. I followed him back down the street. He was a massive man, and he leaned his beefy hands on his desk.

"Anselm, you've got a lot to worry about with Mrs. Roth doing poorly. However, the Schulz's came in the other day saying they are concerned about Miss Adelaide. They think something has happened to her. And they don't think you're telling them the whole story."

"I hoped she'd written to them. But what do they think happened to her?"

"They said you told them some cock-and-bull story about her going to your ranch out west to assist with someone else's baby. Now I agree, that makes no sense for her to go that far when there must be somebody closer—"

"I couldn't tell them the truth."

Sheriff Thompson put his hands on his hips. "Ya need to tell me the truth then. What happened to her?"

I exhaled and sat down in one of his chairs. "What do they think happened to her? That I threw her down the stairs and buried her in my backyard?"

"Well, that's close. You left out the part about attempted rape. At least that's what Helene Schulz imagined."

"God Almighty. I'd never hurt Adelaide. I love Adelaide." *Where had that come from? I guess I do love her.* "I put her on a train going to Sacramento. I had a man meet her at the station, and he said he took her to a place called Claremont House. But they claim she's not there."

"Sacramento? California? Why would she go there?"

I leaned forward in the chair and studied the checkered linoleum floor. "To have a baby."

"A baby?" Sheriff Thompson walked over to the door of his office and closed it. "Helene mentioned that Adelaide and Henry Hoffmann were no longer together."

I scoffed. "It's not Henry's, it's—" I didn't think I'd needed to finish that sentence.

The sheriff pulled up another chair across from me and sat down to get me to look at him.

"Let me see if I understand this. You got this young woman pregnant and sent her all the way to California to have the baby. Did you think the ocean view would make it better?"

"I don't think you can see the ocean from Sacramento. My problem now is I have misplaced her. My letters come back returned to sender." I pulled out one of my returned letters from an inside pocket. I also had one of her letters in my possession. "See, look here. Her return address is the same one I used, but my letters all come back. Is there some way you can investigate where she went?"

I'd given the sheriff all the information I had about my contact with Mr. Fischer and the woman at Claremont House. He hadn't been successful in tracing Addie's whereabouts either. I suppose I should be thankful he didn't arrest me.

My deception caught up with me after Matilde's funeral. We had the service in the local church and the burial at the Hallam cemetery. If I'd ever needed a bottle of spirits because I was feeling down in the dumps, it was that day. Instead of the community supporting me in my hour of grief, they were looking at me suspiciously. My brother, Anton, and his wife, Mary, stood by my side, along with six of their children, but even Mary stole glances across the way at her Schulz relatives.

Instead of going to Anton and Mary's house for a luncheon, I went straight home and opened another bottle of gin. Fifteen minutes later, Henry and Emil Hoffmann barged through my door.

"What have you done with her?" Henry started in without preamble. I saw their shapes against the morning light pouring in from the southern windows, but their faces were in shadow.

"Matilde? She's in the ground. You were there." I took another drink, but the angry young men still loomed before me.

"Adelaide, you drunken ass," Emil barked.

"Adelaide? She left, look around." I walked back to the kitchen and set down the bottle of gin. "You boys want a drink?"

Henry grabbed me by my collar. "Tell us where she is or you'll be keeping Aunt Matilde company in that cemetery."

"I don't know." It was the truth, but it was obviously not what they wanted to hear.

The next few minutes were dulled by the alcohol engulfing my brain. I recall the kitchen cabinet abruptly meeting my nose and blood running into my mouth. My ear started ringing from the blow to my cheek. Someone's fists pummeled my gut, and I was kicked as I hit the floor. I believe the assault would have continued except for a new voice I heard. Samuel arrived, hollering to his stepsons to stop, then they all left. It was dusk when I opened my eyes and hauled my battered body onto a chair. *Addie should have married Henry after all. He's tougher than I gave him credit for.*

That was more than a month ago. I could have retaliated. After all, as far as they knew, I owned the land Samuel and Emil were farming. Still, I didn't blame them. I had made mistakes with Adelaide. And now I could only hope to find her and make it right.

CHAPTER TWENTY: ADELAIDE

Sacramento, California
November 1926,

"Lena! Where are those towels?" Miriam called. The sight of my friend Miriam all but toppling over when she stooped to clean up a soapy water spill made me giggle. I rushed out to the clothesline to gather dry towels. I had no right to laugh at Miriam. I'm practically waddling through the door myself. I had no idea how pregnant women felt until now. And many women I knew have babies every two years.

Despite the frightening expansion of my mid-section, I felt a peculiar kinship here at Claremont House. Every young woman in residence was in the same situation. We were all in the second half of pregnancy and weren't able to raise the child for various reasons. Some of their stories were truly tragic. My story was truly fictional.

Starting with my name. On the train to Sacramento, I overheard two ladies talking about adoption. Naturally, my ears perked up.

"My friend, Annabelle, went to one of those orphanages to try to adopt a baby," a prim matron had said. "They told her that most of the babies are abandoned by mothers who aren't married."

"How shameful! I'll bet the mothers are prostitutes working at one of those dance halls." Her companion had said this in a lower voice, and I had to strain to hear.

"That's exactly what Annabelle was afraid of. She said the child would undoubtedly have an affliction or be mentally unstable with a mother like that. She told the matron of the home that she was only interested in children of married parents, or perhaps one whose father had died suddenly."

That took me aback. I was finally getting used to the idea I was going to have to give up my baby, and now there was a chance no one would want them? Did that mean the child would have to grow up in an orphanage? That had scared me silly.

So, the day I arrived at Claremont House, I had my script ready. I was ushered into a comfortable room and directed to sit on a chintz-covered chair.

"Welcome to Claremont House. I'm Mrs. Bodine. What should we call you, Dearie?" She took a seat at a delicate spinet desk.

"My name is Helene. Helene Schulz, Mrs. Samuel Schulz. I came all the way from Nebraska."

"I see." Mrs. Bodine began taking down every lie I was feeding her. "Is Mr. Schulz here with you?"

"Oh no. He's busy on the farm. He'll be harvesting corn soon." *Not for two months but she wouldn't know a cornstalk if it grew out of her desk.*

"Is this your first child, Helene?"

That stumped me at first. The real Helene had other children, of course. I was only the pretend version. "I have three other children at home. I just can't afford another one."

Helene did have two other children with Samuel and she was expecting another within months. Oh, I forgot to count Henry and Emil.

I forced a laugh. "Oh, I'm sorry. I forgot to mention I had two sons who are grown with my first husband who died. So, this is baby number six."

"You have five children already? And the oldest two are grown? May I ask your age?"

I felt the color draining from my face. *I couldn't say I was twenty-six. The sons would have to be at least eighteen. I'd have to be at least…eighteen plus eighteen is thirty-six.*

"I'm thirty-six. No, thirty-eight." *Better give myself a little leeway. I did say two grown sons.*

"You look remarkably young, Mrs. Schulz. You must take very good care of your skin on that farm of yours." Mrs. Bodine smiled, but disbelief dripped from her voice. "Now then, Helene, did you bring the payment with you?"

"Yes, I have it right here." The broker, Mr. Fischer, had given me an envelope of cash that Anselm had wired to him. "Oh, and no one calls me Helene. I don't like Helene. Can you call me Lena?"

For the first few weeks, I wrote letters to Anselm. I was still angry with him, but I had to admit we didn't have any good options. He had said he would have married me if it weren't for Matilde. I wondered how Matilde was doing and if she was still alive. I just hoped she hadn't been in pain.

But Anselm didn't write me any letters back. He knew where I was. He was the only person who knew where I was. I considered writing to Henry or Emil to tell them what was going on, but I was afraid they would be disappointed. Anselm had sent me away so no one back home would know about the pregnancy, but when I dreamed about my life in Nebraska, it made me lonely. I hoped Anselm would keep his word and bring me home. But the weather was very nice here in California. Maybe I'll look for a job here once this whole thing was over.

CHAPTER TWENTY-ONE: ANSELM

"That's right. We spoke on the phone several months ago. I couldn't travel then. I need to locate Miss Adelaide Schulz. I hired a broker to help her get settled and he told me he brought her here in July."

I tapped my foot on the oriental carpet in Mrs. Bodine's office. It struck me as a prissy sort of place. I suppose she dealt predominantly with young ladies in her line of work, but the abundance of little flowered prints, throw pillows, frilly curtains and dainty furniture made my skin crawl. The chair I was seated on looked like it might break if one gave it a good kick.

"And I believe I told you, Mr. Roth, that there has not been anyone here since then using the name of Adelaide."

"How about the last name of Schulz? That's S-C-H-U-L-Z. No T. Is there a young woman here with that surname?"

I saw the flicker of recognition in her eyes. She diverted her gaze.

"How are you related to the young woman in question? Are you her husband or father?"

Not sure that's any of your business. "No. Neither."

Mrs. Bodine sat up stiffly. "It may surprise you but we have men coming in here from time to time searching for young ladies who have run away. They fled because their home life was intolerable. I like to think our residence is a haven, and we will not be a party to someone who is trying to force one of our residents to return to an environment from which she escaped."

I felt the muscles in my jaw clench. "She would want to see me. She has written letters to me." I pulled out the four letters I had received from Addie and tossed them on her desk.

She picked up one of the letters and read the return address. She nodded. "Do you mind if I look at the letter?"

I gestured for her to go ahead. She began to read. I didn't recall precisely what each letter said but I was sure she talked about what was happening here. I hoped Addie hadn't complained about Mrs. Bodine. No, scratch that. I didn't care.

She folded the letter, returned it to the envelope, and handed the letters to me. "It seems that you have an amicable relationship. However, I'm still not sure you have identified the person you're seeking. I think there is a chance she was here at least, possibly using a different name."

I commanded eye contact as I pulled out a photograph of Adelaide. Matilde had placed a high school portrait of Addie in a scrapbook she kept upstairs. She'd changed a little, her face was narrower now, but her features were recognizable. When I saw that note of recognition again, I pulled out Addie's hair receiver from my pocket. Like many women, she'd saved the hair from her brush to use for stuffing pin cushions or hair art.

"This is what her hair looks like. It's fairly blonde for someone her age. Most of us tend to have darker hair when we grow up."

Mrs. Bodine stood up. "Mr. Roth, why did you come to see her?"

"So, you admit she's here?"

"I cannot say. What is your intention? Are you the one who sent her here?"

I squinted at her. "Of course. Will you take me to her?"

"No." She pulled a piece of paper from the drawer. "Write down how I can contact you if I can identify the girl you seek. She will recognize your name, won't she?"

"Yes, but I came here directly from the train station. How about I come back tomorrow? If you find her, she can meet me here in your office. Otherwise, I'll have hotel information by tomorrow.

"How is it that you have her hair receiver? That is a rather personal item. A woman keeps that in her boudoir."

I shrugged. "It was in her room. She lived with me and my wife."

She pursed her lips and took a sidestep, glancing back toward the doorway. In response to her wariness, I moved carefully toward the door myself and nodded respectfully.

"Tomorrow then."

I returned the next morning, only to be told that Mrs. Bodine was not available. She had more than one resident in labor. I learned that midwives delivered the babies right in Claremont House.

Before I left, I explored some of the shared rooms in the front of the building, since it didn't appear that any workers were securing the spaces. I found a nice library, a parlor with a gramophone, tables for the residents to write letters or perhaps eat meals, and a room that they might have used for visits, with extra chairs. I circled the three-story building. There were two other exterior doors, likely fire exits. I tried to open both and found them unlocked, at least during the day. An idea began to form. I sensed Addie was in there somewhere. Mrs. Bodine wasn't going to get in my way.

It was supposed to be warm in California. That night was rainy and the December wind howled around me, but I didn't think I could afford to wait on the weather. I carried a hand lantern but was afraid the wind might extinguish the flame. I circled Claremont House quietly and tried both doors I had discovered earlier. They were both locked.

I was about to start testing the locks on the windows. It was unknown if the girls in residence slept on the ground floor. Everything looked dark through the first-floor windows. I heard a noise and saw one of the doors opening. Two giggling girls emerged as I extinguished my lantern.

"Don't let any of the guards catch you, Darlene," one said to the other. "I don't want them confiscating my cigarettes again."

"Where's the brick?" The second girl said. "Oh, I see it; someone put it back in the wall." It looked like the second girl pulled a brick out of an adjacent decorative wall and propped the door open so they could return inside. They were so intent on lighting their cigarettes in the wind that they didn't notice me stealthily move to the door and wrap my fingers around it before scooting inside.

Now, what am I going to do? I've probably just committed a crime. Find Addie. That's why I'm here.

I moved quietly through the hallways on the main floor and found no one. Apparently, the sleeping quarters were upstairs. It might be tricky getting up there without frightening the ladies.

When I reached the second floor, I could see this was where the residents were living. The first couple of rooms I passed had closed doors, but there were little signs by each door with the first names of the occupants. None of them were Addie's. The third door was open. A young woman in a pink bathrobe beckoned me inside. It was apparent that she was in a family way, but I guess all these women were. It occurred to me I had not pictured Adelaide as any larger than she had been when she left.

"Are you the new janitor or a night watchman?" she asked.

"I'm here to take someone home. Have you seen this girl here?" I held up Addie's photograph. She had to turn on her lamp to see it.

"Hmmm. That looks like Lena. I think she's the one having her baby today. Two girls were giving birth at the same time."

"She had the baby already? Where is she?" My pulse quickened. Why hadn't Mrs. Bodine mentioned that?

"Her room's way down at the other end of the hall, opposite side. Keep going until you can't go no farther."

I darted down the hall, not worrying whether I was seen anymore. When I got to the room, the door sign said "Lena." I opened the door carefully, hearing voices inside.

A dark-haired girl was hovering over the bed with a wet compress in her hand, dabbing Lena's forehead. But it wasn't Lena. It was Addie. She was sweating profusely in December and moaning as if in pain. The sound she made reminded me of a cow in distress.

I rushed to her side and knelt next to the bed. "Adelaide. What's going on? Did you have the baby?"

"Are you the doctor? I was afraid you weren't coming." The dark-haired girl looked relieved. "She's been like this for a couple of hours. Mrs. Bodine went home and the midwife is with the other girl. I think she's got an infection. I've seen it before."

I put my hand on Addie's forehead; it was as hot as a radiator.

"Anselm?" Addie had trouble getting the words out. Her eyes flitted around the room in delirium. "I had…babies. Two boys. Born today…they said I did real good."

"You had twins?" My heart nearly stopped. I looked at her companion for confirmation.

She nodded. "Lena had two little boys, just sweet as pie. The midwife said they were a little early, but twins usually are."

"What-what happened to them, the babies?"

"I think they had to take them to the hospital because they were small. They don't let the mothers spend time with the babies, it's too hard to let go."

"Where's the hospital? What's it called?"

"It's just down the street. Sacramento County Hospital."

"I want you to come with us. Show me how to get there. What's your name?"

"I'm Thelma, but we can't go anywhere tonight. It's past lights out."

"Get your coat, Thelma. I don't care about the rules. Addie needs to see a doctor, and we need to find the babies."

Addie's eyes were closed and she appeared to have fainted. I wrapped her up in the sheet and blankets from the bed and picked her up. She didn't weigh much.

We didn't run into any resistance until we approached the front door. Someone jumped in front of me and shone a lantern in my face.

"Halt! What are you doing running around this time of night?" It appeared to be the watchman.

"This woman needs to go to the hospital. Thelma is going along to help but she'll be back."

"You the doctor they called then?" the man asked.

I didn't answer, I loaded both women into the car I had borrowed from the hotel. Thelma was right; the hospital was a few minutes away. I wasted no time in finding an attendant.

"Please! You've got to help us. She had twin babies today and she has a terrible fever."

A nurse intercepted me and directed me to lay Addie on a gurney. They wheeled Adelaide into a curtained area. After a few minutes, a doctor came in.

"Wait outside, Sir."

A short time later, the doctor whipped the curtain back. "You said she had a baby today?"

I looked at Thelma.

"Two babies. Little boys." Thelma backed away from the doctor, using me as a shield.

The doctor turned to the nurse. "Probably those twins they put in the incubator room. Did I understand they were to be adopted?"

"No!" I said, surprised at my reaction. "If those are her babies, they aren't available for adoption."

The doctor gave me the once over. "Are you the father?"

"Yes. And no adoption. We've changed our minds."

"Well, talk to the agency. They'll be here tomorrow. We've got to get your wife on mercurochrome. It's a good thing you got here when you did. Blood poisoning has set in."

They gave Addie an injection and she went to sleep. I took Thelma back to the Claremont House and parked the car in the hospital lot.

I stopped to talk to the nurse when I returned to the hospital. "Where is that incubator room the doctor mentioned? He said the twin babies might be there."

"It's up on the second floor, but they won't let you go in. They have to keep the temperature high and make sure it is germ-free. When it's daytime, you can look through the window."

I turned back toward Addie's bed. "Will she be okay?"

The nurse picked up a chart. "Her temperature has come down a bit. That's a sign that the medicine is working. I'll be checking on her all night. Why don't you try to get some sleep over on that davenport?"

I stretched out on the lumpy sofa. I'd found Adelaide. Not a moment too soon, it appeared. Tomorrow I'd fix the rest of the mess.

I tried to sleep and saw Matilde's face. The last time she was lucid, she'd asked for Addie. I'll never forget the look on her face when I told her Addie had left town.

"What did you do?" my wife had choked out.

I found the nursery the following morning. Dozens of babies were swaddled tight onto little beds smaller than the seat of my roadster. It had been a few years since my nieces and nephews were infants, and I'd forgotten how small they were.

"Do you have a set of twin boys here who were born yesterday?" I asked one of the nurses who bustled in and out of the nursery.

"Oh, they're in the incubation room in the back. Come to the back window and you can see them." She pointed toward an area next to the far wall. "We try to keep it warmer in there and put hot water bottles in their beds. They were only a week early; chances are, they will survive. They need a little extra fat on their bodies so we feed them more often."

She went back into the incubation room and opened the curtains. Two babies were huddled together in one bed, a bit smaller than most of their peers in the front room. They both had a shock of dark hair, which looked out of place on their wee heads. I couldn't see much more than their little pink faces, but suddenly my throat ached and tears burned my eyes.

It was unimaginable that I was looking at my sons. *I have two sons born just yesterday.* The whole parent-child relationship made more sense now, how a person would do anything to protect their offspring. Why had I driven their mother away without thinking about their welfare? I had to change that now.

Addie was conscious and sitting up in bed when I went to her. "What are you doing here?" she asked.

I took her hand. "I came to find you. My letters all came back. When I called the Claremont House, they said you weren't there. I worried."

"Oh. I used a different name: Helene. I told them I was married to Samuel Schulz. They called me Lena. I heard that people preferred to adopt babies if the parents were married so I used their names. I should have told you that in my letter."

"How are you feeling this morning?"

She sighed. "I feel very tired, but I ate a little bit. I think I had the babies yesterday. Two of them. That was a surprise."

"I just saw them. They look like Roth's already. Their noses are squished up and they have dark hair."

"They're here? I thought the adoption agency would take them to their new home."

"Let me worry about the adoption agency. I told the doctor last night we weren't going to let them go."

"What? But I signed the papers…"

"Did you sign your real name?"

"No, I had to sign Helene's name," Addie said.

"That shouldn't be legal then. When the adoption people come, I'll tell them we changed our minds. Nobody is taking our babies. We'll just get married. Do you think they have a chaplain here?"

"You want to get married?"

"Yeah, don't you?"

"Aren't you forgetting something? Or someone?" she asked.

I pulled a chair next to her bed. "Matilde died about six weeks ago. She was delirious for the previous two months, and didn't know me or where she was."

"I'm sorry, Anselm. That must have been hard. But don't you have to wait more time after your wife dies before you remarry?"

"It's not necessary. I think it would be better if we are married because of the babies. Once the hospital releases you and releases them, we can find a place here in Sacramento. Stay here until spring maybe, then go back to Nebraska."

"Wait a minute. I think I'm dreaming this. You think we should get married here and keep the babies? And live in California this winter?"

I took her hand in mine and put it to my lips. "I should never have sent you out here. I was worried about what people would think, I guess. And Matilde. I didn't want her to be embarrassed or hurt, but there are things more important than that. Love, for one. I love you, Addie. If you love me, we should get married. We'll figure out the rest as we go."

"I'll think about it," she batted those long eyelashes at me. "When I feel a little stronger."

Two days later, I was able to take her back to the hotel and made sure she had plenty to eat and plenty of rest. The next day, I went to the nursery to see the twins. The incubator room was empty.

I found the same nurse I'd spoken to earlier. "Where are the twin boys that were in the incubator room a few days ago?"

She smiled. "The parents were able to take them home. They were doing much better."

I felt like someone had knocked the wind out of me. "No, that can't be. We're the parents—my…um their mother, she was here in the hospital and I took her to the hotel. We were taking them home. There's been a mistake."

"I'm sorry. I don't know how that works. You can speak to the hospital administrator."

"Where do I find him?"

She directed me to an office on the first floor. I barged in on a balding man studying papers on his desk. His desk plate said he was Mr. Drew.

I stood as tall as I could, looming over him. "My infant sons were taken from the nursery! What are you going to do about it?"

I expected him to show alarm, but he gave me an icy look over wire-framed glasses. "And you are?"

"My name is Anselm Roth. The babies were in the nursery yesterday. Where have they gone?"

"You said babies. Are you referring to the twin boys who were being adopted? They were transferred here from Claremont House. They came in with adoption papers and the agency representative showed up this morning along with the parents." He dangled a piece of paper. "I have their paperwork and it appears to be in order."

I held out my hand. "Let me see that."

"No, I'm sorry. This is sensitive information."

I took a deep breath to calm down. "Look, I understand. Someone else intended to adopt Addie's baby. Then the baby turned out to be twins. We can change our minds, can't we? I mean, they haven't even gotten used to the babies yet. If that deceitful Mrs. Bodine had leveled with me earlier, we could have avoided some of this confusion."

"I assure you that Mrs. Bodine and the Claremont House have stellar reputations for helping poor young women who seek homes for their infants. They work with several adoption agencies."

"Look, Mr. Drew. Just tell me where they took our children and I'll go explain it to this couple. They'll understand it was all a big mistake." I took a step forward and tried to grab the paper out of his hand. He was quicker than I anticipated. His office chair had wheels and he rolled out of my range.

"That's enough Mr. Roth. I'll have to ask you to leave. Otherwise, my security men will escort you out."

I could see he wasn't going to help. My next stop was to return to Claremont House to see the ever-delightful Mrs. Bodine. She was hanging up her telephone when I entered her office. Good old Mr. Drew had given her a warning.

"Mr. Roth. What a surprise." She stood up and crossed her arms.

I didn't think it would be wise to try to intimidate her. At least that wasn't my first tact. So, I sat down.

"Here's what's happened. I had been trying to reach Adelaide Schulz, who was using an assumed name. She didn't receive my letters. I wanted to make things right with her and explain that my circumstances had changed. However, because she didn't receive my letters, she went ahead with the plans for adoption. She didn't sign her real name, so I don't see how that could be legal. I would like the name and address of the couple who have our babies. If you don't have that information, just tell me which adoption agency was involved so I can get it from them."

"Here's what I see," Mrs. Bodine pointed a skinny finger at me. "You broke into our residence hall under the cloak of darkness and absconded with one of the girls. You took her to the county hospital without telling anyone on our staff—"

I narrowed my gaze. "To save her life."

"Then you insisted to the hospital nurses that two twin boys in their care belonged to you. You have no idea if those babies are the same ones that Miss Schulz gave birth to. And just this morning, you told Mr. Drew at the hospital that your babies were stolen from his facility. According to his records, the paperwork was all in order. Adoption is a private matter, Mr. Roth, and we take our responsibilities seriously."

"Do you know where the babies are?"

"Of course not!" she hissed.

"Can you say which adoption agency was involved with Adelaide's babies? You must have a record of that."

"Yes, but that doesn't involve you. Your name isn't even on the birth certificate."

"It should have been! You didn't tell me Adelaide was in labor when I was here before."

"Again, none of the business we do here involves you."

I cocked my head. My patience had just about run its course. "How does this whole adoption scheme work? You ask these young women for room and board, which I paid incidentally, and then you get a kickback from the adoption agencies as well? What happens if the women change their minds?"

"Anyone is free to leave at any time."

"Up until the moment of delivery. If you'd told me Adelaide was here, I would have taken her away before the babies were born. Whatever she signed didn't have her real name."

She rolled her eyes. "She isn't the first girl who lied about her name under these circumstances. It doesn't make any difference. The agencies don't care about the birth mother as long as she's healthy."

"Am I going to have to get an attorney involved?"

"Go ahead. It won't do any good." She wrinkled her nose. "You had nine months to decide to keep these children. Now it's too late."

Her words whipped across my soul. She was right. I should have come sooner. I'd waited on the crops, the weather, foolish pride, and indecision. Without another word, I went out into the cool morning air, which had turned dark and ominous.

CHAPTER TWENTY-TWO: ADELAIDE

I was surprised when Anselm insisted that we get married so quickly. Two days after the babies were born, the hospital chaplain pronounced us husband and wife. It was not the ideal wedding, but I understood why he wanted to hurry. He was bound and determined to make our family legitimate.

I could see the disappointment painted on his face when he returned to the hotel after visiting Claremont House.

"What did Mrs. Bodine tell you?"

"She refused to tell me which adoption agency took our babies. I wanted to strangle her. Only that wouldn't help. I'm going to hire an attorney. Maybe even a private investigator."

"What's that?"

"It's sort of like a policeman but you hire him to work for you. In this case, he might try to snoop around different adoption agencies. I stopped at the hotel desk on my way up here. The clerk said he'd get me a list of nearby attorneys I could call."

Three days later, the attorney Anselm hired, Lionel Stanton, came to give us a report.

"I went to see your Mrs. Bodine at Claremont House. That woman is tighter than a drum. It's going to take some time to track down the adoption agency she used for this transaction. After doing a little legwork on my own, I've identified five possible businesses she uses. I think there might be one or two that don't have a real office, they work under-the-table."

"Are you talking about baby-selling?" Anselm lit a cigarette.

"Well, there have been some accusations. You won't find the law coming down on something like this. The courts are too busy with bootleggers and such. The point is, this isn't going to be easy or quick. That means it is liable to be expensive. Are you sure you want us to try to find your sons?"

Anselm glanced at me. "Yes. We do."

"And you realize that even if we find these twins, by the time we can take this to court, it is likely to be months from now. Maybe even six months. It's doubtful that the judge will be willing to take two babies away from the only home they have known. In California alone, there are thousands of children waiting to be adopted. The judge might tell you to find another child."

"You're saying the odds are stacked against me?" Anselm asked. "I can't tell you how many times I've won in that situation. Do everything you can. Especially if you can wipe the smile off the face of Mrs. Bodine."

I'd seen his expression before when he was attempting to close a deal buying a farm and the seller didn't want to compromise on the price. My new husband could be very resolute. His lip curled just a little bit and his nostrils flared. I suppose his dogged determination made him successful in many areas of his life. Nevertheless, he needed to step back.

"Anselm, can we talk about this alone?" I asked.

Mr. Stanton picked up his hat. "I'll let the two of you discuss this. I'll swing by again tomorrow or you can call me."

After the attorney left, I sat down at the table where Anselm was smoking. He studied his cigarette, not meeting my gaze. "You, of all people, aren't going to try to talk me out of this, are you?"

"When I first learned I was pregnant, I was scared. I know women younger than I have babies all the time, and they handle it. I also knew some of them died having babies. Then when the babies started growing bigger inside me, I felt them move. Of course, I thought it was only one baby who kicked a lot. I learned to love them. I talked to them."

Anselm stubbed out the cigarette butt, blowing out smoke. "I missed that part."

I nodded. "You did. By then, I was already at Claremont House. Mrs. Bodine and the other ladies who worked there told us about the couples who would adopt our babies. They had enough wealth but couldn't have children for various reasons. These couples would love our babies and be able to give them good lives. The children would have more opportunities than any of us ever had. That became the dream. We were sacrificing our pain and our love for our children to give them better lives. I believed in that, and I agreed to the adoption. The decision wasn't easy. The childbirth wasn't easy. Yet I trust those babies are where God intended them to be."

Anselm looked at me with narrowed eyes. He swallowed hard. "You think we should leave them be? What about our family? I understood you wanted to have our own."

I stood up and slipped my arms around his neck from behind him. "I do want that. I can have other children. Or we could adopt a child ourselves as the lawyer said."

He pulled me into his lap so he could see my face. "You want me to drop this investigation?"

"Put yourself in the shoes of those parents. They've been waiting years for a baby, and now they've got two. I'm sure they're over the moon. Do you really want to try to take their family away?"

"But they're not—" he looked away. "You didn't see those cute little faces. I'll never forget—" His mouth pressed into a hard line.

"Have you ever reneged on a contract, Anselm? Once you gave your word, wasn't it as good as gold?"

He sighed and studied me. "This is different, Addie. This is our flesh and blood. I didn't think I'd have a chance to have children, to continue my lineage. When Matilde was alive, it felt impossible. I was wrong to send you so far away. I didn't know how it was going to feel to lose them. I was afraid I was losing you too. I've got to fight for our family. There's nothing more important than that. Let me do this for you."

"There's no point in arguing with you once you've made up your mind, is there, Mr. Roth? Can we please go home though? Let the attorney handle it. I just want to leave the bad memories of this place behind us."

"I'll go downstairs and call Mr. Stanton back. You rest. You'll need your strength to handle two little boys one of these days."

After weeks passed, I decided to write to Emil. I believed he would be the family member who would be the most understanding.

> *December 23, 1926*
>
> *Dear Emil,*
>
> *I have been in California for the past five months. I realize I should have written sooner, but I didn't know what to say. Now that it is over, I can tell the truth and we don't need to talk about it again.*
>
> *Anselm sent me to a very nice place for pregnant girls. I had twin boys a few weeks ago and they were adopted. Anselm came out here to get me and we got married.*
>
> *Please tell the rest of the family that I am fine and no one needs to worry. We will probably be home within a few weeks.*
>
> *Love, Adelaide*

Anselm and I stayed in California until the end of January. When we returned to Nebraska, he sold Matilde's big house to his brother, Anton, and we moved into the remodeled home in

Lincoln. Over the years, he continued to buy and sell properties. Our marriage was a happy one until he departed this life nineteen years later, but we were never again blessed with children.

THE DESCENDANTS

CHAPTER TWENTY-THREE: DARCY

Lincoln, Nebraska
April 2022,

"I can't tell you how excited Tasha and I are that you agreed to meet with us to compare family histories," Trevor Wood said as they settled into their seats at a Tex-Mex restaurant. My dad, Donald Schulz, had made his doubts about meeting these two apparent to me in the car.

Tasha Edmonds took the chair next to me. She looked about my age, maybe slightly older. Her brownish hair was long and streaked with blonde. She wore large purple eyeglasses and dangling gold earrings. She was a pretty woman; someone I could imagine on a reality show based in California. I often wondered if those pseudo-stars came by their Barbie Doll physiques naturally or if a plastic surgeon remained on call doing liposuction, boob lifts, and Botox treatments on them regularly. I would gladly claim Tasha as a relative if it came to that, based on her beauty alone.

I was warier of Trevor. He'd made no secret of his mission coming here, to try to find a connection between his family and ours. He may have been hoping to rewrite history and that had my father's ire up. Trevor was also nice-looking though, and I could see a family resemblance between Tasha and Trevor in their dancing green eyes. I already knew their grandfathers were identical twins, so that was reflected in their appearance. Trevor was tall and fit, with neatly trimmed dark hair and a goatee. He flashed perfect teeth with a generous smile, making me question his sincerity.

This farm girl wasn't born yesterday. I don't always trust strangers, even those claiming to be kin.

"Did you hear from Archer, Darcy?" my father asked. He'd sat across from me, next to Trevor, leaving two empty seats at the end of the six-top.

"I got his text as we were walking in. ETA is five minutes. Cheyenne had to work late."

"Cheyenne is always making that boy late." Dad shook his head. "Maybe his girlfriend needs a watch. Or maybe he needs a girlfriend who can tell time."

Trevor flashed his pearly whites. "Who needs a drink?" The server appeared as if on cue.

"They let anyone in this joint?" Archer asked, one hand guiding Cheyenne's back. Archer plucked his sunglasses off and slid them atop his shaved head. It was a shame that he was prematurely balding while my sixty-five-year-old dad sported a thick crop of gray curls. They took their seats and everyone submitted drink orders. Introductions were made once again.

"What kind of work are you in, Archer?" Tasha asked.

"I'm an estate attorney. I work here primarily, but sometimes my clients live elsewhere although the estate is local. It sounds dull, but sometimes you find out some shenanigans have been going on with the finances. What are you doing, Tasha?"

Tasha was wearing a silver metallic sweater with cutouts placed in only one sleeve. She sat straighter and stuck out her chest, as though that was her principal asset. It was hard not to roll my eyes when Archer grinned. "I'm a show-runner on a daytime talk show based in Los Angeles. It can be very nerve-wracking, but I meet some fascinating people with wild stories to tell."

"I'll bet you do," Cheyenne pulled the lime off the swizzle stick when the waiter set down her frozen cocktail. "I spend half my time with sweaty construction workers."

Archer snorted. "She's exaggerating. Chey is a housing inspector for the city. It's mostly paperwork, right, Babe?"

Cheyenne gave my brother a tight smile and tucked her dark blonde bob behind one ear. "And Trevor, what is it that fills your bank account down there in the heart of Texas?"

"Same thing that brought me to your fair city. Genetics and genealogy. I work at a well-known DNA testing company in Houston."

Banter was the usual method of communication in my family, but this was running a little too flirty for me. Maybe if I had a partner to tease it might feel more comfortable.

My father drummed his fingers on his glass mug. "Trevor, can we get down to the meat of this? How do you think you're related to the Schulz family? I went back through my family records, and I found no one with the last name of Wood. Or Edmonds, for that matter. Isn't that your last name, Dear?" He nodded at Tasha.

"Ah. Well, it might be easier to show you than to talk about it." Trevor stroked the end of his nose. "If you like, I have some information on my laptop that I can share in our hotel suite. In a nutshell, Tasha and I are related because our grandfathers were identical twins, Robert and Richard Wood. When we were growing up, we knew them quite well, and they were a hoot, especially when they got together. Anyway, they were adopted by Radcliffe and Margaret Wood shortly after their birth in 1926. I'm trying to find their biological parents in order to go back further in my family tree. Naturally, these same ancestors would belong to Tasha as well."

"And you think the Schulzes have ties to your grandfathers?" Dad fished around in his coat pocket and came up with a folded sheet of paper.

"My mother did some genealogical research about ten years ago," Tasha said, turning her attention to my father. "She obtained the original birth certificates for the twins. She had a lot of trouble getting them, she said, because adoptions have always been closed in California. The parents of the twins were listed as Samuel and Helene Schulz of Lancaster County, Nebraska. I believe those are the names of your grandparents, Don."

Dad studied the paper he had unfolded on the table. "That's their names, sure. But when did you say your grandfathers were born?"

"Nineteen twenty-six. December sometime, wasn't it Trev?" Tasha appeared to be working on melting my father's prickliness with her warm smile.

Dad smirked. "Well, there you go. My father, Josef was born in 1922. His older sister, Nellie was born in 1919, and his younger sister, Hermione, was born October 24, 1926." He folded his paper and put it in his pocket again. "I don't believe it would have been possible for my grandmother, Helene, to have a baby girl in October and twin boys in December of the same year."

"I suppose someone could get the years wrong," Tasha suggested. "Or maybe ol' Samuel was the father but Helene wasn't the momma. I see that all the time in Hollywood, men having babies with more than one woman in the same year."

My father's face turned red. "Not in this family. Not on your life. Remember, this took place in the 1920s."

"The roaring twenties. I heard they were rather wild." Trevor threw back his cocktail and held the glass up to signal the server for another.

"You couldn't even buy a drink in the 1920s. Read your history." Dad squinted at Trevor. I knew that look well. He disapproved.

"We don't have to solve this mystery tonight." I tried to lighten the mood. "It sounds like Trevor has a lot of information he wants to show us after we eat a nice dinner."

We ordered our meals and talked about some other topics. After a short time, Trevor circled back.

"There is also the issue of the matching DNA, Don. You took a DNA test at Ancestry.com. You and I shared over one hundred centimorgans."

"I don't have any idea what you mean." Dad drained his beer mug and set it down with a thud.

"It means we're genetically related. I'm not impugning anyone in your family, but this is important to Tasha and me. We want to learn about our ancestors."

"You remember taking the test, don't you, Dad?" Archer leveled a look at our father. "Darcy and I bought those for Christmas. We all took the DNA tests."

"Of course, I remember taking that test where you spit into a tube. How dumb was that? I didn't expect distant relations to come crawling out of the woodwork."

Trevor laughed heartily and Tasha joined in. I tried to shield my face with one hand. Archer huffed and gave our father a dirty look.

Trevor leaned over to Tasha and whispered, "He must mean you. I don't crawl much, but you're often on your knees."

She giggled and slapped him playfully on the shoulder. "Hush."

"My enchiladas are delicious!" I said. "Is everyone else happy with what they ordered?"

Cheyenne covered her mouth with her cloth napkin. "Yum! Excellent food here." She turned to Archer. "Are you driving, Honey? If so, I'll have another margarita."

Archer ordered her another drink and asked for a soda for himself. "Perhaps we should table the talk about genetics and genealogy for tonight. How long are you here for?"

"Oh, I have to leave on the afternoon flight tomorrow," Tasha said. "I aimed to get to know all of you a little better before then."

Cheyenne laced her fingers through Archer's possessively. "What do you think, Arch? Do we have time to do breakfast or brunch tomorrow? What have we committed to on Saturday?"

"I think we're flexible. I'd be interested in seeing what information you have on your laptop, Trevor."

I sighed and side-eyed my brother. He likes to make everyone think he has the situation under control. We still had only a clue what these two cousins were dumping on us.

By the following morning, it was laid out. As I expected, my father declined to attend the breakfast meeting at the Residence Inn where Trevor and Tasha had a two-bedroom suite. The center area of their suite was suitable for looking at Trevor's monitor while munching on sweet rolls, yogurt, and fruit. Archer and Cheyenne were in attendance when I arrived, and they'd already drained the first pot of coffee.

Trevor clicked on his laptop to cast the screen to the TV. "The first thing I'm showing you is my family tree, starting with me at the bottom, my parents, Ronald and Joyce Hurt Wood, and my grandparents Robert R. Wood and Mazie Ann Gassman Wood. My grandfather was one of the twins who were adopted. Tasha's family line looks similar, her grandpa is the other twin."

He switched to a different tab. "Now here are the DNA matches in Ancestry. Donald is the closest match I have except for the Wood family that I have already identified. And he is only matching 106 centimorgans, which means he is likely a second cousin once removed, a half-second cousin, a first cousin three times removed, or a half-first cousin twice removed. A half-cousin would mean someone in his lineage or mine had children with more than one mate. That isn't true as far as I know. Is it true in your tree?"

I had my laptop open to my family tree also. "Well, my great-grandfather, Samuel Schulz was married to Helene Dunn, and she was previously married to a Hoffmann and had two sons with him."

"Wait. Did you say Helene's maiden name was Dunn? Wasn't there a different name on the birth certificate that my mother had?" Tasha fumbled through the papers Trevor had laid on the coffee table. "Here. It says the twin's mother's maiden name was Helene Hoffmann. Nothing about Dunn."

"That's a mistake then. Hoffmann was her first husband. We have a copy of their marriage registration." I pulled that document up on my screen.

Trevor frowned at his screen and clicked some keys. "Let's see your profile of Helene Schulz, Darcy."

I pulled up Helene's screen which showed her first marriage to Frederick Hoffmann with sons Henry and Emil, and subsequent marriage to Samuel Schulz, my great-grandfather, which produced three more children, Nelle, Josef, and Hermione.

"And you're descended from Josef, right?" Trevor looked at Archer, then me. We both nodded. "Well, the two of you show up as sharing some DNA with Tasha and me but not all that much, around fifty cM. I wonder if there are descendants of either of these sons Helene had with the first guy, Hoffmann?"

"We wouldn't be related to them, at least not through Samuel," Archer said.

"It might be a way to eliminate a possibility though. What I'm seeing here is that I'm related to the Schulz family, but not as closely as I expected, although DNA isn't completely predictable. If I could test Helene's older sons' descendants, I could be sure that I'm related to her, or not related to her independently of the Schulz DNA."

"Oh! George Martinez. Jorge is his real name. He works at the same insurance company I do. He went to a Schulz family reunion, and we figured out we were related," I said. "I think his grandfather was Emil Hoffmann. I went over to his house when I was putting together the family tree. George's wife had a box of family history information too."

"Do you think he'd do a DNA test?" Trevor asked. "Again, I would pay for the processing myself."

"I suppose he would."

Archer scratched his head. "I'm trying to follow where you're going with this, Trev. If it turns out you aren't descended from Helene, does that mean great-grandpa Samuel had a side chick?"

"That's only one possibility. We'd have to look at everyone in the tree. All I can see for certain thus far is that Donald is the father of you and Darcy by your shared DNA. If we can test other descendants of Samuel Schulz, we'll learn more. Let me worry about who to test; this is my area of expertise, after all."

CHAPTER TWENTY-FOUR: DARCY

The next day, Sunday, George Martinez and his wife Joann invited us to share information at their home in northeast Lincoln. Archer and Cheyenne had other engagements and Tasha had already flown back to California. I stopped at the motel to pick up Trevor, and he insisted on driving his newer rental car.

It was a nice warm spring day, and Joann took us out to their lovely garden in the backyard, where they had beds of vegetables started and many perennials in bloom. Joann was an avid gardener and offered us a quick tour of her plantings, but it was apparent that Trevor wanted to discuss varieties of DNA. Talk about a one-track mind.

When we were settled in their comfortable living room drinking iced tea, Trevor got down to business.

"I appreciate you seeing us today. Darcy must have told you I'm visiting from Houston where I'm a project manager at a DNA testing company." Trevor took out a business card and gave it to George.

"I want to identify the ancestors of my grandfather, Robert Wood. He was born in 1926 and adopted by the couple I think of as my great-grandparents, but they aren't biologically related. My aunt was able to obtain a birth certificate for him and the parents who were listed are Darcy's great-grandparents, Samuel and Helene Schulz. I've compared my autosomal DNA to that of Darcy, her brother, Archer, and her father, Donald Schulz. The results show that we're related, but not as closely as I expected."

I could see he had already confused George and Joann. "What Trevor would like to do is test a descendant of one of Helene Hoffmann's sons, who wasn't a Schulz. That way, he can determine if he is related to our family only on the Schulz side or if he is a descendant of Samuel and Helene."

"Helene Hoffmann would have been what, Joann, my great-grandmother?" George asked. Joann nodded.

"You're a direct descendant of Emil Hoffmann, her son from her first marriage?" Trevor asked, taking notes.

"I think so. I could verify it with my mother if she remembers."

Trevor's brows shot up. "Your mother is living? How is she related to these Hoffmanns?"

George smiled. "*Mi madre*. She's eighty-nine and still feisty. She's in an assisted care facility, and her memory comes and goes. Not complete dementia, but she calls it half-Alzheimers. Her father was Emil Hoffmann, I think. Is that the guy you're talking about?" He pointed to a box that sat next to Joann on the couch. "Look in there, and see if I have the names right. He was always *Abuelo* to me."

Joann started looking through the box. I moved over and sat on the sofa on the other side of the box. I found it interesting to see what families hung onto over decades.

"Would it be possible to do a DNA test on your mother?" Trevor asked.

"What does that mean, like take her blood? They have a hard time getting needles into her veins anymore." George frowned.

"No, nothing that difficult. She would have to be able to spit into a test vial. Or for some testing companies, a cheek swab is enough."

"Oh, like they do for suspects on *CSI*. We'd have to ask her," George said.

"Here's the chart your mother did years ago, George." Joann handed a hand-drawn pedigree chart to her husband.

"What else is in your family history collection?" I smiled at Joann, thinking she may have cultivated these artifacts as she did in her garden.

She started flipping through clippings and greeting cards in the box. "Oh, some of these things go way back. This came out of Sylvie's house. That's George's mother. I couldn't bear to let these old keepsakes go. There's even a letter, I think, that Emil received as a young man."

"Wow, that would have been a hundred years ago, right?" My eyes were glued to the box now, waiting for her to uncover the letter.

"I think so. It even had a dated postmark from somewhere in California." Joann pulled some of the top papers out and placed them in her lap to search deeper into the box.

"California? That's where the twins were adopted." Trevor's voice had a new eagerness.

"I think it mentioned twins. Do you remember, George?"

"I don't remember a letter. Was it from Emil?"

"No, oh wait, I think I found it." Joann straightened her back and opened a yellowed envelope, withdrawing a weathered piece of paper with faint handwriting. "It's on stationery from the Stanford hotel in Sacramento."

I glanced at Trevor whose eyes were big. I think we found a clue!

Joann read, "December 23, 1926, Dear Emil, I have been in California for the past five months. I realize I should have written sooner, but I didn't know what to say. Now that it is over, I can tell the truth and we don't need to talk about it again.

"Anselm sent me to a very nice place for pregnant girls. I had twin boys a few weeks ago and they were adopted. Anselm came out here to get me and we got married.

"Please tell the rest of the family that I am fine and no one needs to worry. We will probably be home within a few weeks. Love, Adelaide."

Joann set the paper down in her lap.

Trevor and I both jumped to our feet in amazement.

"God bless Texas and all her firepower! I can't believe you've had a letter like that for nearly a century!" Trevor paced around the room. His face was flushed. I had no idea he would get so enthusiastic, but this was big. At least I thought it was.

I took a big breath. "Who is Adelaide? And who else did she mention? Anselm? Are they part of your family tree?"

Joann looked at the letter again. "I don't recognize those names. Friends of Emil's perhaps? George, do you know?"

George shook his head.

Trevor piped up. "Well, she said, Anselm married her. She was the mother of twins. But are we talking about the same twins?" Trevor pulled out his smartphone. "Let me take a photo of that document and the envelope. Do you mind?"

Joann handed it over and Trevor took several photographs. I photographed it too. If it turned out to be significant, I wanted my dad and brother to see it.

"Do you still need to do a test on my mother?" George asked. I was sorry we might have given them confusing information, but we may have found something that would solve the mystery.

"Let's talk this through a minute," Trevor said. "Someone named Adelaide wrote to Emil Hoffmann in December of 1926 from Sacramento, California, saying she'd put her twin boys up for adoption. My grandfather, a twin, was born in Sacramento in December 1926."

I nodded. "Adelaide said she married someone named Anselm. Was he the father of the twins or was Emil Hoffmann? Or neither?"

Trevor pointed to George. "We might have the answer to that by testing your DNA or your mother's."

"How so?" Joann asked.

"If Emil Hoffmann was the father of my grandfather, he would be my great-grandfather. And you said Emil was your mother's father, so he was your grandfather. That would make you my half-first-cousin once removed, I think. Your grandmother wasn't Adelaide, was she?" Trevor began scribbling in his notebook again.

"No," George said. "Grandma was Emil's wife, Elizabeth. She died before he did."

Trevor blew out a long breath. "George, would you be willing to do the DNA testing? I have kits in my car. I can walk you through it, but you basically get a bunch of saliva in your mouth and spit into the tube. You aren't supposed to drink or eat within thirty minutes though. When was the last time you took a sip of tea?"

"When we first sat down. It's been that long. You want to do it now?"

Trevor went out to his car and returned with the kit. He instructed George on how to use it. I picked up the missive from Adelaide again and looked at her perfect faded handwriting. The more I looked at those names, the more familiar they seemed. Maybe it was my imagination.

Trevor was getting information from George so that he could contact him when his results were ready. He also had him sign a release giving Trevor the right to view George's results. Then we took our leave. It was getting late.

Trevor opened the passenger door for me.

Suddenly he's a gentleman?

"You're my lucky charm, Miss Darcy. That was unbelievable! And you're the one who found George and Joann. I would have never known about them and that letter! I want to take you out to the fanciest restaurant in this town! Where are we going?" Trevor gushed.

I laughed. His enthusiasm was infectious. "The Cornhusker. They have a nice bar and grille, I think. And it has historic roots in this town. There are fancier places but we're not dressed for that. We can have a nice steak at the Cornhusker."

"Can we have a drink though?"

"I think the restaurant is called Miller Time, so what do you think?" I pulled out my phone. "I should tell my dad I won't be home for dinner though. Maybe we can bring him something. Or, if you like, I could cook at our place for all of us."

"I don't think Donald is my biggest fan. If you're up for it, I'd like to keep it a twosome."

I gave him the side-eye. *He sounds as though this is a date. We're not dating; we're collaborating.*

"Hey, Dad. Trevor and I are going out to celebrate after we found something amazing over at George's house. They had a note from someone named Adelaide, who said she had twins who were adopted. The time and place line up with the twins Trevor was talking about. Have you ever heard of an Adelaide in the family?"

"Nope. If she's one of the ancestors I might not remember her. You watch yourself with that Trevor fellow. He's not what he pretends to be. I see it in his eyes."

I smirked. "You don't need to worry, we're fine. I think there are some leftovers in the fridge. I'll be home later."

"He doesn't trust me, does he?" Trevor shook his head and chuckled. "Or is he suspicious of every man you go out with?"

That insinuation popped up again that this was a date. "As a matter of fact, he was cynical about my fiancé. But then, he was right about Eric."

"You have a fiancé?"

"I did. We were together for three years. Engaged for one. Then we moved in together so we could plan the wedding. Things went downhill from there. That's when I moved back in with my father to save money to buy a house of my own."

"Sounds like a story there." Trevor glanced my way.

"Not a very interesting one. When we first met, it was exciting and romantic. He liked to do adventurous things like race motorcycles and jet skis. We took some fun vacations. By the time we lived together, things became kind of routine. There just wasn't the spark we needed. It was like we were playmates."

"But not in bed?"

"What? Did I say that?" The blush was climbing my neck quickly. "I didn't mean to get that personal. Something was missing in the romance department. We weren't all that well-suited in other ways. When I moved into his apartment, I found out how bossy he was."

"Ha. And you don't like bossy men. I'll try to remember that."

"I mean, I guess everyone is bossy sometimes. Enough about Eric. We're over."

"What about now, Darcy? Do you have someone special?"

"It's a little challenging dating while living with my father twenty minutes outside town. I've dated a little, but I consider myself single."

Trevor didn't comment, he only smiled.

We were walking through the hotel from the parking garage. I gestured to the grand staircase. "This is the second Cornhusker Hotel. The first one was built sometime in the 1920s. I can only imagine what that looked like— very Art Deco. They imploded the old one in 1982 before I was born, but my parents watched it happen live. This version is about forty years old I guess."

"Maybe some of your ancestors walked over this same ground." Trevor surveyed the coffered ceilings.

"Did we tell you that the farm I live on is the same one my great-great-grandparents homesteaded? There have been Schulzes living there ever since 1870-something. So, I tread on my ancestors' ground every day."

After we had ordered our dinner and were drinking wine, Trevor tilted his head back on the chair and shut his eyes. His sigh told me he had finally relaxed. I wondered why he kept smiling at me.

"So now that you've heard about my dismal love life, tell me your story? Have you got a wife and three children back in Houston that you haven't mentioned?"

"Darn it!" Trevor sat straighter and snapped his fingers. "I wanted to keep the wife and three kids a secret until after you'd slept with me."

I laughed. The wine must have given me a buzz because I wasn't annoyed that he assumed I could be so easily seduced.

But he's joking, right? It's been a while since a man flirted with me. I need to chill and enjoy the harmless exaggerations.

"Seriously though. I did have a wife once. No children. We were married for seven years. We were both ambitious, maybe too ambitious for our marriage to survive. She worked for a congressman and followed him to Washington when he became a senator. I tried to ignore the rumors about how she was helping the senator during all those trips and late nights. You said moving in with your man didn't work out. Our long-distance marriage didn't work out. I have been accused of being married to my job. It's kind of funny, now that I see what I'm doing this week. I'm on vacation, yet I have taken my genetic genealogy job right with me."

"But you came here specifically to find some answers. You can take other vacation days to have fun. Don't you ever go to the Gulf of Mexico? That's not too far from Houston." The server set down my salad and I took a bite.

"I have been to the gulf. It's more fun with a bikini-clad woman by your side. My wife left two years ago, and I haven't found anyone I wanted to be with long-term." Trevor shrugged. "My co-worker, Marnie, says I have to be more open to the possibilities around me." He waved his fingers in the air. "I'm trying."

That was more candor than I expected. Maybe Trevor Wood isn't quite as buttoned-up as he pretends. Maybe I also need to be open to possibilities.

When our steaks came, we attacked them like ravenous wolves, and the conversation stalled. Throughout the meal, he kept topping off my wine glass. I'd never been out to dinner with a man who ordered a whole bottle of wine and didn't even care how much it cost.

"You didn't bring your laptop today, did you?" Trevor asked when I had to stop eating.

"No. I didn't think we'd go this late."

"But you could log into your ancestral tree from my computer, can't you? Do you know your password?"

"I think so. My password is on a list on my phone. Why?"

"It occurred to me that we might be able to find either Adelaide or Anselm. Maybe in your tree or maybe through a search of other public trees."

"I guess it's worth a shot. I should let this wine settle before I drive home anyway."

I couldn't miss the mischievous glint in his eyes. Was it what my dad had seen?

"Excellent. Are you ready to leave?"

When we rose to go to the parking garage, I was a little wobbly and should have switched to water before dessert. I'd have a chance to sober up a bit in his hotel room. My father's warning flashed through my brain.

It's fine!

When we got to his suite, he pulled out a bottle of whiskey and poured himself some. He made a quick trip to get ice in the hallway. "I guess you don't want a drink if you have to drive."

"Water for me, please." I sank onto the cozy loveseat. He handed me a water bottle.

He fired up the laptop and pulled up the ancestry site. "Go ahead and log in," he invited.

I stifled a yawn while logging in. "Now what?"

Trevor took over the laptop. "Let's search for Adelaide in your tree." No results came up. "Okay, what was that other name, Anselm? Let's try him." Nothing again. "Too bad we don't have last names." His fingers flew over the keys and another search screen appeared. "Let's try this. I'll put in Adelaide and 1926. She said she was coming home in that letter, so she may have lived near here. We can enter Emil Hoffmann and Samuel Schulz as people she might have had a connection with. Okay, cross your fingers."

There were a lot of results that showed up. The screen lit Trevor's face and I could read the concentration in his expression as he analyzed each record. His eyes went wide. "Schulz! Here's an Adelaide Schulz in the 1920 census!"

We both held our breath when he pulled up the view of the census. "There she is, in a household with Herman Schulz; head of household, Samuel Schulz; son, Helene Schulz; daughter-in-law, Adelaide Schulz; daughter, Henry Hoffmann, Emil Hoffmann; step-grandsons, Nelle; granddaughter."

I tried to piece it together, staring at the entry. "She was Samuel's sister! My great-grandfather's sister! And your grandfather's mother? Your great-grandmother!"

"This explains it! The DNA match is perfect. I am related to the Schulz family, but not how I thought. This is an amazing breakthrough!"

Trevor jumped up again and leaped around the room. He'd done something similar at George's house so I wasn't so surprised this time. I was taken aback when he yanked me to my feet and planted a passionate kiss on my mouth. My reflexes were slowed by my jubilation and the after-effects of drinking wine.

"Trevor, you...you can't do that," I laughed. "You just said we're related."

He swung me around like we were on a dance floor. I was already a little dizzy.

"Stop!" I broke his grip on my hands, but couldn't stop laughing.

"Darcy, Darcy! You solved the mystery! I have been working on this for months! Thank you so much!"

He grabbed me and kissed me again before I could prevent it. This time though, he slowed down: he put his hands around my head, then slid them down my back. He was a good kisser. And it had been a long time since anyone had kissed me. Gosh, maybe not since Eric. Eric did not kiss like this. Trevor could give Eric a few tips. My hands found their way around Trevor's neck all on their own. Then my brain kicked in.

"Trevor, I didn't say you could kiss me." I tried to look admonishing.

"Oh, that's right. You disdain bossy men."

"Darn right," I nodded. "Where are we? Done for the night? Anything else you need to know?"

He raised one brow. "Yeah. This is only half the puzzle. Who's my great-granddaddy? Let's see what we can find out about this Adelaide Schulz."

Trevor plopped down on the loveseat again and began to type. "It looks like several trees have Adelaide Schulz included. This one says Roth-Sherman tree. Let's take a look. I see Adelaide Schulz 1900-1987 married to Anselm Roth 1874-1945. Looks like he was married to Matilde Schulz 1849-1926 first. Do you see those birth dates? Anselm's first wife was twenty-five years older than him, and his second was twenty-six years younger than him? That's strange."

"But Trevor, you have a last name! Anselm Roth. He was married to Adelaide Schulz, who said she married Anslem in the letter to Emil."

"You're right! Anselm Roth. Let's see if they have other descendants. I don't see any on this tree. Let's check some others. No. He had a brother named Anton. Looks like Anton was a couple of years younger. And he married, looky here, another woman named Schulz! A Mary Elizabeth Schulz. This is insane. Were the only women in this county part of the same big Schulz clan? Of course, if they all looked like you, the men were probably breaking down their doors to marry them."

I was startled by that comment. A back-handed compliment. Maybe he had more to drink than I noticed.

Trevor slumped against the back of the loveseat. "My head is going to explode. It looks like Anton and Mary had a bunch of children. Some of them undoubtably had descendants, but the program blocks out the names of living descendants in someone else's tree unless they permit you to see it. How do we get those names?"

"Obituaries." I smiled. He had to have known that simple trick.

"Obituaries. Right. Newspapers.com. Tomorrow I'm going to delve into that ferociously. I think I need some sleep first. Are you off tomorrow?"

"No, sir. Some of us work for a living. Tomorrow is Monday."

"Oh, yeah, you told me about your insurance company job. Call me when you have a chance and I will tell you the latest news."

"All righty. I think maybe I can drive now." I got up and used his bathroom before heading out. "Tomorrow. I'll call you."

CHAPTER TWENTY-FIVE: DARCY

By noon on Monday, I'd forgotten about the excitement of the night before. I was knee-deep in the Monday morning call center backlog when the human resources director, Terry Heston, stopped by my desk for an impromptu chat.

"You heard about Jill Brownbrook's transfer, I suppose?" he asked.

"I overheard something, I think. She's moving to Kansas City?" I gulped some coffee while I had the chance.

"Yes. It's a nice promotion for Jill. She'll do well. However, she was the obvious choice to fill Carl Winston's director job when he retires at the end of the year. Now you're the leading candidate."

"Me? Director of Operations?" I brushed back my hair behind my shoulder. "I suppose it is the logical career path. Would you send me the job description?"

Terry smiled and nodded as he stood to leave. "We may need you to take on some of Jill's team at least until her job is filled. It will give you more experience. You've always had a good rapport with the clients and employees."

My mouth went dry and my pulse vibrated. My gaze flitted to the large corner office where Carl had reigned as long as I had been working there. I could certainly supervise the four customer service teams, and deal with the escalated customer calls. I wasn't certain what else was on his plate. I'd love the salary bump. *My savings account would be flush.*

By the time I took a lunch break, it was one-thirty. I had three missed calls from Trevor Wood and a couple of impatient text messages. The last one threatened to send me a naked photo if I didn't respond soon. He answered my phone call right away.

"I'm working! Keep your pants on, Trevor!" I said. "Monday is the worst day at a call center."

"I don't have to wear pants in my hotel suite. I found some good stuff. What time are you done working so I can show you?"

"I'm off at four-thirty. And don't send me any racy photos. First, *eeeww*. Second, my father looks at my phone sometimes."

"Aren't you a little old to have your old man screening your phone?"

I sighed. "He's not screening it. I show him some of my mom's Facebook posts. She lives in Florida now with her second husband."

"Let me guess. He doesn't have Facebook."

"No, he's got one of those idiot-proof phones. No internet. I might stop by your hotel for a few minutes, but I'm heading to the grocery store tonight to fix dinner after that."

"Okay, but will you do one thing for me first? I've got an email address for the Roth-Sherman tree. Could you send an email asking for contact information? I'm hoping there is a male descendant of either Anselm or Anton Roth who will do a DNA test for me. Oh, and add your photo to the email. That way they know you're not a spammer or phishing."

"Why can't you do that?"

"I don't always have as much luck getting people to respond. I tend to go all scientific on them and I think it puts them off. You can be more down-to-earth. I'm hoping this person is in Nebraska since I'm here now. Ask where they live."

I took the email address from him and tried to compose a concise message. I took a quick photo reapplying lipstick after I ate.

I can't tell by this email address if the recipient is male, female, my age, or much older.

"Hello, I hope you can help us. We're trying to locate a male descendant of Anselm or Anton Roth. They appear in your Roth-Sherman tree. My cousin wants to use DNA to link up an ancestor who was

adopted. Would you mind sending your name, phone number, and location so we can see if a DNA test is practical? There will be no cost to you. Thank you for your consideration.

Darcy Schulz"

I attached the photo and sent the email. I went back to meetings the rest of the afternoon and didn't think about my family tree again.

CHAPTER TWENTY-SIX: DUSTIN

North Platte, Nebraska
April 2022

I'm generally off the clock by two-thirty. That comes with the territory when you work part-time as an agricultural science teacher at North Platte High School. I taught two classes, did some work as the sponsor of our Future Farmers of America club, and now I was killing time on my computer, waiting until after three when Veronica, my nine-year-old daughter, wandered in from the grade school a few blocks away.

Here's an unexpected email from the Ancestry message board.

I clicked through to read it. There's a photo. A nice photo. I double-checked to make sure this wasn't from one of those dating sites my sister-in-law made me join a year ago. No, it looked like it was about the family tree.

My mother was the one who worked on our genealogy. She went on and on about people we were related to. Dead people. Like I cared. The only dead person I cared about was Brittany. Brittany, who should not be dead at all. Who should be home in my kitchen, or down the street managing her fitness center, or doing homework with our child, and spooning with me in bed.

But Brittany was one footnote on the elaborate tree my mother had created. A few years ago, Mom changed the email address on her Ancestry account to mine, thinking I could carry this on after she was unable to. No one had ever messaged me before this.

What did this woman want? She appeared about my age, but heck, this photo could be ten years old. She looked familiar. Did I know her somehow? She didn't say where she lived. She was very pretty; I couldn't deny that. I kept staring at the photo.

Was I a descendant of either one of these men she mentioned? I growled. Now, she's making me look at the damn family tree on the website. After a quick search, I found them both. Yep. Anton was the name of Grandpa Lamar Roth's daddy. My great-grandfather. He never writes, he never calls. Well, looks like he died in 1941. The other guy was his brother. Also dead. Bunch of dead relatives, like I said.

I don't have much tolerance for extended family. Mine was kept tight: Dad, Mom, and me. Brittany and I married and had one child too. I suppose we might have had more if she hadn't…I looked toward the door—no Veronica bursting through to greet me yet. I can answer this email quickly.

> My name is Dustin Roth. Definitely male. Anton Roth was my great-grandfather. I live near North Platte, Nebraska, on a ranch that I think once belonged to Anselm Roth, Anton's brother. I like your photo. What do you need?

I added my phone number before sending it. Ronnie arrived and I shut down my PC.

It was after dinner when I saw her text:

Thank you for your information. Apparently, my great-grandfather's sister was married to Anselm Roth, so we must be distant relatives. I am helping this other distant cousin, Trevor. He came to Nebraska to try to find his adopted grandfather's family. He thinks it might be the Roths. I live near Lincoln. If we came to North Platte, would you consider giving me a DNA sample? This is Darcy Schulz, BTW.

I laughed out loud. I went back and looked at the photo from her email. I started texting without censoring myself:

> **I would love to give you a DNA sample the old-fashioned way.**

No, I couldn't say that. She's likely a lovely girl. I hit the backspace key to erase what I'd typed. Ronnie startled me when she knocked on my bedroom door. I jumped enough that I accidentally hit return. With horror, I looked to see what I had sent. The auto-correct function must have kicked in too. So, it said:

> **I would love to give you a trample**

Jesus, that might have sounded even worse:

> **No, dumb auto-correct. I tried to type I would give you a DNA sample, not a trample. How does that work?**

She must have had a sense of humor. She wrote back:

LOL. You just have to spit into a test tube that comes with the kit. Then Trevor will send it in. Easy peasy. How soon can we come to see you? Trevor is here from Houston.

> **Come anytime. Doesn't sound like it takes long. Do you want to test me or my father too? I work at the high school. I guess you could track me down there.**

Darcy answered in a few minutes:

Trevor and I will drive out there on Wednesday then. If we can test your dad too, even better. I will call or text when we arrive.

Simple enough. A three-hour trip for them but my part should be quick. I'll call my dad tomorrow and get his schedule for Wednesday. I tried to dismiss the whole exchange but for some reason, I kept pulling up that first email with the photo. She was a very pretty girl.

CHAPTER TWENTY-SEVEN: DARCY

Wednesday morning, Trevor was driving west on Interstate 80 heading toward North Platte, about 250 miles from Lincoln. We planned to stay at a motel that night and return on Thursday but I took vacation days for the rest of the week. Trevor assumed I could be at his disposal, and I was up for a road trip.

"I'm sorry I didn't make it to your motel Monday night. I ended up working later and then I had to get groceries. What have you learned since I saw you?" I pulled out a spiral notebook and idly doodled on it. Maybe I'd make a few notes to help with my own family tree. After all, Trevor was a professional genealogist and he wasn't charging me a thing.

"You took care of the most important thing. You contacted a Roth descendant and got him to agree to take a test. That will either be a dead-end or solve the mystery of my adopted grandpa. But let's see. I found a lot in the newspapers. First, I read all the obituaries of everyone in the Roth and Schulz trees. That identified living descendants. This guy we are going to see is Dustin Roth. He is the only son of Louis Roth. Louis is the son of Lamar Roth, who was Anton's son. Anton and Anselm were both sons of Karl Anselm Roth. It looked like Karl stayed in Germany when his sons immigrated, but that doesn't matter. We can test Dustin's Y-DNA. If he and I are a close match it should point us straight back to a common ancestor, in this case, Karl Anselm Roth."

"You said the DNA is less reliable if you must go back more than two or three generations. That's four generations if I counted right."

"That's what is so remarkable about the Y-DNA compared to autosomal DNA. It is constant from father to son. There's no recombining or loss for the most part. Oh, there are a few mutations over thousands of years, but you might find the same Y-DNA if they could dig up a man's caveman ancestor."

"Maybe that explains why men have so much trouble accepting change," I mused. "Why they are so stubborn, inflexible."

"What was that?"

I chuckled. "Never mind. Talking to myself. Find anything else helpful?"

"Yes. They used to put more information about wills in the newspaper. That Anselm Roth must have been wealthy. He owned land coming out of the wazoo. In southeast Nebraska alone, he owned about 2000 acres plus a few houses in Lincoln. In addition, he had over 3000 acres in Lincoln County, where North Platte is located. I'm guessing that's the farm Dustin referred to in his email.

"Of course, the liquid assets he left to his wife, Adelaide Schulz, who as you recall, was much younger than he was. He also bequeathed land to his nieces and nephews, his brother's children. His brother had already passed on.

"At some point, one of those children, Lamar Roth, moved to Lincoln County and took over what was called Rattlesnake Ranch. Maybe he bought out his siblings, hard to tell. I'd have to search for land deeds in Lincoln County. I may have time to do that if we get there early enough."

I looked out the window. "It sounds like this Anselm Roth guy was rich. I wonder where the dough went?"

"Hard to say. Your father still owns some of that land, doesn't he?"

A little snippet of worry buckled my brow. "He owns the 160 acres that were homesteaded by Herman and Lillian Schulz back in the 1800s. I think Dad might have owned some other land but he sold it when my parents divorced, to settle with my mom."

"When did your parents get divorced?" Trevor tapped his fingers on the steering wheel.

"Oh, it's been sixteen years ago now. Right after I graduated from high school."

"That must have been tough. I'm sorry, Darce. I wonder who owns the rest of that 2000 acres now. I saw Adelaide Schulz Roth's will and she left her estate to her nieces and nephews, the children of Samuel and Helene Schulz and Christian and Grace Schulz. The will separated those homestead acres and left that specifically to Josef, your grandfather. Did he farm that ground before your father did?"

"Yes. How did you come up with that?" I felt my brow creasing again.

"Oh, plat maps mostly. I did some library research while you were working yesterday." He glanced at me and smiled. "I'm a history buff—not only genealogy but I like to recreate family settlements, whether it's on a farm or in a city. I think it helps me visualize the people."

I settled back in the comfortable seat of the luxury SUV he had rented. I reclined the seat and relaxed as the miles streamed by. The last thing I heard before sleep overtook me was Trevor telling a story about how people make incorrect assumptions about their DNA relationships.

We stopped for lunch in Kearney, Nebraska, and made it to North Platte by half-past two. I called Dustin to arrange a time to meet and I got his voicemail. He had a very smooth baritone voice.

I suppose he's used to a lot of public speaking as a teacher.

"Hello Dustin, this is Darcy Schulz. I'm here with Trevor Wood and we were hoping to meet with you today to do the DNA testing. I'm not sure when you are done working, but call me as soon as you can. We're close to North Platte now."

He called back within minutes. I put him on speaker.

"Darcy, right? Boy, you sound just like your photo. That was kinda cheesy, sorry. Listen, I would have you come here to the high school, but maybe you'd like to see the ranch. I have to wait for my daughter to get out of school, but we are usually home before three-thirty. My dad can meet us at my place."

I glanced at Trevor. "Hey, Man. I'm Trevor. Sure, we'd like to see your place. Isn't that the same land your ancestors owned? Give me the address and I'll pop it into the GPS."

We found the motel but it was too early to check in, so we drove around town.

At the appointed time we pulled into a long driveway beneath a sign that said, "R&R Ranch." A young girl was playing with a white cat on the spacious cedar deck.

"Daddy!" she called out. "They're here!"

As we opened our car doors, the screen door banged open and a dark-haired man descended the stairs from the front deck. He was dressed in crisp blue jeans, a flannel shirt, and cowboy boots. It all looked custom-made for his broad-shouldered frame. Then I got a load of those chiseled cheekbones and his square jaw. His blue eyes smoldered like they wanted to eat me alive. I hoped I was related to this handsome god. No, forget that. I wanted him to father my children. Would that be genealogy in reverse?

I opened my mouth to introduce myself, but I'd forgotten my name.

CHAPTER TWENTY-EIGHT: DUSTIN

Who was this magical woman standing in my driveway? Those nearly-black curls hovered around her heart-shaped face in the spring breeze. My first thought was that I knew her; she looked even more familiar in person. But I wouldn't forget a face like that. I forced my gaze away from those tantalizing blue eyes and took in the rest of the picture. She was taller than average, not overweight, but curvy in all the right places. Her jeans hugged her hips, topping endless legs. The breeze was also making her knit sweater cling to her enticingly.

Snap out of it, Man.

A lean man in a button-down shirt and khakis stepped forward extending his hand. I hadn't even noticed him until then.

"I'm Trevor Wood, here from Houston, Texas. Thank you for agreeing to help me in my family search." I shook Trevor's hand. His smile was broad, his teeth nearly too perfect.

Trevor had noticed me noticing Darcy. He walked around the car and put one possessive hand around her back. It was a clear statement saying "she's with me."

I dropped my gaze, then beckoned to Ronnie. She scampered over to nestle at my side. "I'm Dustin Roth and this is my daughter, Veronica."

Darcy moved forward then, offering her hand to each of us. "I'm Darcy Schulz. We might be long-lost cousins!"

"Really? Then you should call me Ronnie. Everyone else does."

The smile Darcy gave my daughter lit my heart.

"Daddy!" Ronnie said to me in a conspiratorial tone. "She looks like the lady."

"What lady?" Kids can be a puzzle sometimes.

"In the picture." Ronnie sighed at my blank expression. "In the hallway?"

I looked back at Darcy and Trevor and it all began to fall into place. "Sweet sugar cakes! You're right, Ronnie Rabbit. It's uncanny."

Darcy and Trevor exchanged glances.

"C'mon, we'll show you." I led them into the stylish farmhouse my parents had remodeled twenty years ago, through the kitchen and common areas into a hallway that accessed four bedrooms. Hanging on the wall at the end of the hall was an oil painting. I flipped on the wall switch and the subject's face was illuminated. Her dark blue eyes captured the light.

Ronnie went up to Darcy, who stood before the portrait.

"See, she looks like you. Same hair, same curls, even your chin and mouth are the same," Ronnie teased. "Can you smile like her?"

Darcy turned to assume a pose like the portrait and gave us a sexy demure smile. At least I considered it sexy. It was a match for the one in the painting. Then she laughed at herself. I had to swallow hard.

"I think I've seen this picture before. Not the gorgeous painting but a much smaller version, in brown tones, maybe this big." Darcy held up her hands to indicate about five by seven inches.

Trevor nodded. "I saw it too. It's in your family tree."

"Who is she?" Darcy asked, finally casting those blue eyes on mine.

"Carolina. Carolina Kraus Schulz. I think that's right. I can check with my father."

"She's a Schulz? Then why do you have her?" Darcy asked.

"I'm not sure. My grandfather had the painting. I think his mother was a Schulz."

"Oh, so you do have some Schulz genes hidden in there." Darcy backed up deliberately brushing her shoulder against my chest. "Lucky you."

Feeling pretty lucky right now. Remember to breathe.

I cleared my throat. "Why don't we head back to the family room or kitchen and get started?"

Trevor fetched a laptop from his car and connected it to the ranch's Wi-Fi. He laid a business card on the table which listed his name as a project manager at a DNA testing company. He pulled up the Roth family tree that my mother had created. He could only see the names of the deceased relatives.

"Huh. It doesn't look like that when I log in. Should I show you?" I asked.

He let me log in with my credentials and the whole tree appeared complete with profile photos from Veronica, to Brittany and me, to my parents, Louis and Janice, to my father's parents, Lamar and Emma, and finally to Lamar's parents, Anton and Mary Schulz Roth. Anton's parents, Karl and Maria Roth, were the topmost ancestors listed.

"This is only the Roth side, of course." I glanced from Trevor to Darcy. "My mother's tree, my father's mother's tree—it goes on and on like that. Well, you're familiar with that, if you work with genealogy."

Trevor's face tightened in concentration. "This is the one I'm interested in. Can you pull up Karl Roth? I want to see his other son."

I selected Karl Roth and clicked on Anselm Roth. There weren't any descendants listed for him, but my mother had attached many newspaper clippings and property transfers.

Trevor pointed to an entry onscreen. "See, it says he married Adelaide Schulz in 1926. Two months after his first wife died. We found some correspondence in Lincoln stating Adelaide had twin boys about the time they got married. And I think one of those babies was my grandfather."

"I've never heard anything like that," I said. As if on cue, my parents walked in. Since they used to live here, they seldom knocked. "Oh, good timing. My mom or dad might know more about this."

I introduced my folks to Trevor and Darcy.

My mom's eyes narrowed. "She looks like…"

Ronnie laughed. "Like the lady in the painting."

Mom nodded. "That's it. Are you a descendant?"

"I think so. If she is Carolina Schulz, I'm her third-great granddaughter."

"Imagine that," my dad said. "So, what's all this jazz about a DNA test?'

I snickered. Trevor pursed his lips, then forced a smile. "It would help me if you would take a DNA test. I work at a testing lab, and I can arrange to view your results. You would have access to them as well. You might find other descendants of your ancestors. Other Roth family members, for example."

Louis squinted at Trevor. "What's in it for you?"

Sometimes I really love my dad. No question I've got his DNA.

"As I was showing Dustin here, I think that Anselm Roth is the great-grandfather I've been tracking down. He would be the brother of Dustin's great-grandfather, Anton Roth. This DNA test I want to have you both take would verify that we all three share a common male ancestor, Anton and Anselm's father, Karl Roth."

"If I remember the family tree, I didn't think Anselm had any children." My mother made an open-arm gesture. "That's how his nieces and nephews ended up with his land, like this ranch right here. It used to be called Rattlesnake Ranch, but Louis' dad changed it to R&R Ranch."

"Let's get on with the tests, shall we?" Trevor unpacked the kits and gave one to Dad and me. He gave us brief instructions on what to do, but the printed diagrams were clear enough.

It didn't take long. While we were testing, my mom and Ronnie went to the barn to see the horses. Then Trevor began packing everything up. "I suppose we can check in at the hotel now, Darcy. It's after four."

"Oh," Darcy said. "I was hoping to see a little of the ranch since we came all this way. The country looks different in this part of the state."

I wasn't about to let this chance go by. "Yes, please stay. We can take the ATV and look at the pasture and the wetlands near the river. The view is great near sundown. We can rustle up some grub later."

Darcy smiled. "Is that cowboy for dinner? Sounds like fun."

Trevor's jaw tightened and he gripped his bag with the test kits so tightly his knuckles turned white. "You want me to drive back here and pick you up? What time?"

"She can sleep here," I offered. Didn't expect that to come out of my mouth. "There are four bedrooms, one is a guest room now. I'm sure Ronnie would enjoy having company."

Darcy gave me the once-over. I can see now why ladies don't like that. Then she moved toward the door. "Let me get my bag from the car."

"I'll get it for you," I said. Guess I'm Mr. Helpful tonight.

Trevor sighed, not hiding his disappointment. There goes his dinner date. "If that's what you want to do. Just be careful, Darcy."

"Always," she chuckled.

"I'll take good care of her, don't worry." I followed them out to his SUV. He said something under his breath to her, and she patted him on the shoulder.

Darcy said, "Call me tomorrow morning, Trevor. We can meet up then."

Trevor nodded and got into the car. He gave me a withering look when Darcy had her back turned. Sorry, not sorry, Cousin.

My mom and daughter returned.

"Are you staying longer?" Mom asked Darcy.

"Dustin said we could take an ATV to see the ranch. That sounded like fun."

"Oh, you'll love it," Dad said. "You know, why don't you come home with us, Ronnie? Grandma is making her special burgers. We can bring you home after dinner."

Ronnie beamed at her grandparents, then glanced at me. "Is that okay, Daddy?"

"Sure. Take your homework with you."

It was apparent what my folks were up to. They'd been suggesting I start dating for more than a year. Tonight, I was on board completely.

CHAPTER TWENTY-NINE: DARCY

I swear to God, I never do this. He could be a serial rapist or murderer. Maybe he has women's bodies buried all over the pasture. But would a serial murderer introduce me to his parents and child? Dustin Roth's steel blue eyes shadowed by dark brows took me hostage. And the rest of him was awfully delicious to look at too. Who could blame me if I didn't want to rush off? I felt more secure with him than Trevor anyway.

Although I started questioning my sanity holding onto him as we were flying over what looked like dunes on the all-terrain vehicle. At least he'd given me a helmet. We finally ascended a winding crest and he stopped the machine.

Wow. That was a view all right. We were looking down on some sort of river, or maybe it was a lake with tributaries going out in different directions. After a spring with plenty of rain, everything before us was lush green. Then I heard the honking. Geese were flying over us and in the sky around us as far as I could see. I was thankful again for the helmet. We watched them make a perfect synchronized landing in the water before us. I'd never seen anything like this. The sun was dancing on the water below as though lighting the stage for the waterfowl's performance.

Dustin stepped off the ATV and helped me clear the big tires. He pulled binoculars out of a bag on the side of the ATV and urged me to look closer at the birds. There were baby goslings nestled in with the adults, climbing up onto the sandy shore. It made me laugh.

"This is incredible! I'm surprised you didn't build a house right here."

His eyes danced over a knowing grin. "There's not enough flat land for a house and the barns here. It is one of my favorite spots."

"I'll bet you bring all the girls here," I smirked.

"A few," he sat down on the grass. "It's kind of romantic, I guess." He chuckled. "I remember in college, my wife wanted to go skinny-dipping down there. So, I said, 'Sure, go for it.' Only she didn't realize the water was only about three feet deep where we went, so we were skinny-wading. Kinda hard to hide in three feet of water."

I looked around and then sat next to him. "You still have a wife?"

He blew out a breath. "No, um she died three or maybe it's closer to four years ago. Ronnie was five years old. Pancreatic cancer. It can get in deep before you even realize it's there."

"I'm sorry. That must have been tough."

"It was hell. She was tough. A lot tougher than I was." He shook his head. "After Brittany died, I was in a fog for a long time. My folks helped me through it, and Brittany's sister, who lives nearby, was a big support, especially with a little girl. Eventually, I got it together and learned how to be both mother and father to Veronica."

"What do you mean you were in a fog?"

Dustin bent one leg and wrapped his arms around his knee. "They talk about different stages of grief. I swear I was stuck in the angry phase for a long time. Before this all happened, I was coaching football at the school, junior varsity. I played football in college, which put me through school in Wyoming. I couldn't go back to that afterward; it was too aggressive. I might have bitten someone's head off.

"I couldn't take it out on my kid either, she was much too vulnerable. So, one day I started ranting to the lady in that oil painting; the one you resemble. The first time, I'd had a few beers, but then it got to be a good way to blow off steam. When Ronnie was at school or asleep, I'd say terrible things to that poor great-grandmother, whatever she is. Sometimes stupid things that made no sense, but I knew she wouldn't judge me."

I squinted. "Did she ever have a comeback?"

He stuck his chin out and shook his head. "Not really. One time I answered for her. Told me to cut out the self-pity and go lift some weights." He chuckled. "Now, you probably think I'm unhinged."

"No, I thought you might be a serial killer."

"You thought I could be a serial killer and you came out here with me anyway?"

I nodded slowly, watching those dreamy eyes of his. "I figured everyone I knew would see the news about my murder. When they flashed your handsome mug on screen, they'd understand. They'd assume I had a good time up to a point."

His eyes went wild, and then he burst out laughing. "I think there might have been a compliment in there but…it's okay to be a serial killer if you're hot?"

"Do you think you're hot?"

One corner of his mouth twitched. "I used to be hot in college. Now I'm boring ol' Mr. Roth who teaches agricultural science."

I snickered. "You don't strike me as boring. Now, Trevor, he's a little…" I made a snoring noise.

Dustin barked out laughter this time. "So, the two of you aren't—"

"Oh no. No, no, no. He might have imagined something else, but he's not my type." Dustin studied me but didn't ask the obvious question. "Do you teach full-time or do you work on the ranch?"

"I wear many hats. I teach two classes and sponsor the FFA at school. The R&R ranch is in a trust, and my father and I both do some farm and ranch work, but most of the land is rented out and the farm manager handles things. I had to reprioritize when I became a single parent."

The sun was getting lower, and the geese were settling down for the night. Dustin stood up and offered a hand to help me. He took the ride back slower: it was dusk when he parked in the barn.

"What are you making me for dinner, Woman?" He smirked as he hung up our helmets.

"I think it's my night off. I could be missing a lovely steak at the local tavern with Trevor."

"Can you even cook?" he asked.

"I don't know which is more insulting, that you expect me to cook because I'm female or that you think I can't manage it. Cooking is a basic life skill for everyone. I make dinner for my father every night."

"Your father?"

"Yes. I live with my father. Long boring story, blah blah. Lived on my own since college. Moved in with my fiancé, and moved out three months later. Decided to live with Dad to save money to buy my own place. No husband required."

"Wow, I think I hit a nerve. I can make some food. How do you feel about French toast and scrambled eggs? Maybe some bacon on the side."

I drew in my breath. "I feel fine about that. Thank you. And it was nice of you to give me that tour on the ATV. The lake and the geese were unforgettable."

A smile crept from the corners of his mouth. "It was a slough and those were ducks."

I marched into the house ahead of him to hide my reddening face.

CHAPTER THIRTY: DUSTIN

I don't remember the last time I had this much fun making food. I guess it was teaching my daughter how to toss a pizza. However, ribbing Darcy while getting my hands full of raw eggs for the French toast was epic.

"You're putting too much milk in the mixture," she complained.

"That's what puts the French in French toast. Otherwise, it's egg in a hole." I flipped the first piece of toast in the air in an impressive arc. Except it landed on my sock.

"That one's yours," she quipped.

Darcy took over making scrambled eggs in my ancient cast-iron skillet.

"Not enough oil," I said, setting the bottle of oil next to her hand.

"I'm watching my weight," she retorted.

I let my eyes drift down to her hips. "Why?"

She rolled her eyes. "You've probably never been on a diet in your life."

I shook my head. "Not true. I had to make weight for wrestling in high school. And they were particular about your food intake in college on the football team. They wanted you to be all muscle."

She deliberately batted her eyes. "Did you qualify?"

I pitched my voice lower. "Oh yeah. I told you, in college I was hot."

I got that million-dollar smile in return. And when our gazes collided, I felt the radiant heat.

We settled down to eat at the old kitchen table. It was functional and didn't merit replacement.

"Darcy, we just met, but I feel like I've known you a long time."

"Are we back to the painting thing?"

"No, it's the way you act or maybe how I act with you. Let's get some basics out of the way." I waved my forkful of syrup-dripping French toast at her. "How old are you?"

She narrowed her eyes. Yes, I'd heard that old saw about never asking a woman her age.

"Why do you ask?" She cradled her decaf coffee mug in both hands.

I glanced back at my plate as though pondering it. "If you are that lady in the painting, you'd be close to 200 years old. I have nothing against older women, but I think I might have to draw the line at sleeping with someone more than 150 years older than me."

She pursed her lips. "That would make me a vampire or something."

"I might not draw the line at that." I licked syrup off my lip.

"I'm thirty-five, will be thirty-six next week. Now tell me your age."

"Thirty-nine. I will be that age until November. Then I will be past my prime."

Her eyes widened in exaggeration. "And not hot?"

I smiled. I think I smiled more with her than I had in the past three months.

"Okay, you passed that question. What's your middle name? Let me guess. Darcy Augusta Schulz."

"Do you make jokes when you teach? No wonder they think you're boring Mr. Roth." She dapped her mouth with the paper napkin she'd found in the cupboard. I often used my sleeve. "My given name is Darcelia Christine Schulz." She held up her palm in front of my face. "You cannot mock my name. I did not choose it."

"I wouldn't dream of it. It's a perfectly lovely name. It was brave of you to share that piece of information." She assumed I was being sarcastic by her caustic stare.

She made a c'mon motion with her fingers as though she expected me to reciprocate.

"My full name is Dustin James Roth. Nothing fancy there."

"Are you named after anyone?"

"My mother's father was James. Dustin was a name my folks liked. They called me Dusty as a child and said I had an aversion to baths. Outdoors on a ranch, little boys get dirty."

"Are we good on the personal questions?" Darcy began to gather up the dishes.

"I can wash up. You're a guest." I stood to clear the table. "And no, we're just getting started on the personal questions." I ran water in the sink. "When did you lose your virginity?"

She gasped. How cute was that? This woman did things to me I didn't recognize. I chuckled. "Too personal too soon?"

She regained her composure at once. "Maybe I haven't lost it at all."

"Really? Living with your fiancé? Maybe that's why it didn't work out."

She picked up a dish towel and leaned against the counter next to me. "I did have a special date for my high school prom. My steady boyfriend of two years. We'd been leading up to it. All my friends said it was a rite of passage, and we had a post-prom party at a motel. And we drank beer. A lot of beer."

I squinted. "You had sex with your prom date?"

Darcy shrugged. "No, but he made that same face you did when I turned him down."

"You are merciless." I moved next to her and hip-bumped her playfully. My hands were out of commission holding a soapy plate.

"You keep dishing it out; I'm merely tossing it back to you."

"So that's why you're so familiar. You remind me of me. Is that what you're saying?"

She shrugged. "Well, we do have some DNA in common. Maybe we both got the ornery gene."

I stepped closer to her so we were inches apart. "You certainly did." I moved back to finish washing the dishes. She dried them without saying more, watching me.

When that chore was done, I went into the family room and stood before a large old fireplace. "How about a fire? It's sorta cool outside now. In a few weeks, it will be too warm for a fire."

"Sure, sounds nice."

After I got the logs burning, I threw a couple of pillows on the floor so we could sit closer to the flames. We leaned back against the front of the sofa. When she rested her hand on her thigh, I curled my fingers under hers. Running my fingers along her hand was making my temperature climb. What were we, in high school?

I stared into the blue and gold blaze. "People have sat around watching fire since the beginning of time."

"Or at least after they discovered fire."

"Are we going to do this all night?" I asked. She tilted her head and looked at me. "Make jokes, quips, banter?"

"What would you rather do?" she asked. She made that easy.

I moved into the kiss gently. That used to be my cardinal rule: don't make initial romantic moves quickly. That way, if the girl wasn't interested, she'd have a chance to back away. This attraction was sudden, and I didn't want to be pushy. I rotated my body slowly to face Darcy.

Were the rules different when you were well past the age of innocence? My fingers tingled when I slid them over her chin to cradle her jaw. My gaze pooled on her lips for a fraction of a second before it sought affirmation in her eyes. When our mouths met, she leaned her head back on the seat cushion of the sofa, or maybe I was pushing her head back with mine. No objection, no witty comeback. *Hell, why hadn't I tried this earlier?*

The contact was warm and inviting, a promise of the pleasures awaiting us. But I retreated ever so slightly, to shift position, to run my hand down to her back, to assess whether she was feeling the same way. I only moved back an inch or two. Her eyes fluttered open halfway, in a dreamy haze. She shifted her shoulders toward me and parted her lips, a faint smile playing across her face. When our mouths explored each other again, I tasted the sweet maple syrup and bacon, but my hunger was only for her.

The kitchen door banged open in a burst of crisp air. "Hey Daddy, I'm home."

I was lucky we weren't in view right away. I straightened up and Darcy did the same. "Did you have fun at Grandma and Grandpa's?"

"Yeah. Oh, you made a fire! Can we have s'mores?" Veronica dropped her bookbag on the table.

Darcy laughed. "You make s'mores in the fireplace?"

"Darn tootin'. See if we have any Hershey bars and marshmallows, Ronnie."

Ronnie ran to the pantry, giving me a chance to search Darcy's face. If she was disappointed about the interruption, she didn't let on.

"Let's make s'mores!" she said. Darcy rose to help Ronnie find the components. I found the long forks we use for grilling.

It was another ninety minutes by the time we'd devoured our sticky treats and I'd convinced my daughter to shower before going to bed. By then, she'd given Darcy a detailed tour of her bedroom, including naming all her stuffed animals, even though she insisted she hadn't played with them in years. Watching the two of them was odd. Ronnie had been missing something too.

I returned to the family room after Ronnie said goodnight, and Darcy was stoking the logs in the fireplace, bringing new life to the embers.

I dropped down on the sofa this time. She sat facing me with one knee bent. "Do you have any brothers or sisters?"

"No. Just me and the folks. Brittany had two sisters and a brother. I think I told you one of her sisters lives here. The two of them opened a fitness center. Leslie still runs it. Her husband is the sheriff in North Platte. The rest of Brittany's family lives in Colorado."

"My brother, Archer, lives in Lincoln. He's an estate attorney."

I nodded. "Hmmm. So how was the drive today?"

"Really? We're back to small talk now? We're not going to talk about the kiss?"

I grinned, my gaze landing on her perfect lips. "Not much to say about kissing. You just do it. We can do it some more."

I absolutely want to do it some more.

The last time I'd kissed a woman had been probably two years ago; on my first date after becoming single again. Immediately, it left me feeling guilty and awkward, which was why I didn't contact the recipient again. But being close to Darcy had awakened something that had been recently relegated to late-night fantasies.

Darcy looked down. "But…but we only met today. I generally don't kiss anyone I barely know. I'm not the one-night-stand kind of girl."

"You've never had a one-night stand?"

"Never."

I rolled my shoulders. "Neither have I. I don't sleep with someone I'm not into."

She dropped her leg to the sofa and beamed. "Well, that's good then. We're on—"

"However." I put both hands on her lovely shoulders and ran my thumbs across her collarbones. "I'm into you." I slid my hands behind her head and pulled her mouth to mine. The next thing I knew she was in my lap and had her arms around my neck. The flood of heat coursing through my body told me I'd been out of circulation much too long. I was sampling the DNA on her tongue when she slid back.

"What are we doing?" Darcy asked. "I mean I didn't come here for this sort of thing."

"I think it's fate. Lately, Fate has been a bitch. She owes me another woman."

"What?" With wide eyes fixed on me, she jumped to her feet. "You think I'm some type of replacement for your dead wife?"

I landed that joke wrong. I got up and tried to put my hands on her arms, but she stepped back. "I'm sorry. That might have been in bad taste. What I meant was that I didn't expect to be a widower at thirty-five. Life dishes out bad things, but sometimes good things happen just as unexpectedly. Your appearance on my doorstep today was one of those good things, maybe even a miracle. I don't want to waste the opportunity."

She crossed her arms. "Haven't you dated since your wife died?"

I scoffed. "A few dinner dates here and there. Nothing too thrilling." What I could have said was no *one* too thrilling. "I went on one of those dating sites. I made the mistake of letting Leslie and Ronnie see the photos, where you swipe left or right. They made fun of all the women. It was hopeless."

Six months ago, I'd decided it was time to consider a partnership with a woman again, but my libido had been on such a long hiatus, I worried it had left for good. Strangely, tonight felt very different. Exactly what I needed and exactly what I'd feared. I couldn't stop my pulse from racing or my palms from sweating. I was analyzing every word out of Darcy's sweet mouth; every dazzling look she cast my way. My longing for her dashed wildly around the room trying to do an end run around my common sense. Was this overwhelming desire mutual?

"You like to poke fun at everything, don't you?" Darcy's glower only made me want her more.

"It's a defense mechanism, and it's hard to stop."

"Say precisely what you mean."

I moved in closer, not touching her this time. "I find you very attractive. I think we have things in common other than our ancestors. I'm as confused by this rush of passion as you are, but you're only here one night. Then you go back to your life 300 miles away."

"Right. How could we even get acquainted? We both have jobs, you have a child, family here. I have family in Lincoln."

"Darcy," I said softly, pushing her hair back from her ear and landing a caress next to it. "Couples do that all the time. If they're meant to be together, they work it out."

She made a little moaning sound when I brushed my lips over the sensitive spot on her neck. "Do you have any tattoos?"

I studied her. "Is this part of the 'getting to know you' routine?"

She nodded hastily.

I unbuttoned my flannel shirt and tossed it on the sofa. She watched me closely as I pulled off my T-shirt and landed it atop my shirt.

"Oh," she whispered.

Gotta admit, her reaction was flattering. Maybe I still had a semblance of hotness. I turned unhurriedly, tightening my abs. Who else was going to admire the results of my weight-lifting?

"You have a compass on your shoulder."

"Yeah. I could feed you some bull about needing direction, but the truth is I went to a tattoo parlor with my football buddies, and this looked like the most neutral design they had. I can't even see it all unless I look in the mirror."

She put her fingers over the tat on my right shoulder. That sent a jolt of pleasure right to where it counts. Then she kissed the tattoo. I closed my eyes.

"What's this one?" I sucked in a breath as she teased her fingernails across the tribal band on my left bicep.

"Uh, that one is more recent. After I was married. Brittany's idea." I struggled to make coherent conversation. "You like tattoos? You have any?"

She smiled mischievously and lifted the back of her sweater so I could see a life-size small-of-the-back butterfly and the top of her leopard-print panties.

"Okay, your turn to take something off." My voice came out huskier than I expected.

"We're not playing strip poker!"

"What are we playing?" I made the same c'mon motion she'd given me earlier. "Jeans, sweater, up to you."

"This is all you're getting." She smiled shyly and leisurely dropped her jeans, stepping out of them so gracefully I'd swear she made a living as a stripper. Although her jeans had been form-fitting, her bare legs were nothing short of spectacular. They were nothing short period. Long, silky, and begging to be stroked.

"I want you in my bed. Is that direct enough for you?" I wrapped my arms around her and started to steer her toward the hallway.

"Dustin!" She stopped our forward progress. "We've got to think about this. We should wait."

"Wait?" *Oh, hell no!*

"Let's take the night to think about this more rationally. I'm going to sleep in the guest room as planned." She laid her jeans on the couch and walked ahead of me. At least I got to watch that.

"All right. Just let me show you one thing. In my bedroom. I have this fantastic complicated bed. Most people haven't tried a bed like this, they're too expensive."

I opened my bedroom door and she reluctantly followed me. I was glad I had made the king-sized bed and added the colorful pillows my wife had picked out. I started throwing the pillows on a nearby chair.

"Lay down on the comforter and use this remote control. You can put your back up or your feet up. You can adjust it so it is firmer or softer." I pointed that out on the remote. "And when you're asleep it conforms to your changing position to keep you supported. It's even got a feature so that you can move the other person if they start to snore. That's handy."

She laid down on her back, pulling her sweater down to cover her underwear. She started pushing buttons on the remote. "There's something I should tell you about me. As soon as I lie down somewhere comfortable, I can fall asleep almost instantly. My friends all told me I was the first to conk out at sleepovers." She yawned. "I do like the bed though. It sounded as if you were selling me one. I'm sleeping on the old lumpy mattress I had as a child." She closed her eyes and rolled to her side, which pulled the sweater up a little higher off her exposed thigh. I think I stopped breathing. There is nothing like the curve of a woman's hip.

I stood waiting to escort her to the spare room, although I'm sure she could have found it. Unbelievably, she appeared to be asleep. In my bed. After she said—holy smokes. *Now what am I going to do?*

I laid down next to Darcy on my side of the bed. There hadn't been another woman lying in this bed since Brittany died. Two days before she'd gotten her cancer diagnosis, we'd gone shopping for a new bed. She convinced me to try this one, even though it was three times the price of the bed I expected to buy. We decided to think about it. The next day she was in so much pain, I rushed her to the hospital. When the doctor told us she had only months to live, there wasn't anything I wouldn't have done to make her more comfortable. By the time she left the hospital, this extravagant multi-tasking bed was waiting in our bedroom.

I blinked back tears and looked down at Darcy. Surely, she'll wake up again in a minute. Maybe I should cover her up and let her be. It would be impossible for me to sleep with her right next to me. It's hard to imagine I didn't know her when I woke up this morning.

No, that's not true, I'd seen her photo, and I had messages from her. I sure wasn't expecting... Jeez.

Twenty minutes went by while I stewed. I needed sleep; I had classes tomorrow. I carefully scooted the comforter out from under her and covered her with it. Then I went to the ensuite bathroom and got ready for bed. When she hadn't woken up from the bathroom noises, I went to the guest room, dropped my jeans on the floor, and slid into the bed. I hoped the sun would awaken me at the usual hour.

CHAPTER THIRTY-ONE: DARCY

Where am I? I woke up at 3:00 a.m., according to the bedside alarm clock. The moon lit a corner of the room. I sat up. The bed moved with me. My eyes began to adjust, and I touched the empty bed next to me.

I was at Dustin's house. I remembered. Were these the guest quarters? Why am I not wearing my pajamas? I should have changed into them but I didn't remember where my overnight satchel was.

I turned on the bedside lamp. I was alone. Looking around, I didn't see my satchel, purse, or phone. And I was wearing my underwear and the sweater I had on all day. I ran my tongue over my teeth. Forgot to brush them too.

Where's my stuff?

I hesitated before leaving the room without pants on. I must have left them in the family room. Maybe everything I'm missing is in there.

I wished I had a flashlight, but I took a chance and flipped on an overhead light. Found my jeans and slipped them back on. And my purse was with my coat near the door. My phone was the only thing on the kitchen table. I should have put it on the charger which was in my satchel. My battery was almost dead. No missed calls or messages. I wandered through all the rooms in the front end of the house but couldn't find my satchel.

I returned to the bedroom I'd been sleeping in. This was big for a guest room. A king-size bed. Oh, this is the fancy-ass bed Dustin showed me and then I must have fallen asleep. I'm surprised he didn't throw me over his shoulder and haul me to the guest bed. Or join me. Yikes. He could have done that. But he didn't. I crept down the hall to the other bedroom door. I knew it wasn't Ronnie's; she'd shown me her room. I gently cracked the door. I could hear Dustin snoring softly. That mystery's solved.

I'm going back to bed.

I remembered I had a travel toothbrush in my purse and used that in the adjoining bathroom. What else can I sleep in? Maybe Dustin still has some of his wife's nighties. I opened drawers and only found men's T-shirts, socks, and things like that. And condoms. That was a surprise. I looked in the closet and saw only more of his clothes. It was time to improvise. I took off everything but my panties and put on one of the soft flannel shirts hanging in the closet. It was a brown windowpane design. I could imagine Dustin wearing it. It came practically to my knees in front, but the sides were shorter.

It took me a little longer to fall asleep this time. I was lying in Dustin's bed. Where he must have slept the previous night. Wearing his shirt. How had I gotten so twisted up about this guy I just met? He appeared to be interested in me too. He was an excellent kisser, and just the way he looked at me made my heart jump. At least I didn't have sex with him. When he took his shirt off, oh man. I was tempted. I'd never dated a guy with muscles like his. I shut my eyes and imagined what his fingers would feel like roaming over my ribs.

CHAPTER THIRTY-TWO: DUSTIN

My God, this bed is awful! I should never let anyone sleep on it. Or was I merely spoiled with my smart bed that adjusted to every last movement of my aching muscles? It was light out; time to rise and shine. The clock on the table was flashing twelve o'clock, so it didn't get reset after an outage.

I found my jeans on the floor and pulled them on. Then I wandered toward the kitchen.

Coffee. I needed coffee. Thank goodness it was made. I must have remembered to set it up last night. I wanted to take a shower and get dressed, but little Miss Darcy took over my room and bathroom. Heck, she hadn't intended to. I sort of conceded it to her. I hoisted myself onto the counter and sipped hot coffee, anticipating kissing Darcy again.

I hardly recognized myself last night. I'd never wanted anyone like that, never acted like I wanted anyone like that. I didn't pressure women. If anything, I'd been accused of being too shy, too gentlemanly. Darcy…she'd flipped a switch. And all I knew was I needed more.

My sister-in-law, Leslie, and Ronnie walked in from the front porch. They both wore jackets.

"You're here kinda early on a school day, aren't you Lez?"

"And you'd better get a move on if you don't want to be late," Leslie scolded. "I'm chaperoning Ronnie's field day, so she's riding to school with me. Don't you remember? You signed the permission slip." Brittany used to refer to Leslie as her big sister. She was bigger and sassier than my wife had been, and her presence filled the room.

"Oh, that's today? What time is it?"

"Did you forget how to tell time overnight? It's past eight." Leslie fetched her car keys from her purse.

"Oh, shit—nanigans!" I said, jumping off the counter. I really tried not to swear around my kid. She'll pick up bad habits on her own.

Darcy walked into the kitchen raking fingers through her bedridden hair and wearing my brown flannel shirt. The one I figured on wearing. "Morning."

"Why are you wearing my dad's shirt?" Ronnie asked. Her perky smile was noticeably absent.

"Oh, I couldn't—" Darcy stopped when she spotted Leslie. She rubbed sleep from one eye and looked at me.

"Darcy, meet Leslie, my sister-in-law. She came to take Ronnie for a field trip today. And this is Darcy Schulz, who…uh came from Lincoln."

"She stayed overnight," Ronnie reported. "But why don't you have on pajamas or your own clothes?"

Leslie gave both Darcy and me a wide grin. "Overnight, huh? Well, we'll have to discuss this more later."

Darcy crossed her arms. "I couldn't find my satchel last night where my pajamas were. I still can't find it."

"I put it in the extra bedroom for you," Ronnie said. "Didn't you see it when you went to bed?"

"That's what I stubbed my toe on last night. What did you put in there, rocks?" I leaned back on the counter.

"Why were you in the guest room, Daddy? And where's your shirt?"

"Darcy fell asleep in my bed. I couldn't get to my clothes or the shower."

"I think it's time we left, Ronnie. We don't want to be late. Remember, we're stopping at Daylight Donuts first." Leslie was not going to let me forget this morning any time soon. She turned her head around as she walked out, in case I missed the simper.

As soon as the door closed, I had Darcy in my arms. "I have to hurry now. When can we talk?"

"I don't know. My phone died. Trevor might be on his way to get me. I need to charge it."

"Get your stuff in the spare room. Charge your phone. I'm taking a shower. And I'd like to wear that shirt."

"This shirt? It is nice and soft." Darcy unbuttoned the first three buttons. My mouth went dry.

She pushed the shirt higher in the front so it slid off one shoulder. I saw a flash of leopard panties before I grabbed her from the side and landed my mouth on her soft shoulder. She laughed sweetly. My hand flew to the buttons to continue the progress, but she turned toward me and kissed me. I slid my hand under the shirt skimming over her bare back.

I am going to be so late for school today.

She broke the embrace and moved toward the hallway, facing me so I could watch her unbutton the rest of the shirt. "I'll hang this on the doorknob."

"There's a name for women who tease men like that," I grumbled, following her.

She smiled and raised her brows. "Ornery?" The shirt hit the floor as she slipped through the guest room door. At least she reached around the door and hung it on the doorknob.

I shut the main bedroom door a little harder than normal and jumped in the cold shower.

I figured she'd be dressed when I went to get the shirt off the door, but she was wearing some silky short robe that reminded me of one that Brittany used to have. It was soft and clingy and felt like butter in your hands.

"You're not leaving?"

"I talked to Trevor. He said he wanted to go to the courthouse to do some deed searches. Something about his ancestors. I guess they're your ancestors too. Do you mind if I stay here awhile or do you need to lock the house? I'd like to take a bath in that soaker tub I saw in the front bathroom."

I tried not to imagine her naked in the luxurious tub my mom had installed when she remodeled. "Sure, stay as long as you need to. Indefinitely. Maybe I can call you after my first-period class. I have some flexible time for an hour or so then. We need to figure some things out."

"Nothing to figure out. I'm going back to Lincoln today. I don't expect we'll run into each other again." If she hadn't given me that demure smile, I would have been crushed.

"We both know this—" I wagged my finger back and forth between us, "doesn't end here. You may live a few hours away, but it's not like it's the moon. We're simply getting warmed up."

She walked up to me and finished buttoning the shirt I was now wearing. "I'm so glad you said that. Call me later, Dustin."

Just hearing her say my name gave me goosebumps. Now I wanted her to say it in bed. I gave her a quick kiss and headed out the door. "I will. Have a safe trip back."

I was done with my first class before ten o'clock. I was missing Darcy already. Maybe she was still at my house. I didn't have a text or call from her. I had some time before anyone at school would miss me. I jumped in my pickup and made the twenty-minute drive to the ranch in fifteen.

It smelled different when I walked into my house, like lavender and lilacs. A woman had been there. I didn't see her though; she must have gone. I slumped onto a kitchen chair, dropped my elbows to the table, and put my head in my hands. Why had she had such a dramatic effect on me?

"Everything okay?" Darcy carried her satchel out and put it on the floor near the door.

"I assumed you'd left. I'm happy you didn't." When she came near, I pulled her into my lap. Her dark curls were damp now and cascading loosely over a knit green shirt. It wasn't as long as the gold sweater she'd worn yesterday, and she had it tucked neatly into black trousers.

She giggled. "Aren't you supposed to be molding young minds or something?" She ran her fingers down the side of my cheek.

"I wanted to talk to you in person. When can we see each other again?"

"I'll be going back to work next week, but I can take a day or two of vacation with a forty-eight-hour notice. Won't school be out in a few weeks for you?"

"Yes, before Memorial Day. I'm sure Ronnie and I can come to see you during the summer months."

"Aren't you busy during the summer with planting or harvesting or whatnot?"

"Sure, but I have a farm manager who oversees all of that." I shifted my gaze toward the door, then back to her face. "Does this feel like a runaway train to you? Like things are happening before I can catch my breath?"

"There's no reason to rush anything. Relax, we'll have time to figure things out if we want to."

I took her hand and interlocked our fingers. "It's that sometimes things happen you aren't prepared for." She nodded. "I'm not just talking about my wife. That was the second major catastrophe I had to face. When I was about to start my senior year of college, my father rolled his tractor. It was a terrible accident and for a week or so, it was touch-and-go whether he would even survive. I had to drop out of school and stay home to take charge of the ranch and help my parents put him back together. Finally, he improved, and he can walk and do almost everything he used to but with more pain. Three years later, I returned to Wyoming for my senior year. They even gave me my football scholarship back, maybe out of pity. It was different playing football at twenty-six. I had a decent season and graduated three semesters later.

"But that time I spent working full-time on the ranch showed me that this is my legacy, my responsibility to handle. Up to that point, I didn't take it seriously. We're lucky to have inherited it from my grandfather, Lamar Roth, and he was lucky he inherited it from his uncle. We get offers every year to buy this land, but it's become part of the family now, like in our DNA. The thing is—and I know this is about twenty steps down the road from where we are today—I feel like I need to look ahead in order not to be blindsided. If you and I get involved, how would we resolve the fact that we live so far apart? I mean, how embedded are you in your job and your relationships at home?"

Her brows knit together. "Why are you thinking about that today? We haven't even had a first date. We might decide we don't like each other after a month. Your school might hire a new English teacher next year and you'll be head over heels for her."

"I think I'm doing that head-over-heels thing right now." I ran a finger over her bottom lip and then kissed her. "But I'm also fighting to keep my flaming libido calm enough to be practical. If I was tempted to move, I could leave my teaching job and Ronnie's school. Leaving my folks would be harder, but I did it in college. I won't permanently turn my back on R&R Ranch. If you feel as strongly as I do about your home situation, I think we should both be honest about it now."

She got off my lap and stuck her hands in her pockets. That tighter-fitting sweater emphasized her hourglass figure. "You're talking about something we might have to address two or three years from now. I mean, I like my job. I might even get promoted this year. I'm in a similar situation as you are concerning inheriting land. I expect I'll receive part of the acres that my great-great-grandparents homesteaded. I've lived long enough to appreciate that if you are ready to make a major commitment to someone you love, you prioritize and compromise." She crossed the room to pick up her purse and came back to stand in front of me. "You're scared that something is going to come between us because of what happened with your wife, is that it?"

I blinked. "No! This has nothing to do with my marriage. It's about location, and what happens if we can't agree. I don't want to set up a chain of events that might end in heartbreak for both of us."

"When you put your heart out there, it might get broken. Sounds like you need to think more about this." She locked eyes with me.

I jumped when a car pulled up near the house and the horn honked.

"Trevor's here," Darcy said. "Call me later after you think this through. Or don't. I'll get the message." She picked up her satchel and walked out the door.

My butt must have been glued to the chair. I swear I couldn't move. "Darcy," I whispered.

CHAPTER THIRTY-THREE: DARCY

I didn't say much to Trevor after I got into his car. I was trying not to cry. The last twenty-four hours had been a major roller coaster ride of emotions.

"You'll be happy that I found many deed records for Anselm Roth, and some for his nephew, Lamar Roth. From what I could trace here in Lincoln County, and what I found already in Lancaster and Gage counties, it appears that Lamar Roth bought out his brother's and sisters' shares in the land here and gave up his portion in the eastern part of the state. I also found the deed where the land went from Lamar to his wife, Emma, then to Louis Roth, when his mother died, and it is now it is in a trust owned by Louis, Janice, and Dustin Roth."

"Um-hmm," I answered non-committedly. *How could I have been so stupid thinking Dustin was falling for me? He was probably hoping to get lucky. He may have had a long dry spell and… it doesn't matter.* He wanted to put the cart before the horse, which was dumb. It's hard to decide what to buy at the grocery store because I can't predict what I'll want to eat two days in the future.

Something told me Dustin was still in love with his late wife. A woman had her hand in the décor of that house. It was clearly not a bachelor pad. That massive soaking tub along with three varieties of bubble baths in the vanity was proof enough that a lady's influence still reigned.

Aside from the bath, there were pretty throw pillows, flowered dishes, and family photos on the wall. I'd had time to look at their wedding photo on the dresser in his bedroom. She was beautiful, blonde, and svelte, and they looked immensely happy. Dustin may have packed away his wife's clothes, but she was there to remind him of their love and pain everywhere he looked. Not that it was her doing. He had left those objects there. He was clinging to that part of his life.

Trevor had been quiet for a few miles. "I'd like to hear more about what you can do with the DNA samples you took if you don't mind educating me," I said. I needed him to launch into a long lecture distracting me from the lump in my throat.

"Sure, if you're interested. I'm going to run a Y-DNA test on both Dustin's and Louis's samples. I'll also do an autosomal test and X-DNA sample to see what can be found from the maternal side of the family..." Trevor continued talking but I found myself looking at the passing scenery out the window.

Would Dustin turn down a woman he loved to stay on his ranch? Couldn't he still own it and go back for visits? Did he even consider that?

I reclined the seat back. "I'm going to rest my eyes for a bit, Trevor. You might want me to drive later. You go ahead and keep talking to me if you want. I'll listen."

Of course, I fell asleep within minutes.

I heard my incoming text sound as I was waking up. Trevor had stopped the car.

He laughed. "You were out, Darcy. We're getting gas and making a pit stop." He was parked at a pump and got out to fill the gas tank.

I glanced around—no idea where we were. Then I pulled my phone out of my purse. I had three texts from Dustin.

An hour ago:

Which step is our first fight?
We must be officially on step
two. I'm sorry. I'm a bonehead.
It's good you found that out
early on.

Twenty minutes ago:

Giving me the silent
treatment? I didn't want to call

because Trevor would hear us.

Five minutes ago:

Text me your address. How else will I know where to send the flowers?

I was glad Trevor had left the car when a tear escaped my eye. I grabbed my purse and went into the truck stop restroom. I took a seat and texted Dustin back, providing my address and this:

My favorite flowers are pink, red, and white roses, lilacs, tulips, and orchids. It's good you found that out early on. You're right, Trevor would eavesdrop. I was afraid he'd be mad that I didn't stay with him last night, but he's been decent. Probably because I asked him to tell me all about DNA.

I sent the text and then loaded up on junk food for the rest of the trip. Life was looking good again.

"Do you want me to drive, Trevor?" I asked when we both got back to the car.

"No, I didn't sign anyone else up as a driver with the rental car company. Besides, I like driving, as long as it isn't weeks on end." He was quiet until we got back on the interstate. "So, what happened last night? Did you get to see the whole ranch?"

"Dustin took me on his ATV up to a ridge where you could see for miles. Several little streams branched out from a slough. And thousands of ducks. I thought they were geese, but he said ducks. Of course, he might have been lying."

"What? You didn't trust the guy?"

"No, because he was always making jokes and teasing me. We had a nice time together. I have you to thank for wanting all of us to meet."

Trevor grunted. "Are you saying you slept with this dude?"

"No, I slept in the other bedroom. We're going to keep in touch and see what happens."

"You're interested in him? The farmer? I guess he was fairly good-looking for a redneck. The sort my girlfriend would call rugged."

I sighed, picturing Dustin's tattoos. "Wait. Do you have a girlfriend? You never mentioned her."

Trevor glanced at me. "You never asked. I usually have a girlfriend. This one's been with me for about four months. Longer than most. I get bored quickly."

"If you have a girlfriend, why did you kiss me?"

"Oh, that was the excitement of the discovery. Mainly. I think you kissed me back."

"I guess I shouldn't have, but I didn't have a boyfriend. Now, maybe I do."

Trevor shook his head. "He must move fast. And even if he's a hick, he's loaded."

I laughed. "Dustin isn't loaded. He teaches at the high school to supplement his income."

"You didn't see the assessed value of that land he owns. Of course, his parents own it too, but one of these days, they'll pass it all to him. Somewhere around fifteen mil."

"Fifteen mil…as in million dollars? Holy smokes! No wonder he didn't want to leave it."

"He was talking about selling it?"

"No, he said he's had offers, but he won't sell it. He said the land was his legacy. Like it was in his DNA. I can't believe it is worth so much. Mostly what I saw were pastures and irrigated croplands."

"It's the quantity. Over three thousand acres. I'm guessing it was all once owned by his great uncle Anselm Roth."

Trevor didn't say anything more for quite a while. I think I was in shock. I had no clue it was that kind of investment. I knew from my father owning agricultural real estate that it's not the same as having disposable income. You can use it as collateral to get a loan. But fifteen million dollars was a lot of collateral. Dustin must be making quite an income from the ranch just to afford the taxes. And he said he paid a farm manager. His parents may be retired; they didn't talk about that. So much I didn't learn about Dustin Roth.

I'd left my car at Trevor's motel. I was still mulling over the events of the past twenty-four hours when I pulled into my driveway. After opening the door, the first thing I saw was a huge floral arrangement on the kitchen table. It had all sorts of spring flowers, tulips, daffodils, lilacs, baby's breath, and roses in several colors.

"I suppose that Trevor fella is behind this waste of good money," my father grumbled, then flashed me a smile. "Maybe he's worth another look."

I picked up the card which read, "Still thinking of you. Dustin."

"No, Dad. Someone I just met yesterday." I grinned. "You're gonna like this one."

CHAPTER THIRTY-FOUR: DARCY

I guess we were now in the relationship-building stage, half small talk, half intimacy from a safe distance. Dustin called me every night. It struck me as a little traditional that he always took the lead, but my ego embraced it. I thought about him frequently, and I knew what that meant. I was falling in love with someone I barely knew.

It would be three weeks before we could arrange to meet again. By the last Friday in May, Dustin and Veronica would both be done with school for the summer, and they promised to visit me then. So, our conversations centered typically around that. He'd be forced to meet my father and brother. That might even be step six or seven, but I'd met his parents right away.

"Darcy, don't you have FaceTime on your iPhone?" Dustin asked one evening.

"Sure. I hardly ever use it. Mostly when I call my mom in Florida."

"I'll call you right back." Dustin hung up and my FaceTime signal chirped. It was nice to see that his handsome face had not been a figment of my imagination. His brown hair had gotten lengthy and was mussed from the windy weather. A hint of stubble grazed his upper lip, giving him a sexy male-model vibe. It looked like he wore a gray T-shirt.

"I don't know why I didn't think of this before," he said. "Now we can have phone sex."

"What? No, we can't! Didn't we agree this whole distance thing was better, so it would force us to talk and we wouldn't let our attraction lead us astray?"

"Yeah, but I want to see you. I want to touch you."

"You can see me. I'm right here."

"Is that what you wore to work today?"

I looked at what I was wearing. It was a simple black pullover. Maybe I should have changed or brushed my hair and teeth before I answered on FaceTime. "Yes, I wore this to work."

"Is it sexy?"

"Sexy? No, I don't try to dress sexy at work. It's mostly women in my call center."

"That's okay. Take your top off. I'm sure what you're wearing underneath is sexy as hell."

"No. Dustin, we're going to wait, remember? You're coming to visit in two-and-a-half weeks. We might be ready for that kind of thing then."

"Exactly what is 'that kind of thing?'"

He wanted me to say it. "Getting naked. Whatever words you choose. I'm only engaging in that sort of thing in the flesh. Not on the phone."

He laughed. "In the flesh. I like the sound of that. You're blushing, aren't you?"

"No!" I turned the screen away so he couldn't see my face. Then I realized I'd pointed it at the mirror above my dresser. I was sitting cross-legged on my bed in my shirt and panties, and he probably saw my bare legs. I jerked the camera back to my face again.

"Wait, what was that? I saw a leg. Did you take your pants off?"

"Let's talk about your visit when you come with your daughter." I needed to get him back on more platonic topics. "Do you want to stay with us? We only have one spare bedroom, but maybe Ronnie could sleep on the couch or a blow-up mattress."

"I was expecting to get a motel room. Now I see the problem with that. You and I won't have much privacy if Ronnie is in the same room. I may need two motel rooms, but she's never stayed in an unfamiliar room alone. We'd have the same problem if we stayed with you, except Ronnie and your father would be there.

Ideally, Ronnie could stay at your place and you and I could have the motel room, but neither Ronnie nor your dad would like that when they're strangers. It's going to be tricky to consummate our relationship."

"We could wait until you come by yourself or I go visit you."

He grimaced. "I don't think I can wait that long."

I ran my tongue over my teeth. "I don't think I can either."

His eyes got wider. "You're on board with this now? You want me to jump in my truck and head your way?"

I laughed. "You have work tomorrow and so do I. But hold that thought."

Dustin smiled and lowered his voice. "Should I bring condoms?"

I glanced at the ceiling. Suddenly this was getting real. "I'm taking birth control pills. And I haven't been with anyone for a long time. Is there a reason you think we need a condom?"

"I'm good without one if you are."

The following Friday was my birthday. For the most part, I like birthdays. My family normally gets together to celebrate. It was more depressing last year, turning thirty-five, and having recently broken up with Eric. The ticking clock on my fertility was deafening. My brother's new infatuation with Cheyenne was one of the few bright spots. Maybe Archer and Cheyenne would marry and give me nieces or nephews.

This year my father insisted we go to dinner at Lazlo's downtown. It's a nice restaurant, and the food is excellent, but I was puzzled when he picked it. It was not convenient to where we live and the parking is a little challenging. It was going to be his treat, so how could I complain?

The night before my birthday, I got a text from Cheyenne:

*On your birthday be sure to
wear sexy underwear.*

That made me laugh. Why would she care about my underwear? I wrote back:

Why?

She said:

*I tell all my GFs that. You may
be a year older but you need
to remember you're still
fierce!*

I took her advice. I'd gone shopping and bought a new dress for the weekend Dustin was coming. It was a purple sleeveless sheath with a V-neck that plunged to the empire waist. I bought a push-up bra in a similar shade that gave the girls a nice boost. I hadn't owned anything that showed so much cleavage since prom. I decided that dinner tonight would be the perfect excuse to wear both the dress and bra. I clipped a pink and purple scarf around my shoulders to make it more appropriate for a family event.

My father and I were seated at a table set for five people. "Who else did you invite?" I asked.

He cleared his throat and looked around. "I'm expecting someone else. A lady friend of mine that I would like to introduce to you and Archer."

My mouth flew open. "You have a date? For my birthday?"

He frowned. "Is that so incredible? Your mother and I have been divorced for many years. I can date if I want to."

I turned to see Archer and Cheyenne coming to our table. Cheyenne gave me a huge grin and set a small gift bag in front of me.

"Sorry we're a little late," Archer said. "Cheyenne had to make a stop."

"Should I open this or wait for our surprise guest?" I asked.

"Oh, open it now," Cheyenne said. She didn't ask about the guest. Had my dad already told them about his friend?

I unwrapped the tissue paper in the bag and found three sample-size bottles of French perfume. One of them was a perfume I had bought myself on a trip to Paris after college, and the others were from the same company. "On my goodness, Cheyenne! How did you know that this was one of my all-time favorite scents?"

"Lucky guess."

Archer snorted. "She found the empty bottle when she went into your room looking for a barrette. She's kind of a snoop."

"Well, I found something useful, didn't I?" Cheyenne pouted at him. "I love French perfume myself, but it's pricey. I found these samples online and they weren't so much. I guess they hope you'll love the perfume and want a larger bottle."

"This is a great gift, thank you, Cheyenne." I opened the tiny bottle and dabbed a bit behind one ear and on my wrist.

"I'm buying my daughter dinner, what about you, Archer?" my father groused.

"I offered to do her estate planning as a gift. She didn't sound very excited about that."

We all laughed. I had my back to the door and saw my dad raise his hand in greeting.

Great. Time to meet the mystery lady.

Dad had left the chair empty between the two of us. When someone sat down, it wasn't a woman my dad invited. It was Dustin Roth.

I gasped. I couldn't even speak. How had they done this? How would Dustin even locate us? He had to have been in cahoots with my father, Archer, and Cheyenne. *Wear sexy underwear.* It all made sense now. He took my hand.

"You…you're here." I stammered. "Two weeks early. How…how is that possible? Is Ronnie with you?"

"No. Ronnie is home with my parents. Did you think I was going to miss your birthday?"

I started breathing again. He was really here talking to me. He'd gotten his hair cut since I'd seen him on FaceTime a few days ago. He was wearing a sports jacket in light blue that brought out his eye color, a crisp white shirt, a herringbone-patterned tie, and dark navy trousers. He wasn't even wearing boots; he had on black loafers. He cleaned up well. Exceptionally well.

When I glanced back at my family members, they were laughing at me.

"I think you've got my sister in a trance," Archer said.

Dustin grinned and turned to my father, extending his hand. "I'm Dustin Roth, Mr. Schulz. It's a pleasure to meet you. You look just like you sound on the phone."

"You talked to my dad? And Archer?" I asked. I was still playing catch-up.

Dustin shook hands with Archer and nodded to Cheyenne.

"I spoke to your father and Archer on the phone earlier this week. Archer was easy to find since you told me he was an estate attorney. He gave me your dad's landline number. They said I was welcome to crash your birthday dinner." He took my hand again and pulled it to his mouth for a kiss.

"How long are you here?"

"All weekend. I've got a room—that is, we've got a room—down the street at the Embassy Suites."

The heat flooded my face as my brother and Cheyenne *oohed* and *aahed*. My family was pimping me out, and I didn't know how to handle it. I would have preferred to keep our romantic tryst to ourselves.

"This is all so unexpected," I managed. "I need some wine."

Everyone else laughed. We ordered cocktails. Dustin kept touching me in subtle little ways. He'd hold my hand or drape an arm around my chair. He'd rub his knee against mine. He'd slide my dress an inch up my leg with one finger. If most dates had done that, I would have been annoyed. In this case, it was unbelievably sensuous, making my hormones shimmy. I'd look at him and he'd give me a side-eye as if to say "just wait."

When we ordered our food, I remembered something. "Dad, what happened to your date?"

"It was your date we were waiting on. I have been seeing someone. Her name is Margie. You'll meet her when we have our barbecue."

"Tonight is full of surprises," I mused.

Dustin chuckled. "I think we can count on that."

It was more than an hour before we were alone, walking to the hotel.

"I can't believe you pulled this off. I had no idea you were coming."

"I hope you're happy to see me. You look like a million bucks in that dress. I'm kinda surprised your father didn't lock you in your room."

"I think he might have if I wore something like this ten years ago. I guess he finally realized I've grown up."

"We had a nice chat on the phone. He reminds me a lot of my father. He cares about his work, the land, his family. He told me he'd never seen you so happy."

"My family tends to stick their noses in my business."

"Yeah, join the club."

When we reached the hotel, we went directly to the room. Dustin had already checked in. A glance revealed a small kitchenette and a living room area in the front of the suite. It looked like the bedroom and bathroom were beyond that. The first things I noticed were vases of flowers, in each room. The aroma of lilacs wafted over us. Then I saw all the tealights and larger candles lit in the living area and even in the bedroom.

I frowned. "How are there candles lit? Have they been burning since before dinner?"

He took off his jacket and hung it in a closet. "No, it must be part of the turn-down service. I asked them to light candles about fifteen minutes ago."

"This is so…romantic. I never figured you for…"

Dustin pulled out his phone and opened a music app. "These are supposed to be the twenty most romantic songs of the last fifty years. Somebody made a playlist for us." He set his phone on the counter with the volume cranked up. "Dance with me Darcelia."

The way he said my name made it almost sound sexy, not like someone out of the nineteenth century. I must be dreaming; this is not at all how I imagined my thirty-sixth birthday would end. And he knew how to dance. Some sort of waltz or fox trot, slow but with steps that I tried to follow. The smell of the flowers mixed with his aftershave made me a bit woozy. I rested my head on his shoulder. He nuzzled my hair.

After a few minutes, I lifted my head. That necktie was much too formal. I started to untie it.

"You don't like my tie?"

"Your tie is fine. I like your chest better."

He stopped dancing. "You made me lose count."

"You need to lose your shirt."

He smiled. "This is a new side of you. I think I like it." He pulled the loosened tie overhead and unbuttoned the shirt, keeping eye contact with me while Air Supply serenaded us. He dropped the shirt behind him and pulled me to his chest. His fingers closed over the zipper down the back of my dress and lowered it. Leisurely he pulled the sides of my dress off my shoulders.

"So, the flowers, music, dancing, candles. Did you Google how to seduce someone?"

"Busted," he whispered. "But everything after this is totally original."

In an instant, I was up against the wall, and he was pulling off my dress. His mouth and hands were on my shoulder, then my strap was sliding down, and his mouth was on my breast, his hands on my ass. I pulled his mouth back to kiss mine and our tongues were now dancing to the next song. It felt like forever since I'd kissed Dustin, even longer since I'd felt this kind of craving.

For a split second, I was back in Eric's arms. He hadn't been my first lover, but he'd been with me the longest. I'd once loved him, making it hard to face the fact that my desire had faded for Eric, and I think he felt the same way. Our love-making had been pleasant.

Nothing like this—a chaotic, insatiable, gnawing hunger.

Then I was off my feet. Dustin picked me up and carried me to the bedroom. I knew those muscles were going to come in handy. And they weren't only in his upper body as I'd seen before. When I got a load of his six-pack abs and quads, I melted like butter on the summer sidewalk.

But I had little chance to admire his physique when he kept kissing my lips and then working his hands and mouth down my body. Clothing had been tossed off indiscriminately. By now, we were naked. When he put his hand between my legs I just about shouted with exhilaration.

"You have an incredibly beautiful body, Darcy. Why did you try to hide it from me?"

"No idea," I mumbled. He kissed me again, pressing hard against me. God, he was divine. I think we were skipping to at least step nine, and we couldn't get there fast enough.

CHAPTER THIRTY-FIVE: DUSTIN

After her hesitation a week earlier at my house, I thought I'd have to convince Darcy to lower her guard. But tonight, she was all in. Although her face and legs were irresistible, I hadn't seen the whole picture. I think porn stars would give anything for breasts like hers, and I was pretty darn sure hers were real. I never wanted to take my hands off her ass either. I must have forgotten what sex was like. Temporary insanity made me think I should live without this.

But not anymore. We'd stopped panting like racehorses and were lying next to each other in the giant bed with ten pillows. How many pillows do these hotels think you need anyway? You don't need lots of pillows for a good night. You need a sexy woman like this next to you. Pillows certainly are no substitute.

"Hey, you're not going to fall asleep on me, are you?" I stroked her cheek with my finger.

"Isn't that allowed? You wore me out in the most wonderful way imaginable." She snuggled her head into a pillow.

"I was hoping to start round two pretty soon."

She chuckled. "How do you have the energy? Didn't you drive 300 miles today?"

I kissed her stomach. That was even perfection. The prettiest little navel I'd ever seen. "I daydreamed about doing this with you the whole drive. I'm surprised steam wasn't fogging my windshield."

I twisted my head and shoulders enough to find my trousers on the floor. I shouldn't have left my nicest pants in a heap. I reached down and grabbed my phone, which had landed on them. I scooted next to her and held my phone up for a selfie.

"You can't take naked selfies!" she cried.

"You can see what the camera sees, just our heads and necks. Smile!"

She grinned despite herself. It was a great photo. We were very relaxed and her hair fanned out over my shoulder and the pillow.

Her eyes lit up. "All right, now let's do one where we're kissing. Turn your face like this and don't move. Hold the camera steady and I'll come to you." She looked at the screen and moved my arm slightly to get the angle she wanted. "Can you find the shutter button without looking? Then don't move."

She kissed me gently, then a little more aggressively. My finger slipped but I got at least a couple of shots.

I pulled the phone back to view the results. The first shot was nice, both our profiles, lips touching, a little off-center. Then my shooting arm must have drifted down slightly. The second and third shots were of her arm around my neck and her bare breast.

Darcy howled. "You have to delete those immediately!"

"Not on your life! That's my new phone wallpaper."

She grabbed for my phone and ended up lying on top of me, but my arms were longer and I held my phone out of reach.

"This isn't something I want to joke about." She pushed off me and sat up with her arms covering her. She wasn't having fun anymore.

"Hey, I was teasing. Don't worry. I would never—go ahead and delete them yourself. I think the kissing one is worth saving though." I sat up handing her my iPhone which was similar to hers.

She took the phone and deleted two photos. "You don't have them stored on the cloud somewhere, do you?"

I shrugged. "I don't think so. Not sure how that works. I'm sorry if I upset you."

"It's not you, it's…once before, a long time ago, a guy threatened to post nude photos of me on his Myspace."

"What? Where did he get nude photos of you?"

"We were dating. He was a friend of one of my college friend's boyfriends, Serena and Mark. We went out for about six weeks our senior year. We had sex, and I fell asleep in his room. He took a topless photo of me with his digital camera while I was asleep. He emailed me the photo, and I was horrified. He thought it was funny; I didn't. That's when he tried to blackmail me. He threatened to share the photo if I didn't keep sleeping with him. Of course, by then, I had no interest in ever seeing him again."

"God in Heaven, what a cretin! Where is he now? I'll go strangle him."

She shook her head. "It blew over. As far as I know, he never made good on his threats. I did tell Archer about it. He wanted to go pound the guy too, which was almost funny because Archie is not very macho. My brother prepared an injunction, but I guess we didn't need it."

"The jerk gave up and left you alone?"

She hugged her knees, pulling the sheet around them. "After graduation, he moved back to Missouri. My friend, Serena, told me it was all a joke and I should have lightened up."

"I'm sorry you had to go through that. I had no idea." I patted her knee. That story killed the mood.

"You asked me about losing my virginity." She swept her hair behind her ear and looked into my eyes. "He was the first. So, it's not a story I like to remember."

I closed my eyes and blew out a breath. How do a few monsters ruin things for decent men? I reached out to embrace her, not sure if that were something she would welcome. She hesitated, then let me pull her to my chest, letting the sheet slide away. I laid back down and pulled her back atop me, this time with the side of her head over my heart. It was comforting even for me.

"If it's any consolation, my first time up to bat was not that great either. Senior in high school, daughter of our pastor. We trudged through a field to find a private spot. She brought a blanket but we ended up with poison ivy. Didn't see it in the dark. The sex was quick and dirty. I remember wondering what all the fuss was about."

She tried to muffle her chuckle. "Where did you get poison ivy?"

"Let's just say it was hard to sit down the next day. Thank goodness I was wearing a condom."

She was quiet for a while; she might have fallen asleep on me. Then she lifted her head. "Since you hijacked my weekend, what did you have planned?"

"This. This is what I had planned for two days. We don't leave the bed except to use the bathroom or answer the door for room service."

Her eyes widened. "They have room service? I've never had hotel room service!"

I grimaced. "You sound more enthusiastic about the food delivery than staying in bed with me."

She smiled. "*Au contraire.* I expect to enjoy that immensely. We can hide away in our little love bubble."

I rolled over astride her to throw her off balance. It did feel like a love bubble, just the two of us, not having to worry about how the heck we could make this work between us.

She sighed and stretched her arms above her head. "There isn't much I can do. The only clothes I have is what I was wearing. I don't even have my toothbrush."

"I don't think you need any clothes in the love bubble. Cheyenne did drop off your satchel with some casual clothes in it. Probably a toothbrush too."

"Really?" She tried to get up, but I wasn't letting her go anywhere.

"First, I want to take another photo. Of your tattoo." I gently rolled her onto her stomach.

"Only the tattoo. Nothing below that," Darcy admonished.

I took a couple of photos of her back. This woman was admirable from every angle. I wanted to take dozens of photos, but I knew that might upset her. Then I lay on my stomach next to her and showed her the ones I'd taken.

"Oh," I said. "Now I get it. You put this on your back because it's a BUTTerfly."

She rolled her eyes. "It's not on my butt."

"No, it's flying off your butt," I smirked.

"Why is it that there is always an obnoxious nine-year-old boy trapped inside an otherwise intelligent grown man?"

"You were expecting to find a nine-year-old girl?"

She propped herself on her elbows. "Speaking of nine-year-old girls, how do you expect Ronnie to react to our dating? Has she been okay with other women you've been out with?"

"I think you have the wrong idea about my social life. She's never met anyone else I've dated. I've only been out occasionally in the past few years."

"Then what did she say when you told her you were going to spend the weekend with me?"

"She seems to like you. She told me I needed to get out more, and she'd take care of Grandma and Grandpa for me this weekend."

Darcy bent her head and laughed. I even liked the sound of her laughter.

I am so gone for this chick, it's not even funny.

CHAPTER THIRTY-SIX: DUSTIN

The following Wednesday evening, Trevor set up a Zoom session with my parents, Darcy's father, Darcy, her brother, and me to review the results of the DNA tests he had compiled. At this point, I didn't care if he proved we were related or not; I had papers to grade that night. It was a nice chance to see Darcy and her family.

When he got everyone online, Trevor began what sounded like a business presentation or a class on "What DNA Testing Can Show You."

Yawn.

"Thank you all for joining the call. I'm going to try to keep this to the point and not dwell on too many details of DNA testing, because I could talk about it all night but you'd fall asleep. On the Hoffmann and Dunn side, I had Jorge Martinez do a regular autosomal DNA test, or what we call atDNA. That means we tested him like the tests the Schulz clan did previously at Ancestry.com. Jorge was a descendant of Helene Dunn Schulz and her first husband, Frederick Hoffmann. I wished to determine if I was related to Donald Schulz through the Schulz side of the family or the Dunn side, or both. Jorge Martinez did not match me, my cousin Tasha, my father, or Tasha's mother. So that told me I was on the right track; we were related through the Schulz side. It also told me it was very unlikely that Helene Dunn Hoffmann Schulz was my great-grandmother."

"You're not telling me that my grandfather had a child with another woman, are you?" Donald asked. He and Darcy were both facing her laptop and he leaned in to scowl at Trevor. That amused me, but it also blocked my view of Darcy, the main person I wanted to see on this call.

"Not at all. DNA testing shows at the autosomal level that Darcy and I share about fifty-four centimorgans of DNA, and you and my father share about 213 cM of DNA. That makes you and my dad second cousins and Darcy and me third cousins possibly. Archer and I share enough to make us third cousins as well.

"This supports the theory that began to evolve while I was in Nebraska." Trevor shared his computer screen which showed the shared cM he was referring to and the different relationships those numbers represented.

"If Adelaide Schulz was my great-grandmother, and she was a full sister to Darcy's great-grandfather, Samuel Schulz, the autosomal results would be exactly as they came out. Now these are estimates, and it appears Archer and I match slightly more DNA than Darcy and I do."

"So, are you saying this proves your theory is correct, or is it still a wild guess?" Archer asked.

"It proves we are related. You must compare the DNA results to genealogical records, and other types of substantiation, such as the letter Jorge had. It appears very likely that Adelaide Schulz was my great-grandmother. The better proof is on the Roth side." Trevor switched to a different slide showing his name and mine, and then his father's name and my father's name.

"We did a more sophisticated DNA test on Dustin and Louis Roth. This is called the Y-DNA test. As you know, men have an X chromosome and a Y chromosome in the nucleus of their cells, and women have two X chromosomes. Although there have been some exceptions to this rule, generally this determines if a person is born male or female. What is unusual about the Y chromosome is that it normally passes from father to son unchanged. It doesn't recombine and rarely mutates. So, your Y chromosome should look like your father's, Dustin. And if we could have tested his father's, it would be the same too."

"Chip off the old block then?" I asked. I wanted Trevor to recognize I was paying attention.

"Precisely. We tested both of your Y-DNA at sixty-seven markers. We could have tested more markers if it had been necessary, but normally sixty-seven tells the story. Dustin and

Louis match on all sixty-seven markers. My father, Ronald Wood, and I match on all sixty-seven markers. The impressive thing is that Ronald and Louis match on all but one marker, and Dustin and I match on all but one marker; in fact, it is the same marker. That means we have a genetic distance of one. There's more than a seventy percent chance that we have a common male ancestor within four generations which I believe is Karl Roth, Anselm and Anton Roth's father," Trevor announced triumphantly.

"And what about the other thirty percent?" I didn't think he should be misleading us with statistics.

"What do you mean?" Trevor asked.

"If there is a seventy-percent chance we share an ancestor, is there a thirty-percent chance we don't?"

"Oh, no. We share a male ancestor. There is a thirty-percent chance or less that it isn't Karl Roth, it goes back further in time to someone none of us knows about. This conceivably could go back hundreds of years. Based on the anecdotal data, I'd put my money on Karl Roth."

Trevor pulled up another screen. "Here's the autosomal DNA comparison. You can see that it shows my dad, Ronald, in the range of a second cousin to Louis since they share about 212 cM, and you and I, Dustin, are in the third-cousin range of about fifty-four cM. Keep in mind these same relationships apply to Tasha Edmunds, my second cousin, and her mother. She has the same range of autosomal DNA matches, but of course, we couldn't do Y-DNA testing on her or her mother." Trevor stopped sharing his screen so the gallery of participants was visible again.

"Okay, Trevor," my dad said. "You left me in the dust about twenty minutes ago, but you seem to be well-informed. You do this kind of thing for a living, is that what you said?" I had seen that dubious look on my father's face many times growing up.

"Yes, sir. I deal with it all day every day. Was there something you didn't understand?"

Dad scoffed. "Hell, I didn't understand most of it. What you're saying is that you think your granddaddy was Anselm Roth's son. That Anselm Roth and Adelaide Schulz had twin sons whom no one knew about it. They gave 'em away. Someone else adopted them, your legal great-grandparents, the Wood family."

"Yes, that is correct." Trevor looked at my father.

My father's brow wrinkled. "But why would they have done that? They weren't poor, and they were childless. They didn't live anywhere near California either."

"They weren't married," Darcy piped up for the first time. "Anselm's first wife died less than two months before the twins were born. Adelaide must have gotten pregnant and was sent away to have the babies."

"She didn't want the Schulz relations to know," Archer said. "And it worked like a charm."

"Until now," Trevor said.

"Until now," Dad echoed.

I wasn't ready to get sentimental about the dead relatives. Trevor started droning on about other types of health and wellness tests available at his company. Darcy had distracted me when she'd spoken. Now she was staring at me, or at least she was staring at her webcam. And she had that sweet little smile on her perfect pink lips, the smile just like ol' double great-grandma Carolina Schulz.

It had only been three days since I'd kissed those lips. Three days since I'd had the most spectacularly decadent weekend of my life. I was picturing the first time we took a shower and Darcy dropped her head back and let her dark waves flatten in the spray of the shower head. The stream of water ran over her closed eyelids and down her full lashes. She'd looked like some mythical sea goddess submerging into the brine. In a little over a week, I could see her in person again.

I pulled out my phone and started to type a racy text to Darcy. Would she read it while sitting right next to her father?

"Dustin!" My mother's tone was a virtual bop on the head. It sent me right back to my childhood when she'd caught me dawdling over breakfast.

"What?" I had no idea what had been said in the past few minutes.

"Trevor was talking about genetic testing for cancer predispositions. It's something they're working on with the medical researchers," Mom said. "Didn't you intend to have Ronnie tested for mutations on certain genes she might have inherited from her mother? He just mentioned one related to pancreatic cancer."

"Uhh…" Now I was thrust back into one of the worst episodes of the four months of watching my spouse die of cancer. The day the oncologist suggested that dear little five-year-old Veronica might already be harboring a genetic time bomb that could guarantee her the same horrific fate as her mother. When I believed it couldn't have gotten any worse, it had. I may have to live through this nightmare twice. Ronnie may not.

My father asked, "They tested Brittany, didn't they? Did she have a gene mutation linked to her cancer?"

"I don't…" My memory was failing me. I'd tried to blot as much of that out as I could. "She did have some test, I think. I may have a note from the doctor that tells what to do if we wanted to have Ronnie tested when she was a teenager."

This time I was pretty sure everyone on the call was staring at me. I hadn't been prepared to talk about this at all with anyone. "From what I remember, they weren't entirely sure if Brittany had a mutation on any of the suspect genes. They couldn't rule it out either."

I heard a noise and turned to see if Ronnie was within earshot. "Listen, I don't want to talk about this with my daughter in the house. I'm going to hang up." I clicked the leave call button before anyone could respond.

CHAPTER THIRTY-SEVEN: DARCY

It's become a Schulz tradition to have a barbecue on the Saturday before Memorial Day. Sometimes the neighbors stop by for a beer and a pulled pork or barbecued chicken sandwich. Archer came out early to help Dad get the pork roast ready on the Weber grill. I was responsible for making everything in the kitchen: cornbread, German potato salad, a fresh fruit bowl, and devil's food cupcakes. We had several kinds of buns for those who wanted their pork or chicken in a sandwich and homemade ice cream. Cheyenne brought her classic barbecued baked beans. I preferred to not think of this culinary feat as sexist. I liked playing hostess occasionally, and my father and Archie always did their share, especially with the cleanup.

Dustin and Veronica arrived the night before and stayed at a motel near our farm. We only saw them briefly on Friday, as they wanted to settle in at the motel, and we all had work to do for the Saturday event.

By Saturday morning, they were on hand to help or get in the way, alternately.

"I don't understand how any of you can prepare barbecue when you're not wearing cowboy hats," Dustin complained. He and Ronnie were both appropriately attired, in his opinion.

"I think I should put you in charge of setting up the games," I said when he came up behind me to sample some watermelon I was cutting. He spun me around for a kiss. With the hat and cowboy boots, he towered over me in my bare feet. He pulled me to my tiptoes.

"What kind of games are we playing?" Ronnie asked. She snuck a bite of watermelon too.

"You can pick from whatever you find on the enclosed back porch. We usually play ladder golf, ring toss, lawn darts, and Flickin' Chicken."

Ronnie giggled. "What's Flickin' Chicken?"

I slid melon slices into a large bowl. "You can read the directions, but you throw something like a Frisbee, then try to land rubber chickens on it. You get bonus points or penalties based on the way the disc and the chickens land. It's pretty silly."

"We brought Ronnie's softball and gloves to practice catching," Dustin said. "Her summer softball league started two weeks ago. And the soccer ball is behind the seat in the truck if we have any takers on that."

"Sure, why not? Archer might recall where our softball gloves and bats are. And I was a goalie in high school, so don't think you'll get anything past me. I wonder where I put my shin guards."

"You played high school soccer?" Dustin asked. "Why does that not surprise me, with those legs?"

"My nickname was Spider. All legs and arms in front of the net."

"Ooooh. Like a Black Widow. I can picture it." He wiggled his brows and headed out the back door. While I was finishing up things in the kitchen, I saw Dustin and Ronnie throwing the softball around with Archer and my dad.

My dad's new friend, Margie Conners, arrived to help me with the food preparations. She had short red hair and was a few years Dad's junior. She had lots of funny stories about her children. I could see how Dad found her entertaining.

Everyone had a fun afternoon. We sat around a couple of tables and had our picnic. The neighbors to the west stopped by for lemonade and cupcakes. Archer and Ronnie were kicking the soccer ball around, and Dustin and I were in a heated game of ladder golf when a young man drove up the driveway on a motorcycle.

"Who's that?" Dustin asked.

I shook my head. "I don't recognize him. Maybe someone Archer invited."

He disembarked and removed his helmet, walking up to us with a manilla envelope.

"I'm looking for Donald M. Schulz." The kid couldn't have been more than twenty-two or three.

Dustin frowned. "He's over there, sitting on a lawn chair with a Bud."

The young man looked, then nodded and marched over to hand the envelope to my dad. He turned then and left quickly on his motorcycle.

"What in the world?" I asked. "Was that kid a process server?"

Dustin blinked. Then he pulled his phone out of his pocket. "Uh-oh. I've missed two calls from my mother. I'd better call her back." He headed back towards our house. I walked toward my father, who was shuffling through some papers.

"I don't know what in tarnation this stuff is," Dad said to me. "I don't have my reading glasses on me. Tell me what it says at the top there." Margie was sitting with him and she squinted at the typed documents too.

I read the first few lines. My stomach dropped like a lead balloon. "It's a summons, Dad. For a court appearance. You're being sued by…the families of Trevor Wood and Tasha Edmunds."

"What? I never did anything to either of them! What could they possibly sue me for?"

"Wrongful inheritance. I didn't even realize that was something you could sue for." I kept reading the documents. "It says here that property that was inherited by one Josef Schulz and later by Donald Schulz should have rightfully been passed from Adelaide Roth to her next of kin, namely Richard and Robert Wood and their heirs, Kathleen Wood Edmunds and Ronald Wood, parents of Tasha and Trevor. This makes no sense. Where's Archer? He needs to see this!"

"Archer!" my father hollered. "Come look at this pronto!"

When I glanced up, it was Dustin who was barreling toward us. His face was a snapshot of rage and his glare was focused on me.

"I talked to my father. My brother-in-law, Jace Lassiter, the sheriff, was over there serving him a summons. Your buddy, Trevor, is suing my family, trying to steal R&R ranch out from under us!"

"They're suing you too? My dad got papers—"

"You brought that man to us," Dustin hissed. "You helped him find out all about us, our ancestors, our real estate holdings, everything about my family so he could try to take it all away. How could you have let that snake into our lives? I trusted you. I cared about you."

A chill ran down my spine. He couldn't think I had anything to do with this. "Dustin! He told me he wanted to find his family, his roots. He said he wanted some emotional closure for his dad and his aunt. I never dreamed he'd—"

Dustin's feet were planted a foot apart and his hands fisted on his hips. "Yeah, you never dreamed. The world is full of evil men. Open your eyes, Darcy. Clearly, you don't know who to associate with. It's too bad you didn't check him out more thoroughly before foisting him on decent people like us. Like your own family, for goodness' sake. This is on you. Bad people prosper if good people stand by watching."

My jaw dropped. I couldn't believe my ears. I could see he was hurt but how was any of this my fault? Was I too trusting? Perhaps. But I'd also trusted Dustin when I barely knew him. I thought he had my back, but I could see now where his loyalties lay.

I turned back toward my father as tears leaped to my eyes. Dustin turned on his heel and shouted at Ronnie.

"We're leaving, Veronica! Grab your ball and glove. Right now!" He hustled her out of the front of the house faster than I knew was possible. I could hear her asking questions but Dustin didn't respond. His truck fishtailed out of our driveway spewing gravel.

Twenty minutes later, my family was sitting around the dining table studying the documents. Archer had made several copies of the first few pages so we could discuss them. I tried to make sense of the words on the page. My vision blurred. All I could think about was how angry Dustin had been and how unfair he'd been to take it out on me.

Had Trevor planned this from the start, wanting to take advantage of our families? Had I ignored the warning signs that he wasn't sincere? He'd generously purchased all the genetic tests and acted so pleased that he'd solved the mystery of his twin grandfather's heritage. He'd even invited Dustin and Archer to join an online surname group of Roths and Schulzes, to find other relatives, I supposed.

I tried to tune into what Archer was saying. He was the one with relevant experience in property and estate law.

"I don't see how a judge could give this case merit; it will likely be thrown out because the time limit for contesting a will passed many decades ago. I think that's why it's worded like a property dispute. He's not contesting the inheritance of other family members who don't own the original property. He's concentrating on us because we own land that Adelaide Schulz once owned, and it sounded like Dustin's family is being targeted because they have Anselm Roth's land."

All eyes fell on me. I pushed away from the table and went to the back deck. The pain in my chest and throat forced a strangled cry from my mouth. I heard the door open behind me and was surprised when Margie pulled me into her arms. That put me over the edge and the tears I'd been bottling poured out.

CHAPTER THIRTY-EIGHT: DARCY

I didn't get much sleep that night. The events of the last few weeks played over and over in my head. When Trevor invited me to visit the Roth family, he told me I could help make the interaction more friendly. And I'd sure gotten friendly with Dustin. Still, at no time had Trevor given me an inkling he was out to recapture some inheritance he believed was rightfully his or his father's. Heck, under other circumstances, we might be willing to sell our land to him once my father retired. Why didn't he explore that option at least?

Because men are bull-headed. Dustin surprised me more than Trevor. Last weekend was a dream-like bliss of love-making and pillow talk. We spent most of Saturday and Sunday alone in our hotel suite. I don't think I'd ever been happier. I didn't want anything to burst our love bubble. Now he'd shown me a different side of himself and I wasn't sure I was willing to accept his behavior. It might not matter if he rejected me as an enemy spy.

Archer and Cheyenne became the point people on the lawsuit. They were both consummate researchers and I was happy to let them have the lead. I had promised to take Veronica shopping at Old Navy that afternoon. I wasn't sure if she and Dustin were still in town.

Around ten on Sunday morning, I received a text from Dustin:

What time are you picking up Ronnie to go shopping?

Down to business, huh? What makes him think I'd even speak to him after his tirade last night? Oh, it's the girl. He doesn't want to disappoint his daughter.

I texted back after about five minutes. I wanted him to sweat a little:

Tell Ronnie I'll be at your motel at 1:30. I can't be sorry I

> ever met Trevor or tried to help him find his family. If he hadn't come to us and asked for my help, I never would have met you.

I put my phone away after sending the text and went to the kitchen to do some work. Today I was going to keep a cork in my emotions, no matter what happened. I made myself wait twenty minutes before reading his reply.

At least it made me smile:

Did I mention I'm a bonehead sometimes? I hope we can talk later. See you at 1:30.

Ronnie was ready to go when she opened the motel room door. I didn't even go inside, but Dustin stood behind her, wiping his hands on the sides of his jeans. He met my eyes, then dropped his gaze.

"Oh, you'll need some money, Sweetie," he said, whipping out his wallet and handing Ronnie three twenty-dollar bills.

I narrowed my eyes at him. "I've got this, Dustin. Working women don't need a man to fund their shopping trips."

Ronnie pocketed his cash before he could withdraw it. "Perfect. I need new clothes for camp in July. I'll let you both pay."

I had fun with Ronnie. She knew what she liked and what looked good on her lanky body. She was at the perfect pre-teen excited-about-everything stage. I had never imagined what it would be like clothes shopping with a daughter, I assumed you'd learn about how to do these things as the child grew through each age category. Ronnie and I were having a ball, dancing and singing in the aisles to the music blaring over the sound system and trying on four times as many clothes as we hoped to purchase.

She even made me buy a dress.

I stood in front of the mirror in the fitting room area. It was a sundress made of a pink flowery cotton print. The ruffled scoop neck was flattering and cool, and it was fitted at the bodice and flared out around the hips, a style that was always my favorite.

"My dad would love that on you," she told me.

I sighed. "I'm not sure he'll ever see me wear it after last night."

"He's sorry. He'll talk to you later, but I know he is. He blows up like that and then he always apologizes."

"I think people should be able to control their tempers. Especially grown-ups."

"He does, most of the time. Sometimes he gets mad first, then thinks about it after."

I marveled at her intuitiveness. Her big brown eyes and shoulder-length dark blonde hair made a striking combination. The freckles dotting her nose and arms told me she'd already spent a lot of time in the sun the past few weeks. I flashed back to the wedding portrait of her mother and saw the resemblance.

"Maybe I will buy this. I suppose there will always be another man to charm if I can't tolerate your father," I said with a grin.

"He loves you."

My eyebrows rose as our eyes met in the mirror. "He told you that?"

She shook her head. "Nope."

I turned to face her. "Does he realize that?"

She rolled her eyes. "He's a man, Silly."

I put one arm around her shoulder. "You are wise beyond your years."

"I've seen a lot of romcoms with Aunt Leslie. She said men know nothing about things that matter."

Our damage at Old Navy came to about two hundred dollars, but I had some coupons that took twenty percent off. It might have put a dent in my bank balance, but I felt like I'd gained an ally.

After learning that Ronnie hadn't eaten lunch, we made a run to McDonald's and got food for Dustin too.

When we got back to the motel, he took one whiff of our offering, and excitement spread across his face.

"We bought out the store, Daddy. I think you owe Darcy more moolah." Ronnie charged in dropping packages on her bed.

"You got food. Thank God. I'm starving. Listen, Ronnie, I need to talk to Darcy. How about you eat in here and watch TV while Darcy and I go sit by the pool and talk?" He guided me down the hall and through a door to the outdoor pool. It was still slightly cool for swimming but pleasant sitting at the wrought-iron tables eating a take-out lunch.

I sorted through the bags and put his meal in front of him.

Dustin popped a fry into his mouth. "Is it all right if I eat before I grovel? I might get my hands dirty if I have to get on my knees."

"I had nothing to do with what Trevor is up to. I can't believe I even kissed him." I took a big bite of my chicken sandwich and watched that play out on his face.

Dustin stopped chewing. He swallowed. "You kissed Trevor? You told me he was boring."

A smug smile teased my mouth. "Not when he's kissing."

"You're making this up." He pursed his lips and then took a long gulp of soda.

"No. He did kiss me. Twice, I think. That was the weekend before we came to meet you. He'd gotten very excited about some of the clues we'd uncovered. He even did a little happy dance. He grabbed me and kissed me. I told him not to, but I think he did it again!"

Dustin's eyes became slits. "Real men don't do happy dances." He leaned forward. "And they certainly don't kiss women who ask them not to."

"I might have told him not to after the second kiss. I forget. Too much wine."

"Wine? God, you should not be allowed outside the house without a keeper."

"You should not be allowed to open your mouth when you're angry."

"I can't argue that. Since you mentioned kissing Trevor, did he think something romantic happened between the two of you? Because when I first saw you in my driveway, he put his hand behind your back like you two were a couple. And he was miffed when you said you would stay to see the ranch and sleep over. I couldn't mistake the look he gave me. He was jealous."

I shrugged, "Perhaps a little, at the moment. I didn't want to spend the evening and night with him and send him the wrong signal."

"But maybe jealousy is behind this whole lawsuit."

"I think he might be jealous that his grandfather and father didn't get acknowledged by the birth parents, and some other relatives inherited. Interestingly, Archer and Cheyenne have done some digging since last night and they discovered that those adopted twin babies landed in a wealthy home. Radcliffe Wood was a prominent businessman in Sacramento and was written up in the newspaper for his philanthropy. He had to weather the stock market crash of 1929 and the Great Depression like everyone else but didn't lose his shirt. The Woods have never had real money problems from what they can tell."

"Then why is Trevor doing this? What did he say to you on the way home from North Platte?"

"Well, after I got your texts, I think I said that you and I might be seeing each other again. He told me he had a girlfriend in Houston. It was the first time he'd mentioned her. I slept part of the drive, but when we spoke to each other it was fine. I didn't see him after that."

"I just don't get it."

"I'm not worried about Trevor and his antics. Archer thinks it will go away. You were quick to assume I was to blame. That concerns me."

Dustin sighed and wadded up his food wrappers. "Yeah. My parents told me I overreacted, and they weren't even there. I'm sorry I came down so hard on you. I realize you wouldn't try to take advantage of anyone. I guess I have a sore spot where my family is concerned."

"It felt like you didn't believe I cared about you as though we wouldn't be on the same side if anyone attacked you."

He took my hand. "What do you want me to say? I was wrong. Can you forgive me?"

I looked at our joined hands. "Ronnie said you've done this before, lost your temper and then thought it through. Maybe you should get anger management counseling to help with that."

He scoffed. "I did go to some counseling after I got tired of being mad all the time, after… Well, mostly everyone else got tired of me being mad all the time. My mother convinced me to seek therapy. It helped. I suppose I haven't been using the techniques they told me about for some time now. Maybe I need a refresher." He shifted in his chair. "It's not like I've ever been abusive."

I studied him. I wasn't sure if someone knew if they crossed that line.

He moved his chair closer and leaned over to kiss my cheek, then the corner of my mouth briefly. "We need to go somewhere more private so I can make it up to you."

I put my hand on his chest. "I assumed you had plans to give us some privacy this weekend."

His sigh was exaggerated. "I'd hoped we'd have a chance to sneak back to the motel room while Ronnie was enjoying the games at the picnic yesterday. Or maybe even go upstairs to your room while the others were all outdoors. That didn't work out."

"That's a shame." I curled my fingers under the neckline of his T-shirt. "The only good part about fighting is making up."

He nodded. "I've got an idea. Are you up for a little adventure?"

I wasn't at all sure what he meant but followed him back to his room. Ronnie was sitting on her bed playing a video game on some gadget or controller. The TV was showing a movie, but she wasn't looking at it.

Dustin picked up a couple of pillows from the other bed. "If you need to use the bathroom, there is one down the hall by the desk where we checked in. You remember where that is?"

"Yeah," she said but didn't look up.

Dustin motioned me to go into the bathroom with him, and he locked the door. The bathroom looked to be recently redone and clean enough. It held a good size tub with a shower, toilet, and floating vanity that spanned the width of the room. A few toiletries were scattered around the drop-in sink. Dustin ran his arm across the countertop moving all the clutter to one side. Then he put the pillows on the vanity.

My brows furrowed. "What exactly are we doing in here?"

He looked around. "We could take a shower, but I think the tub is a little small for two. I figured the sink thingy here was the best surface."

"For what?" I asked.

In response, he lifted me under my hips and set me on the pillows.

"You're not supposed to sit on this. I might break it!"

"We'll have to be a little careful, but I think it'll hold. You are going to have to be quiet though. None of that loud screaming and moaning you did last time."

"What? You were the one who—" He cut off my words with a blistering kiss. We'd exchanged a few polite busses in front of other people this weekend, but this was the first genuine heart-pounding contact we'd had for two weeks. It was as if he'd turned the juice on and my body was electrified by the spark he provided. He broke the kiss long enough to jerk his T-shirt upward and toss it toward the tub. Then he pulled my shirt over my head, a little more gently, and threw it aside too.

I was glad I'd worn that nude and pink lace bra when I saw the grin lighting his eyes. This was the romantic lover I remembered. He ran eager fingers down my rib cage watching the anticipation on my face. He kissed my chin, then my outstretched neck and moved slowly down to my cleavage. When he dipped his fingertips into the back of my shorts, a soft groan escaped my mouth. He chuckled against my breasts.

CHAPTER THIRTY-NINE: DUSTIN

What do women do to make their skin feel like opulent silk and smell like a flower garden?

Touching Darcy was so intoxicating. I swear I forgot that my daughter was in the next room; the riptide was carrying me away. And somehow, even though I'd been a colossal jerk, Darcy was giving me the keys to the kingdom once more. I wanted to smother her with kisses, hold her, stroke her, push myself inside her, and never leave. Was this love or uncontrolled lust taking over my brain and my body? Right then, I didn't care.

This woman had some very sexy underwear. Or maybe her very sexy body made it look that way. Those pink lacy cups were in my way now. They had done their job, promoting the amazing plump breasts that strained beneath. My hands were too busy removing her shorts, so my teeth went to work pulling off her bra. I had to multi-task as speed was essential trying to slow the roaring freight train in my pants. No time for joyful anticipation; I needed her now.

Her shorts and panties were on the floor—check. I unhooked her bra to cast that aside—check. Dropped my pants to my ankles—check. Kicked those away—whoa. She somehow pushed herself up to her knees and was leaning over me while we kissed. This was going to be a delicate operation that I had never attempted before. I couldn't have her going rogue on me.

So, I pushed her back a little. She braced her hands on my shoulders. My mouth watered as I saw those full breasts right in front of me. Yeah, I was going in for a taste while I had a chance. She made a high-pitched noise as I cupped both boobs in my hands and my tongue took a stroll around her nipple.

We both were gasping for air when I gently pulled on the back of one of her thighs. "Wrap your legs around me."

"You sure?"

As if I couldn't hold her up. I'd already picked her up twice. When she circled my hips with her legs, I moved the pillows so that they would be under her buttocks on the vanity top. I had to line things up, bending my knees to get the right angle. Made me think I should be doing more squats in the weight room. Darcy arched her back and braced her hands back on the counter, which forced her hips forward, and that opened her up. Oh boy, did it ever.

We were rocking and rolling, and I tried to keep her aloft so we weren't pushing against the vanity. I could picture what would happen if it came loose from the wall. We were bouncing up against it; no way to avoid it now. She moved her hands around my neck, and I could support her weight better.

"You good?" I asked.

She nodded and closed her eyes as if to say she was ready to enjoy the ride. I was so busy concentrating on the positioning that I almost missed the spectacular view right in front of me. When I glanced at the mirror, my face was flushed, her dark waves were rippling down her bare back, my hands were gripping her buttocks like I was kneading dough, and right above that madcap butterfly. With every thrust, the butterfly jumped and fluttered. I'd swear that when I let it all go, the damn thing took flight.

When she became a dead weight in my arms, I had to set her down on the pillows. I was panting like a stevedore and having trouble standing. I leaned my palms on the counter, hanging my head. I heard a faint crack. The caulk was separating next to the wall.

"Shit!" I gasped and yanked Darcy off the countertop, pillows tumbling to the floor.

"What's wrong?" She was glowing with sweat, which somehow made me proud.

"The vanity. The silicone connecting it to the wall, it's giving way. If you'd had one more French fry, this thing would have collapsed."

"I told you this was a bad idea!" She tapped her index finger on my nose. My gaze flickered to her heart still visibly pounding between her breasts.

I sucked in air. "You're seriously going to tell me this was a bad idea? Cuz I'm impressed that we pulled it off."

"We're lucky we didn't pull the vanity off." She laughed softly. "I guess you're not quite past prime time."

I picked her up so her face was above mine and kissed her mouth. "Not yet. We'd better do a lot of this kind of thing before my osteoarthritis sets in."

Later, on the long drive home on the interstate, Ronnie was quiet as though she'd dozed off. Naturally, my thoughts drifted back to Darcy. I was becoming more obsessed with her every day. This three-hour drive was going to get awfully old this summer. By next fall and winter, it would be worse when we had to deal with bad weather. She ought to move in with me. My God, was I considering that? What's the rush?

"Daddy, what were you and Darcy doing in the bathroom?"

Jeez, I hoped I'd dodged that discussion. "We were talking."

"You said you were going out to the pool area to talk. Then you came back."

"Yeah, we wanted privacy. Other people were coming to the pool." There's the first little white lie. "We always said that a bathroom is a place for privacy."

"But how can it be private if you have someone else in there with you?"

"It was private in a different way. Between Darcy and me."

"You sounded like you were lifting weights."

"What?" I jerked the wheel a little bit, prompting the car behind me to pass. Had she heard the sound effects? She's way too young to talk about the birds and the bees. Don't they discuss that in middle school health class?

"Yeah, I heard you laughing and then grunting as if you were lifting something heavy. Like when you work out in the barn with those big barbells. What were you lifting?"

"Uh…Darcy."

"Why?"

I had to think fast. This was getting into dangerous territory and I didn't want to keep lying. "She didn't think I could lift her, but I did. The grunting was…a joke, like I was insinuating she was heavy."

"Didn't that make her mad?"

I shook my head. "No. She laughed."

"She made funny noises too. One time I heard her call your name but you were right there. Are you sure you weren't doing her?"

I was glad it was getting dark because a crimson heat shot up to my scalp. My fingers started jumping on the steering wheel. I waited for a beat before asking, "What does that mean?"

She crumpled up the rest of the bag of chips she'd been munching on, to save for later. "I'm not sure exactly. Stuart Bevins said he can hear his mother and her boyfriend when he's going to sleep. He said they make all sorts of lovey-dovey noises and then the boyfriend says, 'I'm gonna do you right now.' Stuart said it was gross and he had to cover his ears with his pillows. Oh, and he said heard something banging against the wall."

Lord, if this is my introduction to parenting a teenager, I'll pass. My eyes bounced between the windshield and the rear-view mirror, and then I scanned the side mirrors. Possibly I would be better off not commenting at all.

I cleared my throat. "I don't think Stuart Bevins should be sharing information about his family with his friends. It sounds like that was personal between his mother and the man she's dating." I glanced at my daughter. "I wouldn't want you to talk about Darcy and me with any of your friends. Something like that should stay in the family."

That lecture sent her into a silent pout for a few minutes. Heck, none of this was Ronnie's fault. It was unrealistic to think she wasn't going to notice I was getting involved with a woman, and we hadn't been as circumspect as I'd hoped.

I tapped one finger on the steering wheel and softened my tone. "Darcy's going to come to visit us at the ranch next weekend because the two weekends after that, you and I will be in Fort Collins visiting Grandma and Grandpa Hamilton."

"Okay."

"You like having Darcy around, don't you?"

"I like Darcy. We had fun at the store. But I'm used to it being you and me, Daddy."

I took a deep breath. How could I explain why a man needs female companionship? I thought Ronnie and I had done rather well by ourselves the last few years, but now that I had feelings for someone again…There had been a void there. I'd been lonely and hadn't put a name to it. I hadn't wanted to admit it even to myself.

"Darcy might grow on you. I like being with her. And when she comes this time, she's going to sleep in my room with me. I don't want that to surprise you."

"Because she's your girlfriend, huh?"

"Yes. I guess that's true. Darcy is my girlfriend." That sounded like we were in high school. At the same time, "lady-friend" sounded like we were ready for the nursing home.

"Does she know you snore?"

I chuckled. Finally, an innocent question. "I think she's figured that out by now."

CHAPTER FORTY: DARCY

It was about eight in the evening when I arrived at R&R Ranch. My eyes hurt from driving into the western sun for hours, but the familiar long driveway was a welcome sight. My GPS did an excellent job of directing me all the way.

I remembered the first time I'd come here, about a month earlier. Dustin had come through that door and I'd been breathless. He still had that effect on me, maybe now more than ever. This time, it was Veronica who ran out to greet me with a Boston terrier puppy on her heels.

"Hello! And who is this? I don't recall seeing him before!" Ronnie surprised me by hugging me, then she scooped up the puppy and held him up for my inspection.

"His name is Puddles, cuz of what he did on the kitchen floor. We're training him though. Uncle Jace found him on patrol. Nobody claimed him so he decided we needed a watchdog. He's more of a cuddler."

I grabbed my satchel and we went into the house. Dustin emerged from the bathroom in a towel. Not sure why he'd picked up that towel as he hadn't dried himself well. Droplets from the shower fell from his hair and clung to his chest.

Be still my hammering heart.

"Oh, Baby. You made it. I planned to be dressed before…" He walked over to me, gave me a one-armed hug, and planted a quick kiss on my mouth. He kept his other hand on the knotted towel. "Let me get something on and we'll get you settled."

Ronnie and I plopped on the leather couch with the puppy. Dustin returned wearing flannel draw-string pants and rubbing the towel over his hair.

Then he donned a white tee. He sat down next to me and put an arm behind me. "I'm glad to see you. It's been a long week."

He nuzzled my ear, and my hormones shot to life. How much of this should we be doing in front of his daughter?

"I'm happy to see you both too. And it looks like your household has grown." Puddles took that opportunity to climb into my lap and sniff my hand.

"Yeah, this little stinker." Dustin grinned. "I about broke my neck the other morning when I slipped on the kitchen floor. We've been house-breaking him, but he doesn't always remember the rules. Don't leave anything out he could chew on like your leather purse or shoes. Puppies love that kind of thing."

"You said we could have ice cream sundaes when Darcy got here. Is it time?" Ronnie asked.

"You two aren't doing my diet any good. You see that, don't you?" I said, getting up to join Ronnie who was yanking open the freezer.

We sat around the kitchen table dishing chocolate, vanilla, and strawberry ice cream into dishes and topping it with fudge and caramel sauce and fresh strawberries. They even had instant whipped cream to put on top.

"All you're missing are the peanuts," I declared.

"We have peanuts." Dustin gestured with his spoon. "Where are the peanuts, Ronnie?"

"You ate them all, Daddy. You and Uncle Jace ate them watching basketball."

"Oh yeah. Sorry, no peanuts."

After cleaning up the sundae mess, Ronnie kissed her father on the cheek and went off to get ready for bed. "Goodnight, Darcy. I'll see you tomorrow."

Dustin and I got comfortable on the couch.

"Are you okay? It looks like something is bothering you." I watched his eyes as he tried to blink back whatever was weighing on him.

"Well, I did something I'm starting to regret. On Tuesday night, I called that son-of-a-bitch Trevor and told him what I thought of his stupid lawsuit. At the time, it felt good getting that off my chest. I told him to leave us all alone. Well, not in such nice words."

"What did he say?"

"He yelled right back at me. I guess he inherited the Roth temper too. He said he was not going away until the score was settled, whatever that meant. I threatened to drive to Houston to punch him in the face and he said he could make my life a living hell without even leaving his apartment. I assumed we were both spitting out empty warnings. I wouldn't drive that far for the pleasure of seeing him bleed."

I watched sorrow crease his brow.

"Did something else happen?"

"Thursday morning, one of our calves was dead. He'd been poisoned."

"What? You don't think—"

"The security camera feed from Wednesday night showed a pickup pulling up near the barn where the calves are kept. I didn't recognize the truck or the men. Jace is tracing the plate, but we only could capture part of it." Dustin leaned his head back on the couch and covered his eyes with his hand. Do you realize how much we'd invested in that calf, what with insemination fees and the feed? We wouldn't recoup his costs until we sold him at auction. And he was a beauty. To top it off, Ronnie had run out to the barn early, and she was the one who found him. Her scream brought Hank, the farm manager, over to check. It was too late to call the vet."

"Oh my God. I'm so sorry, Dustin. How's Ronnie with all this?"

"She was quite upset. We talked about it for a while. She has seen animals die on the farm. This one was unexpected. I think getting the puppy and having you come this weekend have been good distractions."

"But how could Trevor be responsible?"

"I don't know for certain that he is. I have a nasty feeling that I set him off. My dad said it could be someone else. He had an offer to buy the farm about six weeks ago and the guy was insulted when Dad wouldn't sell after he'd raised the offer three times." Dustin sat up straighter and pulled me into his lap. "We're meeting with an attorney next week about the suit. Tomorrow we're going to be at my parents' house and go through some of the old paperwork to see if we can find anything useful."

"Sounds like fun."

"You know what's really going to be fun?" He pushed my hair away from my face and kissed my jaw.

"Hmmm?"

"Getting your sexy body into my very fancy bed. This time, I'm not letting you fall asleep until I have my way with you."

I laughed and started to retort. But he'd learned how to stop my witty comebacks. His mouth captured mine before I even knew I was surrendering.

Janice and Louis Roth lived in an older home that they had completely renovated down to the studs across the street from Washington Elementary School where Ronnie attended. We went over for fried chicken around noon and then dug into the family paperwork.

"Louie's parents were very good record keepers," Janice explained, pulling out several large cardboard boxes from a back bedroom. "It took us months to go through their things. Some of these records were stored in our hayloft. Most of the important stuff was in the attic where Dustin lives now. Lamar is the one who built that place. There's an older house that was there when his uncle Anselm owned it, but I don't think he stayed there most of the time."

"What are we looking for?" I asked.

Louis opened one of the boxes and stacked its contents on the dining table where we were sitting. "Ideally something that tells us that Anselm Roth intended to leave his land to his nieces and nephews. If we find anything mentioning his illegitimate children, that might help. Just going through what we have, so we are aware of the contents, will prepare us for the attorney's questions."

Louis, Janice, Dustin, and I worked mostly in silence for the next forty-five minutes or so. Ronnie played catch with the neighbor girl in the backyard.

"What is all this stuff?" I asked, picking up a lot of papers stapled together at the top. It was yellowed with age and had been folded in thirds and crammed into a box for years.

"Oh, that's all the deed papers," Janice explained. "Lamar and his seven siblings inherited land from Anselm Roth in the 1940s. Some of it was back east and also the land here that we own. Lamar had to have deed transfers to show that he owned the land in Lincoln County and he gave up his share of the land in Lancaster and Gage counties. I don't think a lot of money exchanged hands, but it all had to be legal. A lot of it is repeated information."

I started looking through it. These people lived in Dustin's house before him. His grandfather had pulled up stakes a few miles from where I was living to take over the inheritance near where we were now. It had been a good gamble. "Did Lamar buy more land than this? This deed only talks about one section. Isn't there more than that now?"

"Oh yes," Louis told me. "My father bought the neighboring farm and part of another. When Lamar started the center-pivot irrigation, I think the value increased tremendously. So even if Trevor Wood was given what his grandfather would have inherited, it was only a portion of the value it had upon Lamar's death."

"And it's worth much more now than when Grandpa died," Dustin said. "You deserve credit for how you have managed the land and the livestock, Dad."

I found reading the deeds interesting. It was like following an evolution. At the end of the clipped papers, I ran across an envelope. The return address was printed professionally in the upper left corner: Sheffield, Williams, Hawthorne, Stanton, and Associates, Attorneys at Law, 145 Beacon Street, Sacramento, California. I pulled out the enclosed correspondence. It was typewritten on what looked like onionskin paper. I was shocked to read the date was May 2, 1927. This paper had held up well for over ninety years.

> Dear Mr. and Mrs. Roth;
>
> In December, you engaged our services to find your twin sons and endeavor to return them to you. Herein is a summary of our efforts and the judgment of the court, as you requested.
>
> Our investigation has confirmed that the twin boys who were in the Sacramento County Hospital at the same time Mrs. Adelaide Roth was a patient in December 1926, were her offspring. We were able to find out that the infants were admitted there on the afternoon of December 1, 1926, by a midwife employed by Claremont House, the same day that Mrs. Roth née Schulz was admitted due to blood poisoning. As you know, this hospital is within a few blocks of Claremont House, where she was living.

We were able to trace the twins' whereabouts after leaving the hospital to the Janey & Price Adoption Agency, which is about five miles from the hospital. By examining some of the Claremont House records and observing the clients who frequented those offices, we identified five separate agencies that used Claremont House to supply children to be adopted by interested parents. We interviewed the owners of each agency and determined that Janey & Price handled the adoption in question. They generally serve adoptive parents in the River Heights neighborhood.

We were then able to secure a subpoena to force them to reveal that the twins were adopted by Mr. and Mrs. Radcliffe Wood of 2400 Watercress Avenue in Sacramento.

The issue came before the county court on April 28, 1927, and I appeared as your representative. According to the testimony of the city director of social welfare, the children were well-cared for and in a loving and bountiful environment. Mr. Radcliffe Wood and his wife are well-to-do and seem to lack for nothing except children.

As a result of these circumstances and the adoption agreement signed by Miss Schulz, who recorded her name falsely as Helene Schulz, the judge ruled in favor of the defendants in this case, namely the Woods, Claremont House, and Janey & Price

Adoption Agency. It is clear from the ruling of Judge Morton that he felt it was best not to disrupt the lives of two babies who were in an ideal setting already.

Mrs. Wood did express sympathy for the parents who had given up their children and suggested that when the boys are fifteen, you might write them a letter explaining the circumstances of their birth and providing information about the families they were born into. She felt that would be the least traumatic way to satisfy their curiosity.

Please find the court documents enclosed, as well as the bill for our services.

Yours truly,

Lionel J. Stanton, Esquire

"Oh, my word," I said. "They didn't want to give up those babies at all."

"What do you mean?" Dustin took the paper from my hands and started to read it. "Have you read this, Mom and Dad?" When they shook their heads, he read the letter aloud.

"Helene Schulz was the name on the birth certificate Trevor had. This is giving me goosebumps, like a message from beyond the grave." I rubbed my arms to ward off the chill.

"So how does this play into the lawsuit?" Louis asked. "If Anselm and Adelaide Roth had gotten their twin boys back, they would have been the ones inheriting all of the property in question."

Janice took the letter from Dustin to review herself. "They didn't have any children after that, so the boys would have gotten it all."

"And Trevor. He wouldn't have been part of the Wood family. Neither would his father." I blinked and looked at Dustin. "Who knows if any of them would have been born? The twins would have married women from Nebraska. This is all a little hard to imagine."

"We don't have to imagine it. It happened. This memorandum explains some missing pieces," Dustin said. "The Roth babies became members of the Wood family. Trevor and his relatives came out fine as heirs to a wealthy California dynasty. Anselm Roth failed to reclaim them, so he left his holdings to the only heirs he had. He obviously cared for his family. He could have sold it off and left the whole thing to charity. We have to honor his legacy."

"Trevor Wood and Tasha Edmunds are also his legacy. Don't forget the Schulz side of this family. Adelaide Schulz and Anselm Roth were fighters. So are Trevor and his cousin. We're all part of the same diverse clan. Maybe this will help make peace," I said.

"We'll show this to the attorney when we meet him," Louis stacked the letter and envelope separately.

"I would like to reach out to Trevor and tell him what we found." I picked up the letter Janice had laid on the table.

"No. You can't. He may have been behind what happened to my calf." Dustin's brows folded.

I nodded. "And he may have just lost his temper, the same way you did. Let me call him, try to smooth things a little. If he gets nasty with me, I will hang up. I work in customer service. I'm quite persuasive on the phone."

Dustin smiled and blushed.

"What are you thinking?" I asked.

"You can be pretty persuasive in person."

Janice said, "I don't know if we should be contacting him at all. Dustin shouldn't have called him when we're on opposite sides of a lawsuit."

"No, I think Darcy has a shot. He kissed her, after all. She might be able to get back on his good side."

His mom and dad looked at me with big eyes. He didn't have to tell them that. Now they probably think I'm easy.

"That was before we came here—before I ever even knew your names. And he didn't try it again." I pushed my hair back away from my face. "Can we make a copy of this document?"

Louis stood up. "Sure, that's a good idea. There's a copy shop down the street about a mile. You want to go with me, Darcy?"

I glanced at Dustin. He didn't object, so I went with his father. He made spare copies so he could give one to each of us and the attorney.

"You've been seeing a lot of Dustin since that first weekend," Louis said, as he programmed the copier.

"We've been trying to. Does that surprise you?" Did he think our dating was a problem?

"Not exactly. I think you're the first woman he's gotten attached to since Brittany died. He had trouble dealing with that, especially with a little girl who needed him."

I nodded. "He told me that himself. I'm not certain what it is about him, but I feel like I've known him for a long time. We sort of click. I've never felt such an instant attraction to anyone else. Maybe we should hang out steadily for a week and see if we get bored."

"I don't think Dustin would get bored. He's apparently smitten." Louis paid for the copies and we got back into his truck. I noticed both Dustin and his dad drove black pickups.

"I'm a good person; you don't need to worry. I work as a supervisor in an insurance call center and help people all day long. I've never been married, but I was engaged for about a year. Then

I decided to move back in with my father and I make him dinner almost every night. He's a farmer and taught my brother and me to work hard and take responsibility. My mother moved to Florida about seventeen years ago, and I don't see her very often. She's remarried and spends time with her husband's grandkids."

"I didn't mean to ask for your resume. I do wonder why such a nice, pretty girl hasn't married. Dustin told us you were thirty-six."

I looked out the truck window. "It wasn't a priority for me. My parents split up right after I graduated from high school. Some kids worry that their parents might have divorced because of something the kid did. I worried they stayed together because of me. Ostensibly, their obligation ended when I turned eighteen."

Why was I spilling my guts to Dustin's father, of all people? I guess he looked sympathetic. I couldn't confess this to my dad. "But now that I'm in my mid-thirties, it feels a little different. If I don't marry, I won't have any children, and then it feels like you're not passing on anything to the next generation of the human race."

Now I must sound deranged. I glanced back at Louis. "Forget I just said that. It sounds stupid when I rewind it in my head."

Louis laughed. "Not at all. I'm flattered that you felt close enough to me to share. Jan and I wanted to have more children. A daughter, ideally. We were close to Brittany, and it crushed us too when she got sick. Little Veronica has been a bright spot in our lives. We'd love to have more grandchildren."

Why did that make me want to cry? I took a shaky breath and looked out the window. This is what families do to you.

After we got back from the copy shop, Dustin, Ronnie, and I returned to his place. Ronnie wanted to check on the puppy.

"Are you still going to call Trevor?" Dustin asked.

"Yes. I need to prepare what I'm going to say. Do you have a piece of paper I can use for some notes?"

"Tell him to drop dead. Oh, I covered that. You're hoping to have a civil conversation? I can't wait to hear how that goes."

"I don't want you to listen. That will make me self-conscious. He doesn't need to know we're together this weekend."

Dustin made a snarling sound. "You're not planning to flirt with him?"

"Not flirt, just be friendly, like a cousin might be."

He flexed his lips and brought me a couple of sheets of white paper and a pen. "Go for it then. I need to check some things in the barn. I want to make sure all the other animals are fine."

I made some notes, then went into the guest room to make the call. Even if Dustin came back and stood outside the door, as long as I didn't know he was there, it wouldn't bother me.

Trevor answered on the second ring. "Darcy?"

"Hi Trevor, how are you doing? Is it hot in Houston?"

"Yes." His tone was guarded. "It's June. It's hot here all summer."

"I wanted to tell you we found something that might interest you. It's a memo from an attorney who practiced in Sacramento in 1927. It appears that Anselm Roth, your great-grandfather, hired this legal firm of Sheffield, Williams, Hawthorne, Stanton, and Associates to try to find the twin babies. Your great-grandparents wanted them back after they'd been adopted by the Wood family. The judge chose to leave the babies where they were since it appeared it was a good home and the adoption was legal."

"What are you talking about? How do you know this?"

"I told you; we found a letter that outlines what happened and how the attorneys tracked down the twins, but the judge ruled against the Roths. If you want, I'll email you a copy of the letter."

"They wanted the babies back? That's not what I expected. Yeah, send it to me. Thank you." He paused then. I heard him sigh. "Darcy, you must think I'm an ingrate after I initiated that lawsuit. You see, I work with clients all the time who are trying to crack adoption mysteries through DNA testing. Their stories are often sad once they find out what happened."

"But your family's story isn't so sad," I countered. "It likely was sad for your great-grandparents who didn't get their children back, but it probably gave your adopted great-grandparents a lot of joy. Your family was well-off and happy, wasn't it? It must have been a comfort during those tough years in the 1930s. And if the Roths had gotten the babies back, they would have been raised in Nebraska, near where I live. You might not have even been born."

"I might not have been born? Well, not the person I am now. I suppose if my grandfather lived in Nebraska, he would have married someone else. Heck, I might have been Dustin. That's a horrifying thought. On the other hand, he's got you. Or did that fizzle out?"

"It's still sizzling, not fizzling. We're taking our time though."

"Well, I envy him there. I like you, Darcy, and I appreciate your call. I can't wait to share this information with the rest of the Wood family. Send me that email, please, Honey."

"Absolutely. I can send it tomorrow morning. Nice to chat with you, Trevor."

I ended the call and said a silent prayer that he might change his position. When I opened the door, Dustin was standing right there.

"You heard?"

"Uh, a few words. Enough to hear you were on the phone. I didn't want to interrupt."

"He was nice enough. I hope he comes to his senses after I send him this letter."

"What are you hoping for?"

"That he will drop the lawsuits," I said. Dustin nodded. "Or at least the one against my family," I smirked.

"Here we go again. Ms. Smarty-pants."

"If this works, you will be thanking me."

"I know how I'll be thanking you too." He pulled me into a long kiss. I could use a lot more gratitude.

The next afternoon, we went to Leslie and Jace Lassiter's house in town. I kept having to remind myself that Leslie was Dustin's sister-in-law, not his sister, as those two picked on each other constantly.

Jace beckoned Dustin and Ronnie into his "man cave" to watch baseball on a large-screen television. Leslie insisted I join her in the kitchen where she was making homemade pasta sauce. It was quickly apparent that she didn't need much help. She wanted information.

I sat on one of her tall stools at an island where she chopped onions. She handed me a knife, cutting board, and green pepper to dice.

"So, you and Dustin? How's that going?" Leslie gave me the side-eye.

"Fine, I guess. It's a little hard dating someone who lives so far away, but we talk on the phone every day."

I studied her as she went back and forth from the island to the stove. She was not as thin as the photo of her sister as a bride, but that had been at least ten years ago, judging from Ronnie's age. I did see how Ronnie resembled Leslie, with the same patrician nose and fair coloring. Today Leslie wore trendy turquoise glasses and I had only seen her with her blonde-streaked hair in a messy knot atop her head.

"Dustin told me you own a gym in town?" I asked. She may not have been thin, but she looked like she worked out. I should have such toned calves.

"It's called 'Buff.' Brittany came up with the concept. We have sort of a collaboration with a nail salon and a hair salon. We offer discounts for those other shops with monthly memberships and they offer price reductions for our services. It sounds antifeminist, but we try to keep our community beautiful, one hot babe at a time."

"You're right, it sounds a little old school. There is nothing wrong with being fit and strong. I should go back to my gym."

"Puh-lease. You're a hot mama. Anyone can see why Dustin was attracted."

My ears burned a little. "Thank you. I'm not a mother. And things are going almost too easily with Veronica. I'm waiting for her to find fault with me or our dating situation. Is she always this easy to please?"

"These are the easy years," Leslie said, sliding the onions into a bowl and starting in on mincing garlic. "We have two sons. Three, the oldest we adopted and he works in Washington. The second got his degree and started working in Grand Island, and the other is in his second year of college at the U of Wyoming. He's still there taking summer school for a few more weeks. They were all good kids. I mean their father was working for the sheriff's department so they had to behave, but it was harder once they hit about twelve. We all butted heads a lot during their early teen years. Then they started sports at school and they didn't have the energy to fight with me or their dad. So at least for my boys, ages twelve through fifteen were the worst. Maybe things improved when they got their driver's licenses and needed to stay on our good side to take the car."

"No daughters for you?"

"No, I wish. Having Ronnie around has been bittersweet. I mean, of course, I wish my sister was alive, but I try to show Ronnie things that I think Brittany would have shared with her. Girl stuff. Cuz, her father is clueless about that."

I smiled. "He does strike me as a man's man."

She scoffed. "A macho man, you mean. They grow 'em like weeds out here in western Nebraska. They have to have their pickup trucks, guns, cowboy boots, and chewing tobacco. What else? Oh, sports for sure. Non-stop football, basketball, baseball, sometimes hockey, and soccer if there is a lull in programming for the others. Dustin was coaching football for a while. He coached my middle son. Then he quit that when Brittany got sick."

"Do you know why?" Dustin had alluded to it but I wanted her take.

"Well, she got sick about March and died in July, so it wasn't football season. He kept teaching but dropped the coaching. Now he's involved with FFA, which wasn't in the school a few years ago. I think he thought the coaching was too much time away from Ronnie."

"That doesn't sound too macho to me, choosing your little girl over teaching boys how to excel at a grueling sport."

She smirked. "Are you saying you don't think Dustin is macho?"

I laughed, "Oh, he is very macho in some areas. He has an impressively masculine physique."

"Now we're getting down to it." Leslie lowered her voice. "He has big hands and big feet so I'm assuming he has…"

"Leslie!" My reddening face seemed appropriate this time and I didn't attempt to hide it. "If you wanted to know something like that, you could have asked your sister."

She swatted the air with her hand. "Brittany wouldn't ever share the juicy details. She was too shy. I'm hoping you might be a little more candid. Let's open the wine."

She kept me laughing, and I even got her recipe for Bolognese. I never would have guessed to add chopped celery or ground veal.

"Is he good in bed? Tell me that much at least." Leslie had opened a bottle of Chianti, and we were both on our second glasses.

"Oh, yeah. He came to visit on the weekend of my birthday." I peeked toward the other room to be sure no one could hear us. "For two days, we didn't leave the hotel room at all."

She squealed. I'd never heard a grown woman squeal but we were both in hysterics after that. I was laughing so hard I face-planted on the island.

"What's going on in here?" Dustin asked. He returned his empty beer bottle to the recycling bin. "What are you doing to my girl, Leslie? Are you two drunk at four in the afternoon?"

Leslie was gasping and crying while laughing. "We're having a nice chat. Making dinner."

I wiped my eyes as they were spilling over too. "And Jace? How does he rate?"

Leslie burst out laughing again, and Dustin looked from her back to me. She gave me two thumbs up. We were both still failing to control our laughter.

Dustin scowled then shook his head. "Don't think I want to know." He pulled another beer from the refrigerator and went back to the other room.

Within the hour, the pasta was done, the salad prepped, and the garlic bread's aroma beckoned the men and child away from the television. I was impressed that Leslie had set the table before our arrival with oversized bowls for the pasta, salad plates, and wine glasses. Bright orange day lilies filled a vase in the center of the table. Everyone filed into the kitchen buffet style and we all sat down to feast.

"The dinner is delicious, Lez, as always," Dustin said.

"Top drawer, Baby," her husband echoed, toasting her with his bottle.

"Absolutely amazing. I can even taste the peppers I chopped," I added.

Dustin was seated next to me and put a hand on my thigh. "You better take it easy on the wine, Darcy. Don't you have to drive home?"

"You're right. How am I going to stay awake? All these carbs and wine to boot. I'd better switch to something caffeinated."

"You want some soda? We have a couple of kinds in the fridge." Leslie started to rise, but I waved her down to stay seated.

Dustin leaned closer to me. "Maybe you'd better stay with me another night. Just to be safe."

Leslie snickered. She and I exchanged glances.

"I did take Monday morning off thinking I'd get home late," I said.

"That's perfect. I can get you up at the crack of dawn to get on the road. You should be home with an hour or more to spare."

I glanced toward him sweeping my eyes down his body. "Another night in your magic bed?"

Leslie lost it again, laughing so hard she was snorting. I covered my mouth, trying not to join her.

Dustin blew out a breath. "She's talking about the controls on the mattress. Because the bed can be raised and lowered and made softer and harder—"

"Don't even try to understand them, Dustin," Jace said, sipping his bottle of beer. "I'm afraid you found another woman as nuts as Leslie. At least they're not fighting."

"I don't understand what's so funny," Ronnie said.

Dustin rolled his eyes. "You should never drink wine, Darlin'. This is what happens when women drink wine."

Later, when we were cuddling in the infamous bed, I said, "No matter what happens with you and me, I think I want to keep Leslie. She is a good time."

Dustin pushed himself up on one elbow. "What are you saying? You think there's an end date on our relationship?"

I combed my hand through his hair. "Not at all. I'm surprised how much I enjoyed Leslie."

He squinted. "Maybe you drank too much."

"I only had two glasses of wine. I don't drink that often, so maybe it was a lot for me. You had at least two beers."

He held up three fingers. "Men can drink more. It's been proven."

"Double standard, if you ask me."

"I suppose. But facts are facts. Men can eat more too— better metabolism. They're stronger, generally taller, faster, more muscular, smarter, funnier, better drivers—"

"Oh, now you're just dreaming. And some of those things are by design. Women need to be able to store fat more efficiently because of child-bearing. Of course, it would be nice to turn that feature off when we don't need it."

"Men wouldn't want to turn that off. It is nice to have a little cushion to grab onto." He cupped my butt in one hand. "And since men rule the world…"

"Now you are asking for it!"

He chuckled. "I am asking for it. You're in the magic bed. You'd better pay your fare."

I was more than happy to.

It was early when I was first aware of the monochromatic light sneaking through the window shades. It was still quite dark so I didn't think I'd missed the alarm Dustin set. I found Dustin sitting up in the bed next to me. He leaned against his pillow propped on the headboard. His arms were crossed over his chest and his head was tilted back. He was still naked.

"What are you thinking about?" I asked, running my fingers down the hollow of his thigh.

He sighed. "Well now that you did that, I can't remember at all."

I sat up and smoothed my hair away from my face. My nightgown had vanished in the bedclothes during the frenzy last night. His smile was constrained, not the reaction I'd come to expect from him in such an intimate setting.

"Tell me what's on your mind." I kept searching his face for more information.

"I was thinking…this weekend was the first time I'd ever made love to a woman in this bed." I was facing him. Naked. But Dustin didn't look at me; his shadowed gaze was fixed across the room.

"Hmmm. How long have you had this bed?"

"Um, four years. I bought it the day we got Brittany's cancer diagnosis."

"So, she was too ill to uh…"

"She didn't do any chemo. Her doctors didn't recommend chemotherapy: it was too late. Some days she felt better than others. One day, about a month into it, we did try to—" He let out a ragged breath. "We were kissing and touching…the preliminary stuff. And then, out of nowhere, she started to cry. Then I started to cry."

He was staring into space, his mouth contorted into a tight line. I waited for him to say more. I put my hand over his.

"That day we both knew we'd lost something: the intimacy of our marriage. We were never going to get that back. Something that had made us so happy had turned tragic." I watched his brow furrow and his chest heave a little as though breathing had gotten harder.

He shook his head and glanced at me. "The day of her funeral, I almost went to the barn and got the ax. I wanted to destroy this bed. She didn't even die here, she died at the hospital, but I think I wanted to lash out at something. Then I realized that was dumb. I wanted to destroy the most expensive piece of furniture I owned. So, I thought I should sell it, and maybe get half the value back anyway. I didn't do that either."

He looked down at our hands. "Ultimately, I let the frustration go. I bought this bed to comfort Brittany. I tried to let it comfort me too." He finally looked back at me. "I'll bet you'll never ask me what I'm thinking about before six a.m. again."

My eyes were rimmed with tears. I climbed into his lap and wrapped him in an embrace. "I can't even imagine what you've been through. You know, you can tell me anything anytime."

It took a second, but he slid his hands across my back, pulling me close and nestling his face in my hair. "How much time do we have before you leave?"

CHAPTER FORTY-ONE: DUSTIN

I didn't see Darcy for two weeks after that. Veronica and I went to Fort Collins, Colorado, to visit Brittany's family. I stayed for five days and then returned to North Platte. The second weekend, I drove back, stayed overnight, and then brought Ronnie back. She usually spends two weeks with these grandparents in the summer.

I called Darcy every night though. She was her usual vivacious self until the last few nights. One night she didn't even answer her phone. I tried FaceTime too, but she didn't pick up. It didn't take me long to decide something was wrong. Was she upset that I'd spent so much time in Colorado over the past two weeks?

Trevor and his family had withdrawn the lawsuit a few days after Darcy called him, so I didn't think that was the problem. Had he contacted her again? The possibilities were endless if she was upset over something. Maybe it had nothing to do with me.

The night after I couldn't reach her, she called me. That was a first.

"I'm sorry I didn't feel like talking last night," she began.

"What's going on?"

She sighed, then she sighed again. "I can't get into it over the phone, Dustin. We'll talk when you get here. You're still coming Friday, right?"

"Yes. Now I'm even more worried. Are you ill?"

"No. God, no, there's nothing wrong with me, it's…I don't think we should talk on the phone until I see you."

Jesus. She wanted me to drive over 250 miles to break up with me? But why? Things had been going so well.

She asked to meet me at the motel. I arrived a good thirty minutes before she said she could be there. All I could do was pace the floor and scan my watch every minute.

When she knocked on my door, I pulled her into my arms. That must have been a bad idea because she started to cry. I pushed her back to look into her face.

"Darcy, you're killing me here. What has you so upset? Were you ghosting me?"

She shook her head and wiped her tears. Then she took a step back and opened her purse. She reached in, took something out, and slapped it on my palm. I stared down at my hand.

It was a pregnancy test. It clearly read "yes."

I'm sure my mouth flew open. I felt like the room was spinning, not like when you're dizzy but when you're in a tornado. A hundred thoughts pummeled my brain at once. A lot of them should never be formed into words leaving my lips. I was oddly aware of that. Things like— how could this happen? You said you were taking birth control pills. Was this something you planned from the beginning? Did Trevor put you up to this? Were you looking for a sperm donor to have a child before it was too late? Could it be anyone else's baby? What the actual hell?

I turned away and faced the window. The weather was calm outdoors; no tornado. I pulled out my wallet and extracted a small card and began to scan the list printed on it. I turned back to Darcy who looked pale and forlorn.

I took a deep breath and spoke deliberately. "Are you sure? These tests can give false positives."

She reached back into her purse and pulled out a Ziplock bag with two more pregnancy tests inside. I didn't need to read the results.

Another cleansing breath. "Have you seen a doctor?" I felt like I was talking in slow motion now, like when you change the speed on an audio recording distorting the voice.

"I went to my doctor today. She said I'd be celebrating Mother's Day before next spring." Darcy sat on the bed. "I realize this is a big shock. I was plenty shocked too. I've been taking birth control pills for years. I've missed a few here and there. But when you sort of kidnapped me on my birthday, I didn't have them with me. I missed taking three in a row. The doctor told me today that missing some can trigger ovulation, and sperm can survive in a woman's reproductive tract for up to five days. I had no idea that was true."

I'd suggested using condoms. She said she had it covered. No point thinking about that now.

I sat next to her and studied the card again.

"What are you reading?" She squinted at it.

"It's sort of a cheat sheet. They gave it to me when I went for counseling. Tips to control your temper."

Her eyes grew wider. "You are angry, I knew it."

I shook my head. "I don't know what I am. Numb. Numb and dumb, I think might cover it. I…I'm struggling to even believe this."

"I was paralyzed too at first. I mean I bought one pregnancy test, and then I didn't believe it so I went back to the store and bought two more. I've heard it was more accurate in the morning, so I did the second and third ones then. It still feels unreal to me also."

"What made you think you were…" God, I couldn't even finish the sentence.

"I'm never late. Especially taking birth control pills; they regulate your periods. I was a week late." She stood up again and in a self-hug. "I have no right to do this to you, but I have decided I am going to have the baby. At my age, I may not be pregnant again, and I think I should consider it a blessing—" She covered her mouth when her voice broke.

I jumped up and swept her into my arms. This was beginning to feel less bizarre. "Of course, you're having the baby. I never considered that you wouldn't."

She attempted to talk through her tears. "We knew each other one week when this happened. How could we have been so stupid? We're not careless teenagers."

"Yeah, I guess we were both equally idiotic. We need to slow down and figure it out." I pulled her tightly to my chest. "Just try to relax. Take some big breaths. We're gonna get through this. Who else have you told?"

She pulled back to look me in the eyes. "No one. The doctor, of course. I didn't tell anyone before you. Funny, I did think about calling my mother. I haven't spoken to her in months, but I suddenly figured she could help me with this. Until I imagined what she would say."

I ran my hand over her hair. "What would she say?"

Darcy scoffed. "She'd ask what Eric had to say. I don't think I have even told her I broke up with Eric."

"I guess this will be a pretty big surprise. We shouldn't worry about anyone else's reaction. This only involves you, me, the baby, and Veronica. I have to think how it will affect her."

"Will she be upset?"

I hesitated. "I think it depends on how we handle it. When she was in first grade, her teacher was pregnant, and the children got to watch this lady's middle get bigger and bigger. She kept teaching almost up until her due date. She let the kids feel the baby moving and everything. Ronnie was excited about it, but then the teacher disappeared a month before school let out. I didn't realize it, but I think Ronnie had developed an attachment to the teacher and her unborn child. Ronnie came home and asked if we could get a baby. Brittany had been gone less than a year, and explaining to Ronnie that she couldn't have a sibling was gut-wrenching."

"Are you saying she'll be happy about this or not?"

"Strictly looking at it from her viewpoint, she'll be delighted about having a brother or sister but not if she doesn't get to—"

If she doesn't get to live in the same household. I walked over to the desk in the motel room and opened the top drawer. I took out one of the pieces of stationery and a pen.

"I feel like I need to map out our options. This whole thing is too emotional." I took a seat at the desk chair and motioned for her to sit on my leg.

"How can it not be emotional? I've been a basket case for days. I feel terrible for dumping this on you. I admit it is mainly my mistake, even if you're not saying so."

I huffed out my breath. "Option one: we go on as we have been. You continue working and your health insurance will cover the pregnancy and birth. Your health insurance is good, isn't it?"

"Yes, I've seen many pregnant employees who have used our insurance coverage. That's not an issue."

"So that option is that we continue dating and you have the baby here in Lincoln. At some reasonable time in the future, we would consider something more permanent, as if this hadn't happened."

"And you'd see your child a couple of times a month? Traveling would be harder with an infant."

"That's the downside. I wouldn't see him and neither would Ronnie."

"You've decided it's a boy already?"

"Him or her. We won't know for a little bit. The point is option one is a much bigger burden on you. I think it would put a strain on our relationship."

"What's option two?"

I put some notes down for option one, then wrote option two. Same as option one, but we set a date to be married, maybe six months after the baby is born. People do that now, wait until the bride has her shape back, and do the whole white-dress, black-tux deal. Or skip the formal wedding and take an exotic honeymoon trip."

"If we got married, where would we live? We've already bumped into this problem before. I think you called it step twenty."

"Okay, let's stop to examine that. You said you like your job. How much money do you make after taxes? Do you know what your adjusted gross income was last year?"

Darcy nodded.

"Write that number down for me up here by option one."

She took the pen from me and wrote a number down. "That's what I remember from my tax return. Of course, there's a pretax deduction for my 401(k) and insurance premiums."

I stared at her figure for a moment. "My income is three to four times that. And I'm socking away a portion for retirement and Ronnie's college fund. It seems to me that we could get along without your income, at least temporarily."

Her brows knit together. "No kidding? Your adjusted gross income is more than three times this amount? Trevor was right. You are loaded."

My laugh came out in a snort. "Trevor believed I was loaded? That's why he tried to sue me."

"Wait a minute. Why are you working two jobs if you don't need to?"

"I like my jobs too. I have been accused of working too much. Something you may need to know."

Darcy looked at the paper. "Option two is we get married after the baby is born. Kind of a long engagement. And I'd have to move in with you once we marry. Is that what you're saying?"

"Yeah. Is that a good idea or not?"

"Not sure yet. What is option three?"

"I think option three is to throw caution to the wind. We've already done that once."

"What does that mean?"

"Get married as soon as possible. We don't need a fancy event, as long as Ronnie gets to attend, anyone else is optional. This summer for sure."

"Get married? We've known each other for seven weeks! I have food in my refrigerator older than that."

"Do you love me?"

She gasped. Not a good sign. "I...I think so. Before all this pregnancy thing came up it felt like...yes. I love you."

"I love you, too. That should work in our favor."

She jumped off my leg suddenly and paced across the room. "You're treating this like it's a business negotiation. You talk like you're deciding which car to purchase. You can't agree to a marriage because it checks all the boxes. There must be romance and candlelight and promises. This baby is not a problem to be resolved. It's a human being. Your DNA and mine jumbled together. It's a wonder."

I tapped my foot. I had been trying to treat this logically, but that might not be a good way to deal with pregnancy hormones. I did have some experience with those.

"Look, Darcy. I'm still playing catch-up here. You've had a few days to accept this change. I need some time to think. Why don't you leave me alone? I will text you tomorrow and we can get together again?"

"You want me to leave? After you drove all this way, you don't want to see me? We're not having dinner?"

I shook my head. "You should eat. I'm not hungry."

She grabbed her purse and flew out the door before I could stop her.

CHAPTER FORTY-TWO: DARCY

My father looked surprised to see me when I got home. He was putting on his shoes.

"I thought you were meeting Dustin tonight, Darcy. I'm going to Margie's soon."

"Don't let me ruin your evening, Dad. Things didn't go well with Dustin. He said he needed a break."

He stood up. "A break from what? I didn't think you'd seen each other in three weeks."

My eye roll should have told him something. "Dustin and I need to figure some things out. I don't even know where things stand."

He put his hands on my arms. "You want to talk about it? I can cancel on Marge."

"No, I need some time to think. It's better for everyone if you spend time with Margie. It's good you're seeing her. I think she's sweet."

"I'm glad you like her. She is sweet. Are you going to be here when I get back?"

"I don't know."

I made myself some soup and a turkey sandwich. I suppose I did need to eat regularly now. I wish I could call someone and talk this out. But until I knew where Dustin and I were, I didn't want anyone else to influence us.

He said he loved me. Only in an off-hand way, not romantically or while we were in the throes of passion. As if it were a prerequisite. We're not allowed to marry unless we love each other. Oh, maybe we conveniently do.

I didn't like any of the options. Maybe option four is that I tell him to take a long hike off a short pier and do this whole parent thing on my own. I'd need that promotion if I had another mouth to feed. Maybe once they realized I was pregnant, I wouldn't get the job—I'd be mommy-tracked. Then my savings for a house would be depleted for childcare.

No, Dustin would have to pay child support. Then he'd have parental rights. Men do not deserve rights. Not when they act like jerks.

That made me think about Eric: the straw that broke the camel's back for me with Eric. He mentioned more than once that he wasn't keen on having children. Kids would get in the way of his fun vacations. No more spur-of-the-moment road trips or canoeing down the river. He dreamed of saving money to buy a house on the beach or a lake. It all sounded exciting, but how could I close the door to having a family?

Then one Friday night a year ago, I'd come home to find him slumped on the couch watching a motocross race. He'd had a towel and a bag of frozen peas on his lap.

"Did you pull a muscle?" I'd asked.

He'd shaken his head as though what he was watching required his full attention.

"So, what's with the ice pack?"

"Doctor appointment. Snip, snip." He glanced at me briefly. "I had a vasectomy this afternoon." Eric had resumed watching the television as though I was the one acting oddly.

I'd picked my jaw up off the floor, strode calmly into the bedroom, and packed a bag. I'd torn up the check I'd left sitting out for half of that month's rent. I had pocketed the section of the check with my signature and left the other pieces on the dresser with my diamond ring on top.

I'd taken the sheets off the bed and stuffed them into a pillowcase. I'd put the comforter into a clean garbage bag. I'd thrown his toothbrush and razor into the toilet. When I had filled my luggage, I had to put some of my clothes into clean garbage bags too. I'd left the kitchen utensils and food but took all the paper plates, toilet paper, and towels. Eric's back was to me when I'd hauled everything out the door, and he hadn't even turned his head. We never spoke again.

That's how I dealt with the last man who didn't respect me. I told no one the truth. Eric had broken me.

The familiar ache was back. The current scenario was close to the polar opposite. Now I had a baby inside that I suddenly desperately wanted. I didn't like the fact that some man, once again, was going to weigh in on my future. Well, only if I let him.

I didn't hear from Dustin the next morning. I took matters into my own hands and drove to the motel with some donuts and coffee. He didn't answer when I knocked. I went to the front desk and asked them to ring his room. No response there either. While they wouldn't tell me who checked into his room, they did tell me that the party had paid for two nights and had not checked out. I scoured the motel parking lot and his black pickup with a county fifteen plate was not there.

I sat in my car and ate two donuts and drank coffee. Where was he? I was not going to call or text him. I waited twenty minutes, then went back home.

It was a hot afternoon, but I figured sweating through my clothes while gardening was therapeutic. The weeds were all hoed and the bushes trimmed back before I went into the house for a welcome shower. I had just finished applying body lotion afterward when my father knocked on the bathroom door.

"Darcy, Dustin's here."

What was he doing here now after ignoring me since last night? I wrapped my hair in a towel, put on my robe, and walked downstairs to see what his problem was.

He looked airbrushed to perfection, wearing a navy-blue suit, yellow shirt, and striped tie. He cradled a paper-wrapped bouquet of red roses. And me in a ratty terrycloth robe. Where was that romcom costume designer when you needed her? I fixed him with a stare.

"Good, you're clean at least. Would you go put on a nice dress? I'd like to take you to dinner."

"Why would I want to do that? I haven't heard from you all day."

"I tried to call you an hour ago but you didn't answer. I wasn't ignoring you; I was getting my ducks in a row. Please come with me. Let's talk."

I walked up to him and took the flowers giving him a blue-ribbon sneer. I went into the kitchen and put the flowers in a vase. No sense wasting good roses. They smelled heavenly and relaxed me a little.

I went back up the stairs and called over my shoulder. "Get comfortable. This may take a while."

He shrugged. "No problem. I'll chat with Donald."

I did not rush. I didn't want to get overheated. I had to dry my hair and press the wrinkles out of that new dress. How many times would I be able to wear this before I got too big? It was nearly an hour later when I came back downstairs, all primped, polished, and smelling as good as I looked.

Dustin's smile covered his face when I walked into the kitchen. He was drinking beer with my father. "That was worth the wait."

He's acting as if nothing has happened. Like he didn't tell me to go away so he could think about the bombshell I'd dropped on him last night. Still, I wouldn't find out anything more unless I spoke to him.

"Where are we going?" I asked when he helped me into his truck.

"You'll see." He gave me a mysterious smirk.

I supposed it had to be nice if he told me to dress up, and I'd never seen him wear a suit. When he pulled into the winding drive of Wilderness Ridge, I looked at him wide-eyed. "We're eating here? I've only been here for lunch once, but it gets good reviews."

He grinned. "I played golf here a few years ago. It was some Cattleman's Association thing, and they had a nice meal after. Cheyenne suggested it."

"Cheyenne? Archer's girlfriend, Cheyenne? You talked to her today but you didn't call me?"

"Cheyenne apparently has quite a few connections. She knew who to contact here on short notice."

When he gave his name at the maître de stand, we were ushered into a small dining room with a fireplace. A sole table topped with a crisp white linen cloth beckoned us. A second bouquet of bursting red rose buds provided the centerpiece and filled the space with their fragrance. The lights were dimmed and burning candles lined the hearth and mantle of the fireplace. A bottle of non-alcoholic champagne chilled in a bucket of ice. We'd barely taken our massive chairs next to each other when a sommelier came in and opened the bottle and poured our drink into crystal flutes.

"Not the real deal, but you shouldn't imbibe with a baby on board," Dustin said.

It looked like the romance bug had crawled up and bit him since last night. I'll ride this a little longer and see where it goes.

The waiter appeared after that. I realized the dinner had already been arranged, as he mentioned "the amour package." We chose appetizers, salads, and steak entrees. Before the salads even came out, a young woman appeared with a chilled silver tray packed with chocolate-covered strawberries. I tried to stop drooling.

I reached for a strawberry but checked Dustin's face. Maybe this was dessert. He smiled like he hadn't a care in the world. He picked up a strawberry and popped it in his mouth.

They were heavenly. Strawberries in season are my absolute favorite. I wanted nothing more than to eat that whole platter. I was famished.

"Darcy," he finally began. "I don't think I handled this whole surprise very well last night. Making lists and drawing things out helps me see things more clearly, but it probably felt kind of impersonal."

"Ya think?" I said, pursing my lips. Then I ate another strawberry.

"I've had some time to consider and I guess you have too." He leaned back and regarded me intensely.

"I don't know which option is best. They all have drawbacks," I said. The pit in my stomach was returning.

"There are going to be obstacles to overcome, no question about it. But we're not young kids, we've been out in the world, and we've experienced relationships. We know a thing or two about life. We can handle whatever comes our way."

I bit my lip. "I didn't expect to be handling this. I didn't even expect to meet you."

"I know. It was so bizarre that we shared common ancestors and yet we'd never met. I couldn't talk to anyone else, so I went back home and talked to my painting of Grandma Carolina, and asked her what to do."

"You went—what? You're saying you drove back to North Platte today? But you're here again."

"Yeah, I needed to pick up some things. Like my suit."

"What did Grandma Carolina tell you to do?"

"Follow my heart."

He took my left hand and stealthily slipped something onto my finger. When I pulled my hand away, my ring finger was adorned with an antique platinum Art Deco diamond nested among a bed of smaller diamonds. The band had a scroll design that enhanced its artistic style. I'd never seen anything so beautiful. It looked exactly like something I'd choose. My lips parted.

Dustin reached for my hand again. "This was my grandmother's ring, Emma Gay Sherman, who married Lamar Roth in the 1940s. I don't think he bought the ring until later when he had more income. My mother wore it a few times, then she gave it to me a couple of years ago. I think she was telling me to find a mate. If you would rather have a new ring, that's totally fine, I just had—"

"I love this ring. How did you know I have a penchant for vintage jewelry? And this is Art Deco. That's from the 1920s when Anselm Roth and Adelaide Schulz got married. It's perfect. What about the options we talked about? What are you proposing?"

He sighed. "I'm proposing marriage, obviously." He stood up and got down on one knee. My eyebrows shot up. "Tell me you'll take a leap of faith. Come back to live with me. I talked to our local insurance agent. We're her biggest customer and she said she could work something out to help you study to be an insurance agent if you want to. She could use a partner; her business has grown. Or maybe you could work remotely for the company that employs you now. We could do this, Darcy. We could have a family. We'll get to know each other whether we're married or not. I've loved you from the moment I saw you. Please, marry me."

I pressed my lips together, trying to stop the tears. "Well, I guess since you said please."

"Is that a 'yes?'"

I nodded and threw my arms around his neck. He smelled so good; like soap and aftershave mixed with beer. How did I think I could live without him? Three weeks of being deprived of physical contact had taken a toll. I could feel how it affected him too. The kiss he laid on me was morphing into something more intimate when his tongue stroked mine and his hands began sliding over my bodice.

I slipped my hands under his jacket and felt the warmth of his back through his shirt. "You still have that motel room waiting?"

He chuckled when he broke my hold and got off his knees to return to his chair. "It has to wait a little bit longer."

"Isn't it odd that we were brought together because your great-grandfather's brother had children with my great-grandfather's sister, and Trevor, the great-grandson, was tracking them down? If that hadn't happened, we never would have met." I sipped my champagne and admired the ring sparkling in the candlelight.

"And now it's come full circle. Another Schulz woman is having a baby with a Roth man. That's got to be destiny." He leaned in and kissed me again.

"That's a good name! Destiny Roth." He looked blank. "For the baby."

That massive grin of his lit his face as the entrees arrived.

All through dinner we talked about wedding plans. We both agreed that having an outdoor wedding in July or early August would work. If we were willing to consider options in both Lancaster and Lincoln counties, we figured we'd find something we could agree on. If nothing else, we'd get married at his ranch or my family farm. I can't remember ever enjoying a meal more.

He said the dinner included dessert, but I'd had several strawberries and was getting stuffed. The waiter came in and cleared the plates.

"Are you ready for the last course, Sir?" the waiter asked.

"Yes, it's time to open it up," Dustin said.

I didn't understand what he meant. He stood up and pulled out my chair, so I stood too. The waiter and another employee unhooked something on the sidewall in front of us and accordioned it back, revealing another room. I was shocked to see family members standing behind the wall. My father, Margie, Archer, and Cheyenne were holding champagne glasses. Dustin's parents,

Louis and Janice, Veronica, Leslie, and Jace Lassiter were there too.

"Congratulations!" Dad was the first to shout out.

I turned to Dustin. "You were pretty darn sure of yourself, weren't you?"

He smirked. "I was born sure of myself. Something else you might need to know. I was hoping I wouldn't have to take my shirt off."

Then I was smothered in hugs and well wishes. Ronnie came up and gave me the biggest hug. "You're going to marry my dad, right? Then it will be two girls against one boy."

I nodded and kissed her on the forehead. "What did your father tell you?"

"That he was going to ask you to marry him. Oh, and he gave you a ring."

"Dustin?" I looked over at him as Jace was clapping him on the back. "What else did you tell Veronica?"

He joined us. Then he held up his hand to silence the room. "Everyone, give us a moment to talk to my daughter."

He took my hand and Ronnie's. "There's something else happening, Ronnie. You're going to be a big sister. Darcy and I are having a baby."

She squealed. She and her aunt must have gotten the same squealing gene because it sounded just like Leslie. Then Ronnie jumped up and down like a nine-year-old and hugged me again first, and then her father picked her up and swung her around.

It took us a second to realize we'd spilled the beans to everyone else, and they were busy chattering with each other.

"You're pregnant?" Janice asked.

"Yes. The wedding will be soon, we hope." Dustin answered.

More hugs and laughter followed. The engagement party had just gotten more festive.

CHAPTER FORTY-THREE: DARCY

It was hours later when we returned to Dustin's motel room. Ronnie's grandparents had gotten a suite so that she could stay with them in a different motel.

"I finally have you to myself," Dustin sighed, moving in close.

"You could have had me last night, but you asked me to leave," I drilled my index finger into his chest.

He grabbed my finger and kissed my knuckles. "You're not going to let that go, are you? I needed time to adjust, just like you did. I made a quick turnaround."

"If you say so."

He ran his hand through my hair, wrapping his fingers around the back of my head, and pulled my mouth to his, so I couldn't say anything more. What could I say that was better than kissing? After the events of the evening, I couldn't get close enough, and I looped my arms around his neck.

"Tonight is our engagement night," Dustin murmured. "Such an occasion requires a strict dress code."

I looked at his clothing and trailed my hands down his chest. "I think we met the dress code. You look great in a suit, by the way. You could be a runway model."

"Thank you. That was the dress code for the dinner date. I'm talking about right now, in the bedroom. The only thing either one of us is allowed to wear is that sparkly ring of yours." He slid his hands down the back of my dress. "And you are over-dressed. How did you get this on? There's no zipper."

"It goes over my head. You've got more clothes on than I do."

He tugged my dress upward to reveal another bra he hadn't seen. Delicate black lace flanked the center plunge contrasted with silver satin on the outside of the cups. My dress landed on the chair.

"Holy moly, Woman. Three weeks is too long to go without sex. We're not doing that again."

He yanked me against him more roughly this time, sliding his hands from the midpoint of my back down my spine to my hips. He tasted my lips teasingly running his tongue across my teeth when I chuckled. Then he moved into the kiss hungrily like a lion cub fighting for his share of the kill. His demanding tongue threatened to cut off my airway and I was momentarily dizzy. Whether it was from passion or asphyxiation, I couldn't tell.

When his lips broke from mine, I gasped for air. His hands were back around my shoulder blades: I had to grip his shirt for balance. His kisses danced down the column of my neck, to my cleavage. Wherever he made contact, seedlings of pleasure bloomed instantly on my skin. When he reached the cramped divide between my breasts, he inhaled, nuzzling me more with his nose than his lips. I'd dabbed my French perfume there, directing him to follow the treasure hunt of seduction.

"You must have stock in Victoria's Secret. How do you have so many sexy bras?" Dustin slowly released me and stood straighter.

I tried to clear my head. "Some women collect shoes. Beautiful shoes are usually uncomfortable. Revealing bras look and feel good, so they are hard to resist buying. I have a whole dresser full; I should warn you."

"Hell, I'll build you a warehouse for them if they all look like this." Dustin had removed his suit jacket and hung it on the chair back. He started whipping off his tie and shirt. When his shirt fell to the floor, I grabbed his belt and started to unbuckle it. His eyes widened but he didn't stop me. A slow grin spread across his face as I unhooked his fly. I unzipped his trousers very slowly watching his eyes. When I traced my fingers over his boxers, he closed his eyes and moaned.

"It has been a long, hard three weeks," I cooed.

"Jesus Christ, Darce. We need to get naked now!"

"But don't you like getting there?" I ran my fingers around the waistband of his shorts, but he pushed away enough to unsnap my bra and slid my not-quite-transparent panties off. It would have been a shame if our evening had gone sour and I didn't get to show off my lingerie. Yet, he seemed to be hell-bent on ridding me of it at lightning speed.

Before I could assist him, he'd dropped his pants and boxers to the floor and toed off his shoes. It didn't look like he was going to bother removing his socks. He yanked me off the floor like I weighed nothing. Some primal girlie instinct made me cling like a rescued princess.

I wrapped my legs around his torso, and he stumbled over to the bed, letting go of me with one hand to pull the covers off. We tumbled forward, and he kicked away the sheet and comforter while climbing over me.

"This is more like it, Mrs. Roth."

I giggled when he started playfully dropping noisy kisses on my eyelids, nose, cheeks, and chin. Then I braced my hands on his shoulders. Feminism poked her way through my desire. "I don't think I agreed to that."

"What? The kissing?"

I shook my head. "The name. I don't know if I want to be Mrs. Roth."

He rolled off me and perched on one elbow. "Didn't you agree to marry me?" The muscles in his face tensed.

"Oh yes, but I'll need to think about changing my name. I've been Darcy Schulz for thirty-six years. Everything is in that name."

Dustin cocked his head. "You'll want to go by Roth in North Platte. The Roths and R&R Ranch are well-known. One of the premier ranches in the county. Women you haven't met will want to throw you a bridal shower just because you're marrying me."

I squinted briefly. "Really? Then why did you have trouble finding someone to date?"

He threw his head back and rolled his eyes. "I didn't lack for offers. Hell, sometimes the eligible women were a pest. I wasn't interested. Until you came along. And now I'm extremely interested. So, you'd better kiss Darcy Schulz goodbye."

"I suppose you could convince me," I smiled slowly moving in to caress him. When I did, he pulled me on top of him and pushed his tongue between my lips again. Then he rolled me over to my back. He began kissing his way down my body until he reached my breasts. He wrapped both hands around them. God, I'd missed this.

"Dustin!" I was surprised I could even squeak out his name.

His face jerked back. "Oh no. Are your boobs tender?"

My brows shot up. "A little. Why?"

"It's part of pregnancy. I didn't hurt you, did I?"

"No, as long as you're gentle, it's fine." My tongue jutted across my teeth. "More than fine. Desired. Invited. Encouraged."

He chuckled and his smoky gaze dropped to my breasts still filling his hands.

When he nudged my thighs apart my hips bucked in anticipation. I let out a high-pitched sigh. Thank God we were getting married.

CHAPTER FORTY-FOUR: DUSTIN

I should be exhausted. We'd stayed up half the night making up for the weeks we'd been apart. I couldn't believe I might get to enjoy nights like that regularly. I turned to look at my fiancé in the king-size bed and snuggled in next to her warm body, rotating her to her side to nestle my morning wood against her silky backside.

"Darcy, you awake?" I kissed her ear.

"Mmmm?" she mumbled, not opening her eyes. When I let my tongue tickle her neck, she wiggled. "Again? I thought we'd gotten that all out of our systems last night."

"It's your fault. Ever since I laid eyes on you, I've turned back into a horny twenty-year-old college kid."

"No, I remember those horny college boys. You're much more thorough." She rolled to her back. "But we need to have some serious discussions today. That means getting dressed. Cuz it's easy to lose control when I have to look at all that." She bobbed her finger at me indicating my face and chest.

I grinned. "It's a shame to get dressed so soon. Maybe we should take a shower."

"You know what will happen if we shower together. We will never make it to the breakfast with our parents."

"I think they'll wait." I planted a tentative kiss on her mouth. She kissed me back and then shimmied away from me and out of the bed. In a moment, the lock clicked on the bathroom door. I guess she didn't trust me not to join her. I wanted to, but she was right. We had to talk about some things. I got up and put on my shorts and jeans. I surveyed my face in the wall mirror. I could skip shaving this morning. Go for that shadow-beard look. Darcy emerged from the bathroom wrapped in a towel. As though I didn't know what she was hiding.

Somehow, we made it to the restaurant across the street in time for breakfast with the relatives who had joined us last night.

When we got back to the motel room, Darcy pulled a Day-Timer calendar out of her satchel. I didn't even know she had one of those.

"We're going to have to start setting dates and making lists. When does school start for you?"

"August 15 is the first day of classes. I'm back at work on the tenth."

"It's almost July. That doesn't give us much time especially if we want to go on a honeymoon."

I sat in one of the side chairs and Darcy sat on the edge of the bed. "What kind of wedding do you want?" I asked. "I already did the fancy version, so I'll go along with whatever works."

Her brows raised. "What? Are you saying you don't care about the wedding details? Been there, done that?"

"I'm saying it's really about the bride, isn't it? You tell me what we should shoot for."

She flipped her hair behind her shoulder. "I haven't contemplated it. The timeline is critical if I'm going to give two weeks' notice at work—"

"About that." I leaned back in my chair. "Tomorrow morning, tell your boss you're running off to get married. I'll wait in the parking lot. Then we'll go to your place and you'll pack up whatever you can get in my pickup and your car, and we'll tow your car back to my place. You'll move in with me."

"Uh…no." Darcy pursed her lips.

"What's wrong with that plan?"

"I've worked there twelve years. I'm in management. A two weeks' notice is required."

I frowned. "Well, that eats up a lot of the timeline. How are you going to plan a wedding when you're working?"

"Most women do that. Of course, they start at least six months in advance. Is there somewhere on the ranch that would be nice for an outdoor ceremony? Maybe we could do the reception in North Platte."

"There's something else going on that I haven't told you about. Well, two or three things. Ronnie has sleepaway camp the second week in July. We couldn't have the wedding that week. And the day after tomorrow, they are digging the hole for our swimming pool. A week later, the kitchen remodel is scheduled to begin."

Darcy looked at me like I'd said I was an alien.

"Back up a minute. Did you mean you're putting a swimming pool in at your house?"

"Yeah. This has all been scheduled since last fall. They're digging the hole, then the cement work will start and they'll do the footings for the kitchen expansion—"

"You're expanding the house? The kitchen is being redone?" The creases in her brow kept multiplying. "You didn't think this was critical information to share with me? Is the kitchen going to be useable during this time?"

"Well, no. I mean the refrigerator might be staying put. They will tear down the wall where the sink and the cupboards are. Pretty much everything is going to be brand new. I'm sure you'll like it."

Darcy's mouth formed a tight line. "Do you have any photos or diagrams of either of these projects with you?"

"Yeah. I have the blueprints in my truck. Some of the sample photos too, I think. Most of it is in my email." I could see her eyes narrowing. "You have no reason to be upset. This was all planned long before we met."

"Yes, Dustin. I get that, but things changed rather drastically this weekend. Let me see the blueprints."

"I'll get them. As long as you understand it's too late to make changes."

"I watch HGTV. They're always making changes."

I huffed. I'd already had my mother and Leslie on my case for weeks as I'd tried to decide on the floor plan and finishes. I couldn't afford to let Darcy throw in a curveball. The construction crew had a tight schedule, and I hoped it would be principally finished when school began. Granted, I had no idea a woman would move into my house in the middle of this. I went out to my truck and pulled the blueprints and samples out from behind the seat. I set my jaw.

When I got to the room, I spread the blueprints on the bed. "Here's the swimming pool. I intend to do the composite decking myself once the pool is poured and they are doing the tiling. The hot tub is here and there will be an exterior door to the new kitchen."

She studied the blueprint. "The kitchen expansion is going to stick out farther into the yard than the bedroom area?"

"Yes. That's where the hot tub goes."

"What if you added onto the house—with another bedroom?"

"No. Why would we—" I stopped. Oh, I wasn't just adding her to the household. The baby—she was making allowances for another family member.

"You could even put a room below it, like a tornado shelter area. Do you have a storm cellar somewhere?"

"No, we have talked about doing that for years."

She pulled a pencil out of her purse and started marking the blueprint. "See, if you took this straight across from the new kitchen wall, that would give you what, ten feet at least. The room could be kind of long and narrow. It would be perfect for Ronnie. She'll be a teenager soon."

I couldn't believe she dared to try to rework my carefully laid plans.

"Darcy, what makes you think I want you to change any of this? Where would you put the hot tub?"

"I don't know. On the other side of the pool. Or just scootch the whole thing farther back."

"They have already located all the utility lines and plumbing. They've ordered materials. It's all set. Maybe we could add a bedroom in the future."

"But you're doing construction now. I wish I'd known about this earlier."

"I didn't tell you because I wanted to avoid all this! I don't need you to come in and start running my life."

Darcy backed off the bed. "What do you think a wife does? If you didn't want me running your life, why did you propose?"

I rolled my eyes. I was beginning to wonder. "I'm not trying to run yours."

"You're not?" Darcy scoffed. "You expect me to quit my job, leave my home and family, and move in with you, to a place where I am a stranger. You took my life in your fist rather quickly. Surely it crossed your mind that something as major as a house renovation would affect me." She crossed her arms. "How were you planning to cook when your kitchen was in shambles?"

I sighed. "My parents have an RV stored behind the barn. We were going to move it next to the house and use that kitchen during construction."

She nodded grimly. "Yeah, it doesn't sound like adding a wedding to this mix is a good idea. The timing is terrible." I could see her eyes filling as she stormed out of the room.

Damn it. I knew this wasn't going to be an easy conversation. Was I kidding myself hoping she'd be thrilled that she was getting a brand-new kitchen and a swimming pool? She didn't even notice I added a dishwasher and an island. I thought women loved kitchen islands.

Her Day-Timer had landed on the floor. I picked it up and looked at the month of June. She'd made notes about our dates. Cute little hearts adorned the weekends we'd spent together. She even circled the date we'd met. Last Friday, she'd noted the doctor's appointment. Heck, she'd have to change doctors too. She'd sacrifice quite a bit to accommodate what I wanted. I could just imagine the response I'd get from my general contractor if I started making changes at this late date. On the flip side, I wasn't in love with my general contractor. He wasn't the one giving me the best sex I'd ever had. Or carrying my child.

I opened the door to find her. She was standing on the other side ready to scan her keycard. I wrapped my arms around her and picked her off her feet. I nudged the door closed and set her down against it. I propped my palms on either side of her head and leaned into her, my mouth finding hers.

"Why did you run off? We're not done here." Before she could answer, I had her mouth on mine again and began steering her toward the bed. Housekeeping hadn't even had a chance to make the bed when we tumbled onto it. I pushed the blueprint aside. "I'm going to keep kissing you until you see things my way," I said, leaning over her.

Darcy put her hands on my cheeks to keep me back. "As much as I like that idea, we need to talk this through. Compromise. Negotiate. Understand the other person."

I rolled onto my back. "I'll call the contractor. Tell him I decided to get married this weekend and my fiancé has a few changes to make. But you'd better be on the call to hear all the colorful language he's likely to spew."

"Maybe we need to go through the entire project before you do that. I'd like to see everything, the finishes, the pool design. Have you picked it all out already?"

"Yes, Darcy. I decided this months ago as I said. I got advice from my mother and Leslie regarding what I needed and what was fashionable. I think you're going to love it."

"Hmmm. A dishwasher?"

"Yeah."

"A new stove?"

"Fancy range with an extra oven."

She nodded. "I'll need room to do my baking. New cabinets?"

"My mother insisted on that. Plus, the island will have storage."

Her eyes lit up. Now that's what I was expecting. "There's enough space for an island?"

"Yeah. The old kitchen is becoming a dining room and the new part is the kitchen."

"Wow. I have never cooked in a new kitchen. This might be worth waiting for. Show me more."

"I showed you the blueprint. You wrote all over it."

"Don't you have samples of the countertop or the backsplash? What about the flooring?"

"Be patient. You'll get to see it all. The sooner you move to the ranch, the sooner you'll see everything."

"That's coercion. I see the game you're playing."

"Speaking of playing games. You can't run off every time we disagree."

"I know. That's why I came right back."

CHAPTER FORTY-FIVE: DUSTIN

40,000 feet above sea level west of Denver, Colorado
July 12, 2022

"You're not a nervous flyer, are you, Babe?" I laced my fingers through Darcy's as our commercial airliner reached cruising altitude over the Rocky Mountains.

"Not normally. This is going to be an extended flight, over seven hours. I remember the long flight when I went to Europe. It's grueling."

"Well, we can nap, watch a movie, or talk about the trip. I arranged something that I should tell you about."

Darcy sighed. "The last two weeks after I put in my notice at work have been chaotic. I was glad to let you plan the honeymoon. Let's hear the itinerary."

She might not agree with this. Sometimes it hit me that we had so much to learn about each other. Was she receptive to sudden changes in the schedule? Or was her Type A factor going to push back whenever I seized control?

"I did some research," I began. "I know we agreed to do this honeymoon while Veronica is at camp, and then have the wedding on Labor Day weekend."

"Yes, I want to lounge on the beach while I still have a beach body. By September, I may be showing, and you'll be teaching."

"Well, um, it turns out you can register for a marriage license online and pick it up when you arrive in Maui. Once you show your ID, they hand you the license and you can get married in Hawaii immediately." I watched her eyes fill with uncertainty. She gulped from her water bottle, dropping my hand.

I plunged ahead, "So, I did that. I paid the fee and made an appointment with an agent to get the license tomorrow. The hotel has arranged for an officiant and we can be married on the beach Thursday."

She shook her head. "I don't understand. We were pulling things together for September. That was soon to plan a wedding. I didn't bring a wedding dress. No one we know will be with us, including your daughter. You said she had to be at the wedding. Why would you want to rush it?"

"Two reasons. One of them is Veronica. After this trip to Hawaii, you'll be moving in with us. It would be a better example for her if we were married."

I let my gaze drop to Darcy's lap. "And then there's the little wrangler you're carrying. Someday he'll be able to count back from his birthday and compare that to our wedding date. Seven months may be more palatable than five."

"Using that line of thinking, we could have married in June, when we first discovered the pregnancy."

"But this way, we can have a beautiful setting. Sunset on the beach. You in a string bikini, me in my swim trunks, barefoot in the surf."

She laughed. "I don't own a string bikini."

"I bought you one."

Darcy gasped. "You're serious about this? It's not some pubescent fantasy?" She bit her lip. "I know I said I didn't need a big extravaganza, but I wanted a white dress, flowers, and my closest family and friends in attendance." Her eyes began to moisten. "A wedding cake."

"You're still going to have that: whatever you and the mothers are planning. We'll have a more formal wedding in September. This wedding in Hawaii will be our little secret."

"What?" Darcy scooted forward in her seat to face me. If I hadn't sprung for first class, she couldn't have managed that. "You don't want to tell anyone?"

"I'll tell Ronnie. The rest will find out eventually, maybe on the official wedding day, when we don't sign the paperwork. For now, it would be fun to keep it private."

She held up her index finger. It was cute how often she wagged her finger in my face. "We don't have the wedding rings."

"I brought them." I glanced toward our feet. "They're in my laptop bag."

She sighed and looked around the cabin. "Are you afraid I'm going to change my mind once I move in with you? You want to seal the deal as quickly as possible?"

I chuckled. "Yep, that's it exactly. You haven't discovered all my bad habits yet."

She settled back in the seat and took my hand again. "I'll have to break you of all of those."

"Are you on board with getting married in Maui?" Maybe this was going to be easy.

She gave me the side-eye. "I'll have to see the string bikini first."

She looked spectacular in that white, crocheted string bikini.

Darcy frowned at her reflection in the full-length mirror mounted on the bathroom door in our hotel suite. "I've never gone out in public showing this much skin. Let's save this for the hotel room. The swimming pool will be finished at the ranch soon, won't it? Maybe I'll wear it late at night when only you can see me."

I stood behind her running my hands down her arms. "Darling, you look better than the woman modeling this on the website. Are you going to deprive the beachcombers at this beautiful resort of this breathtaking view? You'll be glad someday that you have photos showing off your insanely hot body."

She scoffed. "When you lay on the flattery that thick, I know you're exaggerating! I'll make you a deal. If I wear this, I get to pick out what you wear to our very casual wedding. I wonder if they sell Speedos in the hotel gift shop."

"I brought a nice pair of swimming trunks." Our eyes met in the mirror.

"I brought three swimming suits. All of them are much better at holding everything in place. With this flimsy thing, I might have a wardrobe malfunction!"

"I'd really like you to wear this." I pulled her hair aside and kissed her neck and let my hands slide down to where the string ties sat on her hips. "Honestly, it looks great on you. If you want to pick out something for me—fine."

"You don't think these are going to fit me, do you? They look like they're sized for ten-year-olds." I held up one of the size-large speedos in the trendy swimwear shop the hotel had suggested.

"They fit very snugly," the sales clerk said before Darcy could answer. He looked like he might have had Polynesian ancestry, but he sported a fade and six-inch dreadlocks springing from the crown of his head, with one dyed a bright yellow against his otherwise raven hair. "Are you wearing these for any particular activity such as surfing or snorkeling? I can tell you these feel wonderful in the water."

I cleared my throat. "My fiancé thinks it would be fun if I got married in a speedo." I rolled my eyes to express my opinion, then turned back to the rack of selections. They must have some with more than a three-inch side seam.

"Where is your fiancé? If it's his idea, he should get to pick." The clerk glanced around the store, which was mostly empty in the early morning.

Darcy started to laugh and covered her mouth. I frowned at her, then looked back at the clerk. Why would he think—? Oh no. This is not the shop for me.

"Darcy, we're leaving. You failed to mention that only gay men wear speedos."

"No!" the salesman stammered. "I just misunderstood. You're marrying…her?"

Darcy nodded, but it seemed he was insulting her, implying there might be a better choice.

"Just try a bunch of these on, Dustin. Can he come out and show me?" She glanced at the clerk's nametag. "Akoni and I will pick our favorite."

I scowled. "How do the sizes run?"

Akoni shrugged. "Your usual size will work. I suggest large or…extra-large." I tried not to roll my eyes again at his subtle smirk.

I grunted as I tried to pull up the tight black briefs. My old football pants with integrated pads weren't this snug. At least those came down to my knees. I looked in the mirror after I stuffed everything inside. Good Lord. This suit started three inches below the tan line of my jean shorts, and another patch of white skin showed at the top of my legs. And a lot of hair. Anyone wearing this would have to spend hours manscaping.

I peeked out of the dressing room curtain, still wearing my T-shirt, which at least covered my top half. "Darce!" I whispered. "Come back here if you want to see this."

Darcy waltzed into the dressing room, giving me the once-over. She immediately pushed my shirt up, forcing me to remove it. "Come out here by the three-way mirror."

"I don't think so. I feel naked."

She grinned. "Exactly how I felt in that string bikini. Now you're getting it."

I shook my head and marched out to the mirror. Of course, Akoni appeared in a flash.

"Oh, yes. You have the perfect body for this one, Sir." Akoni walked around me as if inspecting one of my prize steers.

I averted my eyes from the mirror. "It's much too small. Don't you have some with more fabric on the sides? Where the legs are longer? Maybe one where the waist part is higher?" No matter which way I tugged at the suit, it just exposed more on top or below.

"Of course, we have board shorts if you want those. You do look smashing in this suit. Clearly, you've been working out. Don't you want to flaunt it?" Akoni waggled his brows.

"I think I can still flaunt it without exposing the family jewels," I said, stomping back toward the dressing room. Darcy followed me, turning me to face the mirror.

She did the one thing that convinced me: the same tactic I'd used on her. She stood behind me and slid her curled fingers below my navel, softly stroking my inguinal crease.

"This, right here, is the sexiest part of the male anatomy," Darcy purred onto my shoulder. "And yours gets five stars, even at the advanced age of thirty-nine. You shouldn't keep it under wraps."

And that Speedo was tight before. It was time to return to the hotel room for some honeymoon action.

In the end, I bought a nylon and spandex swim brief sporting a banana-leaf motif. I'd swear an actual banana leaf would have provided more coverage. I could see how cleverly my bride was retaliating. Akoni also talked me into buying a tube of self-tanner to darken my white stripes.

After all the angst about our wardrobe, the wedding itself went off without a hitch.

Shortly before sunset, we strolled down to the beach below the hotel accompanied by the officiant, a middle-aged woman wearing a massive muumuu and several leis, and the photographer the hotel had arranged. We chose a spot where the photographer could get a good backdrop of the ocean.

As I took off the shirt and shorts I wore over my speedo, it hit me. *This is it. No turning back now. In a few minutes, it will all be legal.*

Is this insane? Maybe.

I wasn't certain I ever wanted to marry again just a few months ago. This woman right here—the stunning brunette stripping off her swimsuit coverup—has turned my whole life upside down.

Yet you could fill this beach with things I didn't know about her. That shining mass of mahogany hair— her natural color? I had no idea. Was she in debt up to her eyeballs? I hadn't asked. Who had she voted for in the last election? My God, we'd never even discussed politics. We were practically strangers. Why the hell should I trust her with my daughter, my home, my assets?

But I never expected to feel this kind of passion or happiness. She'd found the crack in my psyche and hot-glued it without leaving a trace. She was even giving me the family I once wanted: another child— perhaps a son. It doesn't matter really. *Of course, I'm marrying her. It would be more insane to hesitate.*

Darcy reached into the beach tote she'd carried and placed a yellow Pua Kenikeni lei over my head. The smell was dazzling, a lush exotic scent as if you could bottle the hip-twitching of a hula dancer. I suppose it contrasted with my bright green Speedo. She placed a crown of purple orchids atop her long wavy tresses. This felt like a dream.

The officiant began, "We gather here today to unite Darcelia and Dustin in marriage. This contract is not to be entered into lightly, but thoughtfully and seriously with a deep realization of its obligations and responsibilities. Please remember that love, loyalty, and understanding are the foundations of a happy and enduring home.

"Do you, Dustin, take Darcelia to be your lawfully wedded wife, to have and to hold, in sickness and in health, in good times and bad, for richer or poorer, keeping yourself unto her for as long as you both shall live?"

I looked into Darcy's haunting blue eyes. I made her wait a second or two more than necessary. I smiled. "I do."

She repeated the question to Darcy. She was taking this solemnly and responded at once.

The officiant continued, "Dustin, please take the ring you have selected for Darcelia and—"

Darn it! I'd left the rings in my shorts. This is why I'd wanted to wear my regular swim trunks: pockets. I held up one finger and walked back over to fetch the rings from my crumpled shorts.

"We're good now," I said. Darcy shook her head, chuckling.

"As you place the ring on her finger, repeat after me: Darcelia, I give you this ring, as a symbol of my love. I ask you to wear it as a sign to the world that you are my wife. With this ring, I thee wed."

I managed to stumble through it, and so did Darcy.

Then the lady officiant pulled something out of a bag that she'd brought with her to the beach: two pint-size bottles filled with colored sand. She handed the bottle of red sand to Darcy and the bottle of blue sand to me. Then she pulled out a wide-mouth jar that had some natural beige sand in the bottom along with some small assorted seashells. She held the jar between us.

"Dustin and Darcelia, today you join your separate lives to make one. The two separate bottles of sand symbolize your separate lives, separate families, and separate sets of friends: they represent all that you are and all that you will ever be as an individual. They also represent your lives before today."

She nodded to the two of us to pour our sand into the larger container.

"Wait," I said.

The women both frowned at me.

"I need the red sand. My name, Roth, means red in German. I suppose I descend from some fellow with red hair."

The officiant switched the bottles between us but I caught a maternal roll of her almond eyes.

Darcy started to swirl sand into the jar, so I followed suit.

The officiant went on, "As these two containers of sand are emptied, the individual containers of sand no longer exist, but will be joined together as one. Just as these grains of sand can never be separated, neither will your love."

"You're not mixing your sand in with mine, Darce."

"I know. I want a little of my blue to stand out, to make it pretty. Don't you want part of the red to show?"

I dumped the rest of my sand on hers. "Nope. You heard the lady. Blended forever."

When she pronounced us husband and wife, I wrapped my arms around Darcy, hoisted her into the air, and kissed her. That's when I noticed a small crowd of onlookers had gathered at a respectful distance. They cheered. We waved.

After a few formal photos with the officiant, and signing the license papers, it was time to get frisky.

"Are you ready to get into the surf?" I asked my wife.

"You really want to get full of sand and water now? It took me an hour to fix my hair and makeup."

I shrugged. "It's time to replicate *From Here to Eternity*. This is why we're wearing bathing suits."

She squealed when I grabbed her around her waist from behind and sprinted toward the water. The photographer kept up with our horseplay in the surf. Despite her previous protests, Darcy was not averse to splashing and grabbing me, and her long, wet hair whipped me in the face a few times as we cavorted.

Finally, I laid down on the shore on my back and pulled her onto my chest. The first time the tide rushed up, we were close to being engulfed. As I scooted us back toward the shore, the cool, wet sand squished down my tailbone burrowing between my buttocks. Damn speedo!

After several takes, we nailed the kissing scene made famous by Burt Lancaster and Deborah Kerr. We'd watched it on YouTube about twenty times the previous night. The photographer nodded and smiled. He was pleased with his work.

After that, we put the lid on the jar of sand and headed for the hotel room, following the stone path winding through the hotel property.

"Now what?" Darcy asked.

"Hit the giant shower to get all the sand and salt off."

"Dibs on showering first," she said.

I snorted. "You think I'm going to let you shower alone? You're a married woman now, you may never shower alone again."

She shook the sand from her hair, removing the flower crown. "Are you going to wash my hair for me?"

I pulled her closer to whisper in her ear. "I'm going to wash every last inch of you."

Later, we lay nakedly entwined in the massive bed in our suite with the curtains fluttering from a gentle breeze blowing through the open window to the balcony.

"How are you feeling, Wife?" Her head was resting on the crook joining my chest and shoulder.

"Mmmm. I'm amazed that I'm still awake. You were right. It was fun to get married at the edge of the ocean. I'll bet I don't know anyone else who's done that."

I sighed. "I even forgot what I was wearing. It just felt natural. Not like the usual wedding, that's for sure."

Darcy shifted to put her chin on her hands on my chest, studying me.

"Have you been thinking about your first wedding today?"

I blinked. Gosh, that was about the furthest thing from my mind. I hadn't thought about Brittany at all in the past few weeks.

I frowned. "No. why would I?"

"You don't need to pretend with me. It's understandable that you would do that."

My lips pressed tightly together. "Oh, man. That day turned out pretty much the opposite of this one. Except for the result."

She squinted. "What do you mean?"

I sighed and looked at the ceiling fan recalling that day twelve years ago. "The wedding was the social event of Fort Collins. Not what I wanted, but I'd signed off. I was living in Nebraska and I told Brittany to do whatever she pleased. She turned the preparation over to her mother, who brought in a wedding planner. So, I showed up at the gigantic church with over 300 guests. I hardly knew anyone, all her parents' friends and colleagues. I loved standing outdoors in the June heat shaking hands with all those strangers wearing a suffocating black tux. My mother-in-law insisted on introducing me to everyone."

Darcy smirked. "The reception must have been better."

"Oh, no. We had to learn a complicated dance routine. Foxtrot lessons, three days before the wedding. I almost bailed then. On the dancing, not the marriage. As soon as we got to the country club for the reception, my best man started handing me drinks on an empty stomach. I was half-plowed by the time the orchestra started playing. I guess we did okay, I don't remember that part well. We hauled in a lot of gifts, mostly dishes and kitchen gadgets, some such shit. I'd never repeat that scene."

"But your bride wanted it that way?"

I grimaced. "I don't know. Her parents went overboard, which I didn't understand until later. Not until after Brittany was gone."

Darcy sat up. "What do you mean?"

"Her parents didn't expect her to get married. They were celebrating her survival."

"I don't understand. You said she didn't get sick until sometime after Veronica was born."

I sat up too and hugged a pillow to my chest. "Brittany lied to me."

Darcy's brows arched. "What? She lied to you? When? At the wedding?"

I shook my head. This wasn't the time to get into this. I felt something tighten in my gut. Why were we talking about something that tarnished my first marriage?

"You know what? Never mind. Tonight is our wedding night. We shouldn't discuss anything unpleasant. We shouldn't even think about anything but our happiness together."

"Dustin, no!" Darcy scooted off the bed and went to the closet and pulled on one of the fluffy white robes the hotel supplied. "Don't start to tell me something and not finish it." She picked up her brush and sat on the corner of the bed, running the brush through her hair.

"All right, I'll tell you. You need to know anyway. I didn't want to spoil the mood." I sipped from a plastic water bottle next to the bed. "About a year after Brittany died, I was clearing out some of her boxes. I found a letter from an old boyfriend. It was dated years before I'd met Brittany."

"She cheated on you?"

"No. Do you want to hear this? Then listen. I read the letter. He apologized for dumping her while she was in the hospital. Apparently, he expected her to die and he couldn't deal with it. It didn't make sense to me. She told me she was in the hospital long enough that she had to repeat a semester of college, but she'd recovered.

"When I went back to Fort Collins for a visit, I tracked down the boyfriend. He told me he believed she had terminal cancer and only had months to live. I went straight to her parents' house and we got into a terrible row." My throat began to burn. "He was right; cancer had nearly killed her before I came along, but she'd gone into remission. The doctors didn't want her to have a baby. She asked her family not to tell me after the other guy left her.

"I don't think I've ever been so mad in my life. She'd lied to me every day of our relationship, over nine years." I covered my mouth with both fists until I spoke again. "Everyone in her family lied to me too: her parents, her brother and sisters, even Leslie and Jace. I threatened to cut them all out of Veronica's life and said a lot of other terrible things. I didn't speak to any of the Hamilton relatives for months."

"You were that mad at Leslie and Jace? They were just—"

"Whose side are you on? I was devastated." My voice cracked so I took a calming breath before continuing.

"I should have had a choice about whether to marry her based on her genuine health status. I should have had a choice about whether she should risk her damn life to have a baby. I didn't even know our baby could inherit genes that might give her cancer too. It felt like my wife died all over again because I never knew the most important thing about her."

"Maybe she didn't want it to be the most important thing about her. She probably didn't want anyone fussing over her. She dreaded the day she'd relapse."

"Darcy, stop it! You didn't even know Brittany. She deceived me. You know how hard it was to trust anyone after that? Even you. I had difficulty developing feelings for you not knowing if you were playing me for a fool too."

She gasped. Watching the color drain from her face told me I shouldn't have said that last part. She bowed her head and wrapped her arms around her waist.

I reached one hand out to touch her arm. "Baby. I'm sorry. I didn't mean to lash out at you."

Darcy got up from the bed and went into the living room. Her hairbrush fell to the floor. It looked like a tear had run down her cheek but she made no move to wipe it off.

Damn it! This is why I didn't want to get into this tonight. This story always made my blood pressure throb against my temples. I grunted and threw on the other white bathrobe. I found her sitting on the loveseat looking at a letter that had been folded.

"Darcy…look at me," I said.

She sighed. "The doctor's office sent me this letter after they did the pregnancy test. It talks about prenatal care and how often to schedule visits. Of course, they didn't realize I was moving. Do you want to read it? I'm not lying about the baby."

I knelt in front of her nudging her knees apart to get closer. I took the letter from her and laid it next to her on the loveseat.

"I don't need to read it. I believe you. I always believed you about the baby. This is not about us; it is about what Brittany did to me." I took her face in my hands. "You have done nothing but try to heal that wound. I love you. I will always love you. I don't want to think about this anymore, okay?"

She let me kiss her gently, then she wrapped her arms around my neck. She flattened my ear with her tight embrace and held my head captive for a good half-minute. Then I loosened the tie around her bathrobe and slipped my hands over her bare back. Her warmth filled me with a mixture of comfort and desire. My hands slid down her back until I was cupping her bottom. Our wedding night was not over yet.

CHAPTER FORTY-SIX: DARCY

North Platte, Nebraska
September 3, 2022

The night before our formal wedding, I'd checked into our suite in the North Platte motel where we were having the wedding reception. Most of the guests from my side of the family were staying there too. My mother, Rebecca Novak-Singh, as she was now known, sat sipping coffee watching a hairdresser form pintucked curls around the sides of my head. She'd rolled the hair on the back of my head into looser coils placed high on my crown. Then she made large loops with gold brocade ribbon, pinning that to my hair. I wore pearl earrings and an antique pearl choker.

"I don't understand why you're wearing this jacket over your wedding gown. It's going to be hot as blue blazes. And those tight pin-curls in your hair make you look like you time-traveled from the nineteenth century."

"We're getting married at noon because it will be cooler earlier in the day, and we will all retire to the air-conditioned ballroom downstairs for the reception." I gestured toward the oil painting propped on a chair right in front of the hairdresser's table. "This look is to resemble Carolina, Dustin's second-great-grandmother and my third-great-grandmother. The first thing his daughter said when she met me was that I looked like Carolina."

"You're much prettier than the woman in that painting. She's barely even smiling. I suppose no one showed their teeth back then, they were most likely rotten. I think you look much more like my side of the family."

If only I looked like you. My mother was tall and fair, or at least she had been dyeing her hair blonde for as long as I could remember. Her hair hung straightly in a controlled fringe dusting her shoulders. I could see my reflection in her blue eyes, but hers were farther apart, and she'd been blessed with a much wider mouth. I'd spent a lifetime wondering why the DNA gods hadn't given me her regal looks. At least until I'd seen the oil portrait of Carolina. With her, I could embrace my heritage.

"That jacket," I said, "is more of a transparent blouse. It buttons down the back and I'm going to leave the top few buttons unfastened and fold it down like in the painting. I think the artist had a thing for women's necks and shoulders. Dustin and I found photos of his paintings from the 1800s online, and they all expose the shoulders or upper back. Anyway, Dustin's mother made the blouse and ribbon belt for me. The painting has been at her house since we started construction on ours."

My mom scoffed. "That's another crazy thing. Why would you do a house remodel in the middle of planning your wedding? It's hard enough learning to live with a new husband, but you added that construction mess and a little girl into the mix? I could have told you that was a recipe for disaster."

"The construction project was scheduled before I even met Dustin. We survived. The kitchen should be all finished within a week, and the new bedroom is getting ready for paint. We're waiting for Ronnie to pick out which shade of purple she wants on the wall."

"Purple? You can't paint a bedroom purple! You'll need ten coats to cover it with something soothing once you realize you hate it."

"Mother, it's all fine. Relax. There are small bottles of wine in the fridge there. Maybe you'd like one of those."

At high noon classical music burst from the outdoor speakers at the winery. I was hidden indoors but I could peek over the café curtains at Dustin, Jace, and Archer sporting matching navy suits standing in front of his minister. Cheyenne and Veronica were winding up the narrow aisle, wearing pale blue chiffon dresses nearly matching the antique-looking blouse I wore over my strapless white chiffon A-line gown. They too, wore ribbons in their loose hair.

I'd decided against my parents escorting the bride down the aisle. My father and Margie, and my mother and her husband, Dr. Stephen Singh, all sat in the front row across the aisle from Louis and Janice Roth. I also rejected the newer tradition of "first look" photos. I wanted everyone to see Dustin's reaction to my unusual apparel and hairdo. As I approached the aisle, I took a chance he might not make the connection between me and the painting.

I tried to paste the same smile on my lips as my ancestor. My lips quivered when I saw Dustin's eyes light up in recognition. His lips parted, and he started to laugh. He caught himself and pressed his mouth tighter. Clearly, he got it. That may have summed up our whole relationship: we somehow understood each other intrinsically. It could have been our shared DNA, but maybe it was just dumb luck to find someone resembling a soulmate. We quickly learned to sense the other person's thoughts and feelings without even speaking.

For those who wondered why I'd fashioned myself in a long-forgotten style, it made more sense after the ceremony when I posed next to the portrait of Carolina.

"What made you want to impersonate Grandma Schulz?" Dustin asked, pulling me aside.

"Didn't you say you had the hots for her when you were a teenager?"

He laughed. "Ancient history. Now I have the hots for you."

"It's mutual." I kissed him then, right in front of all the guests.

Later, during a brief reunion with the hairdresser in my motel room, I removed the old-fashioned blouse. The hairdresser carefully pulled the pins from my hair and combed out the curls and waves. She placed the ribbon on my forehead and wove the curls through the ribbon and tied it in the back in a style suggestive of the 1920s as well as the 1960s. My dress was modern, if simple, with a corset covered in flowy chiffon with organza flowers embossing the fabric. Faggoting joined tiers on the front of the dress, and the tiers dipped to a short train in the back. This lightweight gown seemed perfect for the occasion and forgiving of my slightly larger waistline.

Dustin reclined on the king-size bed watching this transformation. When the hairdresser left, I stood up and so did he.

The room started to spin. "Dustin!" I reached out one arm and he flew to my side.

"What's wrong?"

"Can't breathe. Unzip my dress."

He unzipped it down to my hips and slid it downward. I took a deep breath and leaned back against his shoulder. I was wearing a strapless bra with a wide band underneath for support.

He slid his hands around my breasts, which were threatening to spill over. He circled his fingers beneath the top rim of the bra. "Should I unhook this too?" He chuckled against my neck. "It feels awfully snug."

I inhaled and let myself enjoy the moment. I hoped my husband would always make me yearn for him like no one else ever had. He tilted his pelvis against my backside. "Oh no. We both know what would happen if you did that. We have a roomful of guests waiting just for us."

He slid his hands around my waist and massaged my ribs. "I know how to work quickly when I have to."

"I have no doubt. Later. Time for that later. I just need to relax for a minute. I had this whole outfit on a week ago when the hairdresser did a trial run and I had the photographer take some photos. Everything was comfortable then. Now my middle has ballooned, and I have been very careful about what I've eaten."

Dustin ran his long fingers over my belly circling my navel. His lips tickled my temple.

"I think this feels different. Someone is making his presence known. You're growing a pregnancy bump."

I sighed. "The baby couldn't wait one more day to expand my waistline?"

"Guess not. When's your first ultrasound?"

"Next Friday. You took off work, didn't you? The doctor insisted the father attend the ultrasound appointment."

"I'm sure I did. It's on my calendar. Will we find out if the baby is packing a little six-shooter?"

I turned to look at him grimacing. "Why are there so many crude slang terms for male genitalia?"

He shrugged. "I dunno. I guess a man doesn't want to be too scientific about something that defines his identity. Anyway, I can't wait to see the baby, whoever it is."

I tugged up my bra and dress. "We'd better get to the reception. I'm a little anxious about the ultrasound. If it is a boy, I'll be sad it's not a girl. If it's a girl, I'm afraid I'll be sad it's not a boy."

He began to try to zip me up. "Stand up tall if you want this to fit. Don't worry about the ultrasound. It's bound to be a girl or a boy. No real surprises there."

EPILOGUE: DARCY

Lancaster County, Buda Township, Nebraska
Thirteen months later

"You are such a pretty princess, aren't you?" I cooed to my eight-month-old as I finished changing her diaper and putting her in a voluminous pink and white dress. The matching band around her head nestled in her dark curls but was no match for a squirming baby. She smiled as I hefted her onto my hip. "Let's go sit with Grandpa for the pictures."

"Is Destiny ready to be captured for posterity?" my handsome husband asked. "It's not every day you get to be the center of attention at your grandfather's wedding. It was nice of Margie to share the spotlight."

He took his daughter in his arms and carried her downstairs and into the backyard where a photographer captured various family combinations.

When it was time for the extended Schulz family to be included, I took a folding chair next to my father, Donald, the groom, and his bride, Margie. Margie's two children, their spouses, and four grandchildren had already had their turn. Dustin sat next to me with Destiny on his leg. I straightened the headband in her hair.

"Where do you want us?" Veronica called out. Dustin patted the seat next to him. She strode up confidently with her half-brother in her arms. I reached over Dustin to snatch red-headed Derek and settled him in my lap. He wore a onesie that mimicked a tuxedo. We smiled at the photographer and tried to get the twins to at least look in that direction.

A baby's wail filled the air.

"Another one?" The photographer asked. We all laughed.

Cheyenne came bustling out of the house carrying her three-month-old son, Donahue. Archer immediately began making faces at the boy, trying to keep him happy. Archer and Cheyenne had gotten married six weeks after our wedding. They took seats next to Margie.

"I must have gone crazy," my father grumbled under his breath. "Why else would I be getting married at my age, and instantly becoming a grandfather of eight?"

"Crazy runs in our DNA," I laughed, "So does the love, and we wouldn't have it any other way."

AUTHOR'S NOTES

I'm sure many of you have done a DNA test now that they have become widely available for matching up relatives. Even if you haven't, many television programs focus on how detectives can use DNA to identify suspects in crimes, and how genealogists use genetics to trace the guest stars' roots. The science becomes more precise every day.

As I reviewed my familial matches from my DNA testing which was loaded onto two different family tree websites, it reminded me of a story that had been passed along by an elderly relative. She told us that her aunt confessed to giving up twin babies for adoption in California although she lived in Nebraska. This must have been in the 1920s or early 1930s. This woman had no other children and she was in her forties when she married.

Was there a way to trace the descendants of these children who had been adopted? I had no idea what their names would have been. I doubted that the mother provided her true name on the birth certificate. Even if I could narrow down the location within California, my understanding was that adoptions were sealed about the time these births occurred.

I have had distant relatives contact me through my public family trees. What if some descendants did have some information tying the adopted babies to our family? We have the same surname as the mother had nearly one hundred years ago, and we are living on the land where her family broke sod in the 1800s. Could DNA testing tie up the loose ends of that story?

So, this book is that "what if." And then I added another. What if I could make it a romance?

ABOUT THE AUTHOR

After leaving the chaos of call-center management and graduating from child-rearing, I'd earned my peace and quiet. Time to write some romance.

I started writing novels in 2019, after spending the better part of the year researching genealogy. I published my first book about my ancestors in 2020. The Twirler Quartet romance series followed, which was set in Lincoln, Nebraska, in the 1960s through 1980s. Some of my tales are set in the present day, others in decades or centuries gone by. Love is timeless. Romance should be endless.

Unfortunately, I'm stuck in the real world, splitting time between several states visiting family, enjoying the itinerant author life. Home base is a farm in Nebraska, smack dab in the middle of the fly-over states, where my husband's ancestors homesteaded over 150 years ago. You're welcome to visit. It's as easy as opening the book cover.

Claudia J. Severin

WHAT'S NEXT?

Authors live and breathe for reviews, so if you enjoyed *The Love Genes*, I would be so appreciative if you would add a short review on Goodreads and the retail website where you purchased this novel.

If you enjoyed meeting Leslie and Jace in this book, you'll be glad to know that Book Two, *The Lost Genes*, is the story of how they found love and laughter.

Was Jace just another one of Leslie's college roommate's discards or should she take another look? It was hard not to look considering what he was wearing. Or. Not. Wearing.

Leslie was clearly going over the speed limit. Should Jace throw the book at her or simply open a prolonged investigation into her misbehavior?

Even Brittany, Dustin's first wife, and Leslie's younger sister found an active role in this saga.

Coming soon!

ALSO BY CLAUDIA J. SEVERIN

Author Claudia J. Severin took things into her own hands when her genealogy research seemed limiting. Follow her foremothers, four mothers plucked from her family tree. She reimagines the lives of ancestral families in this anthology. Ina, the tragic suffragette, traded her college degree and teaching career for a loving husband and children in the 1910s, in the shadow of the Great War, but things did not work out as she planned. Mary, a German immigrant, finds love with an Iowa farmer and crosses the state in a covered wagon with his entire family to become a homesteader on the Nebraska plains in 1869. She didn't know that Indian encounters, prairie fires, and locusts would threaten her and her rapidly growing family. Nellie fell for the bad boy, the Good Time Charley who didn't let a little thing like Prohibition stand in his way. She tries to control his drinking and spending while supporting her family in times of calamity in the 1920s and 1930s traveling from Nebraska to Kansas and back again. Katie finds herself the sole heir to her father's farm in southeastern Nebraska decades after the Homestead Act took most of the land ownership out of play. She enjoys playing the flirtatious games learned from her older half-sisters. But are her suitors interested in her or her inheritance?

It's 1969. Teenage boys didn't scare Yvonne. A beautiful girl like her had her pick: the jock, the party animal, the hippie, the poet. But she wasn't finding true love like her baton-twirler girlfriends. Was it because she'd kept her boyfriends wanting more like a good girl? Or had she craved control too much to let anyone get so close?

Daniel, the boy next door, was the least of her worries. He came as part of a twin set with her lifelong best friend, Debbie. But what happens when the ambitious egghead she used to play games with starts to notice her?

Teetering on the brink of fulfillment a decade later, a medical problem threatened Yvonne's perfectly manicured marriage. Her malady was treated, but serious side effects took a toll. Her happiness kept spinning out of reach just like that baton she once tried to master.

Catch It Spinning is the first of the Twirler Quartet. The turbulent late 1960s and early 1970s provide the social unrest that simmers in the background even in a sleepy Midwestern city.

You'll find yourself transported to 1968 in this slice-of-life look at Yvonne and her three best friends as they navigate through high school and young adulthood. Part fiction, part autobiography, this series exposes a snapshot that baby boomers will remember.

The **Twirler Quartet** series showcases **Yvonne, Debbie, Nancy**, and **Linda**, four baton twirlers from the mythical Capital High School set in Lincoln, Nebraska. Each of them deals with the temptations of young love, as they seek to establish their identities amid the numerous transformative issues of the time such as racial relations, feminism, the draft, student activism, and rebellious social experimentation. *Twirling Fire*, *Learning To Twirl,* and *Spinning Sideways* continue the stories of how their romances and adventures evolved.

Printed in Great Britain
by Amazon